THE URBAN LEGION

Dave Agans

Nancy —
Remember to smile
for the camera!

D

B. MiRTHY & SONS

WILTON NH

For information contact:
B. Mirthy & Sons, PO Box 487, Wilton NH 03086
www.BMirthy.com

B. Mirthy & Sons are not responsible for the content of any website or publication referenced in this book, real or fictional, except for the www.BMirthy.com website.

First edition 2015 — rev 1

Cover design by Jack Spellman, www.jackspellmanart.com
Author photo by Duarte Images

Publisher's Cataloging-in-Publication Data

Agans, Dave.
   The urban legion / Dave Agans.
      pages cm. – (Urban legion trilogy, bk. 1)
   ISBN: 978-0-9861709-0-4 (pbk.)
   ISBN: 978-0-9861709-1-1 (e-book)
      1. Urban folklore—Fiction. 2. Conspiracies—Fiction. 3.
Humorous stories. 4. Adventure stories.   I. Title.
PS3601.G33 U73 2015
813.`6—dc23
                                            2015903097

For my muses Gail, Jen, and Liz

Disclaimer

None of the people, events, technologies, or facts in this book are real, as far as the author knows, and any references or similarities to specific people, institutions, or companies are either accidental or used fictitiously. The author is aware of no Corporation or member cartels in real life. The urban legends are just legends and the conspiracy theories just theories. To the author's best knowledge, there is no Trail Boys organization and Elite Trail Boy candidates do not study Sun Tzu's *The Art of War* in preparation for their Military Strategy skill patch.

And the author isn't just saying all this because two big guys came to his house last March 12th and threatened to microwave his poodle if he didn't.

That never happened either.

Part I

"The truffles were complex, with mysterious undertones."
— Our Zen Gourmet

Chapter 1

Our Zen Gourmet was three bites into the Duck Pâté with Tiny Truffles when she first heard the voice. It seemed to be inside her head, which was surprising, since it was male, with a distinctly French accent.

ZE TRUFFLES, ZEY ARE TERRIBLE, NO?

Lynn Grady froze, listening, wishing she could check what she'd written about the truffles on her hidden notepad. But she was pretty sure the words were *[savory]* and *[delicate]*. She considered adding *[psychedelic]*.

She expanded her awareness to the entire restaurant. Burgundy walls, mahogany columns, and carved-wood furniture provided the Castle on Green Street with its Dark Ages atmosphere. It was nearly empty on this sunny Saturday—everyone else in Cambridge was outside, enjoying the last warm days before the inevitable New England winter.

Lynn often felt conspicuous during undercover restaurant reviews, and not just because she was dining alone; she stood a full head taller than most women, which made her freckled face and flame-red curls even more prominent. But now, she felt invisible. Her server ignored her to flirt with the hostess at the reception station. An overweight businessman crowded a back corner booth and talked quietly on his cell phone. The bartender and two barflies focused on the Boston College game on TV, its closed-captions making no sound. Her crisp reality was suspended in a bubble, cut off from the rest of the Castle, trapping her with a phantom competing critic—

QUITE POSSIBLY ZE WORST TRUFFLES EVER.

—who clearly didn't like the food.

She knew hallucinations could pop up after hours of deep

meditation, but her practice, particularly during a Zen Gourmet session, was not very deep. Her signature style was an adaptation—or perhaps abomination—of good technique; the moment she became one with the flavors and aromas of Here-And-Now, her writer-mind would interrupt to scribble descriptions onto the notepad. When she explained this method to her Zen Master, he called the detours "catnaps" and admonished her to stay awake.

Whatever the voice was, it wasn't real; there was no one nearby. She took a fifty-cent sip of Cambri designer water to cleanse her palate, a deep breath to cleanse her thoughts, and a bite of the appetizer to get back to work. Her awareness flowed to her tongue.

[Pate - rich, creamy, light onion]—
WHERE DID ZEY GET SUCH AWFUL TRUFFLES?

She froze again, instinctively bracing her back; if the Master knew she was still fixated on a French-sounding mental echo, he would have hit her with a stick. She closed her eyes and took another long cleansing breath. As a professional—part time, anyway—she'd get through this. Her bank balance was counting on it.

"Excuse me?"

She flinched, and heard the notepad flutter to the floor as she opened her eyes. A barrel-chested young man towered over her table.

"My name is Roger Landowski. May I speak with you for a moment?"

Great. The Castle's inattentive wait staff was letting street solicitors barge in to harass the guests. At least Roger's voice wasn't French; rather, it carried the slightly nasal whine of a Chicagoan, confirmed by the White Sox cap. His short brown hair, square jaw, and resolute eyes gave him a church missionary look, except for the slight beer belly projecting from his otherwise solid frame.

As one of the few remaining anonymous food critics, she couldn't tell him he was interrupting a review.

"I'm sorry, I don't have time. I've got a busy afternoon scheduled."

"I'm hoping you can rearrange things, Lynn. And don't worry

about blowing your cover—I have friends at the Globe. I pulled a few strings to get you assigned here today."

What? Evidently, Roger's friends were unclear on the concept of "anonymous food critic." She'd have a word with her editor.

"I need your help," he continued. "May I sit down?"

To help another is to discover Oneself, said Zen-mind, the wise inner voice that spoke for her spiritual teachers. She waved Roger to the opposite seat, but he'd already swung the massive carved-wood chair out and back under him with one hand.

"What can I do for you, Roger?"

"Well, that pâté you're tasting? We supply the truffles. We were surprised by some bad feedback from the restaurant; that's why we had you assigned to do a review. We wanted a trusted opinion." He brightened. "How are they?"

Lynn studied the young face across the table.

"You sell truffles…"

"I do." He was grinning. "Come on, whaddya think? Great truffles, huh?"

"Well, yes, the truffles are good, though a voice in my head keeps saying they're awful."

Roger snapped so visibly from cheerful to wary that Lynn wondered if he was bipolar. Except she thought bipolar people had up days and down days; Roger switched like he was having a down minute. He glanced around the room, then returned his focus, now scary serious, to Lynn.

"You heard a voice, in your head. Not your own?"

"Yes. It was male, with a French accent."

"Is he talking now?"

She hadn't thought of the voice as a separate "he."

"No, I only heard him when I was eating the pâté."

"Hmm." Roger scratched his head above his ear. "Please, take another bite, but after you do, hold your fork near your ear like this." He subtly pretended to wave a fork. "Trust me."

He seemed so earnest—Lynn wanted to trust him.

She picked up her fork, carved off another bite, and placed it in her mouth. Then she innocently held the utensil up, while her hidden hand instinctively jotted her impressions.

[Getting warm. Delicious.]—
DISGUSTING, TASTES LIKE MICROWAVED POODLE.
—[Writing on skirt.]

"There he is," she mumbled around the mouthful, while bending to retrieve the fallen notebook and place it back onto her lap.

"Okay, this time hold the fork next to your other ear. Casual, like before."

"That seems kind of awkward."

"You'll think of something."

Lynn did think of something: she took a bite and leaned her chin down onto the back of her hand, so the fork was on the opposite side of her head. The stuff was scrumptious, despite the voice.

PERHAPS—TIME—VOMIT.

"That was garbled, like a bad cell phone connection," she reported.

Roger smiled and looked across the room at the fat businessman.

"I believe I'd like to meet that gentleman," Roger said as he slid back his chair. "I'll be back in a second—enjoy your pâté." He surveyed the restaurant, then wandered around the perimeter of the room until he approached the man from behind. Lynn watched out of the corner of her eye as she took the next bite; the man didn't notice Roger until the big Chicagoan plopped down into his booth.

ZE TRUFFLES ARE—

The voice cut off as the man shrank from the hulk beside him. Roger said something and the man smiled weakly, nodded, and dropped the phone into his breast pocket. He threw some money on the table, and he and Roger slid out of the booth together.

They headed for the exit with Roger's arm on the fat man's shoulder, like they were best friends. But the man was wheezing, and the loose skin around his neck was pulled taut into Roger's hand. He resembled an oversized, red-cheeked bobblehead as Roger steered him out the door.

Lynn tried to enjoy the remaining pâté, but she had trouble getting into the zone again. At least the voice in her head was gone.

She scribbled notes and wondered if Roger would indeed return, or if this was all just a magic mushroom dream. And if Roger *was* real, was he really a truffle salesman? Was there even such a thing as a truffle salesman?

Roger sauntered back in, stopped by the bar for a few words with the bartender, and returned to the table.

"That explains why the Castle says everyone hates the truffles. Good thing I came in."

Lynn set down her fork and dabbed a napkin to her lips.

"You'd better explain all of this. Now."

Roger seemed to recognize the wayward teenager treatment, and with a slight nod, he took on the appropriate contrite demeanor.

"Okay. My people grow hydroponic truffles and sell them for way less than wild French or Italian ones. It's insanely profitable, despite our low prices. The Truffle Cartel doesn't like—"

"The *Truffle* Cartel?"

"The Truffle Cartel. Not as big as the diamond people, and not famous like OPEC; in fact, they're totally clandestine. But it's your basic cartel—they control the supply to keep the price up. They don't like us cutting into their business, and apparently that guy's been hanging out here for weeks, doing the same thing to anyone who orders truffles."

"Wait, I'm missing something. What was that guy doing?"

"Our fat friend was using a cochlear audio transmitter, disguised as a cell phone, to project his voice into your head. It has a directional phased array, which beams electromagnetic pulses directly into your auditory nerves. But a well-placed antenna causes enough reflections to disrupt the signal. I figured out it was him by having you shield each side of your head with the fork and seeing which side blocked the voice. Silver works pretty well—good thing this place is too upscale for stainless steel. Of course, I wear an antenna." He took off the White Sox cap and showed her the inside. "It's lined with a tin-copper alloy—am I getting too technical?"

Lynn couldn't help a snorted laugh.

"My God, tin-foil hats!"

"No! It's tin-copper alloy. Much more effective."

"Against the evil conspiracy putting voices into your head."

"Well, yeah, actually." Roger's eyes clouded. "You heard the voice."

She had. And not since the fat man left.

"Good point."

"The 'evil conspiracy' makes fun of our metalized hats, so people like you don't use 'em. Then you walk out of a store wondering why you bought the most expensive shoes or the biggest TV. The sales sug-jectors they use in the malls are a lot more subtle, and target everybody. But they work; people tend to obey voices in their heads. Julian Jaynes' theory says it goes back to pre-metaconscious humans, when voices from the 'gods' on the right side of our brains told our left brains what to do."

He paused while that sank in, looking very sober. Then he brightened, like before.

Up minute coming, Lynn guessed.

"I picked the guy's pocket on the way out," Roger said, waving the fat man's phone. "He can't bother anyone now."

His enthusiasm was contagious, but Lynn had apparently developed immunity. She wasn't going to let him suck her in.

"Okay, so you've got some kind of corporate espionage going on here. I have no idea how that voice thing works; I'm just a food critic. But I do know truffles, and good ones grow wild, underground—not underwater. These can't possibly be farmed. If you want my help getting your truffle business going, you're going to have to be honest about where they come from."

Roger got serious again.

"I am being honest, and I can prove it—I'll show you the farm. Right now."

"Roger, I can't just drop everything and go look at a truffle farm, unless it's in some back room here at the Castle. I just ordered lunch."

"I'll pay for it." He pulled out a money clip, peeled off a fifty, and laid it on the table.

She stared at the wad of bills. Unfortunately, the lunch tab wasn't the problem.

"I can't do it, Roger. I'm a restaurant critic. I have a review to write."

"That can wait—I'm tight with the Globe, remember?"

"But you're not tight with my landlord—" She lowered her head.

There is no need for appearances, they are not You, said Zen-mind.

"I'll be honest, too, Roger. I'm short this month; I've got to get this in today or I won't be able to pay my bills."

Roger nodded thoughtfully.

"Okay. I'd like to hire you for an inspection of our truffle farm." He counted out four more bills. "How does $200 sound?"

$200 sounded *great*. Lynn tore her gaze from the money and looked up into Roger's brown eyes. She clearly wasn't the best judge of character, but he didn't look like a creep. And having personally experienced his tin-foil hat technology, Lynn couldn't help being intrigued by hydroponic truffles.

Only a beginner sees the truth, said Zen-mind, *without preconceptions, without judgment, without fear of the unknown.* Usually it was preconceptions and judgment that got in the way of Beginner's Mind. This time, it was definitely fear of the unknown.

She went with Zen-mind, and her landlord.

"Okay," she said, stuffing the cash and the notepad into her belt pack. "Lead the way."

At the door, Lynn looked back to see her waiter delivering the Curry Chicken on Mixed Greens entrée she'd ordered but would never enjoy. She didn't know if the gnawing in her stomach was hunger or dread.

* * *

Roger Landowski helped fold Lynn into his VW Golf wagon. It felt like the awkward first moments of a blind date—they were total strangers, and things would probably go downhill from there. He was glad he'd cleaned out the trash that usually adorned the passenger seat, though he knew by the faint smell of rancid oil that a few stray French fries must be hiding under the floor mats.

Fries on the lam were the least of his worries.

Pulling Lynn into the situation was risky—she might still be involved with her ex-husband. He wished that sort of thing would show up on her bio, but of course, that sort of thing never did. He'd have to win her confidence and figure it out for himself, before he dared open up about the rest of the operation.

She asked about his background, so he told her about growing up in Chicago and—to boost his credibility—earning Elite Trail Boy rank. While he talked, he stole a few glances to size her up. Her loose-fitting, earth-toned cotton blouse and skirt, and especially her hemp belt purse, showed she was no slave to fashion; that was a good sign. And the skirt had some kind of ink stain on it, kind of like the grease spot on the front of his favorite jeans. But he couldn't base an alliance on poor laundry habits.

Her bio said she was almost forty, and her pink, freckled skin showed subtle signs of weathering. But even at ten years older than him, she was in much better shape—she'd played center on her high-school basketball team and her athlete's build was still evident. Her interest in Zen and healthy living were two more things they didn't have in common. He'd tried meditation once, but that wasn't exercise; contemplating his navel only reminded him of the belly fat it was sinking into.

On the other hand, he was pretty sure Phil Grady wasn't into meditation or healthy living either.

He navigated to the old brick lab buildings that defended MIT like a castle wall from Vassar Street invaders, found the gap in the ground floor, and pulled the Golf through the underpass to an inner courtyard. He parked and shut off the engine; the diesel coughed and died, but a small whine persisted for a few extra seconds—a minor bug he'd been meaning to fix.

"Is your car okay?" Lynn asked. "It sounds like my Civic; after 200,000 miles it makes a lot of sick little noises."

Roger paused. If Lynn was working with her ex, she'd be driving something nicer than a 200,000 mile-old Civic. And she wouldn't run off with a total stranger for a mere $200. She was broke, unlike any of Phil's associates. He could tell her about his new engine, and it might distract her from the unusual route ahead.

"My car's old, but not sick," he said. "More like mutant. I'll tell you about it while we walk."

* * *

Slightly reassured by the assault-free car ride, Lynn followed Roger along a deserted corridor, past dozens of numbered, pebble-glassed office doors, trying to see everything with Beginner's Mind.

"This is MIT," Roger said, "in case you didn't realize it. I studied Mechanical Engineering here. One of the cool things about the Institute is how it expanded piecemeal over the years, so the buildings don't fit together perfectly—which leaves a bunch of useless, barely accessible spaces at the junctions. As an undergrad, I joined a secret club called the Roof and Tunnel Hackers. We'd explore late at night, finding, mapping, and sometimes even decorating those spaces. We called them tombs—you'll be getting a little tour."

Tombs, Lynn thought. *Wonderful.*

"I should warn you, I'm kind of claustrophobic," she said.

"You'll be fine," came the answer as they descended a ramp into a cramped, dim tunnel. Yellow and red painted pipes ran along the ceiling, and humming metal boxes in cages labeled "high voltage" lined the walls. Lynn could smell electricity, like an underground thunderstorm had just blown through. It struck her that maybe this was all part of some elaborate fantasy game, played out in MIT's hidden high-tech caverns.

"I was a loner on the south side of Chicago," Roger said, "too smart for the guys, not smooth enough for the girls—and at MIT it was easy to stay that way. But one of my fellow hackers, Todd, came from a tough neighborhood in Jersey City, and we clicked. He became my best friend—really, my only friend. We did everything together, including working on a new motor technology, based on the piezo-electric effect."

Lynn shook her head, blank. Pizza-electric? He had to be making this stuff up.

"It's a sandwich of two materials like this"—he put his palms together like he was praying—"and when you put voltage across it,

one side shrinks and the other expands, so it flexes." He curved his
fingers left, and then right, to demonstrate a waving motion. "The
industry used it to make fans and speakers at first, which was
obvious, but we used it to drive motors. The best part is, it's a
capacitor, not a resistor—it stores electricity instead of wasting it as
heat loss. Like how a hybrid car battery reuses braking energy. We
built the first motor into a portable electric winch, powered by four
D batteries, and used it for a world class hack—hoisting a fake
patrol car onto the Great Dome."

At least some of that story was true. Lynn recalled the front
page picture of the car parked atop MIT's prominent dome. It was
the attention to detail that made the news—when the authorities
removed the dummy vehicle, inside they found a dummy cop, and
on his lap a dummy box of donuts.

They wound their way through more turns, up a small
stairway, and down two more. Roger unlatched a cage door and
helped her step through. As she balanced herself with a hand on the
frame, she felt the cold metal under her fingers. It was worn
smooth—many others had come this way before.

Had any of them come back? She really wished Roger hadn't
called these places tombs.

They slid behind a waterslide-sized insulated duct into a
cavernous triangular space. There were murals painted high up on
the wall: a sailing ship, a bug, and a door-sized black and white
whiskey bottle label for "Jack Florey's Old No. 5."

"Roof and Tunnel Hackers use the name Jack Florey to remain
anonymous," Roger said, smiling. "When I was a freshman, Jack
gave me my first tour. Whenever someone got caught, it was Jack.
I've even been Jack myself a few times. But none of the other Jacks
know about this."

The giant pipes fed into what seemed like a boiler given its hot
aura. But it was fake; Roger grabbed a protruding gauge, turned it
like a door handle, and pulled. The beige-painted metal panel
reminded Lynn of a middle-school gym locker opening its jaws.
She felt her throat tighten as Roger stood aside and waved her in.

No way I'm letting him stuff me in there.

"After you," she said politely.

He shrugged, ducked, and entered—to Lynn's relief, it was bigger than a locker—and as she followed him in, he let the panel swing closed behind them.

It was warm and quiet. And dark. *Like a tomb.* Getting there seemed like a lot of effort for a rape and murder, but the ambiance was perfect.

"Your eyes'll adjust in a minute."

Lynn began to make out a line of pinpoint red lights overhead, which disappeared around a corner.

"The tunnel zigzags around a few building foundations. We used to carry flashlights, but I thought built-in LED lighting was more elegant. They only turn on when the door is closed—kinda like a fridge in reverse."

Outlined by the red glow, he started into the dim tunnel. It was wide enough for them to walk side by side as it ramped gently downward. Roger lowered his voice to match the subterranean hush.

"Todd was two years ahead of me and went to William D. Jones Consulting after he graduated. He worked on their oil-to-electricity project. It got some hits on the news—maybe you've heard of it?"

She hadn't, and even if she had, she probably would've ignored it. Reading about technical stuff usually just made her feel stupid. She had to admit that Roger made it all sound simple.

"Todd invented a chemical process to get electricity directly from oil, without combustion or moving parts, so it didn't waste any energy. And it even worked on low-grade crude. But the Refinery and Solar Cartels greased a few palms and W.D. Jones abandoned the project. Todd didn't want to let it die, so he convinced me to install a big version of the motor into an old diesel Volvo, powered by an oil-to-electricity converter. That was the best year of my life, building that car with Todd. And it worked great—the first prototype got 200 miles to the gallon."

That sounded perfectly reasonable to Lynn—coming from a guy with a tin-foil hat.

"I've heard about the 200 mile-per-gallon car, but it's always just urban legend."

Even in the dim light, Lynn could see the tension in Roger's jaw.

"Yeah," he said finally. "Just urban legend. Except you just rode in one. The diesel engine sound is fake, to cover up the technology. That whine you heard was the electric flywheel spinning down."

"I'm afraid that doesn't mean anything to me." Lynn didn't know a flywheel from a fly swatter.

"I admit it's not easy to demonstrate—not as easy as metal hat technology. Technology you didn't believe in an hour ago."

That was true.

"Okay, so you're one for two in the proof department."

"I guess that means we need a tiebreaker," he said, grinning.

They reached the end of the ceiling lights at a solid metal door, where Roger pressed his finger onto a glass panel. A bolt slid back; he pulled the door open and waved her into a brightly lit and somewhat disorganized-looking laboratory.

"Welcome to Muddy Charles Farm."

Chapter 2

The fat man followed the ruffian's orders, huffing away from the Castle on Green Street as quickly as possible given his short stride and considerable air resistance. Once out of sight, he beached himself onto a sidewalk bench; the green-painted slats creaked and the elderly lady at the opposite end bounced noticeably upward. He shrugged an apology—he was breathing too heavily to speak, unaccustomed to such exercise.

His neck throbbed from the young man's grip. He patted his pockets to find his real phone and realized that the bastard had stolen the fake one. He whispered a curse—protocol not only required him to report his failure to management, but now he would have to submit a Lost Equipment Form for the voice-projecting phone. Turning his back on the old lady, he extracted his real phone and dialed his superior.

"François."

François sounded irritated already, and he had not even heard the news yet.

"Zis is Toine. I have had a difficulty. A woman was lunching, tasting ze truffles. I was beaming suggestions as usual, when a ruffian joined her. He attacked me and forced me to leave ze restaurant."

"I do not have time for this. Wait until he is gone and resume the operation."

"I cannot. Ze bastard has stolen my transmitter."

François' brief silence said much.

"I cannot delay our activities for you, Toine. Remain in the area. I shall contact you once we have finished here."

"Oui. I will await your call."

Toine felt some relief—though his endeavor had become

catastrophe, the repercussions, and the Lost Equipment Form, would wait until François' own mission was complete. Thus, there was time to waste, and as usual, his stomach complained of hunger. Fortunately, he was but a few steps from Massachusetts Avenue, upon which he could find La Longe Baguette—not authentic, but comfortingly familiar. He rolled himself from the groaning green slats, nodded adieu to his unappreciative bench-mate, and tottered off—at a leisurely pace this time, despite his eager anticipation of a croissant chocolat.

Or perhaps several.

* * *

François stowed his phone with slightly more force than necessary; he had been aware of the risks when he split his trainee team, and Toine's troubles confirmed his apprehension. But his deeper concern went beyond a failed sug-jector session. Jean-Paul, his other intern, hovered always on the edge of self-control, barely containing a core of inexplicable rage. This volatile attitude had the most damage potential, and thus François had chosen Jean-Paul to receive his constant, direct supervision.

Weekend parking in Cambridge was plentiful; François chose a space hidden around a corner from their objective, and Jean-Paul coerced the black Lincoln into it. The two men checked and concealed their weapons—François carried a specially modified pistol, but Jean-Paul was a traditionalist, preferring the standard-issue 9mm Glock semi-automatic. François reminded his quick-tempered assistant that discretion demanded use of the weapon only as a last resort.

"I should have brought the muffler," Jean-Paul grumbled.

"The proper English word is 'silencer,' M'sieur, and whatever you call it, it is difficult to conceal. Furthermore, even though it does not make noise, it makes corpses, which may be equally inconvenient."

They slid out of the leather seats, brushed their suit jackets flat, and proceeded to the GenTrex Research front entrance.

* * *

The GenTrex front desk supervisor only half-watched the Boston College game on the lobby TV; he was daydreaming of his own long-ago Saturday afternoons, roaming the secondary and knocking heads with defenseless wide receivers. The front door intercom startled him back to his shift at the gene-splicing factory.

"Professor François Spaquel, Université de Nice, and my assistant," crackled a voice through the tiny speaker. The supervisor muted the video and buzzed the lock. The weekend guard joined him at the desk as the researchers crossed the lobby.

Professor Spaquel was obvious—lean, twitching a thin mustache, and leading the way with the nose-in-the-air haughtiness of a French waiter. His assistant was shorter, with the solid build of a football player—or soccer, or rugby, or whatever they played in France. He had dark eyes under dark eyebrows, and looked like he had a score to settle.

Not a guy to mess with.

Both men were overdressed in conservative charcoal-gray suits with white shirts and multicolor pastel ties. They matched the photos on the visitor list, which were noted as VIP status—full access, "Unaccompanied" badges, the whole works. They obviously had connections upstairs at GenTrex. They also knew what they were doing—they signed in, clipped their badges to their lapels, and disappeared into the main hallway without a word. The supervisor waited until they were out of earshot.

"I gotta stop takin' weekend duty," he said. "Last Saturday a guy showed up with a coupla pigs."

"Really? The cops?"

"No, pigs. Oink-oink. On leashes. The pigs were frickin' VIPs too, photos and all. We hadda clip the badges to their collars."

"Pigs," said the guard.

"Right. Frickin' pigs."

* * *

Out of sight of the GenTrex guards, François led Jean-Paul to a stairwell behind the main elevators. They descended several flights, pressed an electronic key into a slot, and slipped into the elevator equipment room. The bank of barrel-sized motors and their controlling relays sat idle for the weekend, but the air still smelled of ozone.

"Now then, M'sieur," François said, "our associates have assured us that the entrance is hidden here somewhere. Let us dig it up and prove them correct."

"We know the passage is behind this wall," snarled Jean-Paul, waving his weapon. "Why do we not just explosion our route?"

François sighed, half with pity for Jean-Paul's mangled English, and half with thinning patience for the young man's complete lack of the same. François' own ability to maintain composure was undoubtedly the reason he had been chosen to train this vicious pup, in the field and at the restaurant. His superiors understood that it requires even more patience to be a French waiter than to be waited on by one. He smiled tolerantly.

"Jean-Paul, your eagerness is admirable—but it will not serve you well here, or in your career at L'Escargot. How will you make a dinner guest wait twenty minutes for a menu when you cannot wait even five to find a hidden entrance? Furthermore, how would we hide the hole in the wall when we have accomplished our objective? Poise, always. We shall search—not shoot."

He waited for a sullen nod of acquiescence.

* * *

Lynn tried to see the underground lab with Beginner's Mind. It was easy, since she didn't recognize much. She didn't know what a hydroponic truffle farm should look like, but this wasn't it.

The main room was large and cluttered, with a dozen gray-and-black tables set with chemical experiments, computers, and complicated-looking electronics. There were several domed chambers with glass windows on the front and machinery inside. Robot arms towered over them like cranes. To Lynn's untrained eye, this was an evil mad scientist's "la*bora*tory," straight out of a scary old horror flick. To a trained eye, she imagined, it looked even scarier. She half expected to see a table with restraining straps ready to welcome a fresh experimentee.

Beginner's Mind, Lynn.

On the left was a windowless door with a bare red bulb labeled "Caution-Plasma Generator in Use." Straight ahead was a hallway with doors on either side. And to the right—

"Hi, I'm Howie Friedman."

Lynn turned to face the New York-accented voice. Her reaction was instant and hormonal—cheeks flushing and a giddy quiver strumming her spine.

Howie was a magnificent young man—he stood a head shorter than Lynn, with curly black hair framing his mouth and continuing up to surround his yarmulke. His nose was crooked, his eyes bulged behind thick glasses, and his stained smile showed he'd spent more time at Starbucks than at the dentist—

She squeezed her eyes shut and reopened them. No difference.

Roger was laughing.

"Howie's our chemistry expert. As you can tell, he's pretty good with sex pheromone cologne. Howie, this is Lynn Grady."

Still disoriented, Lynn reflexively offered her hand.

"Pheromones did that?"

Howie shook hands, leaning back to grin up at her.

"With looks like mine, I can use a little help. In fact," he said, "I can use a lot of help."

Lynn studied this comically-built little man and again felt the shiver—only this time it wasn't sex, but foreboding. Every minute something impossible was happening, and yet she couldn't deny her senses.

"So you're telling me pheromones really work."

"What, I'm not proof enough?" Howie leaned close to press his hip against her thigh, setting off fresh waves of unwarranted excitement.

"Back off, Howie," Roger said, "We've got something else to prove today. Is Meg here? We need to show Lynn the farm."

"Meg won't be too happy about that," Howie muttered. "She's in the middle of cleaning the filters."

"Meg is our biologist," Roger explained, heading off Lynn's

next question. "She runs the farm." Then to Howie, "Lynn won't mind seeing a few dirty filters."

"It's not the dirty filters Meg wants to hide. Have you seen her when she's elbow-deep in plankton sludge? It's not pretty."

"How about you give her a heads-up, and while she's hosing off we'll wait in the lounge?"

Howie nodded a defeated "okay" and shuffled down the hall. As Lynn followed Roger she turned to see Howie disappear through a side door. She felt a twinge of something like disappointment to see him go.

And a wave of conflicted memories welled from her chest and warmed her cheeks.

There had probably been pheromones wafting around the WERS radio studio back then, when Lynn, as an Emerson College journalism student, interviewed the lead guitarist for a hot new grunge band out of South Boston. Phil Grady sat on the stool opposite, the big microphone only half-obscuring his face and hiding none of the playful light in his eyes. Lynn had trouble concentrating on her questions, and he noticed. He invited her backstage that night and the rollercoaster ride began. A daughter, three tours, and six years later, it jumped the rails. She still wasn't sure what she'd done wrong.

She'd spent the decade since the divorce trying to cast Phil out of her thoughts and let stillness take his place. Zen discipline, a full-time day job, and mothering Tanya provided plenty of distraction.

Could one whiff of Howie Friedman undo all that?

The illusion of past causes pain, said Zen-mind; *let it go and simply Be.*

She let the Phil thoughts go, and focused on following Roger.

* * *

François pressed a polished wingtip onto the stirrup of Jean-Paul's interlocked fingers. Steadying himself with a hand on the intern's broad shoulder, he stepped up and reached for the pipe hanger. This solitary piece of hardware, nowhere near a pipe, would have been cleverly inconspicuous, except for the scratches on the ceiling above it. Unlike an ordinary pipe hanger, this one could move.

He tugged the hanger sideways; it flexed along the scratch marks several millimeters but sprung immediately back.

"It is frozen."

Jean-Paul glared up at him.

"You are weak. Lift me up, I can melt it."

François considered the effort required to hoist the solid Jean-Paul to a height at which the intern's short arms could reach the lever.

"I shall try harder," he said.

François pulled violently, causing the hanger to move and Jean-Paul to stagger. But a ceiling panel scraped open, showering dust and mouse droppings.

"Merde!" Jean-Paul shouted, releasing the wingtip to swat the debris from his suit. "It is filthy!"

François dangled from the lever momentarily, then plunged to the floor via his assistant.

"However, it is open." Blinking grit, François admired the panel. The rope and handle of a pull-down attic ladder dangled before his upturned nose. "Devious, to make us go up in order to go down."

He rose, brushed his shoulders, and straightened his tie. His snarling partner did the same, with an additional check of his Glock. François sighed and extended the ladder.

"Remember M'sieur—patience."

* * *

Lynn took stock of the lounge: well-worn coffee table, bookshelves, several couches and overstuffed chairs, a TV, and a minimal kitchenette. Considering the mess in the lab, this space was surprisingly clean, with no obvious signs of mold or insects. Or plankton sludge.

"We have bedrooms and bathrooms down that way, but we hang out here mostly," Roger said, steering her to the couch and continuing to the fridge. "Can I get you a pop? Beer? Zap a slice of pizza?" He paused, frowning. "Sorry I made you skip lunch."

So was Lynn.

"Um, water's fine. You know, soda and pizza are both really bad for you."

Roger rubbed his gut.

"Well, then, I guess I'll stick to beer."

He grabbed a bottle of Sam Adams and hooked his substantial MIT ring under the top; one forward flick of the wrist popped the cap off and into the trash bin. He filled a glass from the faucet and carried it to Lynn.

"Cambridge tap water. It's Cambri before they put it in the fancy bottle." He glanced at the empty couch seat beside her, but dropped into the nearby chair.

Lynn took a sociable sip of the cool water. It was indeed as good as the designer water she'd left at the Castle—but no substitute for the Curry Chicken.

Howie's whine drifted in from the hall.

"For me, you take hours to get ready. A perfect stranger and you're done in minutes."

The response was female, with a Texas twang, from a tiny but shapely twenty-something striding into the lounge.

"That's 'cause she's an expert. You couldn't tell a truffle from a turkey gizzard."

She was short, like Howie, but played the beauty to his beast— an hourglass figure, with an impossibly narrow waist and curves straining at a Blackberry Smoke tee-shirt. Worldly eyes belied her childish face, framed by long chestnut hair clipped back with too many barrettes. She turned to Roger first.

"She's cool, right? Else you wouldn't've cracked a beer."

Roger grinned.

"Nobody's uncool enough to stop me from cracking a beer. But, yeah, she's cool."

The young woman extended a hand.

"I'm Meg Bryson. You must be Lynn."

Lynn shook her hand and leaned to get up, but Meg plopped down on the couch beside her.

"I'm sure you got things t' do, but I was thinkin' maybe you could help me out while you're here."

Lynn glanced to Roger and Howie for help and got a "trust us, don't fight it" look instead. Meg Bryson didn't need pheromones to get her way.

"What can I do for you?"

"I need an unbiased opinion. You know, for quality control. I hear you know your truffles."

"Yes, I do know my truffles. In fact, I had a serving of Duck Pâté with Truffles at the Castle on Green Street recently. Roger tells me they were yours; if that's true, your quality is excellent. I found them delicious—despite the little voice in my head to the contrary."

Meg's eyebrows shot up.

"We didn't tell you," Roger said. "After all the bad feedback, we 'suggested' that the Globe assign Lynn to review the Castle. And she had a little run-in with a Cartel guy. He was sug-jecting bad opinions at her, like he did to all their other customers."

Meg smiled.

"You're gonna need some headgear, honey." She jumped up from the couch and grabbed Lynn's hand. "But that can wait— first, how 'bout we show you what we got?"

Lynn sighed and got to her feet—she wasn't going to finish even a glass of water today. As Meg dragged her through the door and down the hall, Lynn got a close-up view of her "headgear."

"I guess those barrettes are tin-foil, right?"

"Nah. Tin-foil works but it takes a lotta sheets and you gotta cover your whole head. These little gizmos are tin-copper alloy. If I tilt my head like this, I can pick up Country 102.5." She smiled, joking, and then stopped at a doorway. "This here's my little garden."

The room could have been a wing of the New England Aquarium. The walls on two sides were lined with glass tanks that started at knee high and extended above Lynn's head, long enough to hold a good size shark if he wasn't all that into swimming. Green-blue lighting gave them a deep-sea ambiance, dark enough to reveal iridescent sparkles in the water. But these tanks had no fish; instead, clumps of—*well, looks sort of like truffles*—clung to nearly invisible white netting. The near end wall was a single tank, tangled in pipes that hung from the ceiling like roots in a gopher tunnel—truffles would feel right at home. The far wall was blank except for an open doorway into darkness, where dim shapes of pipes and machinery reminded Lynn of the MIT tunnels.

A wooden dinette and chair occupied a corner near the far end. The table was set with a plate, napkin, utensils, and a small bowl of suspiciously-symmetrical truffles.

"This here's the quality control department," Meg said, leading Lynn to the chair. "I prepped a sample for you to taste. You okay with raw?"

Lynn nodded; cooking was the customary way to mask the poor flavor of low-grade truffles. And kill bacteria, she grimly noted, but this operation looked pretty sanitary. She closed her eyes, took a deep, cleansing breath, and exhaled into no-mind.

There is nothing but Here, Now.

She gently lifted one of the delicacies out of the bowl. It had the texture of a wild Black Perigord.

[Pungent, garlicky bouquet.]

It smelled right. She placed it on the plate and sliced it open. The aroma filled her awareness, and her empty stomach purred with anticipation. She carved off a sliver, noting the properly complex inner structure. She hesitantly placed it on her tongue.

[Silky. Earthy. Hint of linden.]

This was the real thing.

Lynn kept a poker face as the truffle melted away. Roger and Howie had joined Meg, and all three hung on her reaction.

"You say you grew this here?"

Meg broke into a wide grin.

"If you're doubtin' that, it must be good."

"It's good. Very good. So good I can't believe it's farmed."

"You must've noticed the shape. Wild truffles are all strange-lookin', but the hydroponic ones are like eggs 'cause they don't have to shove away any dirt. They grow faster than underground, and we don't need French pigs to find 'em."

"Good thing," Howie said. "Lots of pigs in France; in Cambridge, not so much."

"Wild black truffles'll set you back a hundred-eighty bucks a pound," Meg explained, "but we grow these for twenty. Then we sell 'em for a hundred-twenty and make a barnload of money. And that's just the black ones. That corner tank has my first crop of white truffles—those babies go for two or three grand a pound. We'll make a fortune at half that price."

"And really piss off the Truffle Cartel," Roger added.

Meg pointed to the pipes.

"We got taps into the process flows upstairs—it used to be a candy factory, but now it's GenTrex Research. They do biotech work, usin' all the same sugars and starches as candy, so we didn't even have to mess with the plumbin'…"

Lynn lopped off another wedge of the mushroom and popped it into her mouth. As it dissolved, so did her attention to the explanation. *One must experience reality, not history*, the Master would say. Good advice, Lynn decided, when reality is so tasty and one's stomach is so empty.

"This whole setup was built into spare space around the candy process waste collection tanks. The folks upstairs have no idea we're here. We used to come in through a hidden entrance in the factory, but that got a might sticky when the building changed hands. So we dug the tunnel from MIT."

Meg moved to the end wall tank, under the watchful eyes of both young men. Lynn figured with her looks, she could recite the alphabet and they'd be drooling over every letter.

"Truffles grow like crazy in this special soup. It's got a nutrient base of ocean plankton—that's the sparkly stuff—but we throw in some ground tree root to give 'em authentic flavor. We got two tanks of oak, a willow, a lime, and this one here's linden, my favorite, which is what you're chowin' on now."

Between the flavor sensations and the biology lecture, Lynn almost didn't notice the reflection in the glass of the end tank—a reflection from the dark doorway behind her, of two men and the glint of a handgun.

"Meg!" she yelled, pulling herself sideways across the table. Meg ducked as a blast came from the doorway and the tank behind her exploded.

"Patience, Jean-Paul!"

Roger and Howie had jumped back against the pumps, but

Meg was swept up by a wall of blue-green water, nuggets of safety glass, and truffle-laden netting. She rode the wave along the floor, slamming the overturned table into the two intruders. The shooter quickly climbed to his feet.

"There are too many of them, François," he said with a strong French accent. "I will improve the chances." He took aim at Roger.

The gun looked as big as a basketball, especially given his "triple threat" stance. But this guy wasn't gonna dribble or pass. Lynn instinctively played defense, lashing out with an upward flick of her fingers to knock the weapon free. It had her full attention as it flipped up, cleared the table edge and splashed to the floor. Meg snatched it and kicked the table, knocking the men backward again before she leveled the barrel at them.

"I ain't been introduced to you boys yet, but I can already tell I don't care for you much." She rose from the water slowly, dripping, wielding the gun with a steady hand. "Shootin' you'd be as easy as shootin' raccoons—easier, even, since 'coons are cuter and ain't nearly as big a target."

The intruder with the mustache looked down his nose at Meg—impressive considering he was soaking wet and on his knees. Meg motioned to Lynn and the boys.

"I think you folks oughta retire to the lab," she said quietly. "You don't want to see this."

Lynn certainly didn't. She scrambled after Roger and Howie into the hall.

* * *

François showed no fear of this uncivilized waif, even as she aimed the Glock along the line of his nose. He was certain of her female pacifist disposition as well as her lack of firearms experience.

"This thing hefts like my Pappy's .38," said the waif. "Comfy."

Perhaps there was still the pacifist disposition.

"You have not the stomach for such violence."

The waif considered this.

"You're right, I don't want to kill you. And I never shot a 'coon, neither; just tin cans."

François exchanged a satisfied glance with Jean-Paul, and the two began to rise from their knees. The girl responded with a smirk which, had she been a waiter-in-training, would have made François proud.

"Also bottles," she said, backing into the open doorway. "They make a really satisfyin' sound when they explode."

She jerked the pistol sideways and fired a shot that shattered the tank to their right. François' raised arm was a poor shield against the flood of water and glass; both men tumbled to the opposite wall. François dragged his head above water for one badly-required breath before the next shot shattered the tank on that side. That wave was so close it rolled over them rather than pushing them along. From underwater, François heard two more shots and anticipated two more tankfuls as he emerged to gasp for air. He was not disappointed—the waif was gone, the door was closed, and converging waves swept over him.

* * *

Lynn was forced to wait in the lab while Roger and Howie scrounged for makeshift weapons; she knew she could never find her way back through the tunnels. They all froze at the sound of gunshots from the tank room. Was that Meg, or did the other guy have a gun, too?

A door slammed and Meg burst from the hall at a full run.

"Hit the road, y'all!"

They rushed for the exit while Meg hid the pistol in one of the chemistry chambers and snatched a messenger bag from a nearby table. Roger shoved the big door open, grabbed Lynn's hand, and dragged her into the tunnel. Howie and Meg were close on their heels.

"Did you shoot them?" Howie sounded half worried and half thrilled.

"Course not, sugar. If I did, there'd be no cause to run. I just shot up the tanks, to slow 'em down a might."

Once Lynn's vision adjusted to the dim light, she quit hitting the wall at every turn and managed to keep pace.

What's with all the Frenchmen? she wondered.

Watch the turns, said Zen-mind.

They reached the MIT boiler room entrance and Roger shushed them; in the silence, Lynn heard running footsteps from the far end of the tunnel. Roger opened the panel, the LEDs winked off, and from the distance came the thud of bodies against an invisible turn. He held the door open while the others climbed out, then propped it open to keep the LEDs off.

The tortuous path through the tunnel in pitch darkness should slow their pursuers, Lynn figured. But as she raced through the MIT basement passages, she noticed that Meg was sopping wet— and leaving an obvious trail.

* * *

François' face throbbed even after Jean-Paul stopped pressing it into the unseen wall.

"Do you carry a torche?" he asked as politely as possible while attempting to massage the pain away.

"A corkscrew only, pardonez-moi," responded Jean-Paul. It was an admirable answer for an intern waiter, but under the circumstances, not the one François desired.

"Then we shall feel our way."

François touched the wall in front of him, reached right, and slid right until he felt a concrete surface. This was the right-hand wall of the tunnel, which meant they had run blindly into a left turn. He turned left, and with a hand in front and a hand on the new right wall, took a number of steps further down the passageway.

"Place your hand on my shoulder and follow me."

Jean-Paul in tow, he continued along the tunnel. At each right turn his side hand would slide off the corner; at each left turn his front hand would touch (or more precisely, crunch into) the far wall. Sacrificing his fingers allowed them to travel faster, but not fast enough.

Then he anticipated a turn.

There was something—faintly glowing speckles—on the floor,

which he could not see until he had acclimated to the darkness. The hydroponic fluid was iridescent! The waif had been soaked with it, and her speckled trail glowed to a few meters ahead, enough to increase speed and still execute the turns.

"Watch the glow on the floor! Quickly!"

François began to run, with Jean-Paul a few steps behind, soon emerging into the fluorescent glare of a basement boiler room. There were odd murals painted on the walls, but no more glowing trail. He looked around carefully—*Ah!*—no need for iridescence when the water itself was plainly visible.

They rushed through complex tunnels to a main corridor and an outside door. François drew his weapon and pushed through, then dove back as a dark blue Volkswagen roared across his path. He caught a glimpse of red hair in the passenger seat before the car disappeared around the corner.

"It is a catastrophe," grumbled Jean-Paul. "We have lost them."

"Only temporarily," François replied, suddenly in a much improved mood. "The situation is better than we had expected."

"How is it better? Our targets have escaped. They have stoled my weapon. And they have ruined my six-hundred-dollar suit!"

François smiled, wondering if all of the moisture in Jean-Paul's trousers had come from the hydroponic tanks. He holstered his Glock and retrieved the phone from his still-sopping vest pocket. Jean-Paul shook his head.

"That will not work. It is soaked."

How pitiful these young interns could be.

"You are one of us, Jean-Paul, and yet you believe that? I suspect you also mindlessly obey the 'dry clean only' tag sewn into that suit. You have much to learn."

Planned obsolescence had become more sophisticated since the simple days of fragile mechanical components. Now there were chemicals in transmission fluid that begin pink and turn brown over time, making it look dirty and inspiring an expensive transmission flush. Print cartridges had timers to shut off the toner flow after a few months, no matter how little toner was actually used. Mobile device batteries would "wear out" and require "replacement" by the vendor, who would revive them at zero cost by applying a short digital code.

And this—perhaps the most elegant—the moisture-sensing phone. It was completely waterproof, of course, but could sense when it had become wet. After turning off all phone functions, it displayed a realistic image of water droplets condensed on the inside of the screen. François pressed "D-R-Y" and waited for the software to erase the water droplets and return to normal operation.

"While it will indeed be tedious to fill out the Lost Equipment Form for your weapon, consider our advantages," he said. "We have discovered their truffle farm. We—they—have destroyed it. We have observed their vehicle so we can track them down. And most promising, did you notice the peculiar smell of their diesel engine?"

"I smelled nothing."

"Exactly—that is what was peculiar. I surmise, M'sieur, that we have not only discovered their truffle farm, but also a piezo-electric 'diesel' automobile. Our superiors will be quite eager to know this."

François had never possessed the distasteful ruthlessness required to move further up in the organization. But perhaps he could advance through cleverness and strategic thinking. And through the good fortune to be in the proper place at the proper time.

The phone screen flickered to life; he brought up the contact list and selected the Surveillance Center.

"We have several hours before we shall host M'sieur Grady for dinner. Perhaps we can serve him a considerably larger fish than we intended."

Chapter 3

A sudden ring startled the man at the console. The Surveillance Center, as well as the cost to build it, had been cleverly buried as part of the Boston Big Dig—and twenty meters beneath the new Callahan Tunnel on-ramp, it was usually dead quiet except for the dripping of the leaky ceiling. It took him a few seconds to collect his attention from the wall of TV monitors and realize it was the phone. He punched pick-up, keeping one eye on the screens.

"Surveillance."

"François Spaquel here—Truffle Division. We require immediate assistance."

"Keyword?"

There was a pause on the line.

"Barrel of pork Tips."

"Okay, what's yer poison? We got the airport, traffic lights, ATMs; you name it."

"The traffic cameras in East Cambridge. Your target is a dark blue Volkswagen that left MIT on Vassar Street approximately one minute ago, carrying two men and two women. The woman in the front passenger seat has red hair and freckles. The plate number is Massachusetts WSOX05. Can you accomplish this?"

The surveillance man sighed.

"No prob—I was just watchin' the airport. Ya want me to, uh, slow 'em down?"

"That would be splendid."

"I'll text ya back."

The man took a last look at the airport images. No great loss—the view from the women's restroom flush-sensor cameras was a lot better a few weeks ago, when the crowds of coeds came back to school. The last few hours had been a parade of pimply middle-aged asses.

Besides, he could get this done and get back to the airport before the afternoon rush.

He set up the text link to François and punched in the plate number, then brought up the map and selected a rectangle around the MIT area. The monitors flipped points-of-view almost simultaneously and presented Cambridge as seen from the traffic-light camera grid. A dialog box flashed up: "Plate number not found; switch to manual recognition mode?"

He clicked OK and scanned the monitors, quickly spotting a dark blue wagon cruising toward Kendall Square. He zoomed in from the front. As he suspected, they'd sprayed the license plate with camera-blocking lacquer, so the cams couldn't read the number through the reflective glare. His lip curled; that shit might hide the plate, but it couldn't hide the car, and it only pissed him off. He verified the VW emblem, and then checked out the red-haired broad in the passenger seat. If she was at the airport, he'd know if that red hair was natural.

He punched a button and the same video appeared on his computer screen. He right-clicked the car and chose TRACK TARGET; a marker appeared at the car's position on the map.

The Default Traffic Delay was NORMAL, the usual Saturday setting. On weekdays, when there were enough people on the road to affect stress-pill sales, the Default Delay was RUSH HOUR; at the end of the fiscal quarter, he might be asked to kick it up to IRRITATING to goose the Dammitol sales numbers. But this was a special case, for a particular vehicle, driven by assholes who lacquered their fucking plates—he right-clicked on the marker and then on Target Vehicle Delay. With a glance at the string of traffic signals on the map ahead of his victims, he clicked on INFURIATING and returned his attention to the airport ladies' room.

* * *

The car pulled up to a red light, the interior steamy with the aroma of pheromones and wet seaweed. Lynn couldn't tell whether she was craving a Norimaki sushi roll or a roll in the hay. She lowered her window and gulped at the relatively fresh Cambridge air as Roger drummed impatiently on the steering wheel.

"Just run the damn light," advised Meg. "—Shoot, I forgot, Mr. Trail Boy would never commit such a heinous crime."

"Who were those guys, Roger?" Lynn asked.

"François and Jean-Paul?—I think that's what they called each other. Must be Truffle Cartel agents. Probably working with the voice-projector guy at the Castle. At least, they have the same tailor."

And probably carried the same guns.

Lynn felt her palms go clammy. $200 seemed like a nice fee for a truffle farm inspection. But not if it got her killed.

Breathe, Lynn, said Zen-mind.

She took a cleansing breath—and Phil came to mind again. Her stomach knotted even tighter, and the car seemed to shrink. When Roger stopped for the next red, she opened the door and jumped to the curb.

"Look, I'm kind of confused here and I can't think straight with a nose full of pheromones. I need some fresh air." She fished around in her belt pack for the wad of fifties. "I'm sorry I didn't give you a proper review of your truffle farm, but I didn't sign up for getting shot." She tossed the bills onto the passenger seat. "Good luck with your truffle business—they really were very good."

"Wh-where are you going?" Roger stuttered.

"Good question. Maybe I can still get lunch at the Castle."

Not like she wanted to go back there anytime soon. Lynn shut the door, crossed Main Street, and hurried across a small courtyard to the hotel beyond. She settled onto a faux-leather lobby chair and immersed herself in the carefully designed environment. With plastic plants, a waterfall cascading over concrete boulders, and daylight beaming in through chrome light pipes, it wasn't the best place to get a grip on reality, but better than the car.

Why was she obsessed with Phil all of a sudden?

Do not try to understand, said Zen-mind. *Just breathe, and listen, and you will know.*

She inhaled deeply, and exhaled, and knew: She missed Phil. A lot. Howie's cologne made her want a man, and Phil was the only man she'd ever wanted. She longed for that heady time when Phil wanted her.

She'd spent the early days of their marriage touring with his band, the Severed Clown Heads, in their converted Thomas Built school bus. It was just after Tanya was born, and Lynn found it exhilarating to balance bus travel, seedy motels, and passionate sex with being a good mom. She was a successful—paid—writer, too, making the whole experience famous in a series of Spinning Rock Magazine articles. Her "Grunge Tour Diaries" captured the band's originality and anti-pop-culture message, while capturing readers' hearts with endearing images like baby Tanya, backstage, wearing her little pink earplugs.

It wasn't just a time of career success. It seemed like Phil genuinely loved her, drawing her out of her hardened shell and making her the star of his own personal stage. He was everything she could ask for in a man—more than she'd ever dreamed she could have.

But when the reality of raising Tanya kicked in, she settled down as a full-time mom. Phil didn't seem to mind, at first, and his visits home were as exciting as ever. But then something went wrong, and before long he grew cold and distant, and finally he abandoned her. She kept up appearances for Tanya, never admitting how much she needed him. Life was hollow, even emptier than when she was single. And it stayed that way for years.

Her collapsing mental state mirrored her finances. Phil's lawyers had gotten her to agree to minimal child support by offering alimony as a percentage of royalties. That sounded like a good deal, but when the band broke up, the royalties dwindled; after a while you couldn't find Severed Clown Heads music anywhere, certainly not on the radio. And without a grunge-star husband, no one would publish her writing anymore. Desperate, she leveraged her high-school grocery-store experience and a somewhat creative résumé to land a day job at the Momma's Good Food distribution warehouse.

Which was where she met Gerry Rutland.

She called Gerry her bodhisattva. As a veteran co-worker, he'd taken her under his wing, first at the warehouse, and then spiritually, encouraging her to rediscover the Zen of her youth. It was Zen, and Gerry, that finally allowed her to let go of the yearning for Phil.

Now the longing was back. Except this time, things were a little more complicated, with hydroponic truffles and voice projectors and guns.

Still, Gerry would know what to do.

And his organic grocery was in Central Square, a short, brisk, mind-clearing walk away.

* * *

Meg wasn't surprised that Trail Boy Roger would let Lynn get away so easily; he wouldn't run red lights, he sure wasn't gonna assault her and drag her back to the car. But he also wasn't gonna give up. They were headed for the Longfellow Bridge, and the T tracks down the center meant no U-turns. Roger pulled over and twisted around in the seat.

"We can't afford to lose her, Meg. Will you follow her?"

"I'm kinda drenched here—why not Howie?"

"He's drenched in pheromones—that's why she left."

"I'll give you that." *Damn.* She scootched her wet jeans along the seat and hopped out.

"Try to keep her interested," Roger added. "And make sure she doesn't call Phil. Or even Tanya."

"What do I tell her?"

"Up to you." He handed her the discarded money. "Maybe this will help."

Meg nodded, feeling goose bumps rise as cool September air filtered through her sopping clothes. Wrong season for a wet tee-shirt contest.

She rounded the corner behind the hotel and spotted Lynn dashing out of the lobby like a startled rabbit. At first she played the patient hunter, hanging back to give Lynn some space and time, but then she reconsidered. Rabbits don't carry cell phones; it'd be mighty hard to stop a call to Phil from fifty yards' range. She kicked it up to a canter and closed the gap, actually feeling wind chill on her wet clothes. Maybe they'd dry faster.

She shivered and tried to think of a plausible opening.

* * *

Roger felt like a bad cabbie as Howie harangued him from the back seat.

"What, we're hitting all the lights from dumb bad luck? They must be tracking us. We should double back to mislead 'em and then go underground."

It had to be just Howie's paranoia; the license plates were coated, so the traffic cams couldn't possibly read them. But even if the lights weren't being controlled, the car was proceeding so slowly that the Truffle Cartel agents could have followed it on foot—which made the direct route a very bad idea. Roger agreed to abandon the car in Cambridge and take the T.

"After a little grocery shopping," Howie said. "I could use some bagels and lox."

They hit a red light at the Boston end of the bridge and another as they turned left under the elevated tracks. They waited at one more red before roaring back over the bridge, Roger venting his frustration onto the accelerator pedal.

Seeing the line of lights ahead as he entered Kendall Square, Roger turned right and grabbed the first available parking space. He retrieved an electronic coin from his wallet, tugged at the attached monofilament to make sure it was secure, and then slid the coin into the parking meter slot. Within a few seconds, the tiny transmitter woke up and went to work—the time remaining on the meter clicked over to 1:27. It would reset the time every half hour until Roger retrieved it with a yank on its nearly invisible cord.

He started toward the shops, but Howie remained on the curb, hands on his hips.

"Aren't you forgetting something?"

"Uh... no?" Roger answered. "The feeder-coin is working, the car is locked—"

"Shouldn't you set the booby trap?"

Roger hesitated—and Howie went into Howie Mode.

"You don't want to set the trap? Fine. If they *have* been tracking us, and I'm sure they have, they'll find the car, rip it apart, reverse-engineer the technology, and figure out who supplies it. I'm sure Piezomotive Components won't mind when their factory mysteriously burns to the ground and takes all their people with it. And the Wheelchair Cartel will be so happy to know your strap-on robotic legs will never get on their feet. Literally."

Roger couldn't argue. The hyper-efficient motors he used in the car, and now in his experimental robotic legs, required several key advanced technologies. He kept the manufacturers' identities secret for their own protection. If the wrong people got access to the intact car, it would be the end of Piezomotive. The booby-trap mechanism had to be set. He just hoped it wouldn't trigger.

He pulled out the remote and pressed Lock, Unlock, and Alarm simultaneously. The horn chirped twice—which always sounded to Roger like the car was saying "Uh-oh."

It probably was.

* * *

Most of the wall monitors were focused back on the airport, as were both of the surveillance man's eyes and all of his attention, when the computer beeped and flashed a warning.

Damn. They'd stopped. Now he'd have to watch 'em himself.

He brought up the traffic cams on the parked car. Two men got out—they were feeding a short-term meter, so they'd be back soon. He peered into the car from another angle. Empty.

Shit!

He'd lost the women. And the phone was ringing.

"Yeah—"

"Spaquel here. They were backtracking but now the text directions have ceased. Where is the target?"

"They parked the car on Third Street, near Broadway. The men are walking back toward Kendall Square."

"And the women?"

"I dunno. Somehow I, uh, lost 'em."

The dripping from the ceiling echoed like a firing squad drum.

"Then I suggest that somehow you find them. Keep this line open and, please, M'sieur, do not also lose track of the men."

"Yessir."

With one eye on the monitor near the car, he took a last look at the scenes from the airport.

Damn. Just as the ladies' room was getting hot.

Of course, he could always catch what he missed later—all the cams fed directly to the GirlsGoneWeeWee website. He switched the airport monitors to scan the entire East Cambridge area. The female targets would not be lost for long.

* * *

Lynn stayed on Broadway instead of taking the direct route to Central Square, to avoid MIT and the Truffle Cartel agents. So when she heard rapidly approaching footsteps, she spun around, wary. It was Meg, her short legs churning to match Lynn's long strides. Lynn rolled her eyes but slowed the pace.

"Hi," Meg panted, "Sorry to bug you, but Roger thought you should keep your fee." She held out the bills. "Call it combat pay."

Lynn looked sideways at the handful of cash, then shrugged.

"I really can use it. Thanks." She tucked the money into her belt pack. "Does this mean I owe you a write-up?"

"Naw. Your reaction told me how good they are." Her face clouded. "Were."

"They were delicious. I wouldn't have believed they were grown underwater if I hadn't seen those tanks myself. Whatever inspired you to try it?"

"It was Roger's idea. Well, the truffles, anyway—he knew they'd be worth a lot if I could do it. I was already into hydroponics at Texas A&M; when an agriculture major hooks up with a marine biologist, that's what you get."

"So Howie's a marine biologist?"

"No, I didn't meet Howie until I came north. I had a different boyfriend in Texas—his name was Tommy." Meg hesitated. "I lost him."

Lynn tried to imagine what kind of guy would reject Meg—she looked like all those cute popular girls who'd made Lynn's life miserable at Lebanon High.

"That's surprising. Some other girl spirit him away with pheromones?"

"That's not how it happened." Meg paused at the curb to let a bicyclist zip across on Windsor Street, but her focus was somewhere very far away. "Can I tell you about it?"

"Sure," Lynn said, not really meaning it. Why were these people so eager to share their life stories?

"I woke up to a kiss on the cheek—Tommy was like that, always gentle, always makin' me feel special. A real Southern gentleman."

Lynn smiled to herself. Phil was a real Southie grunge star—he would wake Lynn with a kiss somewhere else.

"It was a beautiful day; crystal clear, deep blue sky, perfect for a shallow dive in the Gulf. Tommy'd been researchin' some microbiological weirdness he'd discovered—concentrations of archaea, and the methane they burp off, a few miles off Galveston. Even the Gulf shouldn't be warm enough for such hot water critters. We were dirt-poor grad students, so he'd posted an online ad describin' his research and pleadin' for a cheap ride. When a dive boat operator offered to take us out for free, we didn't think to ask questions.

"By two o'clock, we'd measured lots of archaea and methane and checked out the whole area. There weren't any thermal vents, but that was normal for the undersea geology in those parts. In fact, everythin' was normal—there was no scientific reason for those microbes to be there. We were disappointed but out of time, so we headed up to the surface for our scheduled pickup. I caught sight of somethin' I hadn't noticed before and tried to signal Tommy, but he had his back to me. My curiosity nosed out the buddy system—I went back down alone for a quick look-see."

Meg swallowed hard.

"What caught my eye turned out to be a metal rod stickin' up a few feet from the bottom. I swept away some sand with a flipper, and found a hinged metal cover on a buried base. I couldn't see any latches to hold it closed, and it wouldn't open with a quick pull. It all looked pretty new; I guessed the rod was an antenna, and the rest of it was some sorta measurement gear; it wasn't like any of the closed-up oil well heads we'd been trippin' over all mornin'.

"I turned back to the surface to tell Tommy, figurin' he'd know what research agency was collectin' data there. I was forty feet down, and I could see him kickin' up at the surface, probably wonderin' what happened to me.

"All of a sudden, Tommy ducked his head and rotated down—he got a single dive kick in before the water around him exploded in a wall of bubbles. The shock wave whoomped the air out of me and knocked me backward, but I caught a glimpse of somethin' in the froth—somethin' metal, and huge. The bubbles fizzed away and I saw it was a hull—this giant boat that had suddenly appeared outta nowhere. Then it lifted out of the water; there was nothing left but dissolvin' foam and an eerie hiss.

"Tommy was gone. I thrashed my way to the surface, ripped off my mask, and watched what took him—a huge plane, climbin' slow and drippin' water, like a pelican strugglin' with a fresh catch. I dove again and looked around, but there was no sign of him.

"All a sudden, a boat comes roarin' in, way too fast for a divin' area, but then kills it right overhead. I came up slow, worried he was gonna rev it up again. It was the damn dive boat—the guy shoulda known better.

"He was in the cockpit talkin' on the radio, and didn't see me. And when I heard what he was sayin, I ducked behind the gunwale to keep it that way. He was tellin' somebody their timin' was perfect, that the divers never knew what hit 'em. The guy on the radio asked if he was sure they got both of us, and the bastard said yes. There was some more about payment bein' arranged once they were sure we were gone, and I decided I better get the hell outta there before he saw me."

Meg shook her head.

"I dove again, stayed down until I was out of sight, and swam all the way to Bolivar Peninsula, north of town. I had a lotta time to think—if they were tryin' to take us out, they were gonna try again if they found out they missed one. I decided to disappear.

"I got one good break—Tommy never told the pilot who I was. I managed to hitch back to my apartment and grab some clothes, but I left enough stuff to make it look like I hadn't been there. Tommy's brother reported us missing—he knew we were goin' diving but that was it. There were all kinds of theories about us runnin' off, or bein' kidnapped, or just drownin' in the Gulf. I was hidin' out in Port Arthur, but our pictures were all over the TV news, so I headed north.

"I was standin' by the highway in Virginia with my thumb out when it finally sank in that Tommy was really gone."

Lynn blinked away tears—Meg was a pretty good storyteller. As usual, Zen-mind noted both her sadness and her resistance to it, and let them both evaporate.

"I figured they'd never expect a Houston girl to want to live in Boston, so I settled in here, got a waitress job under a false name. With my looks and my accent, I made pretty good tips and did okay. And one day I was searchin' the Net and discovered what happened to Tommy."

She paused, as if Lynn might not want to know. Lynn gave her a go-ahead nod.

"It was a story about a scuba diver found in the smolderin' remains of brush fire—supposedly scooped up by a fire-fightin' plane and dropped to his death onto the flames."

Lynn narrowed her eyes.

"But, that's an urban legend."

"Right. The story was on all the urban legend websites—rated FALSE."

Which was exactly how Lynn was rating the story. Just another legend, like Roger's 200-mile-per-gallon car. Meg told it well, but something was amiss. Shouldn't she be more broken up about it? Lynn had moped around for years after Phil left.

"I don't see how you can go on as if it never happened," Lynn said finally. "Haven't you tried to do something about it?"

"Oh, I'm workin' on it, and Howie and I are thinkin' of goin' back down there this winter to do a little incognito investigation. But no matter what happens, I don't let it get me down." Meg sounded like a Southern, female Gerry. "You gotta keep your sense of humor, and look at the bright side. It hit me later, that if I hadn't broken the second rule of scuba divin' by separatin' from my buddy, I'd be *in* that urban legend, about *two* dead divers in a burned-out fire."

Lynn pondered that, then saw Meg's expectant grin.

"Okay, I'll bite," she said. "What's the first rule of scuba diving?"

"Don't breathe water."

Lynn had to smile, even as she wondered: was Meg impossibly upbeat or just really good at making up shaggy dog stories?

* * *

"Established brief visual of female targets at Broadway turning onto Norfolk. Last seen headed toward Mass Ave, but can't follow—no traffic cams on Norfolk. Male targets entering deli at Main and Hayward."

"Merci."

François glanced through the windshield at the red brick buildings lining Albany Street and pictured his location on the map. After a quick relative distance calculation, he directed Jean-Paul to continue driving toward Kendall Square. There were enough traffic cams there to keep track of the men. And while the women had disappeared again and were further away, they would likely reappear somewhere in Central Square—where François had reinforcements who would not be recognized.

He called La Longe Baguette. The line rang repeatedly—Saturday afternoon, they had to be open—and after the eleventh, a parochial Boston accent blared onto the line.

"Lah Longe Bahguette. Yvette speakin'."

François leaned away from the phone, suddenly nostalgic for the ringing.

"Yvette, this is François Spaquel—Truffle Division. I have a rush order."

"Yeah? Yah gonna need a keyword for that."

Merde. Even she needed a keyword…

"The béarnaise is burning."

"Hey, that's right! Whaddya know! What can we do for ya?"

"I require two able, ah, helpers, immediately, in your vicinity. What have you available?"

"Lemme tell ya, Frannswah"—he grimaced at the mangled pronunciation—"theah's only me and two guys workin' heah, and the line's 'bout twenty people. So we can only give ya the two guys. But theah wicked big, and mean, too." Her voice faded as she shouted across the shop. "Pieah! And Pieah! Yah needed down the street. Rush ordah." The voice came back to the phone. "They'll be heah in a sec."

"They are both named Pierre?"

"Naw, that ain't theah real names. We all get French names when we work heah, fah the atmospheah, ya know?"

"But... *both* are Pierre?"

"Why not? Everybody's Pieah or Yvette. Cheapah that way—we buy the nametags in bulk."

François shook his head and waited for Pierre (or perhaps it was Pierre?) to pick up the line. He instructed them to proceed to Norfolk and Mass Ave. and locate the targets emerging from the side street.

"One thing in addition," he said before hanging up. "Is there a short, very round man in a black suit and pastel tie in your establishment?"

Pierre hesitated, then answered, "Yeah, he's been waitin' in line, for like, forever. But he's almost to the front."

"His name is Toine. Tell him the chocolate croissants must wait, and bring him with you."

* * *

Walking the last block to Nature's Grocery, Lynn conceded that her Texas shadow was not going to disappear, so she filled Meg in on where she was going, hinting that she'd like to talk with Gerry alone. Meg didn't seem to take the hint. Lynn started to insist as she pulled open the Grocery door, but then she glanced up and stopped talking.

Three men were walking down the other side of Mass Ave.

One was pale with long blond locks and the second black with flat-cut hair, both large and young and wearing white baker's uniforms. The third was the fat businessman from lunch at the Castle, eons earlier that day. He was visibly very upset about something, complaining to the others.

"We've got trouble, Meg," Lynn said, ducking her head away and pushing into the store. "The guy who used the voice transmitter on me is across the street. From the Truffle Cartel. And he brought some friends. Big ones."

"Did they spot you?"

As the door closed behind her, its bell gently ringing, Lynn snuck a glance through the front window.

"I don't think so."

"Well, I'm wonderin' if you really want to get Gerry involved in this. The less he knows, the more likely those thugs'll leave him be."

Lynn's eyes went wide.

"They wouldn't bother Gerry! Besides, they didn't see us come in here."

"Maybe they didn't. How 'bout we just do a little shoppin' and make sure, 'fore we start spreadin' our troubles around?"

Lynn observed Gerry as he cheerfully worked the register. He looked like the sage he was, with a gray beard, a simple ponytail, and sixty years' worth of wisdom inscribed into the kindly lines on his face.

Why would anyone want to hurt Gerry?

* * *

François tapped his phone against his chin. The male targets had disappeared into the Kendall Square T station—where the surveilleur's camera network could not see. They would be aboard a train, bound for an unknown location, before François could reach the platform.

But there was good news, also. The Central Square traffic cams had rediscovered the women once they reached Mass Ave, and more importantly, surveillance had noted that they entered a certain "Nature's Grocery."

He had expected the women would also disappear into the subway. Perhaps they spotted Toine's team, and this establishment was merely a temporary hiding place. But Toine and the Pierres were not involved in the truffle farm attack, and thus could not have been recognized.

A delicious idea began to form.

Perhaps Nature's Grocery was their destination. Perhaps it concealed a secret entrance.

A natural food store would be fitting, if not obvious. The men, conceivably, had split off to draw away any tails, or simply to shop for disgusting delicatessen food, while the women proceeded directly to safety.

They would soon learn that safety was not so easily attained.

He called Toine.

"François here. Your targets have taken refuge in Nature's Grocery, which is located one block from you, toward the square. Proceed there immediately. Cause no public disturbance, but secure the establishment. They will likely attempt to escape by some hidden exit. Allow them to reveal the portal, but do not permit them to use it."

Chapter 4

Gerry Rutland's day always brightened when Lynn Grady came through the door. He didn't see his protégé as much since he'd opened the Grocery, but she made it a point to stop by on occasion and let him know she was still doing okay. This time was different, though—she was with a new friend, a younger, dark-haired girl.

He packed his customer's produce a little faster than usual, and after thanking the woman and sending her on her way, beckoned to Lynn.

"Hi Lynn! What brings you here today?"

Lynn glanced at her friend before answering.

"Just doing a little shopping, Gerry."

"Really! I thought you'd rather eat out than make your own dinner."

"If somebody else is paying. I can't stand my cooking."

"You do have good taste."

He waited, smiling, and Lynn rewarded him with the appropriate sneer; he remembered a time when she was too insecure to handle that kind of kidding. He turned to the newcomer and offered his hand.

"Gerry Rutland, at your service."

"Meg Bryson; pleased to meet you."

The girl's handshake was icy cold—and her clothes were damp.

"You're wet. It can't be raining."

"Ran across a badly-timed sprinkler—don't worry, I'm just about dry."

"I hope so," Gerry said, pleased at her attitude about it. "But you don't want to catch a cold. If you need a towel, the bathroom's downstairs. Lynn can show you. And maybe she can give you a little tour. I could use a new customer." He shot her a playful look, but only half joking.

"Fact is," Meg said, backing away a little, "I'm kinda into synthetic foods." A disappointing answer, but honest, at least.

"Well, you can fix that here. You won't find anything that isn't real and good for you, except the stuff in the cages." Another customer approached the register, so Gerry excused himself. Lynn and Meg nodded and wandered off as he began weighing fruits and vegetables.

He'd always looked out for Lynn. When she'd first come to work at the warehouse with no money, no experience and no confidence, she was a poster child for human suffering—that universal misery of need that the Buddha learned to overcome. So while he started off teaching her practical stuff like how to drive a forklift and repair a dropped pallet so the boss wouldn't notice, he slipped in some spiritual hints, too. As it turned out, she'd grown up with Zen, and she became a willing, though not accomplished, pupil. Over the years, she'd learned to reject the turmoil of modern living, focus on the joys of motherhood, and at least occasionally find the true peace of turning inward.

Recently, though, he'd begun to wonder if he'd gone too far. It was fine for him to live like a monk; he was too old to change and too Zen to regret. But Lynn was still in the prime of life—he hated to think he'd turned her into a nun before her time. He'd even started gently encouraging her to broaden her horizons, but to no avail. She didn't get out much. Even after she discovered yoga, she avoided studio classes, pleading poverty and practicing at home.

He smiled to himself. As any Zen devotee should have known, there was never a need to worry. Lynn was finally breaking out of the rut, finding new interests, and new friends. Meg seemed like a down-to-earth girl, even if she was into "synthetic foods."

* * *

Meg insisted that her tour of Nature's Grocery start off near the back, where she could watch the windows without being seen from outside. So Lynn showed her the cages—a high shelf crammed with wire-frame pens, each smaller than a microwave oven. A sign perched on top said "Cage Poisons, not Hens." Meg grew up with chickens around, but on such a small farm the poultry went pretty much wherever they pleased.

She imagined 'em stuffed into those tiny coops and allowed that maybe there was something to all that free-range stuff.

'Course, better to come up with hen-free eggs—she'd have to work on that.

Trapped in the cages were food items, each with a "poison" sign stuck in it, complete with skull and crossbones, and what made it toxic. There was an apple ("Pesticides"), a bag of mass-produced cookies ("Trans Fat"), an ear of corn ("Genetically Modified"), a dried steak ("Bovine Growth Hormone"), and a bag of white flour ("Irradiated"). The imprisoned foods were what Gerry meant by stuff that wasn't good for you. She wondered what the old hippie would think of her hydroponic truffles; the ingredients were all natural, if not the growing process.

Lynn pointed out the selection and benefits of organic, non-allergenic, gluten-free products. Meg didn't recognize a single brand name, but then, she wasn't their target market. For all she knew, these names were the Swanson's and Oscar Mayer of the New Age. She hoped Gerry's suppliers hadn't been corrupted by the Pseudonatural Foods Cartel like the big organic food chains.

It wasn't all food for the body—there were books, music, and even crystals to nourish the mind and soul. But Meg's mind was focused less on nourishment than on the Truffle Cartel thugs and possible escape routes. She noted a back hall, leading past the basement stairwell to a steel door—the rear exit.

"How'd you get into all this stuff, Lynn?" she asked, casually glancing through the front window for the three men.

"I grew up organic—my folks were authentic sixties hippies. I was raised in the wholesome atmosphere of the New Hanover Academy, out near Dartmouth College in New Hampshire. The neighbors complained about it being a commune, but it was more of a boarding house—we didn't share everything, just the garden and the chores. The real point of the place was Zen training—that's the Academy part. We sat zazen—meditation—every morning and evening, and listened to Master Chuushin lecture after dinner. We also did T'ai Chi after breakfast and played basketball after school."

"I'm tryin' to picture a little Japanese guru takin' it to the hoop in his robe and sandals."

Lynn laughed.

"Master Chuushin was short, but he was African-American, not Japanese; his birth name was DeShawn. He grew up playing street ball in L.A., so he used basketball as a Zen exercise, to help us pay attention to the here and now. It was a fun way to meditate—and I picked up a few moves, too."

Meg glanced down the stairwell—probably led to a dead end. Not every building in Cambridge had a tunnel under it.

"So—the Academy, that where you met Gerry?"

"No, that was later, after—" Lynn paused, mentally wrestling with something. "After my divorce, I took a job at the Momma's Good Food distribution warehouse, over in Watertown. Gerry worked there. He's the one who got me back into Zen. To be honest, it saved my life, too—I was a mess before then. I think Gerry's kind of proud of me, getting myself back together following his advice. He left Momma's a few years ago to open this place, but he still likes to watch over me. He knows I'm stretching to pay the rent and save for my daughter's college, so he helps me out however he can."

Meg considered the old man as he busily served his customers. She was amazed he could afford to help anyone, beyond protecting them from toxic food. All those caged poisons were what made manufactured food cheap enough to transport cross-country, move through layers of distribution, sell in bulk to bulky families, and still clear enough margin to pay the stockholders. Organic stuff cost more to produce and more to transport, so you could only sell it to a few local, wealthy, and enlightened customers.

Of course, that never stopped people like Gerry—every city had a handful of struggling independent natural groceries. And they were all run by aging hippies, trying to keep the Earth Day dream alive, forty years later.

It's a little piece of Eden, Meg thought, catching a glimpse of the fat man creeping toward the front door. *And the snake is right outside.*

She gave Lynn's blouse a yank at the waist, toward the back hallway.

"We'd best be goin'."

* * *

Toine dispatched white Pierre around to the Grocery's back door and posted black Pierre at the front. He found it awkward to call these two "Pierre," but they insisted on using their name-tagged names, no matter how inappropriate. And inconvenient. But at least the Pierres were strong and willing to do violence, which would perhaps relieve Toine of that responsibility. Not that he found any fault with violence, except that it often required substantial exertion.

Toine delayed two minutes for white Pierre to reach his position and then squeezed through the door to Nature's Grocery. A quick scan revealed an annoyingly wholesome-looking proprietor serving a customer, an elderly lady selecting items from a refrigerator, and Toine's targets. The two women, one tall and one short, were edging toward the rear of the store. Toine sucked in his breath—François had neglected to mention the tall one's distinctive red hair, so painfully familiar from the Castle restaurant disaster.

At that moment the woman glanced over her shoulder, so Toine rotated to hide his face. He stuffed his bulk between the dog food and the cleaning products, pretending to seek something on the low shelf—and cursing the emaciated vegetarians who laid out the narrow aisles.

He phoned François.

"Zey are here," he puffed. "But zere is a trouble. One of zem is ze woman from ze restaurant. I know zat she saw me. I assume zat she recognized me."

François' voice was hard.

"It has perhaps become more difficult, but your objective is unchanged. Remove the other customers and keep the women waiting there until we arrive."

"But how will I make zem wait?"

"You are a French waiter, are you not? It is what you do."

* * *

Lynn noted the fat man's struggle to wedge himself between the closely-spaced shelves. He was obviously out of place; Nature's Grocery customers were much too health-minded to gain so much weight. Or perhaps, at organic food prices, they couldn't afford to overeat.

But there wasn't time to dwell on it as she and Meg slipped through the short hall to the back exit. Meg pushed the door open a crack, her face pressed to the edge.

"Shoot," she muttered, easing the door shut. "One of the bakers is staked out back there. Should we try to bust through 'im? He's mighty big, but so are you."

Lynn cringed at the thought of attacking anyone—besides, size wouldn't matter if the guy had a gun, like every other Truffle Cartel agent she'd met so far.

"This is a public grocery," she said. "Customers are around. If the Truffle Cartel is as clandestine as Roger claims, they can't start shooting up the place. Can we just wait them out?"

"Okay, but we'd best let Howie and Roger know what's up."

Lynn shrugged agreement; her attempt to escape the boys was failing miserably. Meg whispered over the phone to Howie about the fat man and the bakers.

"Howie says wait here and act natural."

It would be natural to scream for the police, but that probably wasn't what Howie meant.

They returned to the store area, where the one remaining customer was halfway out the door. Lynn spotted a baker outside, just before the door fell shut and left her staring at the hanging carved-wood OPEN sign—which meant someone had flipped it to read CLOSED to the outside. They were alone with Gerry, and no other customers were going to wander in. Gerry was looking at her funny. She craned to find the fat man.

"No, I am no longer concealed behind ze shelves."

The voice that invaded her head at lunch was now directly behind her. With its usual calm detachment, Zen-mind noted her confusion, anger, and fear. And a disturbing loss of innocence, when she realized how clearly she could picture a pistol by the feel of its muzzle against her neck.

* * *

Roger leaned against the red and white tiles of the Kendall Square station wall, trying to look casual as he counted the minutes until the next inbound train. Howie's quest for acceptable bagels and lox had kept them in the open easily long enough for the Truffle Cartel agents to spot them and follow them into the T.

Between glances at the platform entrance and his watch, he studied the subway chimes—a wall of vertical tubes and hammers between the inbound and outbound tracks. The tubes, attached to a knee-high barrier and the ceiling by tight wires, were different lengths to create a B-minor chord. The hammers were cabled to levers on the platform walls, to be operated by bored subway riders as they waited for their train.

Some Harvard artist had installed them, along with a ring-shaped bell and a rectangular gong, as an innovative, participatory work of social art known as the Kendall Band. But as well-intentioned and clever as it was, the Harvie hadn't gotten any MIT engineering advice—the mechanisms had been chronically broken until a group of MIT students formed the Kendall Band Preservation Society and began to re-engineer them into working order.

He smiled to think of the rivalry between the two schools, just a few miles and two subway stops apart. MIT asserted its dominance by hacking Harvard constantly, from an MIT "brass rat" class ring welded onto the John Harvard statue's finger, to the MIT-logo'd weather balloon sprouting from the fifty-yard line during a Harvard-Yale football game. Poor Harvard never managed to retaliate.

This made him consider, with some chagrin, that maybe the "rivalry" was just an MIT fantasy.

Maybe Harvard didn't give a crap. Why should they? Most likely every one of those MIT hackers graduated and went to work for a Harvard boss.

Howie had moved down the platform toward the cell repeater to get better reception for an incoming call. The news was not pleasant, from the look on his face as he sprinted back.

"That was Meg. She found Lynn, but they're trapped in a grocery by your fat guy and a couple of bakers!"

Roger found this confusing.

"Come on!" Howie prodded. "We have to go!"

"Where?"

Howie pulled him toward the platform's edge.

"Outbound!" he shouted, and leapt down between the tracks. Hurdling the high-voltage third rail, he sprang up onto one of the chime tubes, like Tarzan taking to a jungle vine.

As a mechanical engineer, Roger instinctively analyzed the situation and concluded that:

a) Vines are a lot easier to grip than chimes,

b) Tarzan was a lot stronger than Howie,

c) Tarzan never hopped a vine while carrying a bag of bagels and lox, and most importantly,

d) Tarzan's vines weren't anchored at the bottom.

With a muffled F#, Howie hit the chime and slid straight down, clutching the deli bag and collapsing in a heap on the low center barrier. He began to slide off, perilously close to the hot rail.

Roger jumped out onto the tracks and across to the barrier, grabbing a chime for balance as he dragged Howie upright. His partner was groggy but hung on as Roger pulled him over the wall between F# and E to the outbound side. Roger didn't dare trust Howie to step carefully, so he lifted him over his shoulder into a fireman's carry as he straddled the outbound hot rail.

The tunnel erupted with the screech of metal wheels—an arriving train, diving underground from the Longfellow Bridge. With no room behind him, Roger stepped forward, but impulsively glanced toward the train and its blinding headlight. Seeing nothing but a bright circle, he stumbled toward the far platform until he felt the outer rail snag his toes. He tried to overestimate the distance to the platform edge—this was no time to come up short.

The train horn blared, triggering the burst of adrenaline needed to fling Howie up and forward and then launch himself in the same direction. He bounced shoulder first onto the concrete and pulled his legs in, feeling the whoosh of displaced air but hearing only the horn, nerve-shatteringly loud and Doppler-shifting flat, as the front car blew past.

As his vision recovered, Roger got to his feet and dusted himself off, then helped Howie do the same. The train had slowed to a stop and the sleek gray doors hissed open. The two young men shuffled inside.

Howie glanced at his empty hands, and scowled.

"You made me drop my bagels."

* * *

François smiled as Jean-Paul pulled the car abreast of Nature's Grocery. The sign said CLOSED and the blinds were drawn; a baker stood guard, glaring at every passerby who approached the door. François checked that his weapon was properly concealed, exited the vehicle, and leaned into the open passenger window.

"Park in the lot behind this building. I expect you will find another baker there; enter together through the back door. I shall meet you inside."

Jean-Paul nodded eagerly and pulled away.

François introduced himself to the nametag-economics-christened Pierre and advanced into Nature's Grocery.

Inside, Toine had positioned his Glock behind the ear of the tall redhead. It looked uncomfortable for him, François noted with mild amusement, requiring a considerable reach in two dimensions for such a short, round man. The farm girl who had dispatched the truffle tanks was standing by. She was obviously angry, but also quite helpless, given the redhead's predicament. The third occupant was an elderly gentleman who appeared ready to die of fright at any moment.

Which could be arranged, if necessary.

"Good afternoon, Toine; I see you have everything under control." Unfortunately, he had apparently achieved this situation without exposing any hidden passage. François turned to the others. "Are you willing to tell us where the secret entrance is, or must we perform our own search?"

"What are you talking about?" the old man sputtered. "What are you people doing in my store?"

"I shall accept that answer as a no. I suppose we shall begin investigating that room over there."

The old man sputtered again.

"That's a private office! I'll call the police!" He reached for the phone.

"No, you will not," Toine said quietly. The old man looked up, eyes widening as they locked onto the pistol buried in red hair. His hand retreated from the phone, and pride welled in François' throat.

François strode to the back and opened the delivery door. Jean-Paul and the other American chain restaurant Pierre—this one blond—were marching rapidly from the parking lot, and they followed him inside.

"Pierre, assist Toine in holding our hostages, s'il vous plaît. Jean-Paul, we must locate our second secret entrance of the day. Let us be quicker about this one, M'sieur. We have not the time to be tidy."

"We can begin our searchion here," Jean-Paul said, and casually kicked a hole through the nearest wall. François instinctively flinched; the proprietor began to object but had learned to hold his tongue.

"Pardonnez-moi," Jean-Paul pleaded, peering into the shattered sheetrock. "I am a mistake. There is no secretive door here."

François pointed to the stairway.

"Let us examine the basement. That is where rodents prefer to dig their tunnels."

* * *

Roger huffed up the stairs from the Central Square T station. Howie had taken two steps at a time—he was a lot lighter, and tapped an infinite energy supply whenever Meg was in trouble. But he'd frozen at the top—probably because of the large man in a baker's outfit standing sentry outside Nature's Grocery.

"Can you distract him, Roger?"

"So you can slip inside? Then what are you gonna do?"

"Eh, I'll think of something. Go on, it's not like we have all day."

Roger nodded; he didn't have a plan either. He stepped out from the station canopy and wandered toward the store, sizing the man up. Other than the baker's outfit, the big guy looked pretty tough. When he turned his back on the grocery door to eye Roger's approach, Roger noted the nametag.

Pierre. Had to be some kind of joke. Except Pierre didn't look like he had a sense of humor.

"Pierre! I'm so lucky to find you here—I've been shopping all over Cambridge for some Chicago-style pizza dough. You're a baker; you must know where I can find some."

"Sorry, Jack, I don't do pizza; just baguettes."

"Oh, yeah, I shoulda known, by the name. You're so obviously French."

"Fuckez-vous. I hadda change my name to work at La Longe Baguette."

"Ah. Happens all the time." Roger wasn't lying—he remembered how all the security guards at White Sox games had to change their names to Andy.

While Roger pressed for a bakery recommendation, Howie crept along the storefronts to the grocery door, then pulled it open and dove through.

He hadn't figured on the bells. Pierre whirled around, and back.

"You did that on purpose, Jack! That sucks, asshole, you're one o' them!"

"Did what? One of who?"

Pierre snarled, stepped forward, and planted a hard right into Roger's stomach. His air gone and his stomach in his throat, Roger doubled over, staggering.

What the hell? In public? *Must be a rookie...*

"Pierre!" he gasped, backing off to avoid the next blow. "I'm just trying to make a pizza!"

The baker lunged again, and Roger ducked the shot to his face.

But the swing wasn't a punch, it was a grab; Roger felt a hand tighten on the back of his collar, and suddenly, his view flipped from red brick sidewalk to blue Cambridge sky. As a mechanical engineer, he couldn't help estimating the enormous stress forces required to spin his considerable mass around so quickly. Shrieking nerves in his neck verified the estimate.

Leveraging the neck hold and a painful armlock, Pierre lifted him, swung his feet toward the store, and prodded him forward. Roger took the opportunity to admire the building's intricate cornice work, since that was the only thing he could see. But he quickly decided to forego the Architectural History skill patch review and focus on his Martial Arts patch techniques—in particular, escape tactics against a larger, stronger captor.

* * *

The pain of her arm being twisted behind her back helped Lynn focus on the moment, kind of like Master Chuushin's stick. The fat man—*Toine*—had tired of reaching up so high and transferred the gun to Meg's more accessible neck, leaving the baker to control Lynn. The armlock wasn't really necessary given Meg's situation.

The sounds of François and Jean-Paul destroying the basement flooded her with guilt for getting Gerry involved in this. Her dear bodhisattva was as close to distraught as an accomplished Zen devotee could be.

"Breathe, Gerry."

Gerry nodded at the admonishment. Breathing deeply seemed to help relax him, but he still winced at every crash from below. And Lynn winced every time Gerry did.

The front door burst open with a violent bell-jangle and Howie vaulted into the store. When he spotted Meg and the gun to her neck, he froze.

Toine turned slowly, deadpan.

"Mon Dieu, you have startled me. I nearly pulled ze trigger."

Howie's face betrayed impotent rage, but his voice didn't.

"Alright, so don't get excited. What would it take to get you to let her go?"

Lynn had been wondering that herself.

"Zere is nothing zat would make me act so foolishly. But I find myself growing weak with hunger; I fear I will soon lose control of my trigger finger. So I suggest zat you find me a morsel to eat somewhere in here—buttery, if zat is possible. And do zis soon, before I accidentally waste a bullet—and your pretty little friend."

Howie searched the snack shelf, muttering.

"You remind me of my overweight Uncle Stu, except for the gun. You should be careful; he died of advanced arteriosclerosis. Massive heart attack, right in the middle of Yom Kippur. Left poor deaf Aunt Sadie with no one to shout at—"

"Just find ze food!"

The front door jingled open, gently this time. Lynn glanced up to see Roger, bent backward, tip-toeing oddly across the threshold. Another baker followed, with one of Roger's arms in a painfully familiar lock hold.

They must teach that hold at baker school, Lynn decided.

As the door slammed behind them, bells jingling, Roger snapped his free elbow into the baker's midsection. Air exploded from the man's lungs and his body launched backward like a jet-propelled balloon. He crumpled against the glass, ringing the bells yet again.

Roger dove behind a shelf, and Toine yelled to the basement for help. Lynn heard Roger whispering in her head—he still had Toine's voice transmitter.

LYNN. GET READY TO DUCK.

Roger popped up over the gluten-free crackers, throwing overhand. As Lynn jerked her head down, wincing from the increased strain on her arm, a family-size jar of Mother Carmella's All Natural Comfort Balm whizzed past her shoulder and crushed into the side of the baker's head. His grip went limp; Lynn pulled free as he slumped to the floor. A second jar zipped across the aisles, cleared Meg's head by a barrette-width, and smacked Toine below the ear.

He dropped the gun and clutched Meg for balance. But her tiny frame couldn't offset his tottering bulk, so they tumbled backward into the produce shelf, sending organic vegetables flying and a poison cage plummeting onto Toine's head. The imprisoned bag of irradiated flour exploded, coating Toine, Meg, and the scattered vegetables like a harvest snowfall. A surreal white haze floated above them.

Sneezing violently, Meg seized Toine's pistol and leapt to her feet. As she tucked the weapon into her messenger bag, Howie scrambled around the aisle to yank her powdered arm toward the door. Roger was close behind, nodding impatiently for Lynn to follow. But Gerry stayed at the counter, dithering like a squirrel in the sights of an SUV.

"Run, Gerry!"

Gerry glanced back and forth frantically, but couldn't move.

"Roger, help!" Lynn yelled, rushing to the counter. Roger joined her as the door jangled to announce Meg and Howie's escape.

"Stop!"

Jean-Paul sprinted from the basement entrance to block the door.

"Pierre!" he barked. "Follow the others!" The bakers, just getting to their feet, scrambled after Howie and Meg.

"You're not so tough without a weapon," Roger said, advancing slowly.

Lynn thought maybe they shouldn't remind Jean-Paul about losing his gun in the lab; he might still be upset.

"I am never without a weapon," he snarled. He glanced sideways, spotted the wine shelf and grabbed a bottle by the neck.

"Crystal Mountain Canadian Organic Chardonnay, pyramid-aged," he read from the label. Baring his teeth, he smashed the bottle onto the tofu cooler. White wine and green shards sprayed across the linoleum. He brandished the jagged neck and glared at Lynn.

"Let us see you slap *this* away."

Yeah, he was still upset.

"It's my turn," said Roger, drawing Jean-Paul's intense focus back onto himself. The Frenchman stalked him, waving the bottle like a knife, and smiling. He'd done this sort of thing before. Roger backed off.

"Please," Gerry pleaded. "Someone could get hurt!"

That's the basic idea, Gerry, Lynn thought.

Roger made a quick move at a throwing jar, but Jean-Paul slashed, forcing him back with a shredded sleeve. He kept retreating, scanning side to side, but Jean-Paul yielded no opportunity to find a weapon.

Being a remedial Zen student, Lynn wasn't sure how the rules against violence applied if you needed to save someone else. Just in case, she backed up to a shelf and groped behind her. She felt only light plastic bottles, but one had a spray head; she grabbed it, twisted the tip, and wrapped her fingers around the pump lever.

Jean-Paul slashed again, slicing air as Roger leapt back. But now the glistening blades of glass pointed directly at Lynn. Jean-Paul's eyes met hers for a split second. She could see his hate.

He lunged at her stomach; she jumped sideways, bringing the spray bottle around and squeezing a shot into his face. He cursed and pulled up, his first instinct to claw at his eyes. His second instinct was to drop the glass, after it opened a gash on his forehead.

Blood thinned by Wholesome Pure Kitchen Kleener drained through Jean-Paul's bushy eyebrows as he staggered blindly. His heels found the information rack, and the rest of him collapsed in a shower of New Age books and tranquility CDs. Lynn guessed that the four-inch-thick hardcover Vegetarian Times Cookbook packed quite a wallop.

She felt a twinge of guilt for violating pacifist principles, but the spray was all natural—shouldn't that count for something? She turned to fetch Gerry again, but he'd already rushed to the first aid section for hemp gauze pads and organic eyewash.

"Hold still, this will help," he said, pressing a bandage against Jean-Paul's head. He carefully flushed the Frenchman's eyes. "I told you someone could get hurt."

"Um, sir?" Roger said, "We weren't done fighting yet." He glanced at the door. "And to be honest, we really should get out of here before it's too late."

"It is already too late."

François stood in the basement entryway, with a pistol leveled at Roger's chest.

"I couldn't agree more," Roger admitted.

François shook his head as he looked over the wreckage of Nature's Grocery, the glass fragments floating in Chardonnay puddles, and Jean-Paul receiving first aid.

"You see, Jean-Paul, this is what happens when you respond too hastily to a request for assistance. You lose control of the situation. Now you are injured, and worst of all, you have wasted a perfectly good bottle of wine."

"Good?" Jean-Paul brushed away Gerry's hand and held the pad himself. "It is Québécois piss!" He peered at Gerry though watery eyes. "If you want good Chardonnay, you should stockade real wine. The kind that comes from France!"

"Jean-Paul! Remain calm!" barked François. "The absence of a French label does not establish the absence of quality."

Jean-Paul turned.

"Québécois are scumsacks, François! They make ice wine! They freeze their fucking grapes!"

François bristled, neglecting his aim slightly. It was a weird time to argue about Chardonnay, Lynn thought.

"Never mind about the wine!" François re-aimed and refocused on Roger. "I grow weary of this. There is apparently no secret entrance downstairs, so I shall be forced to extract its location from you."

"I'm not aware of any secret entrance," Roger said.

"Except for the back door to your underground laboratory?"

"Actually, I didn't know that one was open till you barged through it."

"It matters not—I seek something far more important than your pitiful truffle farm. And I assure you, we can persuade you to reveal it."

Lynn followed Roger's cold stare across the shelf tops, along the barrel of the pistol and up into the Frenchman's smug smile.

"Give it your best shot, François," Roger said.

Please don't, François, Lynn thought.

* * *

François appraised Toine, who lay unconscious under a pile of vegetables, everything coated with irradiated flour, according to the sign balanced on the summit of his belly. He looked ready for the sauté pan.

Toine groggily came to his senses, tossed off the vegetables, cage, and signage, and began brushing off his suit. His head was misshapen by a large lump growing below his ear, visibly purple even through the flour coating. He frantically scanned the pile of powder around his feet.

"Where is my weapon?!"

"The farm girl probably stole it," Jean-Paul muttered. "I suppose she has a big gun ensemble by now." He turned to François. "She and the little bowl-head escaped, but I sent the Pierres after them. The girl was spewing clouds of flour; they will find her and deal with her."

François reflected briefly on his interns' shared irresponsibility with guns; the Lost Equipment Forms were beginning to pile up. But the image of the bakers chasing the flour-coated girl gave him an idea.

The front door bell jingled and the two Pierres burst in, breathless. They had taken no prisoners.

"Well?"

"They booked it into the T," said white Pierre. "We were right on their ass. But at the bottom of the stairs, man, all these high-school girls were droolin' on the nerd like he was a fuckin' pop star. He pointed, and they mobbed us. We couldn't get by."

"The targets escaped?"

"Yeah. Got on the train, an' it pulled out before we could get there. We were gonna grab the next one, but figured, shit, they could get off anywhere between here and Braintree and we'd never find 'em."

François considered this. Pierre was half-correct: the targets could indeed disembark anywhere between there and Braintree. But he was wrong to think they would not be found.

"You have done what you could," he said kindly. Then, to Jean-Paul, "M'sieur, how serious is your wound?"

Jean-Paul examined the bloodied bandage, and hastily reapplied it.

"It is just a scratch."

"Good. May I assume that you can manage my weapon with your other hand? And that your eyes have cleared enough to aim?"

Jean-Paul nodded, unable to hide his gleeful anticipation of again handling a gun.

"Splendid. Please take this and aim it at the shop's proprietor." He waved the gun at the old man, who had stood petrified since François' arrival upstairs. "Observe us as we escort our prisoners to the car. We shall be in public and cannot physically force them to come. Therefore, if for any reason we do not leave with them in our car, immediately kill your hostage." Jean-Paul was smiling broadly now. Not so the redhead and her partner, and especially not the old man.

Jean-Paul exchanged the car key for François' weapon and, over the protests of the redhead, pressed the gun to the root of the proprietor's gray ponytail. François turned to the others.

"Now, let us proceed to the car before Jean-Paul becomes impatient. He is not a patient man."

"Breathe, Gerry," said the redhead. "Everything will be okay." Her eyes and voice betrayed her anxiety about the old man's fate. And thus she would not risk his life by attempting to escape.

François and Toine took the hostages, each escorted by a Pierre, through the back entrance and across the parking lot to the car. There were people around, but given the threat to the proprietor, François expected that his captives would not run. He did not expect that the young man would pick his nose—blatantly, several times. Toine glared at him—the young man only shrugged.

"Sorry, got some flour up there. Really itches." He twitched his nose, reminiscent of a large rabbit.

"Do not complain to me about ze flour," Toine responded sourly, gingerly touching the lump on his jaw.

As they approached the Lincoln, François pressed the remote trunk release. The reaction of the redhead was instantaneous, and rather enjoyable—her jaw dropped and her eyes widened in perfect synchronization with the slow rise of the trunk lid.

"Madame, I do not believe we can effectively control you in the passenger compartment without my weapon. Regretfully, we must transport you in the trunk."

Toine and the Pierres tightened the circle around them.

"No!" the woman pleaded quietly. "Please, don't put me in there."

Her partner touched her shoulder.

"They have Gerry. Like you told him, everything will be okay."

François smiled at the success of his hostage ploy.

The woman's breathing became shallow as she watched the young man squeeze into the space, but she allowed herself to be guided in behind him. There was little room for two such large people. François wondered if they were intimate—they soon would be, if they were not already. Toine seemed to take pity; he gave the woman a few extra moments of air and light before he lowered the trunk lid, graciously checking for protruding fingers before latching it into place. Or perhaps he wisely realized that, in traffic, protruding fingers might be noticed.

François considered his resources as they moved beyond hearing range of the trunk. He would need the size of the two Pierres to control the captives. And Toine's flour-covered clothing would be useful for following the others.

"Toine. You and Jean-Paul shall track the two who escaped."

"How can we track zem?" asked Toine. "Zey could get off ze metro anywhere!"

He was François' prize student, but still so unimaginative.

"Earlier today, in a dark tunnel, Jean-Paul and I followed a trail of iridescent water. Now you shall follow something much brighter, although it requires special eyes to see it. There is a Battery Hut on the next block. Purchase an adjustable narrow-band radiation detector. Use the flour on your coat as a standard." He studied Toine for a moment. Sad, and yet comical; not unlike an immense powdered donut. "And then acquire some new clothing."

Toine gaped down at his now light-gray suit, finally comprehending. He turned toward the shop, but François stopped him with a touch.

"Several more items: Continue to retain the proprietor until we are safely out of sight. And before you go, please remind the old man that we have his friends, and harm will come to them if he speaks a word of this to anyone."

Toine nodded and chugged back across the parking lot.

"Remember to keep the receipts for your expense report," François called after him. He faced the Pierres.

"The flour on Toine's coat, and on the girl's clothing, was irradiated. Like all radiation, it has a half-life of many years and thus remains quite intense. With a narrow-band radiation detector, tuned precisely to the residual energy emitted by the flour, we can determine at which station the target exits, and where she goes after that. Unless, of course, she finds an opportunity to shower and dispose of her clothing along the way. But, this I doubt."

He paused to consider likely outcomes. Despite their powdery advantage, Jean-Paul and Toine would almost certainly encounter further security measures. Hence the remainder of the plan required critical timing.

"Come; let us take the next step. Pierre, you shall drive, I have telephone calls to make." He handed the key bob to white Pierre and slid into the back seat.

"What about this?"

Black Pierre was holding an orange parking ticket envelope. François glanced out at the meter, which was flashing "expired" in red, and shook his head. This expense would come out of Jean-Paul's pocket—the accounting department would not reimburse parking fines, and Jean-Paul apparently had yet to learn that American parking meters do not magically feed themselves.

* * *

"I think zat you can understand ze seriousness of your friends' situation," Toine explained to the terrified proprietor. "And so it is clear to you zat to keep zem safe, you must not tell anyone what has occurred here? If you are asked, you will say you were struck from behind and did not see who caused ze damage to your store?"

The old man nodded nervously.

"I will make it easy to justify your story," Jean-Paul added, "by making a bruise for you." He drew back the pistol and slapped it behind the man's ear. The proprietor, too frail for even such a light blow, collapsed unconscious onto the pile of flour.

Toine studied the scene with dismay.

"If zey find him before he awakens, ze story will not hold. Ze authorities will notice zat he has fallen on top of ze mess, not ze other way around."

Jean-Paul pondered this.

"I can fix that," he said. He brought the weapon to bear on the old man's head.

"Jean-Paul, no! Zat is too drastic! Too much blood! François would never approve!"

"But, this is *François'* weapon. Specially modified for managers without spines. It is parfait for the job."

Toine understood. Because François disliked bloody violence, he carried a custom Glock, as did many of his peers. Instead of a bullet, it propelled a tiny but equally deadly pellet. The projectile would penetrate the skin of the victim, leaving a mark so small it would be mistaken for a mosquito bite, if it were noticed at all. And the chemical it released, while undetectable, would quickly cause a fatal heart attack, indistinguishable from a natural one.

"Zey will believe he witnessed ze destruction," Toine concurred, "and perhaps could identify zose who committed it. But zen, ze poor man apparently suffered a heart attack from ze shock."

Jean-Paul nodded, smiling.

"There is no need for a story, if there is no one to tell it."

He squeezed the trigger. The gun spit and the unconscious old man twitched.

"Come," said Toine, "we have work to accomplish."

Jean-Paul tucked the pistol into his jacket and the men proceeded to the rear exit. On the way, Toine took a moment to acquire several packages of lamentably wholesome-looking granola bars.

The proprietor did not object.

Chapter 5

Lynn didn't think the word "spooning" applied to the situation, but it was a pretty good approximation of her and Roger in the darkness. Roger was curled deep in the trunk, his legs folded tightly into the main well. Lynn's back was squeezed against his chest and belly, but she'd draped her knees over his thighs to find legroom in the side compartment. She'd seen a ledge space behind Roger, which promised a little extra air—and at the rate Lynn was breathing, she might use it up fast.

"I need to get out," she panted quietly, then louder, "Let me out!"

Roger's hand found her elbow and slid down, until he could lock fingers with her. She gripped hard.

"Good," he said. "Squeeze."

And breathe, said Zen-mind. *Slowly. Empty your mind as you empty your lungs.*

She tried to pay attention to the sensations and let the panic flow out with each exhale. She began to notice things: the smell of carpet and sweat, a tire iron pressing against her left shoulder. And Roger's body pressing against pretty much everything else.

"Relax," he whispered. "I'm here."

Somewhere in the back of her brain the absurdity kicked in, that this huge man occupying two-thirds of the available trunk space had just informed her "I'm here." Despite the panic, or maybe because of it, the next breath was half-sob, half-giggle, and soon she was crying/laughing uncontrollably.

And the panic ebbed away. *Master Chuushin would approve.*

"Are you okay?" Roger asked, his concern as palpable as his presence.

Lynn caught her breath and calmed down.

"Yes, I'm okay. It just hit me funny that you told me you're here."

"Huh," he snorted. "I guess that's pretty obvious. I was just trying to help."

She turned her head.

"You did! Thank you. It would have been worse to be alone."

The last time Lynn had been alone in a small space was during middle school. It was a basketball team tradition, she discovered, for the seventh- and eighth-grade girls to initiate the sixth graders by stuffing them into a gym locker for five minutes. It was tough for most kids to take, but Lynn was a very big sixth grader, and it took a lot of shoving to get her in there. She sustained bruises that took months to heal, and emotional scars that never did.

After that, she had a hard time trusting her teammates, and she certainly refused to take part in the hazing. They had to play ball with her, of course; they needed her height. But off the court, she was ignored by the jocks and all their popular friends. She lived through middle and high school as an oversized, shy, and somewhat clumsy pariah with a paralyzing fear of small places.

Somehow it wasn't that paralyzing when she had company. It was more like the bunk in the back of the tour bus with Phil—that was cramped, but Phil made it feel cozy.

"I'm sorry about getting you into this," Roger whispered.

"You did what you had to do to protect Gerry," she replied. "Thanks for that."

"Gerry seems like a nice old guy."

"He's not so old. And he's young at heart."

"Like you, right?"

Lynn considered that, feeling her eyes narrow.

"I like to think I'm still young at everything."

"I—I'm sorry, I just meant, well, I admire your—flexibility."

"That's the yoga."

"No! I mean—you've got a great attitude. You're adaptable."

"For such an old lady."

Roger paused.

"If you insist. I'm adaptable, too."

Even in the dark, Lynn could sense his grin.

"So what happens now, little boy?"

"Good question, Aunty Lynn. Sounds like they want to interrogate us."

"Right—about another secret entrance. To something more important than the truffle farm." It finally hit Lynn that with all the violence, this had to be a lot deeper than hydroponic truffles. "What was he talking about, Roger?"

Roger shifted slightly and didn't answer right away.

"I told you about my 200-mile-per-gallon car—the Volvo my friend Todd and I modified while I was still at MIT. But I didn't tell you everything; I was afraid I'd scare you away."

"Well, I'm not going anywhere at the moment."

"True." He paused again. Gathering his thoughts? Or getting his story straight?

"We took our prototype to Detroit that summer to meet with U.S. Motors. Their engineers ripped the car apart looking for hidden batteries and fuel tanks, and even put it into an environmental chamber to measure the byproducts. But of course, there weren't any, besides carbon dioxide and water vapor. As demos go, this one was killer.

"Finally, the managers told us they were convinced. They said it could revolutionize the industry, and how glad they were that we came to them first. Then they asked if we were prepared to sign a contract.

"Todd said 'Depends on the contract,' in his tough Jersey City accent. I relaxed—at least one of us had some business experience. They said they needed a few hours to pull it together, got our information, and promised to call later that day. We were giddy as we drove back to the motel; the future, for us and the environment, was looking pretty damn green."

He paused again, then sighed.

"Around 10 p.m. we started arguing. I said they weren't gonna call, and wanted to go out for a beer—I figured we could try one of the other car companies the next day. Todd insisted we should wait and accused me of caring more about beer than the car. I'd had enough. I stormed out of the room, past the damn car, and three blocks down the street to the nearest open bar. It only took one beer to make me regret it. It wasn't the first time I sat by myself staring into an empty glass. But it was the first time since I'd met Todd. I felt awful.

"I headed back to apologize. Two steps outside, my phone rang. It was Todd. I started to say I'm sorry, but he said forget it—U.S. Motors had just called and wanted to know if we were both available if they came over with a contract. Todd had said yes, and told me to get back there quick. He was asking if I was sober enough to read a contract when a loud pop on the phone cut him off. Two seconds later, I heard the explosion.

"I ran toward the motel, but I couldn't get within forty yards—the Volvo, and the room—and Todd—were a churning fireball. When the sirens started I backed off into the shadows and disappeared. The story in the paper the next day said everything was so badly burned they couldn't count the bodies."

Lynn was quiet for a moment. Was he really claiming Todd was murdered?

"I don't suppose the engine could've exploded on its own," she offered.

"Not a chance. It used diesel fuel, and not much of it, and there was no combustion mechanism. The explosion was huge—it had to be a bomb."

"Planted by U.S. Motors to keep your engine off the market."

"Well, I think the Fuel Cartel did it, but somebody at USM tipped them off. You got the motive right, though. The oil people live high, as long as we're all addicted to gas guzzlers. The new engine cuts fuel consumption by a factor of six, at least—that's a lot of oil profit evaporating in a hurry. At those stakes, they could afford to buy a hit. They didn't kill me, but they think they did."

Lynn shook her head in the darkness.

"The 200 mile-per-gallon car legend always has the oil companies suppressing it. But it's legend."

"That's what the oil companies want you to think. Trust me, it happened. And every day I kick myself for not dragging Todd out of the damn motel room."

Lynn could hear him breathing, quicker and more forceful now.

"On the South Side of Chicago," he went on, "people don't just get pissed, they do what I call EBAR—Escalate Beyond All Reason. Most Southsiders would've torched the USM national offices, and a few dealerships for a chaser. But I've earned my Elite Trail Boy Military Strategy skill patch. In *The Art of War*, Sun Tzu teaches that if you're outnumbered, you hide first, then fight from the shadows. The Fuel Cartel thought I was dead, and I decided it was best that way. If they figure out they missed the first time, they'll kill me for sure.

"I started fighting a guerilla technical battle to get my design out there, posting on automotive forums under a false name, as if I'd just come up with the idea. But my posts got drowned out by noise—other people posted inflated claims about fuel line magnets and hydrogen boosters, and obviously impossible statements about my engine. They planted so much misinformation, nobody would believe my articles anymore.

"One day a couple of guys showed up, saying they'd seen my posts and tracked me down. I was waiting for a bullet, but they'd figured out the truth, and wanted to help me. They signed me up—and now I work for them, along with all the other 'urban legend' survivors we've recruited. We're well organized, but we stay out of sight, fighting any cartel that uses covert technology or obscures the truth with misinformation. François is after us. He knows we have a secret headquarters in the area."

"And who is 'we'?"

Roger hesitated again.

"We call ourselves the Urban Legion."

Lynn stewed in the darkness, finding it all a little too pat to believe. And if it was true, more than a little scary. But it did jibe with Meg's story. She wondered what Howie's urban legend was. And how many others were there?

"How big is this Urban Legion? 'Legion' would imply a few thousand, at least."

"We're not really legion, that's just a cute pun; most people don't survive their 'urban legends.' Around the world, we have about two hundred agents. Twenty-three in the Boston region."

"Any chance some of them could come to the rescue?"

"It's possible. With a little luck, someone was in the area and saw my distress signal."

"What distress signal?"

"In the parking lot, I flashed one of the Urban Legion's secret hand signals. The standard greeting, if we see someone who might be one of us, is to pinch a nostril with the thumb inside and the index finger outside. We usually use that one in the car, while waiting at traffic lights. Index finger inserted means warning, danger nearby. Pinky in—which is what I used—is the distress signal. It means we're in trouble and need immediate help. We can use the signals in public because, to outsiders, it just looks like we're picking our noses. But if any of those people on the street back there were Legionnaires, we've got a tail on us already."

"Do you think any were?"

Roger sighed.

"They all looked at me like I was picking my nose in public."

That didn't surprise Lynn. The secret handshake sounded like yet another fantasy story—just like the Urban Legion itself.

"So we have to deal with this ourselves."

"Yup. I don't suppose they're taking us to another food store, stocked with all those handy weapons. The Comfort Balm jars were, like, designed for throwing."

"That was amazing," Lynn said. "I don't know how you did it—barely missed Meg and nailed Toine right on the ear."

"I played a lot of softball in Chicago."

"Softballs aren't *that* big."

"In Chicago, they are."

Lynn adjusted the position of the tire iron against her shoulder and settled back against Roger's ample padding. If she had to be trapped in a car trunk by a violent band of truffle importers, Roger was probably a pretty good guy to be trapped with. She tried to relax and picture herself lounging in the soft green grass of a wide-open Chicago outfield.

* * *

His phone to his ear and waiting to connect, François took in the view from the Harvard Bridge. The Boston skyline was charming enough, but of course, there was no Eiffel Tower—just the staid Prudential, the rhomboid Hancock, and the bouquet of downtown glass palaces blooming into the clear afternoon sky. The view to the left was idyllic, the Charles River basin dotted with sailboats and crowned with the stately Longfellow Bridge. But beyond that, the scene was marred by the Zakim, apparently a sad attempt to capitalize on the iconic Bunker Hill monument by suspending a bridge between two replicas of it. François chuckled to think of a tiny Eiffel Bridge spanning the Seine. Never would Paris allow such a perversion—a respected original could not be imitated.

The phone picked up.

"Tronics Town tech support, Neil Cherbek speaking. Have you tried rebooting?"

"This is François Spaquel—Truffle Division. I have a priority one escalation."

"Cool. Keyword?"

"Open source sucks."

"Awesome, dude. 'Sup?"

"We have discovered an interesting laboratory. We lacked time to investigate, but we noted that there were computers and machinery. We request that you extract all valuable information— without triggering any booby traps this time."

There was brief silence. François guessed that the usually arrogant young technologist was recalling the previous fiasco, when his team had attempted to retrieve a stolen Neiman-Marcus cookie recipe from a recovered laptop. A sentry program had detected their tampering and emailed the recipe all over the Internet, ruining its value. M'sieur Cherbek surely understood that equally disastrous cyber-mines awaited him in the abandoned truffle farm.

"We'll be careful. Where is it, and when can we get in?"

"It is accessible through MIT, I shall text you directions. You can enter whenever you are ready. The tunnel is dark, so bring torches—ah, flashlights. Also, wear boots."

"Boots? Like hiking boots? Rain boots?"

"Perhaps waders."

François hung up. It was rare to attain access to such a

facility—somehow, the abandoned ones always ended up completely filled with rigid insulating foam. He hoped that before then the young technicians would get in and extract the data. And, if possible, that they would extract themselves as well.

He watched pedestrians cross in front of the car for a moment, then selected another contact.

"Welcome to the Somerville Executive Inn. For reservations, please press—"

He pressed 33.

"'ousekeepeen'."

"Is this Lily?"

"Yes—'oo's askeen'?"

"This is François Spaquel—I have a code red, keyword is—"

"Don' bother, Frenchie. I know eets you."

"I am not Frenchie, Lily, I am François."

"Okay. Whatcha got, Frenchie?"

Obstinate Columbian tart… He shot an exasperated glance at Pierre in the driver's seat.

"A chemical lab that requires cleaning."

"Whatcha speel thees time?"

François sniffed at his still-damp jacket.

"Mostly water, but containing unknown additives. Can you manage it?"

"Frenchie, we 'andle 'otel sheets—and guest toot'brushes after the bellhops pull them outta their asses. We can manage."

"Just the same, I recommend gloves. And boots, there is much liquid." He rubbed his nose. "And flashlights—the access tunnel is painfully dark." His watch showed 3:55 pm. "When can you do this?"

"Tonight, we can work late. Tomorrow ees Sunday, we let the guests sleep een—we don' start bangeen' on the doors till seex t'irty."

"Fantastique. I shall text you directions. A computer team may also be there tonight. They are somewhat immature; please do not disturb their work."

"Geeks? Ah! My girls won' go near 'em."

François ended the call as Pierre wove his way around the

double-parked cars on each side of Comm Ave., scattering several jay-walking pedestrians. One more call was necessary.

"Bunker Hilltop Pre-owned Motors—we got your deals on wheels. Carl here."

"Carl, this is François Spaquel—Truffle Division. I have a special."

"Hey, great; business is stuck in first gear. You got a codeword?"

"I am not making a dime on this."

"How can we make you happy today?"

"A very unusual Volkswagen is parked on Third Street in Cambridge. It must be repossessed."

* * *

Jean-Paul leaned back on the subway bench seat, pressing gauze to his stinging head wound and trying to focus his blurred vision on the Red Line map.

The redheaded bitch would pay.

Toine sat across the car, wearing the largest clothing they could find in Central Square: an XXXL sweat suit, stretched like spandex over his middle. Its purple color matched the bruise spreading across his face.

Earlier, when they delivered Toine's powdered suit to the cleaners, Jean-Paul asked the clerk if it really was "dry clean only." The man insisted it was, but as Jean-Paul left the shop, he thought he heard snickering. He was glad he had not handed over his own clothing, now stained with truffle water, wine, blood, kitchen cleaner, and eyewash. He decided to test François' claim by washing the suit in his home machine. In cold water, to be safe.

At the first stop, the search team stood out, even among the strange occupants of Kendall station—Jean-Paul holding his bloody bandage, and Toine, looking like a giant grape, waving his radiation detector wand. Then Jean-Paul saw a blind beggar sitting against the red and white tile wall. Pretending to drop money into his coffee can, he snatched the man's sunglasses and baseball cap. He wanted the cap to hold his bandage and free up his hand, but once he saw the inside brim, he decided to keep it far away from his open wound. He tossed the hat back at the shouting man and hopped onto the train just ahead of the closing doors.

"You will pretense to be blind." he told Toine, handing him the glasses. "Your detector wand is your cane."

"But, you stole zeze from a blind man!"

"And so, he cannot identity me."

Toine, of course, could not argue with this brilliant thinking. The disguise was successful at Charles and Park stations, but the search was not.

The train arrived at Downtown Crossing; Jean-Paul held the doors while Toine tapped his way along the platform. Though people pitied Toine and gave him space, they ignored Jean-Paul's injuries and complained about his delaying the train. The angry mood was beginning to boil over when Toine began tapping more quickly. He suddenly looked up and waved his cane.

"We have zem!"

Jean-Paul jumped to the platform and caught up as Toine tapped through the exit. They emerged onto the brick-paved pedestrian mall and into a light breeze.

"The wind could be trouble, Toine? Blowing away the flour?"

Toine kept tapping, listening to the signal in his earpiece, and smiled.

"Ze detector is very sensitive, and ze flour is very hot. It does not take much." He immediately turned and poked a channel through the Saturday shopping crowd. Jean-Paul followed, hoping the shoppers would forgive his blind companion for his rudeness.

Also, his ridiculous taste in clothing.

* * *

When Lynn heard the car engine stop, she reached down and curled her fingers around the tire iron. She wondered if she could bring herself to hit someone with it—that seemed too bluntly violent for even a remedial Buddhist. The trunk lid popped open, blinding her with a flood of daylight glaring from the bakers' jackets. She was still blinking when a hand grabbed her wrist and pried the tire iron away.

"Bad idea, lady."

The white baker lifted her out in one motion; either she'd lost a lot of weight skipping meals all day or this kid was really strong. He kept Lynn in an arm lock while the black baker tried to yank Roger out of the cavernous trunk. Roger resisted until a thwack on the forehead with the tire iron convinced him to climb out himself. The black baker locked both of Roger's arms behind him; he'd apparently learned from his experience in the Grocery.

They were parked in a cobblestone alley, surrounded by the backs of brownstone buildings. It was pretty clean for an alley, had to be some upscale neighborhood—too nice for Cambridge, too flat for Beacon Hill; maybe the South End? Then again, Lynn thought, once you'd been taken by force to an unknown location, did it matter where it was?

You are always here, now, noted Zen-mind.

François herded them down granite steps to a basement entrance. He pressed a doorbell, and after what seemed like minutes, a very short, well-dressed man opened the door. François nodded in deference.

"We have a new vintage, M'sieur Tippiteaux, which must age in the wine cellar for a certain time."

The man inside leaned back precariously in order to look down his nose at Lynn and then Roger.

"You cannot bring him in here! Not even to the wine cellar!" He sneered dismissively. "He requires a proper jacket and tie."

The little man disappeared into the basement. François seemed unperturbed, though Lynn thought she caught a subtle eye roll. Tippiteaux reappeared, carrying a bright green sport jacket and a rose-colored silk tie. He and the black baker—well, mostly the black baker—wrestled Roger into the jacket and slipped the noose around his neck. Once Roger was appropriately dressed, the Pierres dragged him and Lynn into the room.

The wine cellar was small but well stocked. There were no windows; instead, dim light glowed from faux-candle sconces. Racks of bottles behind oak-framed glass doors lined the walls, except for the outside door and an inner door, which opened to stairs beyond. Stemmed glasses hung from slots in an overhead rack, directly above a cabinet with brandy bottles artfully placed on its glass surface. The floor was a sort of cobblestone, very rough, almost an extension of the street outside. In the center stood an elegant stained-oak table with four matching chairs—large and heavy, with high backs and ornate leaf-and-vine carvings. Lynn noticed that the seat cushions matched Roger's tie.

Nothing on Earth matched Roger's jacket.

She quickly found herself seated in a chair, hands pulled around its back, where they bound her wrists with what felt like another silk tie. Roger's hands were also silk-tied behind his chair; he had a bloody lump on his forehead and an apologetic smile on his face.

He damned well better be apologetic.

François stood before them, lips pursed, flanked by bakers eagerly awaiting orders.

"I shall return in a moment, Messieurs Pierre," he said, turning for the inner door. He glanced at the black baker's tire iron. "I believe I can find something more persuasive in the kitchen."

* * *

Toine tapped his detector cane down the narrow chasms of Boston back streets with Jean-Paul close behind. They proceeded into the financial district, drawing embarrassing stares from the crowd feeding pigeons at Post Office Square. Toine wanted to sneer back, but that would be inconsistent with his blind persona. Finally, he halted at the Liberty Bank building.

"Here," he said.

Toine removed the sunglasses and looked up at the edifice—thirty stories of prime downtown property, teeming with law firms and financial institutions. He released the door lock with a credit card and they entered. The lobby was deserted—lawyers and brokers do not work on Saturday—so they carefully followed the trail to the elevators. They checked each car for radiation, finding a signal only in the endmost car. They stepped in and closed the doors.

It would be a repeat of the train exercise, except vertical. They would discover the targets in a few minutes.

There were thirty-six floors including the lobby, plus three parking garage levels. They started at the bottom, where they hid against the side walls as the doors opened. The garage was nearly empty; Toine scanned the concrete around the elevator for signs of the irradiated flour, and found none. Mildly surprised, they let the doors close and continued upward.

They repeated the exercise at every floor, growing more concerned with each fruitless search. At fifteen they met a weekend receptionist for a personal injury law firm—ambulances run on the weekends, also—but Toine's blind act allowed him to scan the floor while Jean-Paul pleaded a mistaken button push. At the penthouse they repeated the performance for an intimidating armed guard. It was not clear what the man was guarding, but Toine was not interested—there was no radiation.

They returned to the lobby and proceeded downward to recheck the underground parking levels, but there was still no sign of their prey. Toine could not hide his bafflement. He had complete faith in the radiation detection instrument, and now it had failed him.

"Perhaps we choose the wrong elevator," Jean-Paul offered. "Perhaps they fooled us."

Toine was unconvinced.

"Zis is ze correct car."

He looked at his partner, who had no further suggestions.

"Jean-Paul, let us call François."

* * *

Roger clung to consciousness, his lungs screaming for air, his stomach twisted and primed to explode. He thrashed against the chair and the wrist bindings but there was no escape from the toxic fumes: inches below his face, at the knot of the rose-colored tie, hung a freshly-cut wedge of Herve cheese.

"Such a shame your nose is no longer obstructed with flour!" François taunted, leaning close to Roger's ear. "Now, will you tell me the location of your headquarters?"

"I don't know what you're talking about," Roger gasped. "I run a truffle farm. I was showing it to Aunt Lynn." He panted, then added, "You wiped it out."

François backed away, as if insulted.

"I did nothing of the sort. You should discuss that with your gun-collecting associate if you ever see her again." He turned to Lynn, snarling. "And if you are so innocent, Madame, why is there a coded message written on your skirt?"

White Pierre shimmered into Roger's tear-drenched vision.

"I don't think he's gonna break, François. And I might hurl before he talks. I can't handle this much longer."

"Nonsense, M'sieur. In France, there is much odor—garlic, fish, cheese, unwashed bodies. But these odors are heaviest near the ground. Be a Pierre, and do as Frenchmen do—raise your nose and collect the better air from higher in the room. Then add a slight sneer, which, you will find, reduces the surface area of your olfactory passages. It is quite effective, and thus common practice. In Paris. Of course, they do not teach it here in America."

Roger couldn't raise his eyelids, much less his olfactory passages.

"I got a better idea." It was black Pierre, slapping the tire iron into his palm. "Supposin' I just beat the shit outta the asshole till he tells us what we wanna know?"

"I admire your resourcefulness, Pierre, but this man is so weak I fear he would be unconscious after the first blow. Or dead. Either way we obtain no information."

"Okay," came the response, "How about I beat the shit outta Aunt Lynn till he tells us what we wanna know?"

Crap!

"You can't do that!" Roger wheezed. "She doesn't know anything about the farm! I was just showing her—"

Roger's jaw exploded in pain as Pierre backhanded him.

"I didn't say she knew anything. I said, I'm gonna whack her till *you* talk."

Roger strained to twist his head into a pleading look at François, hoping to reach the man's sense of decency. François seemed genuinely on the fence about the brutal idea. The cellar silently awaited his decision.

As if the cobblestone floor itself had flinched, the bakers jumped at the intrusion of *La Marseillaise*, rendered electronically from François' vest pocket. He pulled out the phone and glanced briefly at the screen, then pressed a button and put the phone to his ear.

"François." He listened briefly. "Excellent. Wait a moment, s'il vous plaît." He returned his attention to the Pierres. "I would rather avoid such messy violence, but perhaps it cannot be helped." He glanced at Lynn and then met Roger's tearing eyes directly. "That, M'sieur, is for you to decide. I shall allow you a short time to talk it over with your 'Aunt Lynn' and then return to hear your decision. The cheese shall remain for you to enjoy."

François nodded to the Pierres and carried his still-connected phone toward the inner door. The bakers glanced at one another and then, menacingly, at Lynn and Roger. François stopped and turned.

"Worry not about them, they are securely bound. Come get some fresh air—you shall need your strength to swing that wrench effectively."

The two bakers shrugged and followed François up the stairs.

"Can you get loose?" Roger rasped. "I can't reach the knots, and my hands are too big to slip out."

"I've got big hands, too," Lynn answered. "I was trying to relax enough to let the tie slip off, until he started swinging that tire iron. But it wasn't going to work anyway."

"Maybe I can turn my chair and back it up to yours."

He pushed sideways with his feet but the heavy chair went nowhere—the cobblestones locked around the legs and wouldn't let it slide. He strained at it a few times, then tried to hop it, to no avail. As a mechanical engineer, he analyzed the arrangement and concluded that his leverage was all wrong—too much weight in the seat and no way to apply lift.

"I can't seem to—"

"Wait, Roger. Please, just be quiet for a minute. Don't you dare pass out on me."

* * *

Breathe.

Lynn had never improvised an Asana sequence. She'd never even done chair yoga, much less any poses involving her hands tied behind her back.

She focused on the act of breathing, ignoring the smell and her nausea and her fear that she'd lose what little lunch she'd eaten. Just breathing. Nothing else. Her consciousness drifted into her belly, until the gentle out-and-in movement of her navel was happening inches in front of her mind's eye. She found herself at her center of gravity, feeling the balance—her weight on the chair, her feet on the floor, her arms wrapped behind her—as if it were all a single sensation.

The only sensation.

She relaxed her back muscles and stretched, lower and lower, until her head was between her knees and her feet pushed back around the chair. She paused, just breathing, then gave a little test shove forward. Now she felt the added weight of the chair, and the slight shock as it tipped back to the floor. She expanded her mind's notion of her self to include the chair, as if it was just a little added weight on her ass.

Actually, she'd been pretty good about keeping weight off her ass.

Focus, Lynn.

This was no time for distracting thoughts. She let her mind slide back down, centered once more. She leaned forward, imperceptibly further, and felt her ass/chair rotate slightly upwards, freeing the back legs from the floor. She paused again, just breathing, then extended her legs slowly, lifting the front chair-legs a few inches. Lynn/chair was crouching now, perfectly balanced.

She glided sideways, feeling the roughness of each cobblestone as it slid under her soles. She was unaware of the passage of distance or time—it is always, only, *here* and *now*. When she sensed the low hiss of Roger's breathing close by, she rotated and flexed her knees until her front chair-legs touched the floor. The movement was subtle, making no sound. She eased backward until the rear legs had also set down.

She breathed, straightened up, and felt for Roger's hands. They were limp, and she couldn't figure out the knot without seeing it.

"Wake up, sleepyhead," she whispered. "I hope the Trail Boys taught you how to untie knots, too."

Roger stirred; she felt his fingers examining the knot.

"It's just a crappy granny," he muttered, and quickly undid it. Lynn shook the silk bond loose, spun around, and worked Roger's knot open. As she helped him out of the chair and toward the door, he tore the tie from his neck and flung it and the rotting Herve into the corner.

Lynn was reaching for the door handle when the tire iron dropped across her chest and yanked backward. She could see black Pierre's hand on the bar and feel his breath on her neck. He jerked the bar down to pin her elbows and pulled her away, just as Roger grabbed for her—and white Pierre's fist flashed by, on the way to its rendezvous with Roger's face.

Mouth bleeding, Roger staggered to the brandy cabinet, grabbed two bottles, and swung them like clubs as he swayed on shaky knees. He looked more drunk than threatening, but it kept the cautious white baker at bay.

François finally joined them.

"It seems that for a mere truffle farmer," he said coolly, "you are quite resourceful."

Lynn struggled against the bar, but like playing low post against a grabby defender, she just couldn't get open.

Unless she fouled.

She modified her long-dormant post-up move—after the sudden pivot and shoulder thrust, she kept going until her head crushed into the baker's nose. He released his grip, howling and lurching backward as the tire iron clanged to the cobblestones. Head and chest throbbing, Lynn lunged for the door. The move energized Roger—he shook the fog from his eyes, flipped both brandy bottles toward the far end of the room, and dove out behind her.

"Catch them!" François shouted.

Chapter 6

White Pierre wasn't always a flunky for a fake French bistro. He'd seen high school glory days as an all-state wide receiver, and he might've even starred in the PAC-10 if they hadn't caught him the night after graduation with two handguns and a trunkload of weed.

Instincts fade slowly—the instant he saw the airborne brandy bottles, he launched himself. They were flipping end-over-end, unlike any good pass he'd ever hauled in, but he slapped his hand onto the base of one and clamped his fingers around the neck. By raw impulse, he forced a foot down inbounds as he twisted around and crashed backward onto the floor.

Even as his helmetless head hit the cobblestone and sparks shot into his eyes, he spotted the second bottle tumbling above his stomach. He'd never done a two ball drill, but he was in the zone. He deflected the other pass with his free hand and guided it into his gut before it could bounce off onto the stones.

He clutched the bottles and exhaled, pain and nostalgia swirling through his brain.

* * *

François glanced at his watch, then considered the floor stones upon which the young baker lay panting.

That was painful, no?

Black Pierre was blotting nose blood into his white sleeve, searching the room.

"They got away?"

White Pierre started up suddenly, wincing but still gripping the bottles.

"My bad! You meant catch the captives!"

François smiled.

"Au contraire, mon ami; I intended the brandies. Both are in excess of one hundred years old, and irreplaceable. I have tasted them—no captive could be worth missing such an extraordinary experience. And I cannot even begin to imagine the paperwork should they be destroyed. You have done well."

François carefully pried the bottles from the baker's grip and replaced them on the cabinet. This American, constantly bombarded by prestige brands offering quality names in lieu of quality products, could never appreciate so fine a liqueur. He offered a hand and lifted the young man from the floor.

Black Pierre was sputtering. "But what about the—"

"Be calm, Pierre," François said, extracting his phone. "Often, a guest will carelessly carry off the jacket he has borrowed from us. But we always find it—we track our property by satellite positioning."

"You planted a GPS transmitter in his jacket?"

"Yes, Pierre."

White Pierre broke into a broad grin.

"You wanted 'em to get away, so we could follow 'em! Just like Jean-Paul and Toine!"

"Perhaps," replied François—the guess was very close to the truth. He pressed an icon on his phone to bring up the tracking app and entered the jacket's transmitter ID. A map of Boston flashed onto the screen, with a green blinking marker in the center. He zoomed in to street scale, and noted the marker proceeding rapidly along Newbury Street.

"They are hoping to be lost in the crowd. Let us follow—maintain communication by phone."

It was somewhat fortunate that they had escaped—François could not have restrained black Pierre much longer. That threat had likely been the impetus for the redhead's extraordinary effort; he noted that she had somehow transported her heavy chair across the rough cobblestone.

He checked the time again—4:45, still too early.

His plan required that they be intercepted, and thus they would again be exposed to Pierre's violent zeal, no doubt amplified by the pain of his bleeding nose and the desire for vengeance. François suspected that, even without the tire iron, the young man was capable of inflicting considerable damage.

* * *

Emerging from the wine cellar's alley, Lynn and Roger quickly recognized Boston's Back Bay and decided the Saturday crowd on Newbury Street provided the best escape cover. Lynn ducked low in an unpromising attempt to hide her torch-like hair. Brahmins, yuppies, and tourists all gave them wide berth, due to either Roger's foul odor or his blazing blazer. Or both.

"Nice head butt in there," he puffed. "Some sort of Eastern martial arts thing?"

"No, too dirty. That was Lebanon High varsity basketball."

After a quick scan for pursuers, Roger pulled Lynn into the Bux Brothers store.

"We need to ditch this jacket and cover your hair. We're a couple of lighthouses out there."

A sales clerk appeared instantly, with the perfect Bux Brothers look—charcoal-gray suit, white shirt, red power tie. The powerful little man confronted Roger.

"Where, sir, did you get that hideous jacket?"

Roger smiled at the dig, peeled off the coat and flung it at him.

"It smells like a porta-potty!" whined the clerk, deftly dodging the fetid garment.

"Doesn't matter—you can burn it. I need a new one, and the lady needs a sweater and scarf. Something dark. And we need 'em in"—he looked at his watch—"forty-five seconds."

The clerk demanded a proper fitting. Ignoring him, Roger lifted a dark green sweater from the fall fashion display table and tossed it to Lynn. As she slid it on, he snatched a navy and green scarf from a nearby mannequin and passed that to her, too.

It matched! *What kind of man is this?*

Lynn tucked her hair under the scarf as Roger yanked a preppie-issue navy blazer from the rack. He had it on by the time he stepped back.

"We're walking out in twenty seconds; figure out what we owe you before then and we'll pay."

The clerk stammered, then blurted a price: four hundred and thirty dollars. Roger pulled out a wad of bills, peeled off five hundreds, and jammed them into the clerk's hand.

"The change is a tip, for forgetting you ever saw us. And for hiding that hideous jacket. Immediately."

The clerk looked astonished and relieved as he picked up the discarded coat. Roger nodded to Lynn, but as they turned to leave the clerk spoke up.

"Sir, will you be needing this pin?"

He held out the jacket, pointing to a small metal object attached under the lapel. Roger's eyes hardened.

"Yes, I will. Thanks for noticing." He unpinned it and buried it in his fist. "Let's go, Lynn."

They rushed from the store into a nearby basement stairwell.

"It's a GPS device," Roger said. "They know we're here. I bet they want us to think we got away clean, so they could track us." He glanced out from the stairwell, waiting, then sprinted to the curb and tossed the device into the open window of a passing cab. He waved to Lynn to come out.

"That oughta take care of 'em."

Lynn suggested they stay hidden until the cab was further away, but Roger was confident the coast was clear and insisted they keep moving. He was starting to relax, looking right at home on the brick sidewalk in his new blazer. Lynn complimented him on his taste in clothes.

"It took me three years to earn my Fashion Design skill patch," he replied. "It was tough to find a mentor, given the Trail Boys policy against gays. I had to—"

Lynn signaled stop; the black baker was coming around the corner of Newbury and Arlington—ahead of them. He hadn't seen them yet, probably thanks to their new clothes. She grabbed Roger's hand and pulled him into the flow of the crowd, headed back the way they came.

"Black baker, a block behind us," she explained. "Don't look around."

They reached the corner and crossed Berkeley. Roger suddenly stooped low and whispered.

"White baker, dead ahead. He's looking in all the cars; they must be following the tracer."

Lynn glimpsed François' distinctive mustache to the left, approaching down Berkeley from Boylston; they were cut off on three sides. She darted right, into a throng of shoppers, and Roger followed. The group flowed across Newbury but then diverted left, crossing in front of a church under repair, its corner towers invisible behind dense green plastic netting. If Lynn and Roger stayed with the crowd, they'd run into the white baker. If they headed down Berkeley, they'd be out in the open. But that was the only path not currently blocked by a French food service employee.

"What now?"

"Sanctuary," Roger said, and dashed into the church portico.

From the portico, Lynn could see that the green netting hid an extensive pipe-and-plank scaffold that encased the corner tower. The fabric shield was arguably for safety, but likely also for esthetics—upscale Newbury Street merchants certainly didn't want shoppers to view the ugly repair structure.

Roger rattled the door latch—locked. Without hesitation, he stepped to the green netting and pulled a section aside.

Lynn tried to step quietly as they climbed. From inside, the view of the street was unimpeded. But Lynn remembered how invisible the scaffold had been from the outside, and assumed that nobody could see in. They reached the top, level with a roof connecting the two towers, and waited.

François and the bakers converged below. Lynn could hear the white baker insisting they were not in any of the cars.

"But the marker was, certainement." François barked, looking at his phone. "They have discovered it and placed it into a passing auto. They must be here. Search the area."

The bakers poked around nearby stairwells and storefronts while Lynn watched, following Zen-mind's recommendation to let negative thoughts go—especially the ones about what would happen if the bakers discovered the scaffold right under François' upturned nose. After five minutes, they reconvened on the corner.

"They split," said the black baker.

"It's like they fuckin' vanished into thin air," said the white one.

"People do not vanish into thin—" François began, looking to the sky. He stopped as his gaze landed directly on Lynn and Roger's hiding place. "Check up there," he said, pointing. "And there," pointing at the other tower.

He wouldn't check the other tower if he could see them, Lynn realized. They were invisible.

The bakers split up, one climbing the scaffold below Roger and Lynn, and one ascending the far tower. François stood at the corner, splitting his attention between the church and the intersection.

Roger ushered Lynn around the tower to the connecting roof. In a crouch, he inched out across the black slate, using snow-melt wires for traction. She followed him out, warily—it was thirty feet down to the brick sidewalk.

He grabbed a green copper downspout and swung from the roof, then shimmied down, hidden from François' view by the tower. Lynn gulped, thinking the pipe could barely hold Roger alone, much less the two of them. But, motivated by the rapid footfalls of the climbing bakers, she clutched the green metal and stepped off the safety of the slate. Using gaps between wall stones as toeholds, she began to work her way down.

Roger was halfway to the ground when the baker on the far scaffold reached the top. Lynn guessed they were in plain sight, from the way he shouted, "François! On the drainpipe! This side of the tower!"

François appeared around the corner, eyes widening, then widening more when Roger leapt from the pipe.

"Tabernac!" François yelled as the side of Chicago beef slammed him into the bricks. Roger got the benefit of the thin French padding, and scrambled to his feet.

"Jump, Lynn!" He held out his arms. Lynn took a breath and pushed away from the pipe.

Roger caught her but stumbled over the still-groggy François. As they untangled themselves they could hear the bakers racing down the scaffolds. Suddenly, François' arm clamped around Lynn's neck; she snapped an elbow into his ribs, knocking him down one more time as she twisted away.

They sprinted toward the Public Garden.

"Another Lebanon High move?" Roger puffed.

"Yeah," Lynn panted. "Tough league."

* * *

On a pleasant Saturday afternoon in the Public Garden, "Boston Mounted Policeman" was more like a Disney World role than a law-enforcement job. Jimmy Dowling understood he was part of the backdrop for the tourists. Maybe his presence would deter some easily-deterred criminal from digging up a duckling statue or tagging a swan boat, but his horse's droppings were enough of a nuisance to completely outweigh any such benefit. So he played the living statue, taking a strategic position at the edge of the Swan Pond—where, from atop his steed and behind his mirrored sunglasses, he could most easily look down women's blouses.

An outburst of cursing and horn honking erupted on Arlington Street. Jimmy swiveled in the saddle to observe a man and a woman sprinting around the curved pathway from the Newbury Street gate, directly toward his position. They pulled up, breathless, at the low pond wall, scanning nervously behind them as if for pursuers. Jimmy glanced around to see who, if anyone, was chasing them. He turned back when he heard the splash.

"Come on! It's not deep!" the man said, and the woman jumped in after him.

What the hell? "Hey, whadda ya think yer doin'? You can't go in there!"

The man flashed a sheepish grin.

"It's okay sir, just my fraternity initiation. My overlord commanded me to do it."

The guy was believable—maybe 'cause he smelled like three days into hell week without a shower. Still, something was fishy, and it sure as hell wasn't the pond...

"What about the lady?"

"House mother!" came the cheerful reply. The pair waded through the shallow water, smiling sociably at the dumbfounded tourists gliding past in the swan boats.

Rapidly approaching footsteps drew Jimmy's attention away from the spectacle in the water. He twisted again to see two men in white uniforms arrive at the wall from each direction of the pond perimeter path. One sported a softball-sized bruise on the side of his face; the other, a bright, fresh bloodstain on the arm of his jacket.

An older man in a suit limped up from the Newbury gate.

"Why did you not stop them?!" he demanded in a snooty French accent.

Cuz I didn't feel like it, asshole. "Just a frat prank, sir; didn't see any reason to."

"It was most certainly not a 'frat prank'." The Frenchman signaled the other two, who took off running each way around the perimeter path. He then looked at his watch, muttered something about urgency, and limped rapidly toward the central footbridge.

Jimmy scanned the opposite bank and located the soaked couple climbing over the wall.

So maybe it wasn't a frat prank.

But they seemed like harmless escapees, and it wasn't Jimmy's job to catch them. Funny, though; he'd always thought "men in white coats" was just an expression.

* * *

As he and Lynn took off toward Charles Street, Roger glanced back to scope their head start. The bakers were dashing around the pond perimeter, and François was fighting his way through a thick crowd across the footbridge, apparently unwilling to wet his shoes twice in one day. Roger checked his own shoes: he was leaving a dripping trail. Again.

They fled through the Common to the Park Street T station, and took the stairs down three at a time. After a frantic search for his Charlie Pass, he ushered Lynn through the turnstiles and over to the Green Line platform.

Escape Tactics skill patch, technique seven: *If you leave a trail, make it lead somewhere else.* Roger stripped off his new jacket and laid it on the floor. He stepped onto it, then removed his shoes and socks and tossed them through the open doors of a waiting train. After drying his feet on the jacket, he jumped back onto the platform surface, barefoot.

"You too," he said, pointing at Lynn's feet. Lynn glared at the grubby concrete and crinkled her nose.

"Eww."

He couldn't blame her—in fact, she probably spoke for everyone in the station, all staring with disgust at his bare feet. He tried not to think about the half-million shoes—*nasty shoes*—that shuffled through here every day, smearing spilled soft drinks and dropped gum into a thin glaze.

But there wasn't time to argue.

He tossed the jacket through the closing doors and as the train pulled away, swept Lynn into his arms and rushed her down the stairway to the Red Line platform. To his relief, a red-and-silver train was already waiting. He carried her across the threshold, smiling back at the annoyed looks coming from fellow passengers as they squeezed away from the damp couple. He counted seconds until the doors slid closed with no sign of François or the bakers.

His right arm was soaked by the water from Lynn's skirt, but he barely noticed; she was staring at him with an expression he desperately wanted to read. He couldn't think of anything witty to say, either, and found himself wondering if strong, silent types weren't so much cool as just tongue-tied. As the train picked up speed his balance got shaky, so he set Lynn down. He'd held her way too long.

Crap.

* * *

François calmly descended the stairs into Park Street station. The bakers reported from beyond the turnstiles.

"The footprints stopped at the Green Line—outbound. Should we follow 'em?"

"No, you have done all you can. I appreciate your help, and

shall be sure to submit a glowing recommendation for your 360-degree performance review. Merci, Messieurs. You may return to your shop now."

Like eager hounds, the bakers were disappointed to end the chase. But, better to keep them hungry for action than feed them too much. They were strong and violent, and would be valuable in the future. As they marched off to the Red Line for the return trip to Cambridge, the T watchman made no move to stop them, apparently deciding against confronting two large, bloodied bakers over some minor turnstile-hopping.

François climbed the stairs into the sunlight and gently lowered himself onto an empty bench, wincing at his sore leg and bruised rib. The afternoon had become considerably more painful than he had anticipated.

He called Toine.

"This is François. I am at Park Street. I have lost the ape and the redhead." *The footprints stopped at the Green Line.* What manner of fool did they think he was?

He rubbed his rib. Though these two had underestimated him, they had proven worthy opponents, especially the redhead. She pretended to be naïve, but she could not conceal her formidable martial arts skills.

He would be better prepared for the next encounter.

* * *

Lynn was startled by a touch to her elbow as the train pulled into Downtown Crossing. They'd only gone one stop, which didn't seem far enough for a serious escape route.

"It's okay, Lynn," Roger said. "They're halfway to Boston College on the Green Line by now. And even if they figured out we're on the Red Line, they can't tell where we get off—we won't be leaving wet footprints."

He lifted her into his arms again and carried her up and out to the street. A cool breeze chilled her wet legs as he set her down and, despite his bare feet, rushed her toward the financial district. When they reached Post Office Square, Lynn pulled back.

"Wait," she said. "I'm tired of running."

Roger stopped and turned, brow furrowed.

"We're almost there."

"Almost where?"

"Urban Legion headquarters."

"The same headquarters that the Truffle Cartel agents are trying to find? Look, since I met you I've been shot at, stabbed at, locked in a trunk, tied to a chair, trapped on a church roof, and forced to wade through the Swan Pond, without any idea why. I think I'd be a lot safer if I stay as far away as possible from you and your Urban Legion."

Roger locked eyes with her for a moment.

"Yeah, you'd be a lot safer. But there's more at stake here, for us and you. We need you."

"I'm sorry, you'll have to do better than that. You and Meg are pretty good at turning urban legends into tear-jerking personal stories just to get my sympathy. But not good enough."

Roger shook his head.

"Lynn, it's the other way around—our 'tear-jerking' personal stories are real, but they've been turned into urban legends by the perpetrators. So nobody will believe us—including you, I guess. But I can do better than that, right here, if you give me a minute."

She glanced around the square. The sun's warmth above her waist fought the Swan Pond chill below, mirroring her mixed attitude about Roger and his claims.

You have all the time in the world to know the truth, said Zen-mind, *but you must begin now.*

A glance at Roger's earnest face brought a glow to her cheeks, tipping the balance to the warm half. She nodded okay.

Roger pulled out a smart phone, and brought up an Internet browser.

"Ever wonder why your writing career fizzled?" he asked.

"I think Spinning Rock only published me because I was Phil Grady's wife. I never had a writing career. I'm surprised you even know about it."

"You sell yourself short," he said softly. "Let's go to the Spinning Rock website." The site came up, and he typed "Lynn Grady" into the search field. The response was:

"Search term not found."

She twisted her head. His eyes were serious, gentle.

"Let's try Grunge Tour Diaries"—*nothing*—"or Severed Clown Heads."—*still nothing.*

"It was a long time ago," she said.

"They keep everything—unless someone erases it."

"Who would do that?"

"Do you know who Phil works for?"

"He started with Omni Music, in L.A., when he quit the band. That was before he left us. I assume he's still there—that's where our child support checks come from."

"He's still there. You probably don't know what Omni does—I mean, besides the whole digital rights management business they hide behind. Omni Music is a primary source of illicit electronics for the retail cartels."

"What do you mean, illicit?"

"Things the public doesn't know about. Like the voice projectors in the mall stores."

That didn't sound like Phil.

"Phil wouldn't be involved in that kind of stuff. Have you ever heard his music? The Severed Clown Heads were all about fighting commercialism."

Roger shrugged.

"People change. He dissolved the band when he went to Omni; you knew that. And I've heard his music, but most people haven't. He and Omni have suppressed it—the lyrics hit a little too close to home. Your articles, and your writing career, got caught in the whitewash."

Lynn chewed on that for a moment. She didn't listen to radio much, but she couldn't remember the last time she'd heard an SCH song. And that might explain why her alimony royalties had dwindled to nothing over the years. She'd blamed that on fading interest in a band that refused to cater to pop culture—she never thought the interest might have faded on purpose. But still…

"Okay, let's say he's gone to the dark side. They can't possibly wipe out history like that!"

"They don't wipe it out—they just make it legendary." He went to an urban legend website, and handed her the phone. "Go ahead, search for Severed Clown Heads."

Lynn typed the band's name as she'd done so many times when writing the articles, and indeed found the term. She struggled to read the words, a lump rising in her throat.

"Severed Clown Heads: Described as a folk-rock protest band out of Chicago in 1961 with a fierce anticommercial attitude. Most versions mention the frontman's wife or girlfriend bringing her baby on tour and publishing a set of diaries in Spinning Rock. Variations include the group as punk rockers from New York appearing in 1985, and a grunge band from South Boston in the 1990s. Inconsistencies begin with the band's name itself, which would have been prohibitively offensive even to the most edgy nonconformists of the early 60s. Most conclusively, there is no record of the diaries in the Spinning Rock archives, and, in fact, the alleged diaries could not have been written in 1961 as claimed, because the magazine did not begin publishing until 1967.

"STATUS: FALSE"

* * *

Jean-Paul crouched in the parking garage shadows, his new Battery Hut laptop open and recording video. François had not delayed the Legionnaires long enough for him and Toine to finish getting ready. But maybe they were ready enough.

They had tapped into the cameras in the lobby and elevators, and the redhead and the ape—who was even barefoot, with hairy toes, Jean-Paul noted with amusement—were clearly visible as they crossed the lobby and entered the elevator. There was no pass key—the ape had pressed a complex code sequence using only his fingers. This was no problem, since Toine had noticed that the buttons looked like fingerprint sensors, and Jean-Paul had coated them with invisible fingerprinting film. He would lift the prints later for a set of fake fingers. And the video clearly showed the required sequence.

But they had not found time to re-aim the cameras into the building, and the floor indicators had not lit up. So when the ape announced "Welcome to Urban Legion headquarters, Lynn," Jean-Paul could not see which floor the headquarters actually occupied.

He called Toine, who was stationed in the elevator equipment room.

"Mon Dieu!" Toine mumbled around a half-eaten éclair. "Of course!"

"Toine! You have them? What is the floor?"

Per François' suggestion, Toine had timed the elevator, comparing with timing they had taken on test trips to each floor.

"Ze twelve-and-one-half floor!"

"What?"

"Jean-Paul, did we not note a slightly longer time difference between floor twelve and thirteen? Zey stopped in between! Zere is an extra floor in zis building. One zat is not on ze elevator buttons, and undoubtedly not on ze lobby directory. While many American buildings have no thirteenth floor, zis one has two."

Jean-Paul sat quietly in the dark, his head wound throbbing. The Urban Legion's underground truffle lab was complex and surprisingly well-equipped. But a whole hidden floor in a downtown high-rise building?

This enemy was not to be taken lightly.

He felt an unfamiliar anxiety—the Urban Legion was far more capable than his superiors had led him to believe. But then he glanced at the video files of the entry code sequence, gently tapped his fingerprint kit, and began to smile.

We shall not take them lightly. We have the upper handle.

Part II

"Nearly authentic French,
with a well-stocked, aromatic wine cellar."
— Our Zen Gourmet

Chapter 7

Given her earlier tour of the MIT tunnels, Lynn hadn't expected to find Urban Legion headquarters in a fancy downtown building. Given the fancy building, she figured headquarters would be in the basement. She hadn't noticed that the elevator was going up. Now, it was pretty obvious.

A modern lobby beckoned, with requisite beige carpeting, reception desk, comfortable chairs, and even business magazines scattered on a coffee table. Opposite the elevator were the glass walls of a conference room. She could see through to a huge east-facing picture window and Boston harbor beyond, framed by harborside buildings mirroring sky blue and sunset orange against the purple dusk backdrop. They were at least ten stories up—this was no underground.

Roger was grinning, like he'd just snuck a cop car onto the Great Dome.

"How do you get away with this?" she asked. "Is it like a front, you pretend to be a business?"

"Actually, this lobby is just in case somebody gets in—we fake being 'Interworld Limited'—but nobody's ever gotten in. That's why we don't need guards. It takes a special sequence of button pushes with the right fingerprints to stop on this floor."

"You have the whole floor?"

"It's easier to hide a whole floor than a part of one."

"Wait. This whole floor is *hidden*?"

"Yup! It's not counted on the elevator buttons or floor indicators, so everybody goes past it without noticing—we even adjust the timing of the dings for the adjacent floors so you don't notice the gap. And nobody thinks to count the floors from the outside; we can leave the blinds open and everything. Nice view, huh?"

Roger steered her past the conference room and into the complex. A hall stretched ahead, with doors and interior windows lining both sides. This was not the kind of place you throw together while nobody's watching.

"Okay, but how did you get it built? Howie used some magic potion on the construction company?"

"No need for potions; we have friends in the Freemasons."

"Oh, come on. They don't actually build stuff anymore—they're just a big fraternity now."

"That's what certain Freemasons—and the popular writers on their payroll—want you to think. But some of them are still the real deal. They've put up buildings with secret sections all over the country for us, and they're really good at tunnels. Like the tunnel to the truffle farm. We had an extensive underground network tied into the New York City sewer system, but we had to abandon it when the cartels caught on and released all those so-called 'pet' alligators."

Lynn would have thought he was joking if she hadn't just discovered she was a legendary alligator herself.

Howie came running up the hall.

"You made it! We were worried sick." He stopped short as he got a closer look. "Barefoot, wounded, and"—he noticed the wet clothes and sniffed—"fresh from a swim in a cesspool? In your clothes?"

"Just practicing escape techniques on our Truffle Cartel friends," Roger replied. "Took the sea route through the Public Garden."

"You sure you lost them?"

"Of course."

Howie examined Roger's bruised head.

"They should pay for this. They should drive French cars till they drop dead from frustration. Come, you need ointment on those scrapes—I'm thinking there's more duck shit than chlorine in the Swan Pond."

Howie led them to a cross between a doctor's office and a pharmacy: drawers and glass-door cabinets, packed with pill canisters and brown bottles, lined the walls. Howie retrieved a sterile gauze pad from one of the drawers, doused it with antibiotic fluid, and held it to the bump on Roger's head.

"You probably deserve this, flinging jars around the store like that. Do you think you could've come any closer to Meg's head?"

"I didn't hit her, did I?" Roger smiled apologetically as he took over holding the bandage. "I think I'll survive, Doctor Friedman. Where's the king? He'll want to brief Lynn."

"Wait," Lynn cut in. "The king?"

"Um, yeah," Roger replied. "The Urban Legion is big. The main organization is divided into nine kingdoms, and ours, the New England kingdom, is one of the biggest. The king is our local leader."

The king. Which again brought to mind the theory that this was all some sort of fantasy game.

A name is merely a word, full of falsehood, said Zen-mind.

"Your timing could be better," Howie said, "he just started the weekend conference call. Discussing the Mall situation, I think. He said he'd be done in about an hour."

"How about Meg?"

"The king sent her shopping—for information—at the Mall. He was afraid for you, not showing up."

"And he's not afraid for Meg? Couldn't he send somebody else?"

"Eh, they cooked up some kind of infiltration strategy. Besides, Meg wanted to go; said she needed to pick up some jeans. Her favorite ones got flour on them."

Lynn smiled to herself. Womanhood; willing to march into mortal danger—to shop. Then she remembered Tanya, and stopped smiling. Tanya was in a training program at the Lexingham Mall.

"You two should get some dry clothes," Howie said. "You'll catch pneumonia—Meg's already sniffling from her dunking this afternoon. I'm going back to work, see if I can get something on the frogs who dunked her." Once Howie headed down the hall, Roger tossed the gauze pad away.

"How about a change of clothes and a little tour? Unless you'd rather rest?"

Rest sounded good. About three days would do it. Lynn was tired, and cold, and hungry, but none of that mattered at the moment.

"I don't want a tour and I don't want to rest; I want to know what mall you're talking about."

Roger took a deep breath.

"The Lexingham Mall," he said, flinching like he knew what came next.

"My daughter is in training there!" Lynn shouted, getting into his face. "What's going on? Why didn't you tell me?"

Roger backed away slightly.

"It's okay, for now. We don't know what's going on, but we have time to find out, with your help. And I didn't tell you because I didn't think you'd believe me yet. But, here, let me show you." He pulled out his phone and punched a few buttons. "We've been infiltrating Omni Music, and we managed to get our mole to caddy for one of their executives this morning. We got a video of him on the third tee, texting the manager of the Lexingham Mall. Here's a transcript." He handed the phone to Lynn.

Lynn examined the message with growing apprehension.

> Re Sunday trainee experiment
> Phil says no danger, but follow procedure
> No publicity
> Equipment and paperwork on the way
> Usual evening arrangements

"Phil? My Phil? What does this mean, Roger?"

"Yes, your Phil. Or your ex-Phil. Like I said, we don't know what's happening. Whatever it is, they don't want the public in on it. And Phil may say there's no danger, but that message sounds like there's room for doubt."

Lynn's pulse hissed in her ears. Tanya's new Mall job had seemed too good to be true—an email invitation out of nowhere, a perfunctory interview that was more about selling Tanya on the job than finding out if she could do it, and an hourly rate that beat Lynn's own wage at the warehouse. It sounded like Phil had pulled some strings. And this mysterious experiment might explain why the Mall was so concerned about whether Tanya could make the training weekend. Maybe that was all they cared about.

"There's no doubt about one thing," Lynn said, pulling out her own phone, "Tanya's not going to be involved. She's coming home right now." She flipped the phone open but it showed zero bars of signal and a "no connection" status.

"Great. You're in a downtown building with no cell service?" Roger shrugged.

"We have service, it's just special—I'll have to hook you up. But Lynn, I assure you, Tanya's safe, at least for today. The message said the operation doesn't go down until tomorrow. And Meg is on her way to the Mall; she'll keep an eye on Tanya anyway." That wasn't reassuring enough for Lynn, and Roger could tell. "Look," he continued, "at least give me a chance to show you around here, and wait until you talk to the king before you decide what to do. It won't be long, and he's way more eloquent about this stuff than I am."

Or he wears some kind of special cologne, Lynn thought. Still, if Roger was right, they had time. And she *was* curious—this was a lot more headquarters than she'd imagined. It might be good to learn as much as possible before meeting his royal highness.

And there was that Zen-mind advice about knowing the truth by beginning now.

"Okay, lead the way."

Roger's relieved smile said he'd gotten away with something. Lynn couldn't imagine what—there were too many possibilities.

* * *

Phil Grady parked the rented Seville at the Lexingham Mall and watched an unmarked truck beep back to a loading dock. Probably his equipment—it was scheduled for just-in-time arrival to minimize exposure and certainly wouldn't be delivered by a brand-name carrier. He looked twice at the truck driver's weathered black dome.

Still shaving his head after all those years.

"Eightball! You're gonna be hauling gear till the day you die, dude!"

Eightball peered at Phil for a few disoriented seconds before his face lit.

"Axe-man? Phil Grady?"

Phil nodded, smiling, as the old roadie flung the door open and hopped down. Eightball quickly wrapped him, and his thousand-dollar navy-blue Armani suit, in a grimy Dickies-and-work-shirt bear hug.

"Jeez, Phil, you're almost as dark as me. And I can't believe you're wearin' a suit!"

Phil couldn't believe he'd just ruined it. He'd have to pick up a new one before the party.

"Things have changed since I joined Omni, Eightball. Now I deal with the deal-makers, not the fans. And I work my magic in the daylight. You still doing concert gigs?"

Eightball shrugged.

"Nah, I couldn't cover the coke. I do point-of-sale gear now. It's hard work, but a lot easier without the coke."

"You loading this stuff in?"

"Yeah, special order for the Mall Manager, Mr. DiSenza. I'm settin' it up, too. It's a shitload of—"

"I know what they are. Treat 'em careful, okay? I want it all working perfectly by showtime tomorrow morning. No glitches."

Eightball grinned.

"No glitches, Axe-man; just like the old days!"

It was a nice surprise to find Eightball on this job; he didn't make mistakes. He also didn't ask questions. Just the same, Phil was glad he hadn't shipped all of the equipment together—even Eightball might get too curious if he got a close look at the key components. Those were tucked carefully in Phil's travel bag, ready for Sunday's festivities.

* * *

Don DiSenza hurried through hidden corridors beneath the Lexingham Mall; Grady was due any moment. As Mall Manager, and the Corporation's top man in the Metro Boston Division, DiSenza was responsible for pretty much everything that went on here, visible and invisible. He was well-rewarded for both, and he wasn't about to derail the gravy train by pissing off a visiting executive.

But he could still resent Phil and this whole fucked-up, last-minute project. Given time, he could've made it run a lot smoother. At least, he would've put it off till after golf season. This time of year, his "golfers" were especially busy, even working late to finish up critical projects.

Don was proud of the setup. He'd combed the area's 19th holes for smart guys, homed in on the ones who'd sell their souls to play more golf, and then arranged for that to happen. Just one Saturday or Sunday a month, tell the wife you're on the links, but show up at the Mall and do some secret design work, or demographic analysis, or whatever the Corporation needs doing. The payoff was enough for top-of-the-line gear and greens fees for the other three weekends. It even paid for all the beer.

The best part was, these guys were hooked on golf—hell, it was Scottish crack, expensive and impossible to quit. Like any good addictive drug, golf made them willing to do anything to get it, without considering the moral implications. That was important—in this case, the ignored moral implications were usually pretty serious.

Don's group was the Corporation's premier technology development consultancy, and the commissions made Don himself very wealthy. But that meant he couldn't just cancel this weekend's work sessions. Instead, he'd let them go all day and then spent the last hour trying to clear everyone out before the trainee program dinner. There were just two teams still in the building, and with a little luck he could kick them out soon.

Tomorrow was another story, though; everyone would be in the basement at the same time. The golfers were used to leering at beer cart girls—Don could guess how they were gonna behave around a couple dozen of the best-looking teenagers he could hire. He didn't dare let them scare the girls off.

He stopped in on the web print project first. Those golfers had long since hacked into all the Internet mapping and ticket services and altered the layouts; pretty much any map or ticket page was one line longer than a sheet of paper, causing a useless extra page to print. The Paper Cartel was very happy with their work. Now they were working on adding an extra square inch of solid black background somewhere on every page, which used as much toner as six pages of normal text—big money to the Toner Cartel. Printer manufacturers were already giving the printers away and making their money on replacement ink cartridges; now they'd make that money more often. DiSenza gave the group a verbal pat on the back and sent them home.

He found the last foursome hard at work in the lab, as usual.

"Sorry guys, you're out of time," he announced.

"C'mon Don, it's not dark yet—we can still get in a couple more experiments. Our wives aren't expecting us for hours."

"It's not about them," the Mall Manager explained. "I've got a special event here tonight, and I can't deal with you guys at the same time. Besides, you've already optimized this thing way beyond anyone's expectations. You're under par—quit while you're ahead, and go have a beer."

The men glanced at each other, shrugging agreement.

Gotta speak their language, Don reminded himself.

He considered the men as they packed up their equipment. They didn't *look* ruthless. But the Terminal Chemistry Team was the shining star of his biochemistry group. Back when the Corporation started looking for a way to assassinate without detection, it was these guys who came up with the "epoxy" method.

It was simple, really. They discovered that trans fat could act like the resin part of an epoxy combination, so they developed the hardener part and named it "T-Reactive Protein." Because trans fat was abundant in commercial foods, and therefore in everyone's bodies, a tiny amount of T-RP in a person's bloodstream would make the dissolved trans fat precipitate out and coagulate, causing a massive, fatal heart attack. But to a medical examiner, it looked entirely natural. Once the weapons division put T-RP into pellets and adapted Glock pistols to shoot them, Corporation agents could finally make undetectable hits.

To ensure potential victim coverage, over the years the Corporation "encouraged" food manufacturers to add more trans fat to more kinds of food. But they were too successful—the side effect of universal trans fat content was an increase in natural heart attacks. And that increase led to legal efforts to reduce, label, and even ban trans fats from the commercial food supply.

But T-RP was too effective a weapon to abandon, so the team counterattacked. They calculated that four-tenths of a gram of trans fat per serving in typical foods was enough for the epoxy effect, and leveraged the Corporation's FDA lobbyists to make sure that up to half a gram could be hidden in foods without labeling. And to get around any hydrogenated oil restrictions, just this week they'd started work on trans-fat-laced xanthan gum.

So for now, as far as label-conscious consumers could tell, everything was zero trans fat. But everyone still got a big enough dose to make the hardener pellets work. That was important to Don, and to the Corporation.

Because you never knew who you'd need to kill next.

* * *

The fuzzy scene crystallized; colorful, snow-covered mountains became flour-coated mounds of organic vegetables, viewed sideways from the floor. Gerry Rutland tentatively lifted his head, but the throbbing in his neck forced him back down. He rolled slowly to the side, drew his knees up, and pushed himself to a crouch. With a hand on the shattered vegetable shelf, he managed to stand.

Nature's Grocery was a battlefield.

He sadly surveyed the destruction: broken glass, puddles of wine, piles of books and CDs and vegetables, all dusted with a layer of flour. The bag of commercial cookies, with its skull-and-crossbones trans fat sign still attached, sat atop the wreckage, mocking him. Avoiding toxins like trans fat all his life didn't do much good once he crossed paths with toxic people. He felt an inexplicable urge to eat the cookies.

Gerry waded to the checkout counter and reached for the phone to call the police, but he froze, just like the last time. They'd threatened to kill Lynn if he told anyone about this. Maybe they already had. He dialed her house instead, but as he feared, there was no answer. He wished he knew her cell phone number—he'd never asked for it, not wanting to interrupt her day. He sure wanted to now.

Breathe, Gerry.

He dutifully took a deep breath and exhaled slowly, letting the panicky thoughts flow out with the stale air. The Way was acceptance—by accepting what is, one does not feel powerless to change it.

But he didn't even know what was going on—how could he accept it?

He took another deep breath and began to salvage the shop, in the purposeful way of his daily cleaning ritual. But this time, he was more intense, more mindful, than usual. Focusing completely on each tiny action distracted him from his aching neck—and the unfamiliar feelings of outrage and dread creeping into his consciousness.

But when he got to the trans fat cookies, his focus dissolved in mouth-watering curiosity. What had he been missing? A few cleansing breaths flushed the feeling away, but he still couldn't bring himself to trash the bag. He compromised by saving the cookies for later, as a reward when the job was done. It wasn't Zen to work toward a goal, but disciplined waiting seemed like a better path than succumbing to a sudden craving for immediate gratification.

Besides, he told himself, he'd waited a lifetime to taste the forbidden snack; a few more hours would only make the ultimate surrender more satisfying.

Chapter 8

Jean-Paul lurked at the bottom of the escalator as his contact, an overly-painted but otherwise attractive cosmetics saleslady, packed perfume boxes into a fancy shopping bag. As the customer took the bag and walked away, Jean-Paul checked that no one else was nearby and casually approached the counter.

"I am having a code red, Phyllis," he said, "the keyword is 'no sweat'."

Phyllis recoiled at the sight of the credit-card-sized bandage on his head, then looked him up and down. She probably thought he should be in the men's department shopping for a clean suit. He wondered what she would think of Toine, waiting outside in his purple pajamas!

"Whatcha got, honey?"

Jean-Paul slid the fingerprint kit across the glass.

"We require a set of fingertip gloves."

"No problem. I can have 'em ready for pickup on Tuesday."

"Tuesday is too late. Can you do it tonight?"

"That'll cost extra."

"We are all well-paid, no?"

"Yeah, but maybe I can at least get a bottle of champagne for my trouble…?"

Jean-Paul smiled—Phyllis was too American to ask for something truly valuable like caviar or foie gras. She would not notice the poor quality and low cost of a certain prestige-name champagne.

"That can be arrangées, Madame." He handed her a business card. "Call us when they are complete."

* * *

François wedged a chair beneath the overstuffed, flower-print-upholstered backside of his first customer. The woman's husband carried equal tonnage, undoubtedly a lifetime patron of expensive restaurants; the image of force-fed foie gras geese came to mind. This would be a typical Saturday late-dinner shift.

Except for one special guest.

François retreated to the waiter station, poured two glasses of ice water, and delivered them to his patrons. This was normally his interns' job, but they were occupied with more important matters. Over the woman's shoulder and through the front window, he could see Jean-Paul and Toine hurrying along Exeter Street.

The two soon appeared on the dining room floor in full dress. François performed a perfunctory inspection, noting the bandage on Jean-Paul's head and the bruise under Toine's ear. Such wounds were not appetizing—the injured interns would have to remain out of sight for the evening. He lowered his head and his voice.

"You have delivered the prints?"

Jean-Paul's nose rose to a height surpassing even the most stringent guidelines.

"Our contact will attempt to produce the prosthetique fingers by later tonight. If she successes, we must reward her with a bottle of champagne. It must be the finest champagne that an American perfume counter saleslady can appreciate."

Toine began to snicker, then caught himself; François suppressed his own amusement more effectively. He waved the interns off to their duties and descended to the wine cellar.

Raising his head and compressing his upper lip in preparation for the pungent blast of Herve, François opened the door. It was unfortunate that the Urban Legion ape had deposited the cheese into a dark corner of the cellar. It was more unfortunate that François had not discovered and disposed of it until just before dinner hour. He retrieved an Henry de Fontenay Sancerre Les Roysiers and quickly exited the polluted vault.

In need of a moment to recover his breath, he leaned against the tightly reclosed door and mused over the day's fortunes. With the exception of the odor, everything had proceeded remarkably better than he could have hoped. And with M'sieur Grady's presence tonight, perhaps the day would turn out better still. François' career had come to somewhat of a standstill, relegated to truffle wars and recruit training. What doors to advancement in the Corporation might one suddenly find open, when one has opened the door to Urban Legion headquarters?

He had no time to dwell upon this, however; the "rush," as the waiters quite facetiously called it, would soon begin.

* * *

Lynn correctly guessed that the women's wardrobe in the Urban Legion headquarters "guest suite" offered nothing large enough for a former basketball center. Digging through the men's closet, Roger came up with a serviceable pair of jeans for her, an even larger pair for himself, and slippers for both. He stepped into the hall while she changed, and then tossed the wet skirt and slacks into the washer. Roger explained that while the king lived in private quarters at the other end of the complex, everyone else had a life outside and stayed over only occasionally.

"We have our own re-identity system, like the witness protection program. We can get a new ID, a place to live, and a cover job that gives us time for Legion activities. Anytime they figure out who one of us really is, we become somebody else. We can even get plastic surgery if we have to."

Lynn examined Roger's face: not bad-looking, but not perfect.

"That's the real you, right?"

He glanced sideways, grinning.

"I guess it's obvious—this is what nature gave me. We don't think the guys who killed Todd took any pictures, so we figured I could get away without surgery. I did change my name, though."

"From what?"

"I forget."

Roger showed her a few offices and laboratories, then a set of windows looking into what seemed like a home theater on steroids. There were leather chairs and couches for viewing assorted large-screen TVs, and a tablet or laptop computer on every coffee table. Headphones hung from the arm of every seat.

"That's our media room. We can watch any video stream, worldwide: Internet, broadcast, cable, and satellite, and a bunch of private news feeds we've managed to, um, stumble across in the network. As the Trail Boy Manual says, intelligent strategy requires strategic intelligence—and we can keep tabs on enemy strategy from the comfort of our living room."

"By monitoring the news?"

"By monitoring the ads."

Lynn's eyes were drawn to the high-definition images flashing in from around the world. She struggled to grasp the scale of the place, especially compared to her cramped living room and tiny, rarely-used TV.

"You built a secret floor in a downtown high-rise, and filled it with more TVs than a TV studio. This must have cost a fortune!"

"Yeah, it's all pretty expensive," Roger agreed, "especially the cable subscription."

"Okay, so how did you pay for it?"

"Remember Howie's cologne? He doesn't just make it for himself. We sell it to generate cash for our operations. Not openly, of course."

Lynn mouth scrunched sideways.

"Let me guess," she said, "you guys have to hide the cologne underground because the perfume companies are afraid you're gonna sell it cheap, so they're out to squash it."

Roger shook his head.

"Nope. Howie's formula is based on a rare, secret ingredient, so the cologne is very expensive; the perfume companies aren't worried about the price. But remember, they don't sell fragrance, they sell the promise of sex. People buy perfume and cologne thinking it'll help 'em get laid, and when it doesn't, they buy different perfume and cologne. If their stuff worked like our stuff, customers would only need one $400 bottle for a lifetime of sex. Actual sex. The kind of sex the perfume executives get when they flash all their money around.

"Money and power," he added, nodding knowingly. "The only effective aphrodisiacs known to man. Till now. Howie's cologne could kill the clothes, liquor, pornography, and sports car markets, too. All those companies would like to squash it. They're all trying to squash it."

Lynn felt like her brain was being squashed—how could anything sound so paranoid and so reasonable at the same time? There had to be a hole in the story somewhere.

"If it's so expensive, how can you guys afford to make it?"

"We're very profitable, because we sell the real thing—even at our high price, a lot of guys buy it. And since we sell it through anonymous email offers, they haven't managed to trace it back to us and shut us down."

"Email? I suppose you also sell penis enlargement pills."

"No, we wouldn't do that. We have ethics—I'm an Elite Trail Boy, remember?"

"But you'd sell them if they worked?"

"Oh, they work, all right. We won't sell 'em because of the nasty side effect. They make the, um, package bigger, but it doesn't grow any new nerve endings. The existing nerves get so spread out the poor guy hardly feels a thing."

Roger apparently noticed Lynn's eyes narrowing.

"Believe that or not, it doesn't matter. If a guy has Howie's cologne, women don't care how big he is. We've got lots of satisfied—sexually satisfied—customers. The only downside is the occasional teenage boy who gets hold of some. Next thing, his teacher gets arrested for statutory rape. It's not fair—she really can't help herself—but that's the law." His cheeks tightened into a grim smile. "We're working on better safeguards, but in the meantime, we have to sell the cologne. It generated the funds to build the truffle lab and about half of this facility."

"How'd you pay for the rest?" Lynn wondered if Howie made facility enlargement pills.

"We had other funding. You know the Nigerian email scam? The original version was real, and we were the ones who got Colonel Saraki's nine million dollars. And one of our earliest benefactors was the lady who tried to dry her poodle in a microwave—well, radar range at the time. She sued the manufacturer and won plenty of money, out of court."

"That *was* an urban legend."

"Nope. But the manufacturers weren't happy about the settlement, and they figured a lot of other people would be tempted to cash in on killing their pets. So they did the usual: planted multiple versions of the story with different, unverifiable details, so anyone looking into it would conclude it was just a legend. But she was very real, very rich, and very pissed off about the cover-up, on top of her grief over losing Gigi. When we contacted her and said we were fighting them, she gave us twelve million."

"You're kidding."

Roger held up two fingers.

"Trail Boy Truth. Plus, we got a really low mortgage rate on the Internet."

Lynn's head was swimming.

"Is there *anything* that's really urban legend?"

"Not much," Roger answered. "Tell you what, let's look some up."

They reached a windowed office at the end of the hall where Howie, intent on the glow of his monitor, was ignoring the glorious view of the South Shore at sunset. Roger sat Lynn at a computer, brought up an urban legend website, and relinquished the mouse. Lynn scanned the Most Popular page for conspiracy theories, urban legends, and Internet hoaxes.

"Did we actually go to the moon?"

"We don't know for sure, but we're thinking probably yes. NASA's a government agency, and it's easier for the U.S. government to land on the moon than to cover up a hoax."

She brought up the "Bill Gates will send you to Disney World if you forward this message" email, and looked at Roger expectantly. He nodded.

"That one actually is a hoax—Bill Gates has no intention of sending a thousand people to Disney World. But it isn't harmless: the part about tracking all the forwards really does work. The original email has a thing called a web beacon—it looks like a single white pixel on your screen, so you don't see it—that blind copies the forwarded addresses back to a tracking site. Sophisticated spammers put web beacons in all their chain emails, usually ending with 'forward this to everyone you know' or 'forward to ten people in the next ten minutes or you'll get bad luck.' They also put them in Facebook status memes; when you repost the meme, the beacon scrapes your address book and sends the addresses back to the spammers. And they don't just use your addresses for their spam lists: they flag you as extra gullible, probably willing to believe anything. So you get even more spam."

Lynn always felt like a party pooper when she didn't forward chain email; now she had a great excuse to just delete it. Unless she was being gullible by believing Roger.

She came across a postcard image of an Arizona Jackalope standing as tall as a nearby cactus.

"Okay, this is just a gift shop joke," she insisted, as Howie got up and looked over her shoulder.

"In a way," Howie explained. "Jackrabbits were crossbred with antelope in Northern California, not Arizona—the background is Photoshopped in. It was an experiment for game restaurants; they wanted something with a lot of meat that would breed fast. But it didn't work out—who knew jackalopes would taste like month-old chopped liver? They released them into the wild, but they didn't last long."

"Hunters?"

"Not so much. Apparently, Bigfoot loves month-old chopped liver."

Lynn frowned, but at this point, she was tempted to believe anything. Maybe Beginner's Mind should actually be called Sucker's Mind?

"Got a minute, Roger?" Howie asked.

Roger nodded and followed Howie to his desk.

"I don't get it," Howie said, eyebrows knitted. "On the two goons—Toine and Jean-Paul—we've got all kinds of data, but on their leader, François, we got nothing. Nada. Bupkis."

"Our data research center," Roger explained as Lynn joined them. He leaned over Howie's shoulder and examined the screen. "How did you find all this?"

"Nothing fancy—I uploaded a few of this afternoon's face shots from my personal witness recording." Howie showed Lynn a tiny camera lens built into the corner of his glasses. "I fed them into the federal criminal database—not a match to be found. Then, I got a little inspiration: I tapped into the Centre Nationale d'Informations in Lyon and hit on both Toine and Jean-Paul. Seems they got into a little trouble in France. After the French Rugby Union banned Jean-Paul for flagrant brutality, he teamed up with Toine; the Wine Cartel paid them to poison the grapevines of independent vintners, until they got caught poisoning the vintners, too. The Truffle Cartel pulled them out before the trial, made them some counterfeit visas, and gave them jobs at a Back Bay restaurant, L'Escargot."

"I think I've enjoyed some cheese there," Roger said.

Howie turned back to the screen.

"I swore I'd find François in there, too, but no such luck."

Lynn smiled to herself. *The Internet doesn't know everything.*

"That's because François isn't French," she said. "He's Canadian. Montréal."

She read the two faces as they turned her way. Roger's was curious, but Howie's, skeptical.

"What makes you say that?"

"We had a little fight with him. Roger jumped onto him from a drainpipe, and when he hit the sidewalk he yelled "Tabernac!" That's a Montréal word—basically translates to 'fuck'."

Both faces flinched.

"I first heard it as a kid in New Hampshire, from a French-Canadian sheet rocker after he dropped a slab of drywall on his foot."

Howie attacked the computer, clicking and typing furiously while Roger scanned over his shoulder. A half minute later they cheered and turned back to her. Roger beamed. Proud of the old lady?

"That was it! Nice work! François Spaquel: Montréaler, U.S. resident for five years, after a stint of fifteen years in France. Currently wine steward at L'Escargot. Spotless record—he stays out of trouble. Clearly the guy to worry about—he's a lot smarter than the other two."

"I didn't see it," Howie chided himself, "I was only thinking he's French."

An image from Gerry's store popped into Lynn's mind, of Jean-Paul waving a broken wine bottle. A broken Canadian wine bottle. And the odd hostility between Jean-Paul and François that followed.

"I bet the goons think he's French, too. And they don't like Canadians."

Roger's eyebrows lifted.

"That might come in handy."

Chapter 9

Meg parked her Impala near the Booster's Diner entrance. The Diner's rocket motif was appropriate; for a farm-raised, down-home girl, entering the Lexingham Mall was like landing on a foreign planet. Some people around her even looked like aliens. She glanced down at the black Widespread Panic tee-shirt she'd swapped for the flour-coated one, and realized she looked just as alien to everyone else, except maybe the goths. It was gonna be hard enough to pull this off without standing out like an E.T.—the shirt would have to go.

Using a Mall map and a Facebook photo, Meg located Tanya in the Demografique store, working a long line of customers at the register. Heavy shopping or rookie cashier? At least Tanya would be stuck there for a few minutes, enough time for a quick trip to The Chasm—which was about as long as Meg could stand the assault of The Chasm's incessant techno beat. She hastily chose a bright pink, waist-baring logo top and a pair of low-cut jeans, paid cash, and headed for the fitting room.

The clerk cleared his throat.

"Most people try the clothing on *before* they buy it."

Shoot. How was she gonna fake being a teenager when she couldn't even shop like one? Meg looked up innocently, raising her voice to a juvenile squeak and toning down the Texas drawl.

"Oh, I know it'll fit, and I, like, love it so much I've gotta, like, wear it right away!"

The clerk responded with a tolerant chuckle.

In front of the fitting room mirror, Meg stripped off her tee and tore the tags from the new top. She slipped it on—it was so tight it looked shrunk.

Perfect.

She slid off her unfashionably-high-waisted jeans, too loose and comfortable to get away with, and tugged the new low-riders up as far as possible. Cool air tickled her exposed waist and triggered a sneeze; she reckoned that staying warm just wasn't in the cards today. At least a stuffy nose would help disguise her adult voice. The alloy barrettes in her hair weren't very trendy, but given the likelihood of running into sug-jectors at a mall, she decided to keep a few on. A last glance in the mirror convinced her she could pass for a teenager, as long as she kept up that innocent, empty look.

She swapped her jeweled flower pin, which housed her personal witness camera, from the Widespread Panic shirt onto the new top, then shoved the old shirt and jeans into the Chasm bag. Spy or no spy, she wasn't willing to part with a favorite outfit, yet. She threw her messenger bag over her shoulder and hustled out of the fitting room; after a quick spin for the very grateful clerk, she rushed out of the store and, as a bonus, away from the music. She dropped the shopping bag in her car and returned to stake out Demografique.

Her disguise had passed the first test, but she still had to convince the real experts: real teenagers.

* * *

Tanya Grady tore the receipt from the slot, set it onto the blouse, and slid both into the bag.

"Thank you for shopping at Demografique. Enjoy your weekend." She handed over the bag and watched the customer disappear into the Mall. The store was almost empty now—most shoppers were at the food court or headed home. It had been a long day, and Tanya was tired and hungry. She turned to her boss.

"Can I go now, Gina?"

Gina glanced at the monitors and then the clock.

"Sure, Tanya. You're done for today. Good job. Have fun at dinner."

"You're not coming?"

"No, that's a Mall management deal. Top secret, exclusive for trainees. They haven't told the store managers anything except to let you go and we aren't invited."

"That's too bad."

"Not really, I hear it's catered by the food court," Gina said, grinning. "Besides, somebody has to cover the stores. And some people"—she nodded toward a totally anorexic-looking girl on the skirt-section monitor—"would rather shop than eat."

"Not me," Tanya laughed, grabbing her purse. She stopped at the dressing-room mirror to adjust a couple of wayward reddish-blonde locks, tugged the bottom of her shirt to make it even, and turned around to check for peeking underwear.

"I'm off duty, right, Gina? I can wear my pendant?" The Mall had made it clear on her first day of work that handmade jewelry was not acceptable when selling brand-name fashions at a Mall store.

"You're on your own time—wear whatever you want."

Tanya dug the chain from her purse and draped it so the silver pendant rested just above the low neckline of her shirt. Guys always noticed the unique piece of jewelry, but she knew that was only because they were already looking there. Not that it mattered tonight—the trainee dinner was rumored to be just girls. The only guys would be bosses; she sure wasn't out to impress them with the pendant—or the low neckline.

That would just be creepy.

* * *

Meg lurked outside the bookstore near Demografique, checking out the bestsellers display. She thought she might actually like *The Darwin Papers*—a hot new thriller about a plot by evolutionists to cover up Darwin's conversion to Creationism. The folks back home would love it. She chuckled that *The Urbane League* was still on the list, wondering who would buy such a silly paranoid premise.

But she kept one eye on the corridor, and when Tanya waltzed out of Demografique, Meg gave her a twenty-yard head start and joined the crowd behind her. Tanya made her way to the food court escalator and rode it to the second level, where a bevy of girls gathered. It struck Meg that they were all good looking—because they all used Mall beauty products? Or more likely, they all met the sexist Mall hiring guidelines. She was amused by all the bare lower backs until a chilly draft reminded her she now fit right in.

A middle-aged man in a white shirt and tie herded stragglers, waving anybody who looked young and confused into the group. Meg did her best to look young and confused.

"Trainees, gather here. I'm Don DiSenza, the Mall Manager. I'll be escorting you downstairs as a group in a moment."

Meg drifted over to Tanya, who stood off to one side, alone.

"Hi, I'm Meg," she said, in her best squeaky voice. "You a trainee too?"

Tanya's expression went from alarmed to relieved.

"Um, yeah. I'm Tanya. I'm at Demografique, how about you?"

Shoot. She'd never go into—

"Upscale Maternity."

They talked for a few minutes; Meg spun a yarn about Waltham High School and a lacrosse-playing boyfriend. Tanya confided that she'd come all the way out from North Cambridge and didn't know a soul at the Mall except her boss.

"But now you know me," Meg reassured her.

Mr. DiSenza shouted over the youthful din.

"Okay, ladies, follow me—we've got a little banquet hall set up downstairs. Don't fall behind—if you miss dinner, you'll miss the special deal we've arranged for you."

He turned and led the crowd down, Tanya and Meg bringing up the rear. At the mouth of the escalator, where the river of teenagers widened out onto the expansive main floor, two manager types stood by, counting heads. The woman could've been an Army drill sergeant, and the guy looked like he'd been drafted from a pro-wrestling ring and stuffed into a dress shirt. They fell in behind Meg as she passed.

That could be trouble—Meg wished they'd hidden in the middle of the crowd. She chatted mindlessly while straining to catch the conversation behind her.

"Three short. You sure you have the right count?"

"Yeah. It's all right—we figured a few would skip the dinner."

Meg relaxed and shuffled ahead. They'd never know they were actually four short.

DiSenza steered them down a narrow hall off the main corridor and around a corner. Meg had studied the Mall map pretty carefully—this was all familiar. But suddenly she was turning left, through a door that was definitely not on the map.

It was a short passage leading to another open door. She twisted to give her personal witness a hi-resolution snapshot of the lock, but the mechanism was electronic—no details to shoot. She untwisted just in time to notice the stairway down—and almost in time to avoid stumbling.

"Watch your step, ladies."

Meg got a glimpse of DiSenza's toothy smirk, and blood rose in her cheeks.

Damn. It was embarrassing enough to trip, but stupid and dangerous to call attention to herself. She decided she ought not take up bear hunting.

From the bottom steps, Meg glanced over the crowd to see a brightly lit corridor stretching away, lined with doors and intersecting with side halls—all underground and, of course, not shown on the Mall map. This was getting interesting.

"Phone, please."

Meg pulled up, face-to-face with a surly-looking guy and his outstretched hand.

"We don't want any distractions," he said, impatient. "Or recordings."

No cameras. What the hell were they hiding? And did they think these kids weren't gonna talk about it? Fat chance of that. Unless they wouldn't be able to?

Meg almost claimed she didn't have a phone, but that would be admitting she wasn't a teenager, so she handed it over. The guy wordlessly tore a numbered claim check and shoved half at her, then stuck the other half to her phone and dumped it into a box. Meg stowed the claim check and moved along, glancing at the tiny personal witness lens in the heart of her jeweled pin.

We don't need no stinking phone cameras.

She took a mental note to thank dear paranoid Howie for setting the high security password on her phone. If the Corporation was gonna plant zombie software into that box of phones, hers would refuse to play along.

The "banquet hall" was a cafeteria crowded with round tables, chairs, and a lectern in a corner. Steam wafted from a buffet line; it smelled delicious, even through Meg's stuffy nose.

DiSenza's voice barked from behind them.

"Grab a seat, girls, and when we call your table number, hit the buffet. There's lots of everything so take as much as you want, and feel free to go back for seconds. After you've got some food in you, we'll present a very special offer—so don't even think about leaving early."

Meg maneuvered Tanya to the only remaining table with a clear view of the lectern. She listened carefully for their table number—she had to admit she was getting mighty hungry. But mostly, she was getting mighty curious about the "special offer."

She had no intention of leaving early.

* * *

Tanya finished off a dripping beef fajita and lamented her Mom's healthy cooking to her new friend.

"Don't get used to it," Meg mumbled between the bites of a fruit torte. "No way they're gonna feed us like this durin' the Christmas season."

Tanya sadly agreed. This was a typical fast-food menu but way better than anything you could scrounge at the food court. Piles of hot wings and teriyaki beef to get them started, with mixed-green and spinach salads for the dieters. The pizza was crisp, the barbeque chicken was tangy, and the fajitas were stuffed with real steak and crunchy veggies. They washed it down with premium bottled iced teas and lemonades, and topped it off with dessert cart treats to die for. There was even a cappuccino machine. Tanya felt like she was being buttered up—or fattened up—for something. Whatever it was, it might be worth it.

She actually wouldn't dare eat like this during the Christmas rush—she'd end up shopping at Upscale Maternity to find anything that fit. But she figured this pampering wouldn't last long—so far, the whole Mall experience felt like a dream, too good to be true. A bubble about to pop. Mom had said there must be a catch—maybe they'd spring it tonight.

She was working on a dark chocolate mousse when Mr. DiSenza appeared at the lectern and tapped the microphone. He looked more formal now, having added a jacket to his shirt and tie.

"Okay, ladies, looks like you're all into dessert, what say we get started? I'm sure you have places to go tonight, so we'll be brief. First of all, I want to welcome you to the Lexingham Mall family"—he switched to a thick Brooklyn-Italian accent and began to twitch his arms—"and you gotta remember one 'ting—you never betray the family, capiche?"

The room went dead quiet. DiSenza scanned the crowd expectantly, then his eyes fell. His voice returned to normal, friendly.

"Hey, lighten up, that was a joke."

Just not a very good one, Tanya thought, as a few charity laughs trickled around her. She smiled at the idea that the Lexingham Mall family, like every family, had an Uncle Don who thought he was funny.

"Seriously, though, we, and now you, are all part of a team. That team is bigger than the stores you work in; it's even bigger than the whole Mall." DiSenza paused dramatically. "You, ladies, are now part of Retail."

Tanya glanced at Meg, who mirrored her own raised eyebrows. The other new members of "Retail" shared their lack of excitement—the room stayed silent.

"It's like the National Football League," DiSenza persisted, like he was talking to guys or something. "Our stores compete against each other, and our malls compete against each other, but the main thing is to sell tickets to the fans. In our case, that means getting shoppers to buy stuff, any stuff, from any store. When one store succeeds, we all succeed. Now, your store managers don't tell you that, and they do their best to go head-to-head with other stores, but deep down, they know we all win when customers spend money.

"Many of the companies in the Retail family already work together to stimulate sales. What we call cooperative marketing has been so successful we want to expand it. And as special new members of our Retail family, you can help us with that—and get a little action yourselves at the same time. We have a special guest tonight, here to explain this exceptional offer. Allow me to introduce the U.S. marketing director for Omni Music International: Mr. Phil Grady."

Tanya, in mid-sip of her cappuccino, nearly choked.

Daddy?!

* * *

Meg noted Tanya's narrowly-averted spit-take when Phil Grady's name was announced. That meant Tanya wasn't in on the plan—as Meg expected. The surprise was that Phil had come all the way from L.A. for this. Meg verified that her personal witness was still recording and adjusted her chair to give the lens a full view of the Corporation bogeyman.

Grady was immaculately groomed, modeling a charcoal-gray suit that looked even fresher-off-the-rack than Meg's own outfit. He was younger than she'd imagined; evil executives should be in their fifties, but of course, Phil was only thirty-eight—Lynn's age. And he stepped to the mike with the stage presence of a young rock star. He hadn't lost a bit of that.

His daughter was staring—probably trying to square this image with all her old memories. According to Howie's research, Tanya hadn't seen her pappy in ten years. Hard to tell how she felt about seeing him now.

Phil looked over the crowd—if he recognized Tanya, he didn't let on when he scanned her table. And if Tanya felt snubbed, she didn't let on either.

"Good evening, ladies, I'm Phil Grady. Before we get down to the fun business, I'd like to tell you a little about mine: Omni Music International." A trace of his South Boston accent had survived the California mellowing. "We're marketing consultants to the music industry. We service all of the major music labels and associations, but recently, we've been cooperating with other marketing groups, like fashion and consumer electronics. As Mr. DiSenza mentioned, we're all part of the same…family.

"Now, for the good stuff. We've developed a new concept in

preferred-customer plans that I'm sure you'll like. We call it the OmniPass, and we're going to let you help us test it out.

"You all know about keychain tags and wallet cards that give you discounts at certain stores—you may have one or two in your purse right now. A while back, we were brainstorming about how to combine them all into one convenient card. But even that wasn't convenient enough.

"You're probably not familiar with inventory control microchips, sometimes called Radio Frequency Identification, or RFID, tags. These things are really tiny, so we can put 'em into products: clothes, electronics, stuffed animals, anything. And when you bring them close to our cash registers, we send them a wireless signal, and they answer back with a unique identification number. We track all kinds of things with that number, which is pretty useful. To the accountants and purchasing departments. But not to me, or to you. Till now.

"We decided to make our preferred-customer card with an RFID chip in it. That way, you don't even have to dig out the card—we'll know who you are the moment you step up to the register.

"Now, we can't start up this kind of program quickly—there's a lot of testing and fine-tuning of the software to do. So we thought we'd start small, with a friendly group of customers. We'd like you kids to be those customers, since you represent our combined markets.

"At first, we created a special deal just for you, as a thank-you for helping us get this program off the ground. You'd be able to walk into any store, buy whatever you want, and the system would automatically discount the price twenty percent—after any other savings."

A buzz of voices swelled. Meg was wary—twenty percent was good, but he distinctly said, "at first." Sounded like a bait and switch.

Grady motioned for quiet.

"But we hit a little snag. Our partner stores were worried that the cards would get stolen, and they'd be giving discounts to the thieves. So we kicked it around again, and somebody asked a really great question: why not eliminate the card completely?"

Meg leaned forward.

"We came up with the ultimate convenience: subdermal RFID tags. Special RFID microchips can be injected under the skin—they've been doing it for pets for many years. The microchip is smaller than a grain of rice; it's FDA-approved for people, and it's quicker, easier, and more comfortable than getting an ear pierced. The best part is, you never have to remember your card or worry about it getting lost or stolen. You *are* your card."

Grady paused, seemingly unconcerned, as the conversation in the room went from squeaky excitement to ominously low murmuring, except for a few girls with tats who exchanged nods of approval. Meg glanced at the personal witness record indicator again—she'd hate to lose this.

Subdermal microchips. *Damn!*

The murmuring quieted down a little, and Phil continued.

"Now, OmniPass is a pilot program, and we understand you might have doubts about being on the leading edge. So we decided to sweeten the deal even more: anyone who joins the program will get an automatic discount at participating stores, for the next thirty days, of forty percent."

The buzz fired right up again; the tat kids looked ecstatic.

Forty percent off gets a girl's attention—Meg caught herself thinking about how much she would have saved on her jeans and pink Chasm top. Even an adult Legionnaire, actively trying to bring Grady down, wasn't immune to his pitch. The teenagers were dead meat.

"Are there any questions?"

A few hands went up. Meg was tempted to raise her own hand. *Where the hell do you get off planting microchips into innocent children?* She thought better of it.

The girls were asking about whether it hurts (no), does it cost anything (no), does the discount apply to everything (no, just clothes, media, and electronics), and most important, where do they put it and does it show? Phil smiled at that one.

"The microchip goes under the skin on your neck, here." He pointed to a spot behind his earlobe. "We use a quick-injector, completely safe and totally sterilized. It goes about a quarter inch deep, and it doesn't show at all—well, the injector leaves a little red mark, about the size of a pin-head. But it's inside your hairline, and disappears after a few days. After that you can't see any trace of it, even with a magnifier."

That seemed to satisfy the teenagers; they broke into animated discussions about their newly expanded shopping plans. As phrases like "sick boots" and "purple iPhone" floated past her, Meg silently seethed at the social-network-generation's lack of caution.

You can't see a trace of it, but they can trace everything you do!

"Whaddya think?" she asked Tanya. The question startled the teen—she'd been quietly focused on Grady.

"I—I don't know… I've got a lot to think about."

Grady scanned the crowd, smiling like a preacher watching his collection basket fill to overflowing. When he stepped aside, DiSenza took the lectern and waited for the chatter to fade.

"I'd like to thank Mr. Grady for making this possible. You'll get a chance to thank him personally tomorrow, but how about a hand for him now?" The discount-crazed girls applauded wildly; Meg pretended to join in, wincing at every clap.

"Remember, this is totally voluntary, but we hope the deal is sweet enough that every one of you will take part." He nodded toward the battleaxe lady from the escalator, who was guarding the doorway with a sheaf of papers in her arm. "Take a permission form home with you, and consider it overnight. If you decide you want in, have your parent or guardian sign the form and bring it down here tomorrow. Your managers will give you an unscheduled break for the test marketing program, and someone will be in the hall to let you in—in case you didn't notice, this is not a public part of the Mall. Tell 'em you're here to pick up your OmniPass— that's kind of a codeword. Keep it to yourselves.

"And one last thing. No matter what you decide"—he paused and scanned the room, a cruel little smile forming—"you're still due at your stores for training tomorrow at 10 a.m. sharp."

Meg swore he was gonna add 'capiche?' again, but evidently he'd gauged the crowd by then. DiSenza backed away from the microphone, smack into a bear-trap of animated conversation with Phil. Grady didn't look quite so happy, or calm, as he did at the lectern. Meg had noticed his mood go into the crapper right when DiSenza mentioned the permission forms.

Meg guessed those weren't Phil's idea.

She recalled the text message the Legion intercepted, which mentioned forms and some equipment. Was Grady in the dark about the equipment, too? It seemed strange that he might not be privy to the whole scheme; she had him pegged as a key player.

The girls shuffled toward the exit, each taking a permission form and picking up her confiscated phone. Meg pasted on a smile and dawdled, trying to stay back with Tanya, but the teen was out-dawdling her. As they joined the stream pouring into the hall, Tanya glanced over her shoulder then darted back into the room. Meg tried to follow, but the head-counting wrestler thwarted her with a thigh-sized arm.

"But I thought of another question!"

"You can ask it tomorrow."

Meg talked herself out of worrying as the man forced her up the stairs. Tanya'd be okay; there was no way Lynn would ever sign that paper.

* * *

The moment the girls pushed back their chairs, Phil grabbed DiSenza's cheap jacket and pulled him aside. It was all he could do to keep his voice down and his hands off the mall manager's neck.

"What the fuck are those forms?"

DiSenza frowned, looking confused and a little scared.

"They came in this morning by email, Phil. From L.A, with instructions—we can't chip a kid without a signed release. You didn't know?"

"I didn't know. The bastards were supposed to stay out of this."

"Hey, you know how hung up the brass is on paperwork. They're just covering their asses. We can't do this without permission."

"No, we can't."

Phil studied DiSenza's face. How much did he know? He got only the cover story, Phil guessed. He released the man's sleeve.

He couldn't believe those L.A. assholes. No surprise they'd set up DiSenza to babysit, make sure Phil didn't take any shortcuts. But Christ, a fucking permission form? That was more like sabotage. How the hell was he gonna get Lynn to sign *that*? He couldn't sign it himself; his parental rights were ancient legal history.

Lynn would probably go ballistic when she read the form, assuming it stuck to the official story. He didn't want to think about what she'd do if it told the truth.

* * *

Tanya barely heard Phil talking about microchips—she was too busy dealing with being overlooked. He hadn't seen her in so long; did he even recognize her? Then again, she always thought he didn't want any contact with his ex-family—he might pretend he didn't know her. Out of resentment, she was tempted to leave it at that. But part of her hoped she was wrong, that he just didn't see her. At the last moment, she decided to at least try to say hello, and dashed back into the room.

Phil was arguing with Mr. DiSenza. Tanya was about halfway there when she caught his eye—he definitely recognized her, but she couldn't tell if he was happy about it. He growled something that sent DiSenza away, then smiled and opened his arms.

"Tanya? Is that you?"

She gave him the biggest hug she could, considering her mixed feelings.

"Yes, Daddy. It's me."

"I didn't expect to see *you* here. My God, you've grown. I hardly recognized you."

Duh. He hadn't seen her in ten years.

"It's been a while."

"So you're in training here? That's fantastic! You get to take advantage of the new program."

"Is that the only reason you're here? For this microchip thing?"

"Yeah. I just flew in today and I'm going back tomorrow night."

"So you weren't gonna stop by."

He flashed the look of a guy who'd forgotten her birthday.

"I realized a long time ago that your mother doesn't want me to visit."

Slick. It was all Mom's fault.

"Did you ever even try?"

Maybe if he'd tried to visit, he could've, and she could've had a father all those years, even if it was just on weekends—

His face softened. Or maybe just blurred though her watery eyes.

"Look, I'm here," he said. "I'll visit. I've got a dinner meeting, but I'll cancel and take you out instead—ah, shit, you just ate. Let me just take you out, we'll get an ice cream or something. And talk."

Tanya blinked and sniffled once, feeling her vision clear. *Your timing sucks*, she thought.

"I can't tonight. I'm going to a concert—with my friend Michael. He's been looking forward to it for months."

Her father raised an eyebrow.

"Boyfriend, huh? With privileges?"

Daddy!

"It's not like that. He's a good friend. We have a lot in common—social outcasts and no money."

Her father gave her a soothing smile.

"Well, I'll leave the shotgun in the cabinet for now, then. But I bet you'll outgrow guys like that." His smile turned up slightly at the corners. "Maybe sooner than you think."

Tanya didn't know what to make of the twinkle in his eye.

"Can we get together tomorrow?" she asked.

"We're both working tomorrow, remember? And my plane is at four… Tell you what, I'll try to change my flight. What's your cell?"

They exchanged numbers, and he promised to call her in the morning. Then came an awkward pause, like they had nothing more to say, even after ten years apart. But it sure seemed like he had something on his mind.

"So, what do you think of the program, Tanya? You gonna do it?"

"It sounds great, Daddy, I need new clothes for work, so I can use the discount. But you know Mom's never gonna sign this." She waved the permission form, and he glared at it so fiercely she thought it would catch fire. Then he smiled.

"I'll take care of that. This is my program, honey, you don't need a form."

She handed him the paper, which he folded and tucked into his pocket, more carefully than she expected for a worthless form.

"So how is your mother these days?"

"She's okay. Keeps her head down, works a lot. We've got college coming up."

"She seeing anybody?"

Tanya tilted her head to look into his eyes. He seemed sincere.

"Not really. She's got friends, but no men, except once in while she goes to some new-age lecture with an old guy from the organic co-op. I think he's weird."

"From an organic co-op, he must be. Sounds like you're already becoming a good judge of men, even if you're not dating a rich, popular quarterback yet."

He grinned and gave her a California cheek-kiss.

"Got to go, babe. I'll see you tomorrow."

He spun around and walked out through a rear door, where he was immediately surrounded by a Mall posse. After watching him disappear, Tanya turned and shuffled toward the hall. Mr. DiSenza waited to take her upstairs.

"He's my father," she explained. "Or at least, my ex-father."

DiSenza seemed taken aback at first but gave her a sympathetic look, like somehow he understood.

He didn't.

* * *

Tanya checked the rear-view mirror for cruisers as she merged her mother's Civic into Route 128 traffic—she was underage for using a cell phone while driving, but she didn't have time to stop. The phone rang six times before the machine picked up.

Mom wasn't home?

"…please leave a message at the beep!"

"Mom, it's Tanya, I'm, um, about to leave, to meet Michael at the concert. You'll never believe this, but Daddy was at the Mall today. He's doing a marketing program there. He offered to take me out to dinner tonight, but I had the concert. And I might see him tomorrow. It was sketchy—we should talk later. Bye."

She pressed END, waited a few seconds, and dialed Mom's cell. That call went immediately to voice mail—Mom was totally out of reach. Weird.

"…exhale, and leave a message—thank you!"

"Hi Mom, I didn't expect you to be out—I already left a message on the home machine. Just wanted to talk about the news, but I guess it can wait till I get home. Don't worry, I'll be in before my license turns into a pumpkin."

She hung up and dropped the phone into her purse. She couldn't talk, anyway; she was too busy dealing with headlights and taillights swapping lanes around her.

But as hard as she tried to focus on the road, she couldn't help replaying her father's words in her mind. It was an old habit, one she'd almost forgotten in the ten years since they'd last talked—back when she tried to stretch their rare conversations for as long as possible, even if only in her imagination.

I JUST FLEW IN TODAY AND I'M HEADING OUT TOMORROW NIGHT.

Always on the go. Never any time to be my Daddy.

I REALIZED A LONG TIME AGO THAT YOUR MOTHER DOESN'T WANT ME TO VISIT.

Right, Daddy. Except, what I remember is how we both couldn't wait for your visits. And when they stopped, how much we looked forward to your phone calls. And how sad Mom was when those stopped, too.

GOT TO GO, BABE. I'LL SEE YOU TOMORROW.

I won't get my hopes up.

Things had really changed—now even her imaginary conversations with Daddy were a letdown. She came up on a pair of taillights—some asshole crawling along at sixty-five in the middle lane. She leaned on the horn and swerved around him.

* * *

After Meg watched Tanya drive off, she pondered what to tell HQ. The girls all had permission forms; in the next few hours, their parents would hear everything she'd heard so far. It was outrageous, but not secret; if that was all there was to it, there wasn't a whole lot to report. The Legion couldn't do much for people who willingly gave away their privacy.

But like an old buck surviving years on the run, Meg had honed a keen sense of danger—and there was a bad scent on the wind. She kept coming back to the intercepted text message, which said there was new equipment involved. What was it for? The cash registers already had RFID readers; why install new stuff? Seemed like an awful pricey way to fire up a preferred-customer program.

She pulled out her phone to check in, but reconsidered. Howie's spyware blocker could stop any software, from Trojan apps to viral text messages—even the factory-installed keystroke tracker. But these guys were fixing to plant microchips into people—what if they already planted one into the phone? If she called HQ, the Corporation could be listening in; and even if she didn't call, they could track her movements. Kind of like hitching a radio collar onto that old buck.

She decided to dig around, maybe get some pix of the gear. She could report back to HQ later. In person.

In the darkness of the parking lot, Meg slid the back off her phone, then laid the battery in her palm and slapped it across the edge of a concrete trash barrel. It snapped in half like a frozen Charleston Chew. She did the same to the phone, tossed the pieces into the barrel, and headed to her car for a change of disguise.

* * *

Phil smiled at the mountain of boxes outside the freight elevator. Eightball had been busy—and he always was the quickest roadie in the business. But there was a lot of gear to be installed and not much time.

"Tell me about deployment, Don."

"I've mobilized eight guys from the wireless stores," DiSenza replied. "Trusted—they'll keep their mouths shut. They'll be down here right after their shift. I told them they could grab some leftovers from the dinner here before they get started; they'll be going all night."

"What, Saturday night and the phone guys don't have a date?" Phil smiled, waiting for a laugh.

"I guess not," Don answered, oblivious. "Plus there's the contractor; he's unloading all this single-handed."

"Yeah, he used to work for me," said Phil. "He's sharp." He lowered his voice. "Is he on the payroll?"

"Nope—just a contractor. Installed all our other RFID gear. Which works great, by the way—how come you need to put in all this new stuff?"

"We have our reasons."

Phil would have been surprised if Eightball were part of the Corporation—the roadie always had strong moral character, except for the coke. And he was off that, now. DiSenza, on the other hand, was a model Corporation employee and could have been tipped off by the bosses, despite Phil's wishes. But apparently he hadn't.

"By the way," Don said, "you probably noticed the crowd was full of lookers tonight. Carefully chosen eye candy, per instructions from L.A. Care to tell me why?"

"It's in my contract, Don—I don't have to deal with ugly women."

"Okay, but what about your daughter? They told me to make sure she went before the other girls. What's up with that?"

"No big deal. A coupla safety nuts in L.A. pushed back when I proposed this. I had to stake something personal to get the green light. Betting the family did the trick."

"But it's just your ex-family, right?"

"The Corporation's my family now. Speaking of which, I'm supposed to have a nice family dinner tonight, right? What have you got?"

Don's expression hovered between amazement and disgust.

"We've set you up for dinner at L'Escargot in Boston," Don said. "French, high-end."

"Yeah, I've been there. High-end date?"

"Very high-end. Her name's Fiona—blonde, hot. HR insisted we use her."

"Nice. What time?"

"Eight. The limo picks you up outside at 7:15—you've got time to relax. Considering Fiona, I suggest you go upstairs to Pierside and down a dozen oysters."

"I'll do that."

Down some oysters. But not relax. Phil fingered the pocketed permission form, which put the whole project in jeopardy. He was satisfied that Eightball and the Mall geeks would set up the equipment and take care of any technical problems. But he couldn't tag any of the girls before he tagged Tanya. And despite what he'd told her, the Corporation's Legal Cartel wasn't gonna let him put a microchip in her neck without Lynn's signature on the fucking form.

That was a decidedly nontechnical problem.

He considered his options.

Chapter 10

Lynn had never seen anything like the Urban Legion communication center. The back wall was lined with racks of electronic boxes, each frantically blinking dozens of yellow and green lights. Cables climbed up from the racks and spread out along the ceiling like multicolored vines on an arbor of gray plastic channels.

Between the channels, Lynn noticed what looked like tiny security cameras and sprinkler heads, and jokingly asked if that was how they watered the cables. Roger would only tell her that if the Legion had to abandon the building, the devices would make sure it didn't fall into enemy hands.

A pair of glass cubicles stood like pillars at the gate of the electronic garden. Visible inside each were chairs around a table, with a speakerphone and tablet in the center. But the glass walls, and especially the glass domes, made them look like little modern cathedrals—pews might have been more appropriate than chairs. As they sat inside one, Roger explained that the glass was actually a piezo-electric sound barrier that suppressed all sound waves coming into or out of the cube by generating exactly opposite waves.

"It's a giant noise-cancelling headphone," he said. "You could have a shouting match in here and no one would hear you. The king calls it the 'cone of silence,' but I don't know why —it's not cone-shaped at all."

Like a cathedral, the silence was absolute; Lynn felt like she should whisper.

"How come this stuff isn't all over American businesses? The Earplug Cartel suppressed it?"

"They tried, but they're not very well organized yet. Mostly, it just never caught on with business managers."

"Really? I'd think this would help all their cubicle workers concentrate."

"Yeah, but they don't want to help them make personal phone calls without the boss overhearing." He shrugged. "Some companies use 'em—for construction trailers, airport planners' offices. The snowmobile, motorcycle, and leaf blower manufacturers have 'em in all their design centers."

Roger pointed to a metal grid visible through the dome.

"That's one of our cell phone trans-locator antennas. It's like a little cell tower: while we're in the building, our phones get connected to the in-house cell network. We relay that through a cloud of mobile antennas around town, so it looks like we're somewhere else to the wireless provider."

"Where do you put the mobile antennas?"

"You know those pizza delivery signs that stick onto the roof of a car? Some of them are specially manufactured just for us. The pizza guys have no idea they're running our remote relay transmitters. As you can imagine, we don't want anybody triangulating on our location here. And that's why your phone doesn't work; we shielded the whole floor with carbon nanotube paint, so no cell signal can get in or out."

"Kind of like a cone of silence for cell phones. Is it piezo-electric?"

Roger gave her an odd look—half pleased, half amused?

"Actually, it's an electromagnetic Faraday shield. But that was a very good guess—in a way, they both do the same thing."

Lynn checked her phone—still zero bars.

"It's not like we ever have visitors," Roger said. "And if we did, we wouldn't want them calling home—unless they're on our side." He hesitated. "Should I add you to the system?"

While she might not be on Roger's side yet, Lynn certainly wasn't on anyone else's; she handed him the phone. He pulled the battery, scanned the bar codes with his own phone, replaced the battery, and passed her phone back.

The display showed five bars. And the message symbol.

"I've got a voicemail from Tanya. Should I take it?"

"I insist! May I intercept it and put it on speakerphone?"

Lynn nodded okay; Roger pressed buttons on his phone as she connected, and Tanya's voice soon filled the cube. She wanted to talk about the news? What news? The message ended.

"I'll call her back."

"Wait," Roger said quickly, "she mentioned another message on your home machine. Let's hear that first."

"It's on my home machine."

"Right. It must have remote message retrieval. They all do. Using a code number. Do you know it?"

"No. I've never used it."

"No problem, I'll just multi-tone it."

"You'll what?"

"Multi-tone it. The machine is listening for a certain sequence of touch tones. But if it gets extra tones at the same time, it ignores them; as long as one of the tones is correct, it's happy. So if we give it all ten tones for each of the four code digits, it'll let you in." He was grinning as he slid the speakerphone toward her. "I'll show you. Call your home phone."

Lynn dialed her number. He waited for the answering machine to pick up, then mashed all ten keys at the same time, producing a cacophonous chord. He played the chord four times.

"You have two messages. First message: Saturday... five... fifty... one... p.m.... To listen, press two, to skip, press three."

Lynn pressed two, and Gerry's voice pleaded with her to call him back and let him know she was okay. He didn't mention any trouble with the Frenchmen—they must have kept their word and let him go once she cooperated. She hit three to skip, vowing to get back to him as soon as she came up with a passable explanation. He wouldn't believe the explanation so far. Lynn didn't believe it herself yet.

Next was Tanya's message. Hearing that Phil was at the Mall was like chugging an emotional cocktail of protective mother, jilted lover, and second-string teammate. She focused on the teammate part.

"Did you know Phil was in town?" she demanded.

Roger shook his head.

"No. But this is great, Lynn. He's here, he's seen Tanya. It gives you a reason to call him without raising suspicion."

"You want me to call him?" Lynn felt another nervous surge, this time straight jilted lover. It would be a big surge if she actually had to talk to Phil. "That would be very awkward. I don't think I can do it."

"Oh, yes you can. You moved a heavy chair across a cobblestone floor, while tied into it. *That* was awkward."

And Lynn would never have believed she was capable of it— until she did it.

There is no can do or cannot do, there is only doing or not doing, said Zen-mind.

"Maybe. What would I talk about?"

"I bet the king'll have some ideas about that." Roger glanced at his watch. "He should be ready for us now." As they emerged from the cube, Lynn almost put her phone away.

"Now can I call Tanya?"

Roger frowned, and then shrugged okay. They walked toward the lobby together, Roger playing with his own phone as Lynn dialed. Tanya's number rang a long time with no answer.

"She's at that concert, probably can't hear it." Roger suggested.

"But it didn't even go to voice mail."

"Must be a phone company problem."

Lynn glanced up to catch Roger glancing away. Around here, he *was* the phone company. He'd already showed that he could intercept calls. She wondered if all Trail Boys were such terrible liars. And why he didn't want her to talk to Tanya.

* * *

This would be Lynn's first audience with a king; she half-seriously wondered if she was expected to wear a hat. She and Roger met Howie in the lobby and proceeded through it to the king's quarters, which apparently occupied an entire wing of the Urban Legion HQ. He had his own conference room, smaller than the main one, but with an equally stunning view of Boston Harbor and Logan Airport beyond. Pretty luxurious setup for a guy supposedly leading the fight against greedy cartels.

Then again, the walls revealed a humble side; a framed retro pop art poster and two black-and-white portraits with a down-home touch: a plain woman in a plaid shirt and a businessman sporting a cowboy hat.

The eastern sky had darkened, and Logan's runway lights sprouted like rows of glowing violets. Lynn was admiring the reflections on the harbor when the drawl came from behind her.

"Hello darlin'! Welcome to the Urban Legion!"

Lynn turned to meet the king. He was an old man—she guessed about seventy—with a full head of gray hair, sparse but extended sideburns, and a twinkle in his eye. He looked familiar. It was the white-sequined jumpsuit.

Not the "king"—"The King"!

He was smiling as he offered his hand. Lynn stared as she shook it, then she came to her senses.

"I'm sorry, I'm being rude. Glad to meet you, um, King?"

"That's the name everybody uses. Don't fret none, Lynn. Happens to all the newcomers."

"A few hours ago I'd have considered this a joke. But after all I've seen… You're really Elvis Presley?"

"I wouldn't 'xactly say that. The Legion has a lotta well-trained impersonators, and it suits us if nobody can tell if we're the real thing. We all talk like we are, and with plastic surgery, we all look like we are. So I'll just leave it as a maybe, if that's okay by you."

Lynn had a hundred questions when she walked into the room. Now she had a thousand. The King pulled back a chair for her.

"Have a seat, darlin', and I'll start you off with a little history lesson."

Despite countless history courses in high school and college, Lynn suspected this lesson would not be a review.

The King spoke with a disarmingly easy manner, as much like Elvis as Lynn could imagine. She was instantly enthralled; the man had natural charm that put Howie's cologne to shame. It occurred to her that he might be the source of Howie's secret ingredient.

"It all started in the nineteen-sixties; I first noticed it in the record business. See, in the fifties, when they decided I was the next big thing, they pushed my records and made me a lot of money. But then they started milkin' it. Now, I'm not talkin' about the movies—they were bad enough. This was worse. They made all the fans who bought 45 RPM singles switch to LPs. Then they made the folks who bought 8-tracks switch to cassettes. Lemme tell ya, my fans were big into 8-tracks.

"'Course, there was always somethin' shady goin' on in the record biz. The labels wanted their records played, so they hooked the DJs on money or drugs or women. The spinners cued up whatever the labels wanted, to keep their fixes comin'. I didn't pay no mind mostly; I was just trying to play my music. But after they put me out to pasture in Vegas where they figured I couldn't do no harm, they went a step further. A step over the line, in my opinion."

The old man shook his head sadly.

"They invented disco."

He stared blindly for a moment, as if remembering the very day.

"It was new music, new bands, new records to buy, the usual stuff; but there was somethin' else, somethin' sinister. See, up to then, music stood on its own. Sure, Pink Floyd wrote *Dark Side of the Moon* to sync with *The Wizard of Oz*, and *Thick as a Brick* underscored *Gone with the Wind*, but you could still enjoy those albums without watchin' the movies. Disco was different. It was good for dancin', but deliberately designed so you couldn't just listen to it. And that added a whole 'nother dimension: to dance, you had go to a disco, and to get into a disco, you had to dress up. No more tee-shirts and blue jeans and sneakers; now it was leisure suit and platform shoes and gold chains. You needed a closetful of expensive threads just to tap your feet. I discovered that the music and the fashion folks had joined forces into an evil coalition they called the Corporation.

"It wasn't a big thing, but it was the first time two groups worked together—the first consumer products conspiracy. And I thought, well, that can't be good, and I decided to fight it.

"That's when I got the idea of goin' underground. I recruited some impersonators, and now there's nine Kings in nine hidden headquarters all around the world. They get one of us from time to time, but they never know if they got the right one."

Lynn looked the old man directly in the eye.

"There's a right one? So the real Elvis is still alive?"

The King's impish grin returned.

"Everybody knows Elvis Presley died at Graceland in 1977. Who can deny that?"

"It could have been faked, or an impersonator."

"I s'pose…"

"And all those sightings?"

"We all look alike. Sometimes one of us slips up and gets spotted in public."

The King described the Legion's early days, raising millions by selling motorcycles inscribed "To James Dean from Elvis."

"But the big cash came from flea markets—we sold a lot of velvet paintings. We mostly spent the money tryin' to expose the Corporation's marketing tactics, like makin' airline meals so bad you'd be willin' to spend a fortune on airport snacks, or changin' the "in" color every fashion season. But then we noticed that they weren't just marketing, they were payin' attention to technology, too. They suppressed stuff that threatened 'em, like cold fusion and Roger's two-hundred mile-per-gallon car, and developed their own stuff, like the voice-to-head-projector or fluoride in the water."

"Hold on," Lynn said, "What does fluoride do for them—besides prevent cavities?"

"Funny story about that—when researchers discovered that fluoride hardens kid's teeth, the dentists were in a bind. They couldn't very well come out against it, but they knew it would hit their filling and long-term crown business pretty hard. Then somebody figured out it also gives kids a hankerin' for sugar—perfect for the soft drink producers. So the soda folks added enough acid and sugar to keep the dentists going, and the dentists were willing to recommend fluoride."

Lynn nodded, then dissonance set in—this was too much.

"Car manufacturers. Record companies. Dentists! So many corporations. You fight them all?"

The King exchanged a glance with Roger and Howie.

"There's only one Corporation, Lynn."

The King leaned forward and lowered his voice, as if he might be overheard.

"There are cartels, from every industry. They run their own businesses, and the brands in each compete, but underneath they're after the same thing: convince, train, or even force consumers to buy what they're sellin'. So the cartels work with each other within the Corporation. They're like divisions in a big company—they all have their own profit and loss, but they share Corporate policies and management infrastructure, and fund overhead operations that benefit them all. They even have consulting groups that offer services to the cartels, for a fee."

"What kind of services?"

"Whatever they need. Research and development, government bribes, hit men. There's even a Wacko Conspiracy Group that pushes theories like 9/11 being an inside operation—they give conspiracy theories a bad reputation so no one takes the real conspiracy seriously. The wackos are very well-funded and get the job done."

"Where does the money come from?"

"It gets siphoned off from legitimate companies by Corporation people embedded at the highest levels. They hide it all with a financial trick called GAAP—Generally Accepted Accounting Principles."

"And who's the CEO of this Corporation?"

The King paused, his expression sinking a little.

"Good question. We can follow the chain of command up a few levels, and then it stops. The top managers are taking orders from somebody, but so far, he's invisible."

After a few more war stories, the King got down to business: uncovering Phil Grady's plan for the kids at the Mall. He was pleased to hear about Tanya's message; like Roger, he immediately grasped the implications. Lynn could see a resemblance between Roger and the King: dedication, quick thinking, and youthful energy, despite the King's age. No wonder they liked working together.

The King suggested that since Phil had proposed dinner to Tanya, maybe he was free for the evening.

"In which case," Roger said, "you could actually meet with him."

"No way I'm doing that." Her mouth was going dry even at the thought of seeing Phil in person.

Roger ignored her answer, persisting with his eyes; Lynn stood firm with hers. He blinked first.

"You've got to help us, Lynn! You know Tanya's in the middle of it!"

"Tanya will be safe if I keep her away from him. You won't let me call her, but unless they kidnap her from her concert, she's coming home tonight. And that's where she's going to stay tomorrow."

Roger stared at her, debating something in his mind, long enough to make her uncomfortable. Finally, he lowered his head.

"I have a confession to make, Lynn. I haven't told you everything. I did stop you from calling Tanya, because if you just keep her home tomorrow, we won't ever find out what's going on."

The King shot Roger a stern look.

"You didn't tell her?"

"No, I didn't." He turned to Lynn again. "That text we intercepted—I didn't give you the whole message. I left out the part about Tanya being first on the list."

"What?!"

"Apparently, Phil made a deal with his boss about the experiment on the mall trainees. He agreed that Tanya would go before any of the other girls. To"—he lowered his head again, and his voice—"to prove it's safe."

Disbelief rose in her throat as she scanned the men's faces for some sign of denial.

"Please understand," Roger pleaded. "We won't risk Tanya. I just figured if I told you, you wouldn't help us—you'd just pull her out."

"You got that right!"

The King took this in quietly.

"Lynn," he finally said, "We're worried about Tanya, too. But we're also worried about all the teenage girls Phil has in his sights right now. A rock star like him knows how to sway 'em—believe me, I've been there. But the Corporation isn't just cookin' up a fake fan club here. Whatever they're doing is so illegal or immoral they gotta keep it secret, and we need to find out what it is. Now, if you pull Tanya out, Phil can't keep his part of the deal; he'll have to shut the operation down and bail out of the Lexingham Mall. But eventually, he'll convince 'em to set the scheme up in another city without constraints, and exploit God knows how many kids before we get another chance to stop 'em."

"You want me to choose between my daughter and everyone else's…"

"No, Lynn. You don't have to choose—if you're willin' to help. If we can find out what's happenin', from Phil, tonight, we can shoot the whole thing down before bedtime. And not risk anybody's daughter."

She took a deep breath, and as she exhaled, Zen-mind noted the pounding of her pulse in her ears. And under that din, the tiny, pleading voice of Lynn the rejected lover.

But what about me?

It hit her then: she wasn't just afraid for Tanya, she was afraid for herself. Years of spiritual discipline had helped her forget Phil but not get over him. She was sure her old flame could mesmerize her, and scorch her, as badly as ever.

Then again, Master Chuushin would remind her that saving her "self" was saving an illusion—a figment of her ego's imagination—that was better lost anyway.

To sacrifice the self is to sacrifice nothing, and gain everything, said Zen-mind.

You make it sound so easy, grumbled Lynn-mind.

"Okay, what do I have to do?"

* * *

Lynn never dreamed she'd see Elvis at a whiteboard, waving a dry-erase marker. But there he was, writing "Phil Grady" at the top, then two column headings, "Weaknesses" and "Approaches." He snapped the cap onto the marker.

"A lot of what we know about Phil came from your Spinning Rock articles. Pretty good writin', by the way."

"Thank you. That was a tough time, on the road with a new

baby. I'm glad you found them before they turned into urban legends."

"We found 'em all right. We were keen on recruitin' Phil for the Legion. We thought he had potential."

"So did I."

Sympathetic looks flashed from the King and Roger and Howie. The King cleared his throat.

"Yeah. Unfortunately, the Corporation saw his real potential and lured him to their side. And after they wiped out all his music they kept him out of the spotlight. So fill us in, Lynn. What can you tell us about Phil? And, ah, focus on the weaknesses."

I could write a book.

Let it go, said Zen.

She felt the bitterness ebb. Zen-mind was right; this was better handled without emotional scorekeeping.

"Well, he cheated on his wife, for starters. And I don't know about lately, but he was a big fan of booze, weed, and coke. Plus he's arrogant, conceited, and interrupts people to talk about himself." Lynn took a breath; this was kind of therapeutic.

"He's rough in bed, doesn't shave or trim his fingernails often enough, and couldn't find a G-spot to save his life."

Okay, maybe that was Too Much Information.

Roger and Howie looked a bit shocked, but the King was deadpan as he turned from the whiteboard. He'd written it all down under Weaknesses: cheats, booze, weed, coke, arrogant, conceit, interrupts, talks/self, rough, grooming, and a circled "G" with a slash through it.

"We oughta be able to take advantage of that," he said.

"On second thought, let's leave my G-spot out of this."

"No, not that. He likes to talk about himself—which is just what we want him to do. Lynn, how'd you find out about his cheatin'? That's the kind of thing he'd want to hide, just like he's hidin' the plot at the Mall."

Lynn thought back ten years. She'd had suspicions.

"I was worried; he was spending three weeks at a time on the West Coast, and when he came home for a few days, he wasn't very interested in either me or Tanya. Tanya was about five, just starting kindergarten. She didn't know what she was missing, I guess. But I did. I remember I made a nice dinner and opened an expensive bottle of wine. I can get a little forward when I drink, so I was sort of trying to seduce him, and he was just rattling on about all the deals he was into. I finally came right out and asked him why he didn't want to come home anymore. And... and why he didn't want me anymore."

She felt her cheeks flush.

"He looked at me kind of funny, like with pity or something, then calmly told me he'd been screwing three different Los Angeles beach babes for almost a year. He was proud of it: told me how they were all over him out there, and said he just got tired of fighting them off. I asked him what I had to do to get him back. He said, 'You can't.' "

She blinked away a few tears, but Roger noticed—he was at her side, squeezing her hand.

"I'm sorry, Lynn. You shouldn't have to go through this."

"It's okay. I better get it out of my system before I see him, right?"

His eyes shone.

"Yeah, Lynn, get it out of your system."

"I think I got it," the King said over his shoulder. He stepped back. Under Approaches, he'd written "drunken sailor."

"You pegged him as talkative, arrogant, and not too sly when he's drunk. So you invite him out for a drink. You heard he was in town; you thought you should talk, about Tanya, or about—yeah, about Tanya gettin' involved at the Mall. He starts talkin' about that, and we play it by ear, see if we can lead him to spillin' his plans. God knows what it'll take, but if you get him drunk enough, he might open up."

"Um, but if I get drunk enough, I might open up about the Legion."

Roger and the King both turned to Howie, who was nodding and grinning.

"Not to worry," he said. "Doctor Friedman's miracle drinking cure to the rescue."

"Howie was developing a hangover preventer," Roger

explained, "as a money-maker product; we were sure the pain-reliever companies wouldn't sell it. But it doesn't work like we wanted—instead, it neutralizes the neural interaction of the alcohol, so you don't even get tipsy. Needless to say, it wouldn't sell very well. You'll be cold sober. Can you act drunk?"

Three faces were fixed on her. Counting on her. And Tanya was counting on her even more. "I'll give it my best shot."

"That's all we can ask," the King said. He set the marker in the tray and motioned for everyone to move. "We oughta make the call before party boy finds himself a groupie."

On the way to the communications room, Roger pulled out Toine's voice-projector phone.

"Tell you what, Lynn—we'll listen in on the call, and I'll use the voice projector to give you advice. It's electromagnetic, so it'll go through the cone of silence, right into your head. Phil won't hear it. And if you can get a meeting, we'll give you a hidden microphone and transmitter so we can listen in then, too. We'll be with you the whole way."

They set Lynn up in a conferencing cube and retreated to the other. Lynn tried to get comfortable. She was nervous, like calling a boy for a first date. A boy she'd had a crush on for fifteen years…

CAN YOU HEAR ME LYNN? AM I TOO LOUD?

She nodded yes, and Roger played with the projector phone.

BETTER?

She gave him a thumbs-up.

OKAY, DON'T WORRY, PHIL CAN'T HEAR ME. AND WE CAN HEAR BOTH OF YOU. TAKE YOUR TIME AND WAIT FOR US TO COACH YOU. THEY SAY THE SECRET TO GOOD ACTING IS HONESTY—IF YOU CAN FAKE THAT, YOU'VE GOT IT MADE. SO BE HONEST. YOU REALLY WANT TO SEE HIM TONIGHT.

Lynn knew that a part of her wouldn't be faking. She stared at her phone, swallowed the lump in her throat, and took a deep breath. As she exhaled, she punched a number she hadn't dared call in a very long time.

* * *

Phil Grady sat at the Pierside Seafood bar, knocking the edge off his coke buzz with a Positiv Martini. In the old days, he'd have ordered house vodka, figuring he couldn't taste the difference after a few spoons of nose candy. Now, he knew better—the top shelf tastes the same as the cheap shit even when you aren't already high. But it wasn't about the taste, it was about the image. He liked the image, and his bosses were willing to pay for it. It was part of his price for doing their dirty work. Just like the nose candy. And the girls.

Of course, like all expense accounts, this one came with strings attached. In-fucking-particular, the release form. Phil was tired of getting jerked around.

His attention bounced between figuring out how to get the form signed and figuring out whether the bartender was wearing a thong under her tight skirt. He'd come to no conclusion on either when his phone vibrated against his chest. He hoped it wasn't important—the limo was due in a few minutes, and he was looking forward to meeting the blonde. The caller ID was just a number, not somebody in his address book. He was about to punch IGNORE when the digits trickled though the cocaine and vodka filters and tickled a dim memory.

Lynn?

He hovered his thumb over the ANSWER key—wishing he had a plan—then gently pressed. He put the phone to his ear and smiled.

"Lynn! What's up, babe?"

"Hi, Phil. Sorry to surprise you like this—I'm sure you're busy. I was—"

"I am pretty busy, but I can always make time to talk to you."

"Right. Um, I heard from Tanya that you're in town."

"Yeah, I happened to see her at a training session here. Did you know she's working at the—what am I saying? You must know."

"Of course. Look, I was thinking of calling you anyway, but since you're in town, maybe we could get together… for a drink or something. I'd really like to see you."

"Really. Let me check my calendar," he stalled. This *was* a surprise. The child support payments were up to date, if his assistant was doing his job. And Lynn didn't sound angry.

And she wanted to meet over drinks.

He wondered how many drinks it'd take to get her to sign a permission form that profoundly violated her fundamental principles. And then a very entertaining thought popped into the base of his brain. He'd had it easy with Corporation-supplied girls, but they were all marionettes, yanked by the same Corporation strings that kept him in line.

If he was his own man, he could get laid without their damn help.

He checked his fingernails.

"Uh, okay, how about tonight? I've got a dinner reservation in Boston. You eat yet?"

Lynn blurted "No!" then, after a moment, "I've been running around all afternoon, and haven't had a bite. I'd love to have dinner tonight."

Phil smiled at the bartender, and winked. She was clueless, but he had to wink at somebody.

"Okay, I've got a limo waiting, I'll pick you up. You at home? Still live at the old North Cambridge place?" He wouldn't know if she'd moved—his assistant handled everything.

"We're still in North Cambridge. But I'm in Boston"—a pause—"downtown. I've been shopping."

"Shopping, huh? Great!" *Problem.* "How are you dressed? The restaurant's kind of upscale—you should be in something that passes for evening wear."

Another pause.

"I can handle it. I'll pick up something at Pricy's while you're headed in."

She was gonna buy a new dress for this. A scene from a classic video flashed into his head, where Candice Bergen tries to seduce ex-husband Burt Reynolds by baring some tit. He'd be golden if Lynn showed up in a see-through.

"This place is worth it, babe—I guarantee you'll love it. I'll look for you in forty-five minutes, on Tremont across from the Park Street station. That enough time?"

"Yeah, that's good. Thanks, Phil… I can't wait. Bye."

"Bye." He hit END and distractedly dropped the phone into his pocket. He liked this kind of improv—reminded him of jam sessions in the old days.

His reverie was broken by Don DiSenza slicing through the bar crowd with a stunning blonde in tow. Her fur-collared jacket was open and midriff-short, revealing a spandex dress that could've been painted on.

Watching paint dry isn't always boring, he thought.

"Phil, I'd like you to meet Fiona. She's prepared to show you a proper 'welcome back' to the Boston area."

Phil extended a hand.

"Nice to meet you." Firm handshake—clearly a take-charge kind of girl. Phil quickly decided she'd make an interesting contingency, in case Lynn didn't pan out. "But there's been a change in plans. I'm getting together with an old friend for dinner tonight, so you're on your own."

Don sputtered a protest; Phil talked right over it.

"If you eat here, I recommend the wood-plank ahi tuna, rare— it's only somewhat endangered. Goes great with a good Chardonnay. Then stick around the bar at the Hyasson—I might be back in time for a nightcap. If I don't see you by last call, have a good life." He opened his wallet and slipped twin Franklins into her hand. "That'll take care of dinner and a few drinks at the hotel. I assume Don has your time covered?"

Fiona flashed a professional smile.

"That'll be fine, Mr. Grady. Have fun at dinner." She turned to Don. "I'll need a cab, Don. Seafood is for cats."

Baffled but dutiful, DiSenza took Fiona to the reception station and spoke to the hostess. Phil smiled at them as he strolled into the Mall corridor to meet the limo. DiSenza stormed up behind him.

"Phil, what the hell are you doing? Do you have any idea how much we're paying for her?"

"I assume it's enough to keep her around in case it doesn't work out with Lynn tonight."

"Who's Lynn?"

"Tanya's mom. I used to be married to her."

DiSenza's flabbergasted reaction was remarkably satisfying.

"You're gonna pass on Fiona, to nail your ex-wife?"

Phil smiled reproachfully.

"Please, that's such a crude term. I prefer 'nail my ex-significant-other'."

"If I were you, Phil, I'd save it for Fiona. The woman's a pro."

"Yeah, but Lynn has that hippie-free-spirit amateur spontaneity. Sexy as hell. Plus she's been saving it for ten years. She wants me." *And I want her—to sign this fucking form.*

Phil grinned and raised an eyebrow for emphasis. He felt like a teenager—lying and trying to get laid at the same time. DiSenza glared, and then nodded his head toward the parking lot.

A long, black, presumably custom-equipped limo pulled up outside the atrium.

* * *

Lynn leapt from her cube to confront the men.

"Only guys would think I can buy a dress and make it to Park Street in forty-five minutes! I couldn't buy a dress in two hours, even if Pricy's had something in my size. Which they don't."

The guys didn't seem worried.

"Howie?" the King said.

Howie stepped forward; his knowing smile was becoming familiar.

"Have we got a dress shop for you! And an expert tailor." He waved his finger for her to follow, and marched into the hall. Roger nudged her along.

"It runs in Howie's family," he said. "Though in this case, it's his chemical talent that makes the difference."

They followed Howie to what could pass for a tailor's storefront, with mirrors, a changing room, shiny dress forms, and racks of assorted clothing. Howie threw a yellow tape measure over his shoulder.

"Welcome to the costume shop," he said. "There's more in the back, but this is the most useful stuff. Please, stand on this platform while I take some measurements."

Lynn hesitated, but Roger whispered in her ear.

"Never feel embarrassed in the presence of your doctor or your tailor."

Lynn took vague comfort in the fact that at the moment, Howie was playing tailor and not doctor, and stepped onto the box. He seemed a long way down as he approached with the tape measure, craning his neck and scratching his beard.

"The box is traditional, but for you, we don't need it." He pointed to the floor.

Lynn stepped down, then at Howie's request, held her arms straight out. He measured her bust, waist, and hips, then from the nape of her neck to various points on her back. He paused and cocked his head.

"What do you think, above or below the knee? It's warm enough to go either way."

"Well, Lynn," Roger asked, grinning, "you think Phil would loosen up more if you show some thigh?"

"He didn't care when we were married," she replied, not grinning back. But she thought about it. "It couldn't hurt. Just not too far up—nothing slutty, I'm sure he gets enough of that."

Howie finished the measurement at three inches above the knee, a modest hemline for her long legs.

"I'll be back in five seconds," he said, and disappeared into the racks.

Ridiculous, Lynn thought. How could he find something that fit, much less with exactly that hemli—?

In five seconds Howie was back as promised, with a classic "little black dress" on a hanger. Lynn scowled. It was little, all right.

"That's at least four sizes too small."

"Ah, yes, but not for long. This is special fabric. It has give."

"You stretch that onto me and I'll most certainly look like a slut. And maybe get arrested for indecent exposure!"

Howie indignantly carried the garment to one of the metallic dress forms. It could handle the dress, because it, too, was way smaller than Lynn.

"Stretch? What stretch? I said it has *give*." He slipped the dress over the form and attached a bunch of clamps, then punched keys on a nearby computer.

A deep electronic hum emanated from the dress form, which began to expand, as did the dress. Lynn could see it taking on her measurements—the neckline rose and the hemline fell, the clamps holding everything in the right proportion.

When the humming stopped, the form collapsed to its original size, but to Lynn's amazement, the fabric didn't. Howie removed the loosely hanging dress, placed it on a bigger hanger, and handed it to Roger.

"It's an electro-plastic synthetic," he said proudly. "It expands under tension when exposed to a strong magneto-electrostatic field, which is generated by the dress form. Maybe you heard the humming? Without the field, it holds its shape. We don't know of any other device that generates the same M-E field; so there's no need to worry about the dress snapping back in the middle of dinner."

Lynn would have worried. In fact, she'd keep her ears peeled for that humming sound.

It occurred to her that this would be a great product.

"I suppose the Fashion Cartel is suppressing this."

"Of course! Not to mention the Fitness Center and Diet Plan Cartels."

Roger passed the hanger to Lynn.

"There's a nice bathroom in the ladies' quarters; you'll find everything you need. What you don't have is much time."

"Um, I also don't have shoes. A dress like this needs something, oh, strappy, I guess."

"Ah!" Howie muttered, slapping his forehead. He dove to measure Lynn's foot. "Forgive me—the world's most thorough tailor I'm not." Measurements in hand, he pushed her toward the ladies' quarters. "One pair of strappy shoes coming right up. I'm guessing you want low heels?"

Lynn glared down at him.

"Low heels, Howie."

* * *

The dress in the mirror fit Lynn's body perfectly; fitting her personality was a different story. Even before she'd withdrawn into Zen living, she wouldn't have owned anything so high-tech or sexy.

Now, it was hard to believe she was even willing to wear it. She noted the irony of getting the truth from Phil by being untrue to herself: the clothes, a hidden microphone, faking drunk. And maybe her intentions—she wasn't sure exactly what those were.

She padded into the hall on bare feet and met Howie, who handed her a pair of black flats with strap heels. Another perfect fit, of course. She decided not to ask.

He held up a dime-sized stick-on bandage.

"This looks like a Band-Aid, but actually, it's a two-function bug. There's a microphone and radio transmitter, so Roger can hear your conversations from a half mile away. Plus, it's a GPS transponder that continuously transmits your position, so he can find you and get close enough to use his voice projector."

Lynn squinted at the tiny stick-on device.

"How can it do all that? Doesn't it at least need a battery?"

"Battery? Who needs a battery, when you've got human chemistry? This little bug does have a capacitor, but that only stores enough juice for a few minutes. When it's stuck to your body, it recharges the cap with galvanic skin current, like what lie detectors use. Luckily, the flush you get from alcohol helps—the more you drink, the more current it can draw from your skin. So be a good charger and drink up tonight!"

He peeled the backing from the sticker and reached up to affix it just behind her ear.

"I matched the color of your skin exactly; Phil won't see it. About it coming off, not to worry—it's got special waterproof adhesive that'll stick through a shower. But you can peel it and restick it a half-dozen times if you need to move it for better sound pickup. Roger will tell you if he can't hear well enough."

He gave her a once-over, seemingly satisfied that the bug was invisible, and glanced at his watch.

"You've got ten minutes to get over to Park Street. It's not good to keep an important man like Phil Grady waiting."

"Where's my purse?"

"Roger took it; he's shopping for a proper bag. He'll catch up with us on the way over. Oh, and don't forget your anti-drunk tablet."

He handed her a tiny orange pill, and as she glanced around for something to drink, he somehow produced a small bottle of generic spring water.

"So what I'm not a Trail Boy—I can still be equipped."

She shook her head, opened the bottle, and washed the pill down.

As they raced along Franklin Street, the night air felt cooler, and the dress skimpier, by the minute. At the corner of Hawley, Roger intercepted, carrying two Pricy's bags.

"I bought you a nice pocketbook—hemp is bad enough, but a belt purse simply won't do. I already moved your wallet and a pack of tissues into it. And I thought since you've been 'shopping,' you should have some purchases." He handed her the two bags. "There's a sweater, and a pair of gloves. I hope you like them."

Roger actually looked bashful. It was kind of cute.

"Your old purse and clothes are in there, too. You've been on your own all day, right?"

"Right." *The secret to good acting is honesty.* Or something like that.

"Good luck," Roger said when they reached Tremont Street. "I'll be near."

Not near enough, she decided.

Roger and Howie hung back at the corner, while Lynn turned left toward the Park Street T station and a double-parked limo. The passenger compartment windows were blacked out.

Breathe, Lynn.

Feigning composure despite her adrenaline-fueled heartbeat, she casually glanced across the street to the Common, where she'd so recently escaped from François. What a difference a few hours made here at the border between park and city. In the daylight, the park ruled; hundreds of people milled about, their kids chasing squirrels and twittering like the birds. Colorful clothes rivaled the flowers in the Public Garden.

At dusk, the city took over, and the Common became a foreboding emptiness. If there were animals, they were hiding, silent. There were no children and no colors. This was a place for adults, with shadowy purposes, wearing black dresses and meeting men in black limousines.

Chapter 11

Phil Grady tucked Tanya's permission form securely into his jacket pocket, adjusted his tie, and stepped from the limo. Lynn was dressed as hot as Fiona, and when their eyes met, he saw fire.

Damn! She meant business!

He recovered his composure; he meant business, too.

"Lynn! Baby! I can't tell you how good it is to see you again!"

He gave her a California hug-and-cheek-kiss; this was no time to act horny. He'd let her make the first move tonight.

"You're looking good, Phil. Tan. I'm jealous."

"Hey, you couldn't tan if you camped out on Malibu. You look great, though. Got some sun, even here on the Massachusetts tundra. I can tell by the freckles." On her face, her arms, and her neck, down to that low neckline; not see-through, but close enough. He helped her into the limo and offered champagne.

"Dom Perignon—only the best for you."

She accepted, insisting that he join her—another good sign that the evening might work out okay. He poured for them both and raised his glass.

"To a long-overdue reunion."

She clinked her glass against his, and smiled.

"I've been looking forward to it."

* * *

Once the limo whisked Lynn away, Roger hustled back to HQ, where he accepted Howie's car key and invocation of good luck. Roger hadn't counted on luck since his Games of Chance skill patch cost him three months' allowance in a poker game with his Trailmaster. But he'd take whatever luck he could get.

As he pulled Howie's green Sentra out of the garage, the GPS tracker showed Grady's limo turning onto Berkeley from Tremont. Traffic was heavy; they were out of audio range but hadn't gotten far. He jockeyed through the Saturday night theatre-district crawl, keeping one eye on the GPS.

The limo turned west on Newbury, proceeded a few blocks, and stopped. Roger noted the location, at the corner of Exeter—where he and Lynn were tied up that afternoon, in the wine cellar of an undoubtedly fine French restaurant. One that undoubtedly catered to Corporation brass and employed one undoubtedly pissed-off Canadian waiter.

He had no way to warn her—the voice projector had to be set up and carefully aimed. Besides, a warning wasn't much use, she was committed. He could only try to help her get through it—if he could get there in time to help at all.

He accelerated, barely noticed the red light, and stomped the brake. The Sentra screeched to a rocking stop, just short of a crosswalkful of petrified pedestrians in near-death poses. Roger waited for the green, drumming his fingers on the wheel and ignoring the rude hand signals sprouting from the crowd.

* * *

Lynn shivered in the cold air—and then again when she recognized the fancy façade of François' home turf. The open iron gate invited her into the enemy fortress, or perhaps the dungeon. Again. She considered running, but that would be awkward in the little black dress, and even more awkward to explain. She hoped the dress had enough give for chair-lifting yoga.

"Ah, L'Escargot!" she said, in case Roger could hear. "Traditional French; excellent food, a well-stocked wine cellar, pungent cheeses. Don't miss the truffles."

Phil cocked his head.

"You've eaten here?"

"In this case, the proper word would be dined. I'm a restaurant critic, remember?"

Phil's forehead snapped back as if slapped by an invisible hand.

"I forgot, sorry. So did they like the review?" He smiled, kidding. "Or are they gonna poison our dinner?"

Good question, she thought.

"I do my reviews anonymously—but it's possible they could recognize me."

"Well, don't sweat it," Phil assured her, "you're with me, they'll treat you right. My organization has ties with this place. I spend a lot of money here whenever I'm in town."

Lynn detected a slight flinch as he said that—maybe he didn't want her to know he was in town so much? Score one for the drunken sailor ploy. But would he get sloppy enough to tell her more about his "organization"?

The image of Phil as a Corporation big shot gave her an idea for how to handle François. Not a great idea maybe, but worth a try. It all depended on how important Phil was to François. And how well she could lie.

As a fortuitously unfamiliar maitre d' led them into the main dining room, Lynn kept an eye out for the Montréaler, and finally spotted him uncorking wine at a table in the back room. The moment she and Phil were seated, she excused herself to go freshen up.

"Shopping all day, you know how it is."

Phil smiled and waved her on, idly perusing the wine list. She wandered off to find the ladies' room—and François.

* * *

François Spaquel poured the fourth glass of Chateau Piètre and carefully set the bottle on the table. It was always an exquisite pleasure to move a six-hundred-dollar Bordeaux, especially when the buyers were tasteless nouveau-riche, buying only the name and price. He twirled the corkscrew across his arm towel with a flourish and spun on his heel.

He started for the wine cellar to retrieve a chilled Dom Perignon for table deux; Phil Grady would be arriving at any moment and would want to commence with his usual. François intended to meet M'sieur Grady's every mundane culinary expectation. The stunning presentation of the Truffle Team's strategic breakthrough would be the evening's only surprise.

That, and the sudden appearance of the red-haired monster, blockading the door.

François tensed for a battle, though she was not dressed for one—at least not the same flavor as earlier in the day. Even so, this could not be good. She seemed impatient but under control; he approached warily, the urge to throttle her tempered by his professional decorum and growing curiosity. What could she possibly be doing there?

She spoke, barely above a whisper.

"Good evening, François. I thought I'd fill you in before you make a fool of yourself again, and this time in front of Phil Grady. You're aware he's here tonight?"

How did she know...?

"Oui, Madame, I am always aware of M'sieur Grady."

"Your actions today make it clear you're unaware of my partnership with M'sieur Grady."

Incredible! But if true, fortunate that he had resisted the inclination to throttle her.

"I have served him here numerous times, Madame, but you have never accompanied him."

"Well, I'm with him tonight—a miracle, considering how you rudely interrupted my operation today. I'll fill you in on a little information that you have no right to know but might help keep you out of my hair."

She lowered her voice further, forcing him to lean in.

"I've been infiltrating the Legion for months, and they finally trusted me enough to show me that lab. I suppose I should apologize for the elbow to your ribs, but I had to keep up pretenses. You understand, I'm sure.

"I intended to get—further information—and deliver it to Phil tonight, as a surprise present. But your ill-timed attacks ruined that. It meant a lot to me, M'sieur Spaquel"—he winced at the realization that she knew his last name—"I'm not happy you got in my way."

François kept a blank face. So they were not enemies, but rivals; he wondered which Corporate division employed her.

"My apologies, Madame. I was unaware of your operation. What would you like me to do?"

She seemed to be calculating, perhaps unprepared for his well-practiced deferential attitude.

"I'd like to proceed with my plans without further interference, including any more of your clumsy attempts to find the Legion headquarters. Phil doesn't know what happened to me today, and I'd prefer that he didn't. I want you to pretend you've never seen me before, and treat me like you would any other guest of his."

Like a bimbo, certainement, François decided.

"Furthermore, I suspect that your associates will find it difficult to stay out of this. I'll let you convince them to cooperate; if you don't, they'll quickly learn that you're not the Parisian you pretend to be but grew up in the bad part of Montréal washing down poutine with dep wine."

Tabernac!

"Have I made myself clear?"

François attempted to maintain a professionally indifferent visage, but he was certain he had betrayed his anxiety. He did not wish to face Jean-Paul and Toine as a Québécois.

"Oui, you are clear, Madame. And please, enjoy your dinner."

As she strode away like a predator after a kill, François surveyed L'Escargot in a new light, acutely aware of the authenticity of the décor, the china and silverware, the wine and cuisine. He alone was an imposter, and she alone knew it. She also knew that exposing his fraud would destroy his standing, not only with Jean-Paul and Toine, but with M'sieur Tippiteaux and Corporation management. His entire career was in jeopardy.

But he had his own advantage in this competition for Corporate favor. She wanted him to abandon his search, which implied that she was racing him to deliver the Urban Legion headquarters to Phil Grady. She already knew the location, as evidenced by her unmentioned visit there today; that she had not yet won the race could only mean she had not yet acquired her own access key. François not only knew the location but would soon have the fingerprint gloves to execute an incursion.

He would proceed cautiously. The redhead's naïve persona had fooled the Legionnaires, but François recognized that such escape and combat skills as she possessed must be taught. And now she had bared her hidden claws: strategic secret knowledge and the threat to reveal it. She understood the power of blackmail and did not hesitate to wield it.

The Corporation had trained her well.

* * *

In a nearby alley, Roger listened to the Band-Aid monitor as he backed into a makeshift parking spot. Squeezing a Sentra-sized space out of the gap between the building and the mini-dumpster was difficult; hearing Lynn nail François made it impossible. The abrupt laugh forced his foot onto the accelerator, and the car leapt backward into the narrow channel. Going slowly, he'd've had an inch to spare on either side, but at that speed he missed by two. With a sickening scrape of bumper-on-dumpster, he slid halfway in before finding the brake.

He glanced around—nobody had seen it. He might've nudged the dumpster over into the parking space on the other side, crowding the BMW parked there. No problem, as long as the dumpster didn't actually hit the luxury car. Or if he split before the owner showed up. He shook off an inconvenient twinge of Trail Boy guilt.

The location afforded him a clear view across the alley and Exeter Street to the front windows of L'Escargot. He could see his partner returning to her table. His very resourceful partner.

He killed the engine and pulled out Toine's voice projector, then checked the glove compartment for something to hold it steady. He found Howie's universal toolkit—duct tape and vise grips—and chose the tape. With the antenna aimed at Lynn, he taped the phone to the dashboard and set the beam width as narrow as possible. With any luck it wouldn't reflect off anything; he was pretty sure Phil didn't wear metalized headgear, and very sure he didn't want Phil to overhear the transmissions.

Lynn's voice, discussing Dom Perignon, radiated from the monitor. He plugged in earbuds to avoid feedback, and hit the voice-projector key.

"Hi, Lynn, I'm here. I heard you hog-tie François—nice work. I wish I could've seen his face."

The transmitter seemed to be working—she hesitated, distracted from her conversation.

"I'll quit bothering you, sorry. But please confirm you can hear me. Say something about... about the wine cellar."

She was commenting on the parity between California and French wines.

"But the French still have a monopoly on good brandy. There are several very nice old bottles in the wine cellar here; or at least, there were the last time I visited. I hope they haven't finished them off—or broken them."

Roger smiled and relaxed a little. Lynn and Phil, and the fly on the wall, were in for an interesting evening.

* * *

François guided his interns to a corner where the front windows, and particularly Phil Grady's guest, were not visible.

"We have a special visitor tonight. One who requires special handling."

Jean-Paul fidgeted.

"We know this. You have told us about him already. What is your point?"

"My point is that M'sieur Grady's guest is also special. You have seen her earlier today. You believe that she is the enemy, but she is not. I was unable to tell you before—I did not want to compromise her infiltration into the Legion."

Jean-Paul's eyes became slits.

"The gun collector or the redhead?"

"The redhead. She has gained the Legion's trust but is actually employed by the Corporation. More importantly, her operation is attempting to capture Legion headquarters—"

"But we are doing zat!" Now Toine was roiling.

"Precisely, Toine. You have done fine work today, and thus, I believe we shall succeed before she does. We *must* succeed before she does—and she must remain unaware of our progress. But she is very influential with M'sieur Grady, and we dare not lose his favor. You must treat her as if you do not even recognize her—give her every courtesy you would an important guest. Do you comprehend this?"

The two young men nodded solemnly. But Jean-Paul's bloodshot eyes simmered with hate.

* * *

Phil poured Lynn another glass of Dom Perignon. She was thirsty tonight; she'd never kept pace with him like this before. Maybe she never needed courage like this before. In any case, he figured the drunker she got, the better his chances were, on several fronts. He filled the glass to the rim.

"Excuse me, M'sieur et Madame." The wine steward, François, suddenly overshadowed their table, two small plates in hand. "Our Chef has modified the 'degustation du vin' menu tonight, in your honor. We begin with a special appetizer. Chef insists that you shall love it."

François placed the dishes in front of them.

"Pâté de foie gras de Strasbourg with wild Black Perigord truffles. Only the finest for our most important guests."

Phil noticed Lynn and François exchanging a glance before the steward spun and disappeared, but he couldn't tell if it was friendly or hostile. He turned his attention to the artfully arranged appetizer. It *looked* safe.

"Let me ask again, they wouldn't poison you, would they?"

Lynn mulled the question way too long.

"If they were gonna poison me, I think they'd do it with something less expensive." She picked up her fork. "I really shouldn't eat this—foie gras geese are treated very badly. But I wouldn't want to offend the Chef—you know how irritable Frenchmen can be."

"What was going on between you and François? I saw a look."

"Is that his name? I figured he just wanted to see if I was impressed with the appetizer. You must be a VIP here, Phil; they're aiming to please." She took a taste, closed her eyes, and sighed. He couldn't help staring—and when she looked again, she caught him and let out a tipsy giggle. Phil never thought pâté was sexy before, but it sure was now. He grabbed a fork and took a man-sized bite.

Liver.

He made a point of smiling and nodding approval as he sipped the Dom Perignon, swirled it around like mouthwash, and swallowed the god-awful shit.

"So, you've been doing well with this restaurant critic gig?"

"Yes, I have. The paper pays for the meal and then pays me for the review. It's not much, but it's a weekly column, so I eat well on Saturdays at least. Except today."

"For someone who's been eating well, you look great. You work out?"

"No, except for a little yoga when I get the chance. Eating well doesn't mean overeating."

"So what keeps you busy these days?"

Her face hardened. *Shit.*

"I'm a single mother, Phil. I work full time shuffling crates at a co-op warehouse, besides keeping a home and bringing up Tanya. And now we've started looking at colleges, and none of her choices are cheap. I don't know what I'll do if we can't get some loans."

"You should find some rich guy to marry—" *damn, that was stupid.*

"I tried that, but he got tired of me before he got rich."

"Hey, I'm sorry. I shouldn't'a said that—it was just a bad joke."

Tired of her? Phil searched her eyes. They had the fire he remembered, but at the moment, he didn't feel that happy campfire glow—more like being burned at the stake. If he didn't take the heat off soon he wouldn't get through dinner, much less get her signature on the paper. Or the rest of her in the sack.

But was that all he was after? In the dozen years since the Corporation hooked him on extravagant living, drugs, and girls, he'd had a lot of fun. But it was all fake—just his salary for performing marketing magic. He couldn't remember having a single genuine emotion in all that time—and he certainly never saw fire in anyone else's eyes. Now here was Lynn, who'd always genuinely loved him for what he actually was. And maybe she still did.

And maybe he'd had too much champagne to be thinking about this shit.

But she blamed herself for the breakup; she clearly didn't understand what happened. He owed her the truth.

He took a long, deep draw of champagne, and swallowed hard.

"May I tell you what really happened to us?"

* * *

Lynn didn't answer right away. It was tough enough to deal with her feelings about Phil now, even without dancing on the unexploded land mines of the past.

The past can only hurt you if you go there, cautioned Zen-mind. *LET HIM TELL YOU. GET HIM TALKING.*

Roger's voice in her head tipped the balance. She sipped her champagne and cranked her vocal inebriation up a notch. Howie's pill was amazing; she was three glasses into the evening and didn't feel the slightest buzz. The bubbly could have been ginger ale.

"Phil, I'd love to hear how it happened. I always thought I'd have to wait for the Phil Grady episode of Rock Star Stories on the History Channel." Not that he'd ever let that go to air.

His expression was intense, like he was wrestling with the truth; she hoped he was drunk enough to lose the match. He cleared his throat, and spoke softly.

"You know I loved it when you and Tanya toured with us. She stayed up late back then."

"She still does—it's natural now. I can't get her to go to bed."

A smile crept onto Phil's face but quickly flattened.

"Guess I trained her well for teen life. Those were the best years—we were the bad boys, fightin' the man but married with children. They couldn't pin us down. And your diary made Tanya famous—when you guys stopped comin' on tour, fans would ask me, 'Where's baby Tanya?'"

"That kept me straight, for a while. Till the *Leadfoot Feedback* CD came out, and I started getting calls from Omni Music. They wanted me to quit the band and join the company; said I could help 'em reach the alternative audience. I told 'em to stick it where the sun don't shine—they stood for everything I hated.

"But, uh, they don't give up so easy. Visitors started showin' up after the shows—very sexy visitors, with piles of coke to chop. I wasn't into the girls or the blow, but the band was. And one night I was drinkin' pretty heavy and they got me to do a few lines."

He took another deep slug of champagne.

"It's hard to believe what a difference that one taste made. I can't say I had a great time that night, but afterwards, I had this powerful feeling that it *was* a great time, and I couldn't wait to do it again. 'Course, the girls were there again, after every show, with more coke, and pretty soon I was a regular. Finally, I found myself doin' spoonfuls off a blonde's belly. And then, I was doin' the blonde."

Lynn felt tears gathering.

HANG IN THERE, LYNN. THAT'S HOW THE CORPORATION RECRUITS.

Great. I didn't lose my husband; the Corporation stole him.

Phil downed the last of his glass and exhaled.

"I felt guilty afterward, but mostly I wanted more blow. They were the only connection I had, and they wouldn't bring it out without the sex. Then they pulled the trigger—told me they'd stop coming if I didn't talk to Omni. Lynn, I swear, by then I was hooked on the coke and the girls, and when they promised me I could live like that all the time if I gave up the band, I just did it. The guys were pissed, but I didn't care. Then Omni told me I had to stay in L.A., and I did it. You were pissed, Tanya was sad, but I still didn't care. I was an addict and didn't give a shit about anybody.

"I've been thinking a lot about addiction lately. It gets you by the neurons, is what happens. It got me so I couldn't think straight—I just followed my neurons. I couldn't help myself."

Lynn wiped her eyes. Was it too late for rehab?

"You still do coke?"

"There's always coke; in L.A., that's still how business gets done. But it's not important. They needed me to be useful; I had to cut back."

"On the girls, too?"

"They're around, but it's not the same. And never as good as it was with you."

HE'S LYING.

Shush, Roger.

She realized Roger couldn't hear that.

"Why did they do it? Couldn't they find somebody who was willing from the start?"

Phil raised an eyebrow.

"Yeah, why me? I wondered about that myself for a while. And I realized, they're addicted, too: to luxury. They saw me as the best person to help 'em get their financial fix. And I do that by pushing products to consumers. It's like the whole damn system is just a giant pyramid scheme; people creating need in the people below 'em."

He laughed abruptly.

"Funny thing is, when I realized that's how it works—and that's how it always worked, everywhere—I knew I couldn't fight it. I bought in big time. I just do my job, and I'm very good at it. Omni nailed it—I do have the power to hook an audience, even if it's not a live concert. My part of the pyramid's getting taller and wider all the time."

Phil looked into the distance.

"Sometimes I miss writing music, but I don't miss performing—I sleep at night now. Just gettin' old, I guess."

"We both are, Phil."

NO, YOU'RE NOT.

Shush, Roger.

Roger had a point, though—Phil looked as good to her as he did when she first fell in love with him. And just being with him made her feel like a giddy college girl again.

If she could turn back the years like that, couldn't he?

Chapter 12

Lying low in the darkness of her Impala's back seat, Meg changed back into the Widespread Panic tee-shirt and old jeans. Afraid her flowing hair might still be familiar, she rummaged around the glove box for a scrunchy.

A minute later, she reentered the Mall looking unfashionable again. The black tee-shirt covered her waist, and her hair hung in a ponytail tied just below the barrettes with a ragged strip of pink cotton. The Chasm bag, containing a brand-new pair of intolerably low-riding jeans and a ripped-up pink fashion top, was hidden in the Impala's trunk. Her personal witness was pinned to the tee and recording.

Meg made a beeline for the private basement entrance; the outer door read "Teabury—Authorized Personnel Only" and wasn't locked. She slipped into the anteroom but couldn't open the inner door; she'd noted earlier that the lock was electronic, so she looked around for a keypad or card reader. Nothing. Maybe a sentry with a hidden camera? She ducked her face and hastily retreated to the outer hall.

She probed deeper into the back alleys of the building, finally peering around a corner to see a bald black man unloading boxes into a freight elevator.

Pay dirt.

Once the man headed back to the loading dock, she slipped into the elevator for a closer look. She found stacks of brown cardboard cartons, all completely blank—no manufacturer label, no address label. No barcode. Seemed like they oughta have RFID tags at least.

Unlabeled boxes, delivered on a Saturday night. Seemed a little fishy.

The truck door slammed—damn, he was fast! She cat-jumped the stacks and curled up on the floor behind them. She put a hand over the pink scrunchy, thankful she'd ditched the rest of the shirt.

The elevator bounced as the man dumped more boxes. Swirling dust started her nose tingling again, and she desperately jammed a finger against her lip to suppress the sneeze. She heard buttons click and the door close, then felt a slight shudder and a sinking sensation—both of which were only partly the elevator's doing.

It bounced to a stop, by Meg's reckoning at the level of the secret cafeteria, and not far from it. The door opened to the voice of Mr. Don "Retail Family" DiSenza.

"That was quick, Eightball. Is this the last of it?"

"Yeah. I'll unload it and then move the truck." Eightball sniffed. "'Cept, I sure could use a bite. The kids gone?"

DiSenza laughed.

"Yeah, they're gone, and there's tons of leftovers. All those dieting girls—hardly touched it. But you should go in now and beat the phone geeks to it—they'll be bulking up for the installation. They're scrawny, but they can eat."

"I can eat, too." Eightball's voice faded as he spoke; Meg figured he was headed for the chow.

"Enjoy," said DiSenza. "I'm needed upstairs." A door closed and everything was silent.

Time to move.

Meg slithered over the boxes into a shipping room stocked with flattened cartons, packing tape, rolls of bubble wrap, scales, and hand trucks. A miniature forklift parked in the corner reminded her of a lawn tractor—just like a real tractor, only cute. The rest of the room was occupied by previous loads of unmarked boxes.

On the left, open double doors led to a hallway. The footsteps had gone to the right, to a heavy-looking door. Meg opened it a crack to see the tables and chairs of the cafeteria, and "Eightball" filling a plate from the buffet. She considered her escape choices: bolt through the caf past Eightball and up the stairs, or walk through the unguarded double door to trespass in unknown, hostile territory?

The stacks of mystery boxes suggested a third choice: don't escape at all. She was here to find out what was in those cartons. And that'd be a lot easier if she got Eightball to help her.

Phone geeks would be doing the installation; she'd passed for a fashionable teenager already tonight, how about an unfashionable one? Hoping the black Widespread Panic tee was geeky enough, she took a deep breath and ambled into the cafeteria.

* * *

Eightball was knuckle-deep in Buffalo wings, grateful that the girls hadn't wiped out the good stuff, when a sweet drawl floated past his ear.

"Mind if I join you?"

He spun around to find himself face-to-graphic with a flaming red guitar stretched across a black tee-shirt. He looked up into the eyes of a knockout teenager, and his internal red alert klaxon began to whoop.

This might be Massachusetts, but Eightball still felt an instinct to avoid being alone with a young, Southern white girl. The hair on the back of his neck would've stood up, if he had any. Eightball set down a half-eaten wing and swallowed quickly, wiped a napkin across his sauce-covered face, and lifted himself from his chair.

"No, not at all, Miss. I was just enjoyin' the free wings." He began to offer a hand to shake, but thought better of it and apologetically withdrew the orange-tinged fingers. She smiled and took a seat—to his relief, a little ways around the table.

"I'm Meg Bryson," she said.

"George Shipley—but everybody calls me Eightball." He glanced upward. "For obvious reasons. Good food here—you havin' some?"

"No thanks, I'm watchin' my weight."

So was Eightball—her weight was in all the right places.

He resumed his meal, deciding it'd be more polite to work on a beef fajita, with the sauce on the inside. Not that jailbait was gonna sit there quietly and let him eat.

"I guess I'm kinda early for the RFID installation?"

"Yeah, the other kids won't be down here for another hour. You work in a phone store?"

Meg looked a little forlorn.

"Sorta. I'm on an accessories cart, upstairs, in the north wing? I sell chargers, headsets, batteries and things? They didn't actually invite me—guess they don't think color-coordinating skins makes me a phone geek. But I know my stuff, and I'd like to help." Forlorn morphed into determined. "I'm not as dumb as I look."

Something told Eightball he ought to believe her.

This was supposed to be a stealth operation, but she was all over it already—so they couldn't ding him for the leak. As for her skill level, he'd had his share of dissing at the hands of younger, whiter, better-educated twerps who wouldn't know a Leslie from a Peavey and couldn't lift either one. Maybe he could get some good work out of Meg—and she sure would make the long night ahead more picturesque.

* * *

The equipment boxes were lighter than sacks of feed but there were a lot of them. Meg had buried the little forklift under a pile of empties, and her sinuses were completely plugged from the cardboard dust, but she didn't complain. Eightball seemed to value honest work, if that's what this was. He didn't seem like a Corporation kinda guy, but you never could tell—Corporation insiders didn't wear name tags. Her only chance to flush out the purpose of all this equipment was to play innocent, work hard, and win his trust.

They counted the gear against a bill of lading; there were electronic modules the size of personal pizza boxes, flat antenna pads, cables, and handheld electromagnetic field meters. The meters came with test cards, each with a glued-on RFID microchip: a little glass bead, pretty much the size of a grain of rice, as Grady promised. But looking at it, even a grain of rice seemed too big to plant into your neck. At least, not without hurting like hell.

They also found two injectors, which had handles and triggers like an ear-piercing gun but no injector needles. Eightball said he'd done lots of RFID installations but hadn't handled subdermal tags before; he guessed they'd be preloaded into sterile, disposable injector tips. But even after rooting around in the packing peanuts, they couldn't find any tips, or microchips, except the ones on the test cards. Meg noted they weren't listed on the bill of lading. Eightball wasn't concerned.

"I bet they keep a close eye on that kinda stuff—don't want nobody stealin' account numbers for their own use."

She asked him how everything worked. He seemed to debate answering for a moment, but then he pointed to one of the pizza boxes.

"Okay. First, the control module connects between the cash register and the network, so it can intercept and modify all the data. That's so it works with all the old registers—costs too much to replace 'em."

He picked up one of the flat pads.

"This is the antenna. The control module sends a radio pulse through here into the air, and the RFID tags pick that up. The microchip draws power from it, and uses that to send back a digital code number. Usually the power supplies are smaller, but they want to sense the tags from far away. See, you need a ton more power to cover a little more distance—transmitted power drops off by the square of the—"

He shot her a condescending look that simultaneously insulted her intelligence and applauded her acting.

"I'm sorry," he said, "I'm goin' over your head. You probably don't get that stuff in high school math."

Meg recalled the A+ she'd pulled down in Electromagnetic Wave Physics at Texas A&M, and held her tongue.

The awkward silence was broken by a commotion on the stairs—Meg recognized Don DiSenza's voice, herding teenagers. She could probably handle the teenagers, but DiSenza might remember her from dinner. And from tripping on the stairs. And she'd be plainly visible through the propped-open cafeteria door.

She claimed an urgent need for the ladies' room and slipped through the double doors at the opposite side. From there she overheard DiSenza turn the whole bunch over to Eightball; when she was sure the boss was gone, she sauntered into the cafeteria. Eightball was surrounded by a pack of scrawny boys, all in various stages of acne breakout, and all wearing black. Widespread Panic could fit in.

She swallowed her maturity and bounced toward the crowd.

"Hey guys! What's up?"

They stammered and squawked like startled geese—unnerved to the last little man by a female in their midst. Granted, the tee-shirt *was* tight. Eightball's resonant voice squelched the fuss.

"Dudes, chill. This is Meg; she's helpin' us do the install tonight."

In a blink, scary woman became incompetent girl. The honking morphed into sarcasm about her technical skill, or lack of it; Meg pictured them thumping their tiny chests.

"Don't give her no shit," Eightball snarled. "She's into this already and she's smarter than you think. She'll do fine tonight; you better hope you do half as good."

His glare sealed the deal. He was older than them, and bigger. And black. Even bald, for cripe's sake. Skinny white kids weren't gonna mess with him. They shut up and started getting dinner, conspicuously ignoring both Meg and Eightball.

That was fine by Meg; since the geeks were in the dark about the equipment, they weren't much use to her anyway. She grabbed a seat beside her newfound champion—who might or might not be on her side, looking at the big picture.

"So what's the plan? Split up and have ourselves a little horse race? First team to finish without any bugs wins?"

Eightball looked up, grinning. He probably didn't care much for these twerps, either.

* * *

Eightball supervised as the phone geeks practiced with a handheld field meter. Together, they'd installed the first of the new RFID readers in the Demografique store and proceeded to run a verification program. They waved a test tag near the register and confirmed that the tag ID number appeared on the screen. But a kid with an Xbox tee-shirt started whining as he punched buttons on the meter.

"Something's wrong here. This isn't an RFID signal. It looks more like some kind of modulated WiFi."

"What's the problem?" Eightball knew damn well what the problem was. He'd hoped these kids were too ignorant about RFID to notice the deviant signals. The geek clicked his tongue in shorthand for "duh!"

"RFID chips don't need this kind of bandwidth. They just have to transmit a 256-bit code."

Eightball hemmed. All the signals were correct according to the installation guide, but he'd never seen an RFID system like this before. He hated to look stupid, but he couldn't even guess why they'd designed it with 5GHz WiFi, never mind using a ton of power. It was Meg who covered his ass.

"You think these are ordinary microchips? So you like, don't mind walkin' down the street, broadcastin' your credit card and Social Security number to every identity thief with a portable reader? I'd rather keep my data private. I'm like, okay with a reader that uses high-bandwidth encryption, thank you. Jeez!" Eightball admired the artful mix of pity and disrespect.

Xbox backed down; he hadn't thought about data security issues. Not many people did, unfortunately.

Eightball finished the training with a cleanup of the tools and scrap packaging, then paired up the boys and divided the stores among them. The teams moved out along the Mall corridor, each dragging a dolly full of gear and accompanied by an apathetic mall cop. Eightball was a little miffed that management felt an armed guard was necessary—he'd never given them reason to doubt his honesty. 'Course, the kids might be a different story.

Eightball and Meg—and Ed, their own chunky mall-cop chaperone—proceeded toward the Battery Hut at the top of their list. Eightball leaned over and whispered.

"Thanks for the prop back there, Meg. You *are* smarter than you look."

"I made that stuff up."

"I know."

Meg's explanation was a good bluff, but not a good explanation. Even 512-bit encryption didn't need WiFi data rates—and WiFi made the system even less secure. If hackers could figure out the modulation scheme, they could tap into the chips anywhere in range of a WiFi router.

There was something funky going on.

Chapter 13

At nine-thirty, Lynn noted they were only halfway through the twelve-course degustation. The meal was exquisite, each tiny serving more extravagant and flavorful than the last. But it took forever, so the whole thing became a tease—a little food, then a big wait, repeat until annoyed. Or starved to death. Lynn was so hungry she considered sending Roger out for pizza.

Phil was getting pretty smashed, and talkative about everything except the goings-on in Lexingham. Lynn steadily acted drunker as the wine flowed freely. It wasn't easy, with the meal taking so long and Howie's anti-alcohol pill working so well. She was still perfectly sober.

François had taken over waiter duty, probably to keep Jean-Paul and Toine away from her. He had just served the Millefeuille of Ris de Veau, when Roger intruded again.

TRY TALKING ABOUT TANYA SOME MORE. BRING THE MALL UP.

Lynn picked at the sweetbreads.

"So, you saw Tanya today?"

"Yeah! Lookin' pretty good, all grown up and all. Got your beautiful genes."

"I don't know, are my genes beautiful?" She giggled foolishly as best she could. "But you know, she got your talent genes."

"Yeah? She's musical?"

"No, no, she does pictures. Painting, sketching, computer graphics. But she has your rebellious attitude. Never wants to do it the way the art teacher thinks she should—"

THE MALL, LYNN.

I'm getting there!

"—so it's sort of a surrender to work at the Mall. All that crass commercial stuff—oops, I guess that's why *you're* there, huh?" She let slip an embarrassed laugh.

NICE.

"Rebels don't make money, babe. Shit, I never made much till the Corpor—" he stopped, shaking his head, laughing nervously— "Jeez, I can't talk tonight—the, uh, *commercial* instinct took over."

"Really? Do you think it—"

HEY BUDDY, WHAT THE FUCK DID YOU DO TO MY CAR?!

This was an unfamiliar, angry voice in her head. She tried to ignore it and keep talking.

"—do you think it's the—"

WHAT? I'M JUST WAITING FOR—

NO, YOU'RE JUST PARKED ON MY FUCKING SIDEWALK AND YOU PUSHED THE FUCKING DUMPSTER INTO MY BIMMER!

"—it's the artist's comm—"

LOOK, I DIDN'T REALIZE—

I DON'T GIVE A SHIT, BUDDY. NOW GET THE FUCK OUT OF THE CAR BEFORE I RIP YOUR FUCKING HEAD OFF!

"—commercial instinct—"

CRAP! SORRY LYNN—

DON'T CALL ME LYNN, DICKWEED—

The argument in her head abruptly stopped; Roger must've turned off the voice projector.

"—or do commercial interests kill the"—this was tricky— "artist's... artistic... instinct?"

Phil was looking at her like she'd sprouted a third eye.

"You okay? I thought *I* was havin' trouble talkin'. You kinda blanked out there for a minute."

Lynn smiled weakly and made a show of sipping some water. It'd be a disaster if Phil figured out she was wearing a wire and taking instructions from a spy coach.

"Sorry, I was just distracted. The sweetbreads are so tasty, reminds me of a restaurant in... oh, who cares? We were talking about commerce... versus art."

"Yeah, we were." A chilly glaze spread across Phil's eyes. "Look, babe, art's great, but it doesn't do squat for the economy. It's greed that makes everybody happy. You're greedy, you wanna make good money, you crank out cheap crappy products. But you pay a lotta people to make 'em, and then those people go spend all their tiny-ass paychecks on other people's cheap crappy products. After a while, ya got commerce, and everybody's got enough money to get by.

"But artists don't hire anybody, and they don't sell much, so they don't contribute jack to the economy. And sooner or later, they get tired of standing on the sidelines starving, and they toe the line. Even Tanya. You'll see."

Phil knocked back his remaining half glass of Muenchberg Grand Cru. The drunken sailor became a morose cynic, forcefully chewing the sweetbreads, which would otherwise melt in his mouth.

Surprisingly, Lynn understood.

Even your enemies believe they are right, said Zen-mind, *so who is wrong?*

She thought about the organic food business—only a few people worked at the Momma's warehouse, and only Gerry at Nature's Grocery. Business was okay, but not great, at both. And the natural food chains were so expensive not many people could shop there, either. So, the food was healthy for people, but not for the economy. She wondered if art colleges were so expensive because their graduates don't make enough money to become big alumni contributors.

She caught herself morosely chewing the sweetbreads, too.

SORRY, LYNN, PARKING DISPUTE—I HAD TO HAND THE GUY TWO GRAND IN CASH TO GET HIM TO LEAVE ME ALONE.

IT'S PRETTY QUIET UP THERE; SORRY IF I BLEW THE MOOD. I HAVE AN IDEA. HOW ABOUT YOU LEAVE THE MONITOR STUCK TO THE TABLE AND GO TO THE LADIES' ROOM. IT'LL TRANSMIT FOR A FEW MINUTES WITHOUT SKIN POWER. MAYBE PHIL AND FRANÇOIS WILL TALK.

The plan seemed reasonable to Lynn; at this point, neither she nor Phil was interested in chatting about the Mall. After finishing her portion, she casually reached behind her ear and peeled the Band-Aid. She palmed it, brought it to her lap, and stuck it to the edge of the table.

"I think," she announced in a tipsy, mock formal voice, "I must use les toilettes." She grabbed her purse and lurched to her feet. "Dooo send for me if the next course arrives before I return. Au revoir!"

Phil nodded. Lynn waved goodbye and carefully staggered off.

* * *

François felt his assistant's nudge and looked up to see the redhead wobble to the ladies' room. Toine's grin rivaled his ample beltline.

"She has finally had enough of ze wine, perhaps?"

"Perhaps, Toine. She most certainly has drunk more than any of M'sieur Grady's other guests could consume. And yet she walks—unsteadily, but without aid. However, dinner is only halfway complete, and she is attempting to impress him by keeping up. If she continues to drink such strong wines, she will not remember the Legion headquarters by tomorrow morning. She will not even remember her name."

Jean-Paul had approached.

"Her name is Lynn, I noted it. She may not remember it, but I will."

"Remember also, Jean-Paul, that she is on our side."

"She is on the Corporation's side. But she competitions with us, no? And she seems far ahead of you with M'sieur Grady."

Jean-Paul was correct about François' status versus the redhead, but more alarming was the intern's obvious challenge to his leadership. Perhaps his best chance to solve both problems was to converse with M'sieur Grady alone. François dismissed the others curtly and hurried to table deux. He glanced back via the wall mirror. Jean-Paul was intently observing his progress.

M'sieur Grady looked rather subdued, not unexpected of a man well into his second bottle of wine with a ferocious dinner partner.

"M'sieur Grady, is everything satisfactory?"

Grady looked up slowly, as if considering the question in more than the polite way it was offered.

"Yeah, everything's peachy."

"Your companion seems a bit, er—"

"Wasted?" He laughed weakly. "Nah, she's a big girl—she can handle it."

"I hope so; there is considerably more to come."

Grady's eyebrows drooped slightly.

"I thought I might take this private moment," François continued, "not knowing the status of your guest, to speak to you about our strategic discovery."

"Which is—?"

"Today, we have unearthed and eliminated an Urban Legion laboratory. It was producing artificial truffles which undersold our Cartel by forty percent, not only reducing our profits, but providing substantial funding for the Legion."

"Really. Well, lemme tell you what *our* Cartel did today. We launched a new program at the Lexingham Mall, and by the time I get to the airport tomorrow there's gonna be a lotta young ladies providing substantial funding for *us*. And that's just the beginning—once this thing goes big time, the Legion won't be able to stop us, with or without those truffle profits."

"But, they are troublesome just the same. We are all in this together, are we not?"

"Yeah... Look François, the Corporation's a big tent—we let in anybody who wants to make a buck. But we can't tie each other up. Face it: I'm too busy pushing pop products to give a rat's ass about you snob-culture guys. Lemme know when you find somethin' important to me, like a pirate video server."

François felt his blood rise, but in deference to his location in the L'Escargot dining room and the couples at the other four tables, he lowered his voice to a whisper.

"We have found something else, which is important to all of us. In our dealing with the laboratory, we tracked several Legionnaires to the entrance of their New England Legion headquarters."

"Yeah, I bet you did. Ya know, they got decoys all over the fuckin' place, big guy. You been inside yet? You're just gonna find the back door they slip out of the second you knock down the front. Tell ya what, you find an old man with sideburns singin' "Love Me Tender" in the shower, then come talk to me." He guffawed at his own joke.

"We are certain it is the real thing!"

"Sure it is. Listen, can you bring these courses a little more, how you say, rapidement? I got business with my guest tonight and I don't want her starvin' to death before we get to it."

Swallowing his initial response, François nodded politely and returned to the kitchen.

* * *

Roger stabbed the volume-down button when Lynn rustled the sticker back onto her skin. He'd heard only the first part of the conversation—before François lowered his voice and the power faded. He did confirm one thing: that the operation at the Mall was somehow going to corrupt teenage girls. Phil Grady was playing just the kind of sleazy game they'd feared.

But he had no idea how the girls were going to "provide substantial funding."

"Lynn," he voice-projected, "Phil told François he was gonna get the kids to make money for the Corporation. You've got to find out how." He could see her through the window. "Signal me if you're hearing this."

Lynn kept talking, but casually put her fingers to her nose and pinched the nostril.

"I got it, Lynn. Now find out what's going on. Do whatever it takes."

* * *

Phil looked away. Nobody in L.A. would pick their nose in a restaurant, no matter how drunk they were. On the other hand, her lack of inhibition might be a good thing—later.

The next course, glazed pork medallions, was delivered by a much more intense François, who must've gotten the *rapidement* message. Lynn seemed pretty happy to see it arrive so soon. She ate with gusto, so much that Phil worried she wouldn't hold it down after all the wine. But she seemed fine, slurring away relentlessly about Tanya.

Then something brushed the back of his calf.

She was looking him right in the eye, still chatting as if nothing was happening. But something sure *was* happening—her toes stroked up his calf to the back of his knee, played there for a moment, then wandered along the inside of his thigh. All of a sudden, despite all the wine, his pants were tight.

Jeez, keep yer cool, Phil.

Lynn was combining yoga balance and amazing long legs to thrill him under the table without any noticeable movement above. She continued to yak, but Phil could barely concentrate.

It was a twelve-course degusta-whatever, and they'd had, what, seven? No, eight…

Four more to go before he could get her alone.

* * *

François delivered the Poire Belle Hélène to table deux, sensing both guests' relief. Dessert meant the meal was nearly over, and these two appeared anxious to leave—as was François anxious to be rid of them. Hoping to salvage M'sieur Grady's favor, he selected the older of the brandies that his baker apprentice had rescued, and two snifters. He relished the irony of serving it to Lynn.

"Armagnac de Saint Pastou 1900, over one hundred years old. Compliments of the house, for our esteemed guests."

"Ssmellss like shit," slurred Phil.

François bit his lip imperceptibly and carefully poured the liqueur.

"Ah, yes, M'sieur, our cellar boasts a state-of-the-art climate control system, which precisely simulates the musty conditions of an authentic underground French wine cellar. We have taken extreme measures to preserve this rare and valuable bottle." He was surprised, and grateful, that Lynn did not smile at the excuse; perhaps she was too drunk to appreciate it.

Apparently, she was also too drunk to leave it at that.

"Arma—Armagnac, François? Thass' great. But thiss's the real thing, right? Not jus' some Canadian knock-off?"

François bit again and forced a smile. *Monster!*

"Aha, but Madame is joking. Of course, it is genuine. Very French. And very old."

Phil took an inappropriately large swallow and gulped it down.

"Funny, babe! As if thiss high-classs joint would sserve anything from that piece-a-frozen-shit country." He winked clumsily at François. "To Frencsh brandy!" He reached out to clink the glass, sending a shudder down François' already stiffened spine. Lynn remained infuriatingly deadpan.

François turned on a heel and marched to the kitchen. There were limits, even to the patience of an experienced French waiter; between M'sieur Grady's arrogance and the redhead's evil manipulations, François had reached his. Shaking off the indignity as a duck sheds water, François straightened his shoulders, tipped back his head, and sniffed disdainfully. He glanced down at the silver tray; the Armagnac de Saint Pastou 1900 did, indeed, smell like shit.

Apparently, the quiet revelation of his discoveries was not enough to impress his superiors and advance his career. Something dramatic must be done, he decided.

Tonight.

He stepped to a quiet corner, retrieved his phone, and initiated a call.

"Phyllis. May I help you?"

"This is François Spaquel. How are you proceeding on our 'cosmetic' project?"

"We're about halfway done. Fingerprints are finely detailed; we wouldn't want to make any little mistakes. I'd say we'll have 'em all by about two. That too late?"

François considered this. It was later than he had anticipated, but it would do, assuming—

"It is fine, if we can pick them up downtown at two thirty."

"That's easy. I'll wait in the Washington Street drop zone. Don't forget my champagne."

"Agreed. Do not be late."

He hung up and selected another contact.

"Bunker Hilltop Pre-owned Motors—we got your deals on wheels. Carl here. We're closed now; can I have someone get back to you in the morning?"

"This is François Spaquel—"

"Yeah, François, the car. I got two repo guys headed over there tonight."

"This is regarding a different operation. We shall need a team—twelve should suffice. Bring crowbars, stunners, and restraints. Nothing lethal."

"Crowbars are lethal enough for my guys. When?"

"Tonight. Meet me here at 2 a.m."

"A dozen guys at 2 a.m.? This better be good!"

"It will be good, Carl." He hung up and tapped the phone against his chin.

It will be very good.

* * *

Lynn leaned on Phil as they wobbled through L'Escargot's wrought-iron gate, though she was actually supporting him. Her footsie-work had him ready to rock and roll, just like the good old days in the back of the tour bus—assuming she could lug him to the limo.

She glanced across at the alley and spotted Roger, shrunk down nearly out of sight behind the dash. He'd been complaining in her head about the fruitless small talk for a half an hour—but he had no clue what she had in mind, or what she'd been up to under the table. And she wasn't in a position to fill him in.

If he knew, he'd just try to talk her out of it.

* * *

Once the limo pulled away, Roger followed, close enough to smell the luxury exhaust. He could've backed off; Lynn's wire had enough range for him to hear the conversation from a thousand yards. What kept his foot on the accelerator was: there wasn't any conversation.

He wished he hadn't told Lynn to "do whatever it takes."

* * *

Lynn marveled at how smoothly Phil and his chauffeur operated—this was a well-practiced drill. Phil recited Lynn's North Cambridge address, adding "no hurry." Then, as the limo began to roll, he pressed a button and a black soundproof privacy panel slid closed between the chauffeur and the passengers. After a few more switch presses, reddish light and soft jazz bathed the compartment. It was warm enough to eliminate any excuse to remain dressed, which Phil demonstrated by casually removing his jacket and tie. For the pièce de resistance, he pressed another button, and the rear seat extended outward to the width of a double bed. Lynn stifled a smile as she pictured a couple of roadies in the trunk running cues for the whole show.

She felt herself drifting with the current, which was how she got tangled up with Phil in the first place. Her newfound lover had been a tough townie on the outside, like all the boys she'd had crushes on in high school, but inside, he mirrored her own nonconformist ideals. Combined with rugged good looks and killer charm, he was easy to love, especially for someone who'd been denied through high school and college. And this time, like then, she didn't think about where it would lead—her mind was focused on him and her own craving. The wine might have been neutralized, but Phil was just as intoxicating as ever. And who knew, maybe she could be as intoxicating as his L.A. beach babes. This would be her first chance in ten years to find out.

She started slow, with gentle caresses and light kisses, which he accepted coolly. That surprised her at first, but considering he'd sipped up more than half of three bottles of wine and a snifter of strong brandy, it made sense—she'd have to be more aggressive. She slid the dress up high enough to spread her knees and straddle his lap, then pulled him to her and kissed him deeply. She sat back and began to unbutton his shirt.

"Wait, babe, there's ssumpin' I wanna talk about firsst," he said.

"It can wait," she whispered, fumbling with the next button.

"No, no, really, I'm sseriouss."

"So am I."

Lynn tore the shirt open, sending buttons flying, and combed her fingers upward through his lush chest hair. God, she missed this. He started to sputter another protest, but her hands were already around his neck. In one fluid stroke, she swept the open shirt halfway down around his thick Irish biceps. She returned his shocked look with a hungry one, then reached around him and pressed his face into her breasts. She moaned lightly, feeling his warm breath through the thin fabric.

He was finally getting into it. With any luck, he was hot enough to overcome the alcohol—and too hot to notice her sticking the tiny electronic Band-Aid directly between his naked shoulder blades.

Chapter 14

This is workin' out pretty fuckin' well, thought Phil as Lynn's left nipple hardened against his lips. Except, maybe, that he was too fucking drunk to get a chub down there under her gyrating ass. Amazing, though—as drunk as she was, she was still revving up like she used to. That was one fond memory of his married life: once she got going like this, she wouldn't shut down till she was done. And that, even his alcohol-impaired brain could see, might solve his other problem. The more important one. He had to make his move before she figured out she wasn't gonna get laid tonight.

He flicked the nub with his tongue a few times, nuzzled its neglected twin, then grabbed her arms and pushed her back. Her eyes locked on his.

"What? Don't stop!"

"Babe, wait. I sswear, I will make—f—fantasstic—love to you tonight, but firsst—you gotta do ssumpin' fer me. Fer Tanya."

She stiffened.

"I got thiss—permission form—you gotta ssign. Iss no big deal, just sayss—she can join our—marketin'—disscount—program."

What was that look? Disappointed? Pissed? He shoulda skipped the fucking brandy.

"Let's see it," she said, her nipples flattening.

He grabbed her ass for balance, stretched over to his jacket to fish out the form, and handed it over.

"Iss like I said, s'no big deal. 'Cept for the big disscount she getss on sstuff at th' Mall—clothess—moviess—electron—"

"Shut up, Phil."

She was reading it in the dim red light—way too wasted to see the small print about the subdermal—

"What does subdermal RFID mean?"

Shit. "Iss, um, an ID microchip. Sso we know iss Tanya—but iss just sso she getss the disscountss!"

She was looking at him funny as she thought about it. Then her eyes lit up. Not in a good way...

"Subdermal! That means under her skin! You want to implant our daughter—my daughter—with a fucking microchip?!"

Lynn twisted around and punched buttons until the privacy panel retracted. Her knee was wedged in his crotch—good thing he couldn't feel it.

"Where are we?" she demanded of the chauffeur.

Circling North Cambridge, if he was doing his job—

"Cedar Street, ma'am, we're very close—"

"I know how close we are. Stop the car."

The driver glanced at Phil, who nodded okay.

Fucked it up, Phil.

The limo glided to the curb. Lynn threw the form onto Phil's naked chest, grabbed her shopping bags, and glared back one more time before climbing out of the limo.

"I guesss this meanss you're not gonna ssign it, huh?" he said to the slamming door.

* * *

It was only a few blocks to George Street, but Lynn soon doubted the wisdom of walking home alone late on Saturday night, especially given her outfit and shopping bags. Not to mention wet boobs in the chilly night air.

But anything was safer than staying in that limo with—*him.* God, he was like a drug—she'd gone cold turkey ten years ago but shot up again the first chance she got. She still craved him. She always had.

I always will.

Funny that mentioning Tanya pulled her back from the brink of passion; the same passion that brought Tanya into the world in the first place. She wondered if she overreacted—maybe Phil's discount chips would be as common as cell phones someday. She hated to think she missed out on some much-needed sex because of some harmless little gadget.

Rolling tires crunched behind her. Tensing, she sidestepped and glanced over her shoulder as a green sedan pulled up with a very distraught-looking Roger at the wheel. Lynn had the passenger door open before it stopped, and she collapsed into the seat. She dropped the bags into the footwell and smiled.

"Hi, Roger. Time for a debriefing?"

"Lynn, I'm sorry!" You didn't have to do that! I said do what it takes, but I didn't mean you should do *that!*" His face was twisted up. She touched his shoulder.

"Nothing happened; nothing was gonna happen," she lied. "I just wanted to get his shirt off and distract him so he wouldn't catch me sticking the transmitter on his back."

Roger's face untwisted.

"The transmitter?"

"You know—Howie's magic little Band-Aid? On his back, right in the middle where he can't see it or reach it. He's so drunk he sure won't feel it. Howie says it'll stick through a shower, and Phil always steams up the bathroom before he gets in, so he won't even notice it in the mirror in the morning. You can listen in on him for the next few days if you want."

"That's fantastic! You get 'im to admit they're injecting kids with RFID beacons, and then you plant your own bug on the piece of crap! Talk about fighting fire with fire! And I was so worried about you."

"That's sweet, Roger. But don't you think after all the trouble I went to, you ought to follow him and listen in?"

Roger got flustered again, and checked his GPS.

"You're right, I should—crap, I was so upset I didn't notice the beacon wasn't on you anymore. We've gotta hurry." He pulled the gearshift and the car jumped away from the curb. Lynn glanced over at him. He was so intense, and so oblivious to anything but his mission. She, on the other hand, had a different mission.

"Um, Roger, I can't go eavesdropping with you. I need to get home and wait for Tanya."

Another flustered look.

"Yeah. Of course."

She guided him in silence to the triple-decker, where he parked and hopped around to help with her bags. He waited on the porch while she found her key and opened the door. She faced him, and he hesitated.

"Well, nice work, Lynn," he said finally. "We really appreciate it."

"I'd say anytime, but I'd be lying. Am I off duty, now?"

"Yeah, you're off duty." He hesitated again. "Even retired, I guess."

"What about Tanya? She'll be home in an hour. What do I tell her?"

"I'm not sure," he said, face clouding. "I still don't think we have the whole story—subdermal microchips are pretty scary, but it's been done before. And it's not like they're keeping that a secret—I mean, they're having parents sign permission forms." He cocked his head. "You didn't sign it, right?"

"Of course I didn't sign it. But I bet he can work around it. He's capable of anything."

"Except, if he had another way, he wouldn't have tried to get you to sign it, or at least not, um, at that particular moment."

He was blushing. *So am I,* Lynn realized. Roger cleared his throat.

"So, I think Tanya's safe. On the other hand, if Phil can't implant her, he can't implant her first, and he'll have to cancel the operation. So it won't matter—you can keep Tanya home if you want. Maybe I can still get some clue from the bug before they shut everything down. If I hear anything important, I'll call you right away, okay?"

"Sure," Lynn sighed. "What if I need to call you?"

"Any time, day or night. I put my cell on your speed dial while I was shopping. Eight, five—for U.L."

"Okay."

Roger turned to leave, but at the bottom of the steps he stopped and turned back.

"Thanks, Lynn."

"You're welcome, Roger. Good night."

He nodded, spun, and headed down the walk, picking up a little more spring with every step. He gave her a little wave as the car pulled away.

Desperately parched, Lynn went directly to the kitchen and chugged a tall glass of water. She refilled the glass, took it to the living room, and collapsed onto the couch; Bodhi, the cat, was on her lap in a twitch. Lynn sipped the cool tap water, at the moment far finer than any imported champagne or ancient brandy. She closed her eyes and idly scratched the purring marmalade furball behind his ears.

It *was* strange that Phil had brought up the permission form at a time like that. She'd done her best to get him interested again, but apparently her best still wasn't good enough. Of course, he was addicted to his new life, his company, and their stupid forms; it might take more than a limo lap dance to break that addiction. Some kind of a twelve-step program, maybe. Or an intervention. He seemed like he really regretted getting hooked by the Corporation and abandoning her—did that mean there was hope to cure him? To win him back?

And did she want him back badly enough to "do what it takes"?

* * *

Roger caught up with the GPS Band-Aid at the Hyasson Lexingham and set up in the parking lot. Audio reception was good; Phil was so drunk, the transmitter was drawing as much skin current as it could handle. The rustle of clothing swamped the voices occasionally, but Roger got most of it.

Unbelievable. The guy went straight to the bar and picked up a woman, Fiona. It sounded like she was waiting for him. Or working for him.

Roger settled in to listen, hoping to make sense of this new player. What was her role? How much did she know? He felt like he was watching a baseball game without a scorecard. No, more like a cricket match—in baseball, at least he knew the rules.

* * *

Phil transferred the "Do Not Disturb" sign to the outside door handle, latched the deadbolt, and followed Fiona's fine ass into his suite.

"You don't want a drink first?" Fiona asked, flipping her jacket onto a chair.

"No thankss, I'm good," Phil said around a thick tongue. Last thing he needed.

"Well, you could have let me finish mine."

"Hey, ssorry, I wasn't thinking. You *are* hot."

"Of course I am." She kicked off her shoes. No pantyhose. Probably no underwear.

"And to think you could have spent the whole evening with me," she cooed, touching his cheek. "Was your dinner date so important?"

"It wass businesss, acshually; I hadda get ssomebody to ssign off on ssumpin'." He also had to quit saying "s"es.

"So she signed it?"

"What?"

"Your ex-wife. Did she sign Tanya's permission slip, or do you have to cancel the operation?"

"I dunno what you're talkin' about..."

Fiona struck a hands-on-hips magazine cover pose, except without the smile.

"Come on, Phil, you think I'm in the dark here? HR insisted on me for a reason. You know the Corporation won't let you run around without some eyes and ears on you." She crossed arms and peeled the dress off in one fluid motion.

No underwear.

"Wait, yer not jusst a hooker? You're a fuckin' sspy?"

Fiona laughed.

"That says it all, doesn't it—a fucking spy." She started undoing his surviving shirt buttons. "Think of me as the sexiest auditor you could ever hope for. Clearly your boss doesn't mind if you enjoy the audit." She helped him out of the shirt and tossed it away, her tits bouncing.

Phil decided she had a point.

"Well, you can tell my bosss I'll be perssonally chippin' Tanya at the Teabury Center tomorrow. She's gonna be firsst in line, like they fuckin' told me, with a ssigned fucking permission form, like they didn't tell me. It'ss all gonna go down without a glitch—sso they can sstop fuckin' with me." He kicked off his shoes as she unbuckled his belt, but he stopped her to retrieve the vial from his pocket. Fiona glanced at the tiny brown bottle and shrugged it off.

"No thanks, I'm not into it," she said, and slid his pants down.

"Really? That'ss a firsst." He set the vial on the nightstand and sat on the edge of the bed. "Sso, if you don't do thiss for the blow, why do ya do it?"

"It pays for my shopping habit—I have expensive tastes. But I admit, I love sex." She removed his shorts as he lifted his ass, and then pushed him down onto the mattress. "I bet you can't wait till tomorrow, when all those girls become just like me."

Damn, he thought as she went to work. She must've been fucking his boss, too. She knew everything.

Chapter 15

Howie munched a freshly-toasted bagel, delivered courtesy of the King to replace the bagful he'd donated to the Kendall Band. It could use some lox, but they were out and who could find a deli open at this hour? Certainly not in Boston, and there wasn't time for a foray into Manhattan. No matter; he expected that the goings-on at the trashed Cambridge truffle lab, seen and heard from multiple camera angles, would be amusing enough to compensate for the salmon shortage.

He clicked on the last menu and checked the live views of the lab. It had an eerie glow—the motion-sensitive lights were off, but a few emergency lights remained, and the floor was an inch deep in iridescent hydroponic fluid. Since the water came in along the floor, none of the wiring got wet. Howie confirmed that the instruments and computers were all working fine.

The only possible glitch was if nobody showed up.

"Expectin' company?" The King stood behind him, studying the monitors.

"Was Christ Jewish? Of course we'll have company. You could do a lot with the technology over there. But before I hose it, I thought I should see who comes by to grab it."

"That's a mess o' water. Musta emptied all the tanks."

Howie's jaw tightened.

"Meg put a lot of work into that farm, and those bastards destroyed it. They should all choke on the plankton."

The King touched his shoulder.

"Meg is fine, don't worry."

"How can I not worry? She should have reported in by now."

"She's a Texas girl; they don't come tougher than that. I bet she's too busy grabbin' Corporation secrets herself right now."

Howie didn't care about any Corporation secrets at the moment.

"In case the bad guys don't all drown," the King said, "you got our data out of there?"

"Yeah."

Howie had already transferred the Legion software and data, and replaced it with misleading decoys. Once the Corporation "discovered" those, he planned to destroy the hardware. He had several, spectacular ways to destroy the hardware.

With a little luck, he could catch a few of the bastards nearby.

* * *

Neil Cherbek and his tech pirates crept into the deserted MIT basement complex. They found the boiler panel and entered the tunnel, turning off their flashlights when a strip of overhead LEDs lit up. Neil was determined to be neither impressed nor intimidated by any of the MIT technology; his crew was carefully chosen from the elite Tronics Town technical support staff, and they could hold their own. In a few minutes they zigged the last zag and approached the lab door. The latch was blocked by a knotted silk handkerchief. François had thought ahead on his way out.

As he reached for the handle, he felt water soaking through his sneakers and realized François wasn't kidding about the boots. Cursing, he yanked the door open, creating a little wave that sloshed up onto his ankles. He cursed again, this time joined by the others.

But their wet sneakers were quickly forgotten as they splashed into the lab and the lights came on. This was an information toy store, full of running computers just waiting to be looted. He pointed out a machine to each of the others, and the team split up.

Neil yanked the topmost thumb drive from his bandolier, plugged it into the PC, and settled onto a stool to see what he could find. The screen saver looked like blood, randomly splattering against the display. Graphics could be better, he thought.

He bumped the mouse, and the screen flashed to a normal

desktop. No password. Apparently, those ivory tower college guys didn't think they needed to protect their data.

He downloaded everything he could onto thumb drives, swapping in fresh ones from the bandolier as needed. There was a ton of good stuff—in particular the maps of two Urban Legion bullion storage bunkers. He'd be a hero some night when the Corporation dug up millions in gold bars from under the John Harvard statue and Caltech's Beckman Mall.

Neil found a directory of recipes he didn't understand (a cologne formula using sulfur and mare sweat) and some he did (oatmeal-garlic-habanero cookies). He was downloading the last of them when he heard a knock at the lab door.

WTF?

The entire team exchanged anxious glances. They weren't expecting help.

"Who is it?" Neil finally asked.

"'ousekeepeen'!" came a Latina voice. Neil relaxed—François was messing with them.

"Go away till later. We're busy. And when you come back, be sure to check the toilets, something's plugged up in there."

Chuckles from the others rewarded his wit, and Neil returned to the download. But as the laughter faded, he heard splashing, and whirled to see a half-dozen hotel maids march into the lab. Their leader, a tiny Latina with curly brown hair and a tight white uniform, smiled.

"We don' have time later. We won' get een your way, don' worry."

The woman directed her girls to the back section, as they dragged a cleaning cart (*how the fuck?*) across the lab. Neil cursed himself for not relatching the door.

"Who are you?"

"Leely, an' in case you na' so good at leesteneen', we from 'ousekeepeen'."

She waited expectantly, as if for another question to swat away, but Neil decided to let it slide. He clearly couldn't stop them, and, besides, what harm could a bunch of maids do?

Lily accepted his silence with a shrug and joined the others in the back section, where they commenced mopping and jabbering in Spanish. It wasn't distracting, because Neil couldn't understand a word of it. He returned to the fun at hand: a fascinating set of clinical trial data, on the use of all-natural porcupine-quill-suppositories for the treatment of hemorrhoids.

* * *

Howie and the King watched the geek pirates uncover every planted document: plans for a rodential rotary cage engine, a tooth-cancer cure, and a detailed scientific Grand Unified Theory proposal relating all the fundamental forces using the constant A_{LUE} = 41.9. Howie fed the audio of the maids' chatter into Google translator and enjoyed their constant ridicule of the geeks, who obviously didn't understand Spanish.

The geeks did some ridiculing of their own—the little shits were dissing the Legion the whole time. The thought of "little shits" reminded Howie of the huge subwoofers stationed in the corners of the lab. Maybe hit 'em with the brown note? They did look a little constipated.

But when they started poking at the robotic devices, Howie decided time was up. He couldn't just flood the lab with polyurethane foam; the jets had safety sensor cameras and wouldn't trigger if they saw people around. But he had a variety of other, equally effective weapons at his fingertips—mechanical, electrical, chemical—even nuclear, if he got really worked up.

"Okay, so we have a few choices," he mused. "The boring thing would be to have a robot grab the gun Meg stashed and start shooting. But with Meg blasting the tanks, there's probably not enough ammo to take them all out." He pointed at the screen. "We could make the robot at the end fling steel bars into the other three robots, knocking them apart and taking out a nerd or two. Then it could give them the finger before it rips its own arm off. Not much body count either, but still fun, right? Like bowling." He pointed again. "Or, I could have the long-arm robot knock out the plug on a few fire sprinklers and soak the whole place."

When Howie looked over at the King for his opinion, the old

man stared back for an uncomfortable extra moment. Like he was judging Howie, not the idea.

"I dunno, son, the water thing's getting' kinda old, don't ya think?"

"Ah, but here's the shocking twist—once they're all wet, I flip on the high-energy plasma generator. They're all so nicely grounded."

The King appraised the underground scene.

"I'm not much of chemist, son, but, can I make a suggestion?"

* * *

Ignoring the team banter and the back-room Spanish, Neil photographed a tiny milling machine fitted into an airtight glass box. He had no clue what the Urban Legion would mill that carefully, but maybe his bosses would. He barely noticed the humming until someone shouted.

"Neil! Behind you!"

A robotic gripper arm was telescoping out from the center table. Mesmerized, he watched it grab a half-full, black-stoppered beaker from a chemical shelf.

That would be bad.

He leapt up to kill the robot's power, but the arm swung too quickly. It smashed the beaker onto a hard tabletop, splashing liquid and broken Pyrex across the surface. Neil tensed; the room went dead quiet except for the pounding of his pulse.

There was no explosion. The table didn't dissolve. Neil started thinking poison gas, a notion reinforced by a second robot arm, which rotated over to the soaked surface and blasted compressed air onto the pool. The fluid atomized like perfume, and in three seconds the entire lab was cloudy with a mist of… well, something. It was too late to put on hazmat suits, or even gas-masks.

The banter had choked off, everyone immobilized with fear, waiting for the effect. Paralysis? Unconsciousness? The stuff didn't burn, not even the eyes. In fact, it smelled kind of nice, like… cologne. They waited half a minute, in silence except for the distant chatter of the maids. Nothing. Neil looked around.

"What *was* that? Anybody feel anything?"

The answer from all was a shrugged "nope" and the banter resumed. Just some glitch in the system.

Neil went back to his photography, concerned that the camera was a little damp from the chemical mist. He was wiping the lens when a shadow fell over him, followed by a hand stroking the side of his neck. His back stiffened; it struck him that the Spanish babble had stopped.

The maids were fanning out around the room, draping themselves across his equally tense teammates. A lusty voice whispered in his ear.

"I can' help eet, you guys are so 'ot. We put fresh leenens on de beds. Come, you make lav wi' me." Lily ran her hands down his chest and brushed the top of his belt buckle. He tried to protest, but when he opened his mouth she filled it with her tongue. It was his first French kiss—the protest was forgotten.

"Queeck, I can' wait no more." The tiny maid grabbed him by the loose end of his belt and dragged him, sloshing, across to the back hall. Three other couples were following, and the remaining two maids were stripping the shirts from their stunned victims where they sat.

Nobody resisted.

Lily found an empty bedroom; she had Neil's clothes off in seconds, and hers in seconds more. She pushed him onto the bed and jumped on top, straddling his knees and lightly running her fingers from his neck to the hardest hard-on he'd ever sprung. She looked like a porn star in 80-inch 3-D High Definition, only not as tall. But Lily was real—he could feel her wet heat on his thighs.

She bent over him and stretched forward on hands and knees—he felt her breasts brush his belly and chest, and then her hair cover his face. Her moist breath swirled around his ear, curling his toes. She pressed against him, softness everywhere except for the pubes scratching his stomach.

One last rational thought flashed through his head.

"What about protection?"

Lily licked his earlobe.

"I take the peell—and I'm clean. Are you clean?"

"I'm a virgin," he croaked.

"Mmm," she moaned, and then sank down onto him so slowly he forgot to breathe. Somewhere amid the tingling rush he heard a throaty whisper.

"Na' no more."

Chapter 16

Tanya kissed Michael goodnight and climbed into the Civic. He waited until she'd gotten under way before going off to his father's car; he was gallant, even if he was poor, and a little weird. Her dad's prediction echoed in her head.

YOU'LL OUTGROW GUYS LIKE THAT.

Will I?

She checked out the other kids streaming around her as she waited to exit the lot. The Actual Musicians weren't very popular, and there weren't any fashion slaves in the crowd. Dad's business probably didn't make a cent off the band or any of their fans.

But Tanya liked the music. It was new and creative. These guys didn't care if they were popular or not; they had fun playing whatever they felt like playing. Kind of like when she painted her Goth Venus with tats and piercings, or set the table at The Last Supper with Chinese takeout. Her art teachers hated it, but it was fun.

Phil Grady was an indie musician once; couldn't he relate to that?

If not, how can he relate to me?

* * *

Gerry Rutland tossed the last bag into the dumpster and returned to Nature's Grocery. Cleaning the store had taken all evening, but with his Zen focus on the task at hand he hadn't noticed the passage of time. At this hour it was disconcertingly quiet, especially without the babbling brook sound from the CD player, whose flour-choked pieces were now buried in the trash. He'd have to get used to the silence—he couldn't afford a replacement. Same went for the damage to the back wall; all he could do was drag a spelt barrel over to hide the hole.

He grabbed the commercial cookies he'd been saving to celebrate finishing the cleanup. It was pretty late for a snack, especially something as unhealthy as mass-produced chocolate chip poison pills, but he was tired of the constant craving. He'd been acknowledging it and then letting it go every half hour, all night.

Cookie in hand, he walked around the store one last time to make sure he hadn't missed anything. He'd thrown away so much produce that even without the smashed shelves, the rest of the store looked pretty sparse. His regulars would notice, of course—he made a mental note to call Momma's on Monday for a restock delivery.

And then it fell on him like a dropped pallet of brown rice; Lynn might not show up at Momma's on Monday. He groped for a stool and collapsed onto it.

Should he have called the police? That French man was willing to knock him out even after accepting first aid; he was probably willing to kill Lynn if Gerry disobeyed orders. No, the only way to avoid trouble with people like that was to avoid getting involved in the first place.

He wondered how it could happen. How could Lynn manage to get tangled up in all this? She'd been so steady, so devoted...

So boring. And Gerry was the one who urged her to break out of the rut.

She'd broken out of the rut, all right. And now she was fighting for her life. Because of him.

He glanced down at the cookie, which was now deeply dented from his tense grip. Eating it was going to be his own little breakout, his little act of defiance against The Way. But clearly, The Way was the correct path—the moment Lynn strayed, she began to suffer. And that was his fault. He was obligated to help her find the path again; this was no time to lose his own balance, even for something as harmless as a chocolate chip cookie.

He put the cookie back into the bag and, after shutting off the lights and locking up, dropped the whole batch into the dumpster with the other poisons. Vowing to call Lynn one more time before bed, he started out on his first-ever anxious walk home.

* * *

Lynn was dozing when the chain reaction began. The phone startled her, which startled Bodhi, who dug in all four sets of claws to launch himself from her lap. That caused her to flinch, which threw Bodhi off balance, widening the gashes as he executed his escape. She winced at the wounds and grabbed the phone. It was Gerry.

"Lynn, thank goodness you're safe. I called, I left messages. What happened?"

"Gerry, I'm sorry, I got tied up—I mean, things just got out of hand. Are you okay?"

"I'm okay. Are you okay?"

"I'm fine. The store? I'll make good on the damages."

"Forget the damages. Who were those people? Why were they threatening you?"

Here was a loose end Lynn hadn't thought about. She didn't want to lie to Gerry, but he had such a stress-free life. Telling him the truth was like telling a little kid there's no Santa Claus—or that Santa shot and roasted the Easter Bunny. Better to stick with the fairy tale.

"Trust me Gerry, everything's fine. It's weird, but fine. Someday maybe I can tell you about it. But for now, just relax and get some sleep."

There was silence as he considered it.

"You're not going to tell me what you've gotten yourself into, then?"

"I—can't. Let's just say I'm trying new paths, like you suggested."

"I wish I hadn't."

"No regrets, Gerry."

Another pause.

"Okay, but call me if I can help in any way."

"I'll call you if I need you."

Gerry hesitated again, then said goodbye and hung up. Loyal friends were good to have—especially ones without claws, her stinging legs reminded her. She shuffled into the kitchen for something to soak up the blood on her thighs.

As she reached for the tissue box, her cell phone rang.

"This is Lynn."

"Lynn, it's Roger. Is Tanya home yet?"

"No, not yet. Roger, what's wrong?"

"Okay, I just overheard some disturbing stuff. Phil's got a hooker in his hotel room."

"He's a sex addict—I'm not surprised."

"Yeah, you told us so. But this hooker's like, Corporate management or something. She knows what's going on and warned Phil not to screw it up. He told her he was still intending to chip Tanya first—personally—and that the permission form was all set. You were right about that, too, he found some way around it."

"So, you thought the plan was off, but it's still on. Let me guess, you want me to let Tanya go tomorrow, so you can catch them in the act. Whatever act it is."

"Uh, actually, no. You should keep her home."

"Good, 'cause there's no way I'm gonna let her go. But you don't need her?"

"That's not it—we can't risk her. Those microchips— ...well, I can't be sure what they do. Let's just say they give the girls something more than a discount."

As Lynn grappled with that, she heard a car door slam.

"Okay, Roger, Tanya's home. And she'll stay here. I'll talk to you tomorrow."

"Thanks again, Lynn. Good night."

The phone went silent. Lynn finally grabbed the tissue; by now there were rivulets running down her legs. As she dabbed at the wounds, the front door latch clicked and Tanya bounced in.

She had Lynn's red hair, Phil's good looks, and something neither of her parents had anymore: blissful innocence.

"Hi, Mom!"

Lynn stashed the red-stained tissue and went to greet her daughter. Lynn was truly grateful to see her, especially in such a nice, normal, un-sinister situation.

"Hi, Tanya! How was the concert?"

"Fun."

Tanya gave her a hug, then stepped back to check her out.

"So what's with the little black dress?"

Lynn couldn't lie to Tanya. At least, not much.

"I went out to dinner. Someplace fancy. With your father."

Tanya's reaction was not what Lynn expected.

"So you got my message and called him, huh? I can't believe you wore that dress!" She cocked her head, taking in the whole picture. "But next time, you really gotta wear nylons. I know you hate 'em, but your legs are too pink. ...and bleeding?"

"Bodhi got a little clumsy... Tanya, let's talk for a minute."

They went to the kitchen, where the teenager tossed the car keys onto the table. Lynn got another tissue, and they sat down together.

"Your father told me about his program at the Mall."

"Sick, isn't it? It's like, huge discounts on practically everything!"

It was also, like, something else. Something "disturbing," Roger said. She wished she knew what it was. She'd have to stick to her original objections.

"I won't let you do it."

Tanya's face fell.

"Why not?"

"Tanya, do you even know how this program works? Do you know they want to implant you with an ID microchip?"

"Mom, it's like an ear piercing. I can deal."

"An ear piercing doesn't let them track you everywhere you go!"

"Them? Who's them?"

"The Corp—...I don't know, anyone. It's a bad thing, Tanya. It's like Nazi tattoos or the Mark of the Beast; I don't want you branded for life by your father and his cronies."

Tanya glared at her. Cold.

"Musta been a tough date. Now Daddy's Hitler and the Antichrist, rolled into one."

That's about right, thought Lynn.

Tanya set her jaw.

"So what do I tell him tomorrow?"

"You won't see him tomorrow."

"Um, hello? He's at the Mall, and I'm working tomorrow."

"Not any more, you're not. You can call them in the morning and tell them you quit. I never liked this Mall job anyway. It's too far away and it's a bad influence. We'll find something around here."

Tanya jumped up, kicking the chair backward.

"No way! It's an easy job and the pay is huge! I'm gonna need the money for school!" She whirled and stomped toward the hall. "You can't just mess up my life like this! I'm going to work tomorrow whether you like it or not."

"Well you'd better leave now; it'll take you all night to walk."

As Tanya stopped and turned, Lynn made a show of sweeping the car keys into her fist.

"You won't find them."

"Auugghh!" Tanya rolled her eyes and resumed her march down the hall. Her bedroom door slammed.

Lynn fingered the keys. Tanya was really angry. Angry enough to find the keys and go anyway?

Yes.

She scanned the kitchen for a good hiding place; Tanya would check her purse, the junk drawer, the desk. Lynn tiptoed into the living room, and her eyes were drawn to the laughing Buddha statue on the corner table. It was hollow, open underneath—she'd caught Phil hiding coke in there once, during one of his brief trips home before the divorce. She'd been pissed off, but it was better than letting five-year-old Tanya find it, and Tanya never went near the Buddha. It was the perfect spot, especially given the irony of thwarting Phil with it. She listened for a moment to make sure Tanya was still in her room, then tipped the statue up and set the keys underneath.

Once she climbed into bed, Lynn felt a wave of exhaustion and relief wash over her. She'd managed to keep Tanya out of Phil's clutches; things could go back to normal now. Except for her reignited feelings about Phil—those might take a while to settle back down.

Did she want them to?

She'd asked that question before, ten years earlier, and the answer at the time was yes. Now she found herself wondering what would have happened if she'd said no, and fought harder to win him back. Or, it suddenly dawned on her, if she'd fought the Corporation, instead of Phil. Maybe things would have been different.

Do not long for what might be, but accept what is, said Zen-mind.

Yeah, thought remedial Zen student Lynn, *but maybe if you fight for what might be, it becomes what is.*

* * *

Tanya sat on her bed, the wall posters a blur.

She has no right to keep me away from my own father!

Mom was always strict, especially about anything that didn't fit into her hippie-organic dream world. No HBO, no logo clothing, no sugary snacks. Now no Mall, and no father!

No wonder I'm such a freak.

She began to doubt her picture of Daddy—since it was mostly painted by Mom, who wasn't gonna cut him any slack. Tanya always blamed him for not coming around, but maybe it wasn't Daddy's fault. How did he say it?

I REALIZED A LONG TIME AGO THAT YOUR MOTHER DOESN'T WANT ME TO VISIT.

Suddenly, her mental portrait of her father turned into abstract art, open to subjective interpretation. Maybe Mom didn't let him come around. And maybe it was time Tanya stopped letting Mom control her life. It was time to figure out the truth.

She pulled her phone out and started to dial, but stopped in mid-button-push. Mom could easily hear a phone call through the thin walls of the triplex. And she'd had been quiet for a while—maybe she was right outside the door, listening.

Tanya smiled, opened a text message, and silently punched the keys.

* * *

Phil watched from the bed as Fiona slipped her jacket on.

"Oh, I'm not disappointed, Phil. I've done my job tonight; I get paid no matter what you do—or can't do."

Phil winced and leaned up on one elbow. He was sobering up, but not quickly enough.

"I, uh, guess I just used it all up on my ex. I thought I had somethin' left for you, but, well, too much expensive wine. You know."

Fiona shot him a look of pity. With a body like that, she probably wasn't used to guys not performing. Except maybe when they drank too much. Which he had. He wondered if some blow would've helped; it had been a long time since he got laid without it. And he was 0 for 2 so far tonight.

Ah, well, he'd be sober in the morning.

Fiona snagged her purse and stepped to the door.

"Next time put me first on the list. I cost enough; you might as well enjoy it. Just remember, I'll be following your progress; if you don't pull this off tomorrow, there won't be a next time." The heavy snap of the hotel door latch punctuated a bad evening.

As Phil lay back, head swimming, a bent guitar note announced a new text message. Who the fuck would text him at that hour? It had to be important; he rolled over and grabbed his jacket, extracted the phone, and hit the message icon.

Tanya> Daddy are you up? We gotta talk

He dragged himself to the bathroom to splash his face with cold water, then filled a glass and drained it—he was heading for a serious hangover; now was a good time to start the cure. He refilled the glass and went back to the bed to type his response.

< Okay, call me

Tanya> Can't call, mom listening. She's freaking out. Won't let me go to the mall tomorrow

Phil sipped his water and considered this. Lynn was freaking out—that took some of the sting out of the past few hours. But the stakes were way bigger than minor sexual skirmishes; in the big war, this would put Lynn on the verge of total victory. If Tanya didn't show tomorrow, the Corporation would shut down the operation. They'd write him off and find somebody else to do it—somebody who could deliver on a promise. And Phil would wind up in some Hollywood legal department, negotiating film credit font sizes for two-bit supporting actors.

He typed:

> < Come anyway I bet she sleeps in
>
> Tanya> I want to but she hid the car keys

Phil closed his eyes and tipped back his head. Where would Lynn hide the keys? He was too wasted to think—and that reminded him of something. He sifted through the stems and seeds of his memory and finally came up with the old rule: *Never get too wasted to remember where you hid your stash.* The answer was obvious.

> < Is Buddha still in the living room?
>
> Tanya> Yeah why
>
> < Wait till mom is asleep and check under the statue. I
>   bet the keys are there
>
> Tanya> How do you know
>
> < We used to hide stuff there
>
> Tanya> What stuff
>
> < Never mind, see you tomorrow. Breakfast at peppers
>   at 9?

Tanya> Ok will text if keys aren't there

< Alright good luck

Tanya> Thanks bye

Phil put the phone away and smiled. Using text messaging to outmaneuver his technology-hating ex-wife was pretty damn satisfying. And after a shower and a couple of spoons to clear his head, he'd take care of a little business downstairs. This war was far from over, and his arsenal far from empty.

* * *

Roger felt like the Cheshire Cat, sitting in the dark Sentra with only his huge grin visible in the parking lot floodlights. The concern he'd had about Lynn going too far with Phil Grady had turned to relief, then pure vengeful joy as he listened in on the aborted tryst with the hooker.

He heard a few guitar notes, which he assumed were text messages; unfortunately, this time there was no Urban Legion mole around to get a video capture. All he could do was listen to silence.

After a while he heard the shower running.

Nice and steamy, Phil.

* * *

Phil stood dripping ice-cold water, wide awake now, shivering and covered with goosebumps, which, sadly, were more erect than he'd gotten with either Lynn or Fiona. He stepped from the tub and reached for a towel, briefly catching sight of his own back in the kaleidoscope of luxury-suite bathroom mirrors. Not that his back was particularly interesting, but the small, pale-pink circle, standing out like a beacon against his deep L.A tan, sure was.

He strained to touch it, but it was placed perfectly out of reach. Snarling, he backed up to the door edge and scraped at the sticker until it caught and peeled away. He plucked it from the door and held it close, quickly recognizing a bug. Planted by someone who would soon regret it.

He recalled Fiona, arms wrapped around him, grinding away long after it was obvious her efforts were wasted on his limp dick. But she'd done her job—which was "to put eyes and ears on him." Ears especially. That's how she intended to follow his progress.

These Corporate games were beginning to frost his ass. It was hard enough to keep this shit a secret without the Corporation tipping all these people off. Who else was in on it? Maybe he was wrong about DiSenza being in the dark. Or even Eightball, for chrissake.

He held his Band-Aid-tipped finger to his lips like a stage microphone.

"Nice try, guys. I keep telling you, the system is foolproof—nobody's gonna figure it out. So there's no need to bring your fucking babysitters into it. How about instead, you back off so I can do my job, okay?" He looked around for something to smash the device, then got a better idea. "Enjoy your tour of the sewer system," he said, folding the sticker in half and dropping it into the toilet. He hit the flush button.

"Say hi to the alligators for me."

He grabbed a towel and headed for the bedroom. It was time to deal with the damn permission form.

* * *

Even through earbuds, Roger found drowning by swirly an unnerving experience. He was relieved that Phil didn't peg Lynn for planting the bug, and curious why Phil's own people would spy on him.

But the bug hadn't lasted long enough to get any real information. Just tantalizing clues: Phil saying "nobody's gonna figure it out" confirmed that there was more to the microchips than discounts. And the hint that they'd make the girls "just like the hooker" was almost too appalling to believe. He regretted withholding that lurid detail from Lynn, but it didn't matter—Lynn wasn't going to let Tanya leave the house. And that meant the Corporation would pack up their program and take it somewhere else.

He'd blown it.

But at least Lynn and Tanya were safe.

* * *

Phil Grady sat alone in the Hyasson business center. The night auditor was perfectly happy to let him in and leave him be; in this modern era of electronic tactics, it was nice to know that old-fashioned hundred-dollar bills were still effective.

Phil's mind was sharp, thanks to the coke and the cold shower, but his fingers were struggling to keep up. He entered his backdoor password into the signature clearinghouse site and typed "Lynn Grady" in the search bar. A few moments later, the result screen popped up. He was only slightly surprised.

Most people had hundreds of captured electronic signatures on file, for everything from groceries to electronics. But Luddite Lynn had only one, for a bookshelf at Hye's Home Center. He realized he'd dodged a bullet—if she hadn't succumbed to that one impulse buy, he'd have lost another round to the all-natural bitch. Good thing all he needed was one.

He examined the scrawl. Like most e-sigs, it was distorted and nearly unrecognizable. But credit card companies didn't care about that. Phil was betting that DiSenza and the boss didn't either.

He set the color printer's advanced properties to ballpoint mode, then entered the coordinates of the signature line. He fed in the permission form and watched it slide back out, now signed by Lynn in what looked like ordinary blue ballpoint ink. With the paper safely tucked into his pocket, he headed to his room for a little sleep. He and the girls had a big day ahead of them.

Chapter 17

Rocco popped the driver's side door lock and hopped in. Why anybody would repossess a geriatric VW Golf, a wagon no less, was beyond him, but he never questioned the jobs Carl handed him. Every repo story was long and involved, and Rocco didn't give a flea's fart. He and Vinnie got paid by the delivery; reasons just wasted their time.

As usual, his partner waited in the van in case of trouble, but this was a pretty easy pickup. Nowhere near a residence, no car alarm, no LoJack, no nothing. He pried out the ignition switch and hot-wired the connection, expecting the gurgle of a diesel engine. That's not what he heard.

"Excuse me?" asked a slightly German-accented voice. "What do you think you're doing?"

He looked around, expecting a cop, or worse, the Registered Owner. There was no one.

"It's me, the car. Given your unorthodox entry method, I am forced to conclude that you are not my owner." The voice sighed. "So you are probably unaware that I'm booby-trapped, set to explode if anyone tampers with me."

Explode, right. That would be a pretty stupid way to protect a car from theft.

"Unfortunately," continued the voice, "I am in no position to negotiate this. If you continue to attempt to steal me I'm afraid I can't be responsible for your injuries or death." The voice lowered to a more confidential tone. "To be honest, I don't really want to explode here—I'm not one of those 'car heaven' believers. So please, do us both a favor and just go away, okay?"

Rocco considered this for a moment, then laughed out loud. What kind of noob would fall for such a cheap-shit alarm? He reexamined the ignition cable and crossed a different pair of wires.

"Now you've done it, tailpipe. The countdown is started and I can't stop it—in about thirty seconds I become a copper nitrate fireball. I suggest you be at least twenty yards away by then. You know, what really grinds my gears is that they made me warn you, so you can get away before you get hurt. But what about me, can I get away? Noooo, I just have to sit here and count off the seconds to oblivion. You really piss me off, you know that?"

Copper nitrate. Nice detail—almost made it believable.

Rocco reached under the dash, feeling for a cutoff switch. When hot-wiring didn't work, it usually meant a cutoff. He'd never met an anti-theft he couldn't beat.

* * *

Howie Friedman wasn't so much the voyeur. So after his atomized cologne got the lab party started and the King insisted they turn off the monitors, he was fine with it. He had no desire to watch his enemies having fun, much less getting laid, especially since it was his doing.

But when the King suggested he go talk to them, he stopped being fine with it.

"Roger has my car, and the T is closed."

"It's a nice night, Howie. You can walk."

"Walking is overrated. So is chatting with Corporation assholes while they're busy looting our lab."

"They're not lootin' anymore, they're makin' love," the King reminded him. "And they'll be mighty grateful to the guy who made it happen. Which makes 'em ripe for recruitin'. Mama always said you catch more flies with honey than with vinegar."

Howie knew that the Legion occasionally enlisted former Corporation soldiers, and double agents could be more valuable than the regulars. But he worried that even after their schtup therapy session, these guys might still want to be enemies. Howie still did.

"And tell you what, Howie—when you get to the bridge, take a moment to peel that chip off your shoulder and toss it into the river. The Legion needs you to be flexible. And we need those recruits."

So Howie did as he was told, and took the brisk walk through deserted downtown Boston to the Longfellow Bridge. When he reached the center he dutifully leaned against the railing to contemplate his metaphorical "chip." In front of him, the Charles River basin glittered in the moonlight, almost a mirror except for the light breeze. The lights of Storrow and Memorial Drives shimmered along the edges—their rare moment of glory in the absence of the usually dominant CITGO sign.

In Boston, they shut off the big signs at midnight. Not like Las Vegas, where they leave them on all night—mood lighting for the decadent things that "happen in Vegas and stay in Vegas." Howie knew about that stuff firsthand; in his case, one of the few things that didn't stay in Vegas was that chip on his shoulder. He wondered what the King would think about the real chip he was carrying around as a result. He hadn't told anyone else about that, knowing they'd just accuse him of being paranoid. And maybe he was, but that didn't mean his hate for the Corporation wasn't justified. How could the King forgive Corporation soldiers after the crimes they'd committed, not just against him, but against the whole fucking world?

Howie's inner rant was cut short by a muffled explosion somewhere across the bridge. A plume of smoke rose in East Cambridge, lit moon-white from above and flickering green from below. Copper nitrate green.

Roger's car.

The thief must have laughed as he escaped—only Urban Legion pansies would build a warning into a booby trap. Wouldn't want any Corporation people to get hurt! Howie imagined Roger's reaction: lenient, just like the King. *Oh well, I'll just build another one.* Easy to say when all you've lost is a car. Roger lost his best friend once—how could he forget? *That's all in the past*, he'd say. *You've got to look to the future, protect the living.*

A chilly gust and a cold thought snapped Howie into the present.

Meg hadn't reported in.

Despite the King's reassurances, that wasn't like her. And God only knew what she was dealing with at the Mall; the possibilities, amplified by his own scarred imagination, were too gruesome to think about. But he finally saw his associates' point about the future and the living. And to Howie, those both meant the same thing: Meg.

He had to rescue her.

And he needed help, even if that meant forgiving and accepting the newly deflowered nerds at the lab. If nothing else, those potential recruits could give him a ride to the Mall. Roger's VW was no longer an option.

* * *

Roger arrived at headquarters to find the King relaxing in the media room, a bowl of popcorn in his lap, a Pepsi in his hand, and *Top Secret* on the big monitor.

"Ya know, this movie's not so bad, but it's kinda unrealistic," he said, eyes twinkling. "That Val Kilmer guy acts more like a rock star than a movie star. Reminds me of Jimmy Morrison for some reason." He clicked the TV off and pointed to the mini-fridge. "Pepsi?"

"No thanks. Where's Howie?"

"He's on an outreach mission, attendin' to some ripe-for-conversion prospects at the lab. I expect he's gonna head for the Mall after that—we still haven't heard from Meg. How's Lynn?"

Roger fell into the chair opposite and described the evening. The King was amused by Lynn's charade with François, and a little shocked by her seduction ploy. The idea of RFID microchips and hints of a deeper purpose than mere discounts brought a frown to his face. He was disappointed with Roger's limited information.

"So the drunken sailor strategy didn't work. You sure he had enough to drink?"

"I'm sure—he was drunk enough for Lynn to risk climbing all over him."

"That bother you?"

"Uh, yeah, actually."

"Jealous?"

"King, she's ten years older than me."

"That don't matter none. She's young at heart—a free spirit, always in the moment."

"That's not it. I got her into this, I'm responsible. I didn't want her to sleep with that jerk on my account."

The King nodded.

"You're a lot like me on that score. You take responsibility and care about your people. I've trained a lotta folks in the last thirty years, but you're the first one to come along who has that."

He took a sip of Pepsi and stared into space.

"You know, I'm gettin' too old for this. I thought I was gettin' too old a long time ago, and started lookin' for a replacement. At first, we thought we should keep it in the music biz family—that's why we looked at Phil Grady before he turned to the dark side. But even if he stayed clean, he was too hot-tempered. Kinda like Howie. Turns out, we don't need a musician, but we do need somebody who can improvise without losin' his rhythm. Somebody who can go with the flow. Like you."

Roger's cheeks were warm.

"I'm fixin' to retire soon; so are the other Kings. We're gonna head for a private little place in the Pacific we call Paradise Lagoon. We aim to do a lotta singin' and guitar playin' and girl watchin'. Bikinis sure have gotten skimpier since the beach movies!"

The old man was grinning, and Roger grinned back.

"They're called thongs now, King. You'd better pack some Viagra."

"Good thing there were too many old men in the Corporation to suppress that." He got serious again. "So when the time comes, think you'd be willin' to take over for me?"

"Will I have to wear sideburns? I look like crap in sideburns."

"Nah, you won't have to impersonate anybody. Just do your own thing."

Roger shrugged, and nodded, and shook the King's hand. It was a laid-back response to a laid-back offer; they really were two of a kind.

"What about tonight, King? You're still in charge. What do we do now?"

The King glanced at his watch, and pushed himself to his feet.

"Seems like all we can do is be wide awake and ready for anything tomorrow morning. I'm fixin' to take a shower and hit the sack. I suggest you get some shut-eye, too."

"I'll think about it. Good night, King."

Roger watched through the media room window as the old man headed for the Graceland suite. He looked pretty spry for an elderly short-timer. Maybe it was the sequined jumpsuit. Or the gel pads in his blue suede jogging shoes. Roger hoped the King was spry enough to hang on a while longer, because his replacement wasn't as caring and responsible as the King believed. Lying to Lynn all day was proof of that.

He'd already been feeling guilty about withholding the text message details and not letting her contact Tanya. Then, when he called her from the hotel, he deliberately didn't mention that the microchips would make the girls "just like the hooker." He'd always taken Trail Boy Truth seriously before—what the hell was going on here?

Of course, his Military Strategy skill patch training taught him that there's a time and place for lying: to mislead an enemy. But Lynn wasn't the enemy, was she? He smiled as it suddenly struck him, after all these years, why other guys could lie so readily to women. They simply considered women the enemy, to be misled and conquered; lying gave them a strategic advantage over someone they didn't care about. Or even hated.

But he wasn't trying to mislead her. Maybe he was protecting her ignorance—trying not to burden her with nasty details. Just a Trail Boy good deed, like relieving an old lady from the burden of carrying groceries?

That wasn't it.

The King had it straight: Lynn was no old lady. And Roger had denied his feelings about her like a fifth grader getting teased about a crush. A pubescent rush set his ears aglow.

His training wasn't much use here. The Trail Boy Manual didn't cover helping an old lady across the street, then realizing she's the lady you've been looking for all your life.

* * *

Howie surveyed the compromised facility from the dim tunnel. There was no one in sight, but he heard conversation from the back rooms. The aroma of cologne, sex, and—Chinese food—drifted through the door crack. He slipped in and waded quietly across the lab, thinking maybe he should grab Meg's gun; but then again, he was outnumbered at least ten to one. And what did he know about guns, anyway? He could only hope everybody was calm and happy by now. God forbid they were looking for a fight.

The geeks and maids were scattered around the lounge, having what looked like an ordinary party, albeit a wild one, given the general disarray of their clothes. They were sitting on laps, eating microwave eggrolls, and drinking Roger's beer. Howie stepped through the door and waited to be noticed. Eventually the chatter, a mix of tech and Latin-tinged-English, trailed off. One of the maids—Lily, according to her name tag—climbed off her geek's lap.

"'ere's another one," she said to the group. Then to Howie: "You look like you wanna smash papas yourself." She gave his beard a playful tweak; he flinched away.

"No thanks, I can pass."

"Whatever you like, papi." She backed off and redraped herself over the grateful nerd. The group afterglow felt like a sunny day at the beach.

Howie hated the beach.

"Mind if I take a little survey? A little while ago my remote control robots dispersed a beaker of cologne in here. What do you think of the stuff?"

There was a sudden cacophony of "Awesome!" "Phat!" and "Sick!" from the crowd, followed by a lone "My boyfriend ees better lookeen'." There was a hush as her already undersized partner shrank from her critical eye. "But 'e don' 'ppreciate me like thees," she added, bringing smiles to both of them.

"Such a shame, don't you think," Howie continued, "if the Corporation wipes out that cologne, not to mention the recipe?"

A wave of grumbling and protests washed over him.

Such a deal I have for you.

"Who needs those schmucks? What, they give you a little money, so you can buy porn on the Net and watch it on a big HD monitor? Or you, ladies, you take the money home to your ungrateful boyfriend so he can spend it on other women?" Guilty looks confirmed direct hits.

"You don't have to take their rotten deal. You could join us."

Lily's nerd raised his hand.

"Why would you want us? You're MIT. We're just Tronics Town."

Howie offered a grandfatherly smile.

"Actually, I'm not MIT, I'm Cooper Union. But you, us— we're all techies. We all have a little geek inside." *Sometimes even you girls.*

"What d'you pay?" It was the unappreciated maid.

"We can't match the Corporation," Howie began, watching her lips purse and her eyes harden, "but it's a living. And you'll be blessed with a boyfriend who treats you like the goddess you are."

She cocked her head and considered this, with a questioning look at her new fan. He was nodding, vigorously.

"So, what do you say? Should I write the cologne off the books, and all of you with it? Or will you join the Urban Legion?"

They glanced around at each other for reinforcement, until everyone was focused on the hesitant maid, who was still evaluating her smitten nerd. Suddenly, she smiled and kissed him, and in the next moment the silence was broken with shouts of "Join you!" "Si!" "I'm in!"—and one "I love you, man!"

That one was drinking beer for the first time, too. Howie actually felt a twinge of nostalgia for those exciting days when he'd lost his own various virginities. It dawned on him that these guys weren't so much evil as immature.

He got contact information from the leaders, Lily and Neil, then issued anti-HIV tablets and post-coital birth control pills—up till now, these guys had no reason to carry condoms. Then he sent the maids home; once the foam jets kicked in, a little water on the floor wouldn't make much difference.

He called Roger at HQ, debriefed, and asked about Meg. Still no word.

"I'm going to the Mall to find her. If she's hurt I'll rip somebody's baitsim off."

"Go ahead, Howie, but stay calm. No baitsim-ripping."

"You sound like the King."

"Yeah. You should take the VW. Got your key?"

"Funny you should mention that. I saw a green explosion on my way over here."

"Crap."

"Is that 'crap, my car blew up' or 'crap, Howie was right about setting the booby trap'?"

There was a defeated pause.

"Both. So how're you gonna get to the Mall?"

Howie looked over at Neil, the sergeant of a small but happy squad of geeks, and now his partner.

"I'm riding with the troops."

A few minutes later, the troops marched into the MIT tunnel. Howie took one last look around the deserted lab—a pleasant place, while it lasted. But it was time to close it up forever.

He spoke clearly toward the microphone in the ceiling.

"Armageddon twenty-four!"

Now armed, the system would give the Legionnaires time to clear out. Once the motion detector cameras in the ceiling hadn't seen any activity for 24 hours, a final evacuation warning would sound, and foam jets would fill the lab in minutes. An hour after that, the entire complex, including the shattered truffle tanks, would be a rigid mass of insulating foam.

Meg put her heart and soul into those tanks, Howie thought, distractedly picking at his shoulder.

* * *

François kept Jean-Paul and Toine at bay as Carl organized his team of pre-owned-vehicle salesmen. There were twelve as requested, armed with tasers and crowbars, but dressed for their day jobs. Each man's sport jacket and tie were loud, and clashed; François idly swapped ties around in his mind but could not find a single combination that worked.

They stopped along the way to meet Phyllis, who offered a small Pricy's box, such as for a pair of gloves. For these keys to the fortress, Jean-Paul traded a chilled bottle of expensively-named champagne.

Jean-Paul donned the fingertip gloves and the group proceeded to the Liberty Bank building. The light was dim, but these people would stand out in total darkness. François urged haste.

Toine credit-carded the lock open and the attack force poured into the darkened lobby. At the rightmost elevator, Jean-Paul pressed the up button four times with his latex-disguised finger. When the door opened, the men glanced at each other—the conveyance was not very large.

They were like the SUVs they sold, François mused, chosen for brawn and destructiveness, not travel efficiency. But without knowing how many defenders they faced, there was no choice but to strike simultaneously.

"All of us, into this car."

They crowded into the tiny box, François last, Toine whining, and Jean-Paul at the keypad, pressing the button combination he had memorized from the hidden camera recording. The elevator groaned under the load but carried them upward.

"Remember, stealth is of the essence."

"Huh?"

"He means shut up, guys."

"Oh."

The elevator shuddered to a stop, the door swished open, and François stepped out, scanning for defenses. It was quiet. Quiet and plush, with a stunning view of the harbor, and the airport glowing in the moonlight.

This was no decoy site. The Legionnaires lived in luxury!

François felt a vague discomfort—was he jealous of the Legion's wealth, or insulted that their legendary poverty might only be Corporation propaganda? Or perhaps the Corporation was not aware. If the latter was true, delivering this HQ to his superiors would serve his career very well indeed.

"The lobby area is all clear," Jean-Paul reported after a brief tour of the immediate environs. "There are delocked doors leading to both wings of this floor."

Carl split his salesmen into two squads.

"We'll send one team in each direction. Keep a chase man back to get help if you encounter Legionnaires. We'll wait here for you to return or request help. Stunners ready?"

The men all checked their tasers and nodded.

"Steve, your team goes to the right. Lloyd, take your guys to the left."

François leaned in.

"We have described the Legionnaires we encountered this afternoon. But most especially, if you find an old man with sideburns singing *Love Me Tender* in the shower, secure him and bring him directly to me. Bon chance, Messieurs."

* * *

Steve led his squad into the south wing. They proceeded down the hall, checking rooms along the way: an infirmary, offices, labs, and living quarters, all unoccupied.

He was beginning to relax when he spotted flickering light escaping a room on the right. He crept up to an inside window and peered through the corner. A large young man was sprawled across a couch, engrossed in some kind of Eastern culture documentary— a large-screen TV flashed images of Buddha, watercolor paintings, and ancient temples, accompanied by annoying sitar music. Steve motioned to the others, who ducked below the window and stationed themselves outside the door. Once they were in position, he gave the signal.

Four men burst into the room and rushed the Legionnaire. He rolled to his feet and yelled.

"Turtle! Two-three-three!"

They surrounded him in seconds, but something bad was already underway. All the monitors went blank, and so did the laptop computers. Machinery at the back of the room began to whine, like a transmission grinding itself to pieces.

Needs sawdust, Steve thought.

The Legionnaire held up a hand.

"I just shut down the whole complex—there's not a byte of

usable information here anymore. But you might like our machines or our people, and we don't want you to have 'em. I can say one more keyword and emitters in the ceiling will blast this facility with high-energy gamma radiation. That'll rupture the cells in every living thing it hits—turning you, me, and the houseplants into a thick broth. The carpets will soak up what's left of us." He paused, surveying the frozen circle of men, saving the last glare for Steve. "It's the party-size version of the old cyanide pill. And since you're gonna kill me eventually, I've got nothing to lose. Unless you decide to back off and go home."

Steve tried to read the guy. Vinnie's report from the hospital about the booby-trapped car proved that the Legionnaires weren't afraid to draw blood. But killing Rocco didn't mean they were willing to kill themselves. It was time to rely on his training.

"Don't move. I'll have to check with my manager."

He relayed the situation to Carl. Word came back: He's bluffing; take him.

"Sorry, we can't see our way to accepting your backing-off terms. Our best offer is for you to come with us."

Steve motioned to the others, but none of them moved.

"Outstanding Service plaque for the first man to take him down!"

They all jumped.

"Armageddon twenty-four!" the Legionnaire yelled.

Steve cringed, as did the others, even as they tasered the guy into submission. There was no flash, no sound, except for the zapping of the stun guns.

How long do gamma rays take, he wondered. Can you feel your cells rupture?

* * *

Lloyd crept through a doorway, stunner ready, and found a huge executive suite. No one about. The next door led to a simulated Southern mansion vestibule, complete with marble undercarriage, oriental floor mats, ornate plaster trim package, stained glass mirrors, and high-intensity chandeliers. It even sported a fake staircase leading up through a painted-on opening in the ceiling. Lloyd made a mental note to see if anyone made stick-on sunroof frames; maybe customers would pay extra without checking for an actual sunroof.

The invaders fanned out, keeping each other in sight and peeking into each of the rooms off the vestibule. One by one the men signaled "nothing," until finally Lloyd saw a thumbs-up. They converged on a master bedroom suite, its plush interior dominated by a huge square bed with a red crushed-velvet bedspread. Light from a side room highlighted steam drifting along the ceiling.

Lloyd peeked around the door into a roomy master bath, with fogged-up front and side mirrors, and a running shower with somebody in it. He couldn't tell what the occupant looked like through the enclosure, but he was singing—*Don't Be Cruel*.

Damn. Wrong song.

He checked with his manager, and a minute later, had a deal: Take the guy anyway.

Chapter 18

Meg inched away from the E-Mart checkout area while Eightball busied himself with field strength readings. This was their fifth install, and she noted that he'd muttered to himself every time he checked the meter. He clearly didn't like it; the signal was weird, and the boxes were pumping out too much power.

She considered the fact that all the girls in the program were Mall retail trainees. That meant they'd be working behind these registers; maybe the antennas weren't aimed at the customers after all.

Meg figured Roger could explain it—he was an expert on Corporation technology—if she could ever get word to him. She'd captured video recordings of all the equipment, how it was hooked up, and even a field-meter session in her personal witness, but she hadn't found a way to upload it to HQ. Ed MacGregor, their mall-cop guardian angel, took his job way too seriously: he hadn't let her out of his sight all night.

Now she spotted a laptop at the end of the computer aisle. It was online—the Google logo was up in a browser window. It would take her twenty seconds to send off an encoded message through the Google query autocomplete database; even if the Corporation could trace it, it wouldn't look significant. She drifted over, real casual-like, and reached for the keyboard.

"I wouldn't touch that if I were you."

Meg spun to find the round mall cop a few feet away, glaring at her with unnerving intensity.

"I was just gonna check Facebook—"

"Step away from the computer, Miss."

"But—"

"I said, step *away*." His holster snap was open and his shooting hand was hovering over the revolver handle.

Ohhh-kaaayyyy…

She stepped back, *slowly*, raising her hands in the universal gesture for "I'm unarmed, please don't gun me down in cold blood."

"I s'pose Facebook can wait."

* * *

Howie mustered Neil and his troop of Tronics Town geeks in the Lexingham Mall parking lot. It was almost deserted; the early-morning light revealed lone cars scattered about, including Meg's Impala, and a cluster around the loading docks, to which they added their own vehicles. A large box truck—"Northeast Industrial Powders and Processed Foods"—was unloading at the only unsealed bay. Howie's plan was to get inside, and then split up and search; how hard could it be to find one tiny woman in a two-story mall? Hard, he admitted, but it wasn't like he had other options.

They crouched behind the truck cab until footsteps faded into the dock interior, then they scrambled onto the platform. When Howie turned to lead the team inside, he found himself face-to-chest with the delivery guy: Bob, according to the stitching on the coveralls just inches from Howie's nose. He scanned upward, hoping for a friendly face atop the thick neck.

"What are you guys doin' here?" snarled Bob's unfriendly face.

"Just taking a cigarette break, Bob." Howie glanced around to elicit murmurs of agreement from the others.

"You ain't got cigarettes."

"Right. We gave up smoking. But we're union—you want we should give up our break, too?"

"I'm with ya on that." Bob rolled his dolly into the half-empty truck and began to wrestle a 30-gallon fiber drum.

Howie and the geeks pushed through double swinging doors and emerged into the hall beyond, the doors flapping behind them. Howie felt like the leader of the Urban Legion gang, just rode into town and looking for trouble at the local saloon. And they found it as they rounded the next corner into the Mall's east wing: a crowd of black-clad, acne-plagued boys.

"Phone-store guys!" hissed Neil.

A short kid with an Xbox tee-shirt halted his comrades and stepped forward.

"Well, what's this? Tronics Town refugees, if I'm not mistaken. What's the matter, dronies, need to buy some real technology?"

Howie assessed the odds: his team was outnumbered, and the maids had drained what little aggressiveness they started with. He whispered to Neil.

"Can you keep them busy for a few minutes? Thanks for the ride, and I'll be in touch. We'll do lunch."

Neil nodded and Howie retreated to the back of the group, near the base of an escalator. Neil stepped up to Xbox.

"Phones are phones—you don't have technology."

"Well, if you had phone technology, you could've called ahead and found out the Mall's closed now. This time of day, this is our turf. And I say you guys are roaming!"

"We're on the nights and weekends plan. We'll roam where we want." Neil waved to his crew and started to walk past the mall gang. Xbox cut him off and shoved him back with both hands.

"Sorry, your plan's been discontinued."

"Oh, yeah?" Neil caught his balance and countered, pushing the kid backward into the rest of his posse. Both groups charged forward into the fight, which, to Howie's amusement, involved little more than shoving and shouts of "Oh yeah?" After the gun-wielding French goons, this was pretty easy to take. He kept an eye on the melee while slipping around to the far side of the escalators.

The phone-store kids used their numbers advantage to push the Tronics Townies toward the Mall exit. Just as it seemed the Townies would be overcome, Neil scaled a brick planter and raised his arms.

"Halt!"

In a superbly deep and dramatic voice, Neil proclaimed that he was a level-seven wizard; then, with a wave of his hand, he summoned the Daemons of Enfeeblement and cast a strength-sapping spell on the Phonies. They froze, helpless.

Xbox recovered first.

"Don't believe him! He's not a wizard, he's just a troll!"

The home geeks tentatively raised and flexed their arms, as if testing them for power. They apparently found it full strength, so to speak, and rushed the intruders again, sweeping the short-lived wizard from his pedestal. Howie caught a hand-wave from Neil as the Tronics Townies were herded into the parking lot, where they clambered into their cars and sped off.

Xbox led the Mall defenders back inside.

"Time for breakfast, men!"

Howie stayed hidden as the warriors strutted down the hall for their victory repast. He was wondering how to track down Meg when it hit him that the food court was upstairs; there was nothing down that hall except the Mall offices and loading docks. Somehow, he doubted they'd be eating packing peanuts for breakfast. He decided maybe he should see for himself.

Once the kids rounded the next corner, Howie followed, getting there in time to see a door swing shut a little ways down the side hall. It was windowless steel, with a stenciled sign: Teabury— Authorized Personnel Only. He heard an inner door slam as he tested the outer door. To his surprise, it wasn't locked.

* * *

Meg stacked the last empty box on the dolly and wheeled it out of the store. It had been a long night, but at least trash disposal duties had been assigned to the mall cops, allowing her and Eightball to head right to breakfast. Meg was as hungry as a farmhand after sunrise chores, and craved huevos rancheros to open her sinuses. She was pretty sure there wouldn't be any Bloody Marys, with or without horseradish.

As they approached the Teabury entrance, she glanced at her personal witness status. She had several hours of recording time left and needed only a few seconds to record how Eightball opened the basement door. Then, she figured, she'd grab a bite, hit the road, and report to HQ.

They entered the Teabury anteroom and found a short man in a yarmulke examining the inner door.

Shoot, it's Howie! He'd blow her cover—a teenager wouldn't know this obviously older man. She'd have to pretend she didn't. Howie spun around.

"Meg! Thank God I found you!"

Great. Umm—"*Uncle* Howie! What are you doin' here?"

Howie's face twisted up for a moment until he caught her "work with me" eyes. He was off balance but used it to his advantage.

"I... I was worried about you. You go out, you don't come home, I worry!"

Not so thick, babe, Meg thought. She hoped Eightball was too tired to wonder how a Texas girl could have a New York Jewish uncle. She was glad she hadn't used a fake name.

"Sorry, Unc. I thought I told you I was workin' overnight. We had a special project." She turned to Eightball, and back to Howie. "Uncle Howie, I'd like you to meet George—or Eightball, as everybody calls him. Eightball, my uncle and guardian, Howie." She gave them a moment to nod hello. "So, Unc, we're gonna get some breakfast, and then I'll come home straightaway. So don't worry; just head on back and—"

"No way, girl," Eightball cut in, "the man came all the way here to make sure you're okay, the least you can do is invite him in for breakfast!"

Before Meg could think of a way out of it, Eightball pounded on the inner door three times, and seconds later it opened, courtesy of Don DiSenza. Meg's cover was wearing mighty thin, fast. She avoided eye contact, and took special care not to trip on the stairs. Getting her evidence-laden personal witness back to HQ was getting tougher by the minute.

"All done, Eightball?"

"All done, Mr. Dee—all tested, all working perfect. Tell Axe-man 'no glitches'."

"Axe-man?"

"Sorry, dude, that's an old nickname. Phil Grady."

So he knew Phil. Maybe he *was* Corporation. Did she read him wrong?

They made it down the stairs and into the cafeteria, which was already occupied by the phone-store installation teams. She could see the steam from the eggs, bacon, and pancakes but couldn't smell a thing. With all those hygiene-challenged nerds in there, her totally-plugged nose was probably for the best.

She heard DiSenza ask the dreaded question.

"Who's that?"

"That's Meg's uncle Howie," Eightball said. "He's just a 'copter parent, checkin' up on her. Thought I'd invite him in for some grub."

"Not a good idea—" DiSenza said, "—and who's Meg?"

It was time to go.

Meg pressed ahead to get some separation from DiSenza, scoping the distance to the shipping room door. It was about nine steps, but Howie'd have to go for it at the same time to catch everyone else flatfooted. She tried to signal the break to him, but he was already occupied—the phone-store geeks had circled him, menacing. A kid with an Xbox tee-shirt poked Howie in the chest.

"You look kinda familiar. You look like the kind of guy who works at Tronics Town. In fact, I'd swear I saw you a few minutes ago with that crowd of T.T. turds."

The other boys snorted and Howie stammered a denial as DiSenza pushed his way into the crowd.

"What's going on, James?"

The Xbox kid told him about chasing some other kids out of the Mall, and apparently Howie'd been with the group. The accused did his best sputtering uncle.

"I was in the hall, looking for Meg. I don't know those other kids; they just pushed right past me. Such manners, I tell you, it's a crime—"

"Shut up." DiSenza turned his attention to Meg. "Looking for Meg. And who, might I ask again, are you, Meg?"

"She's the best tech in the bunch, Mr. Dee," Eightball said. "Helped me—"

"Shut up." DiSenza's eyes were burning holes in her. "I didn't hire you. In fact, I don't even know you. Except"—he reached around her head and pulled at the torn pink hair ribbon—"I think I saw you at the dinner last night. Wearing the rest of this shirt."

Meg jerked her hair from his grasp and stood defiantly mute.

The path to the packing room was open; she tensed her legs, hoping Howie would follow her lead. She couldn't wait for him—getting her personal witness out of there was more important.

But DiSenza moved first, grabbing her wrist and wrestling her into an arm lock. Howie jumped to help, but he barely got a hand on DiSenza's shoulder before the boys pulled him off. If Howie'd been Roger, he'd have flung the whole gaggle of geeks across the steam tables.

Eightball looked confused and disappointed. He'd trusted her.

"Mr. Dee, I thought she was one of your kids. She did a fine job in the stores—you sure about this?"

"No." The big man's grip remained firm. "But we don't have time to discuss it—you've got to finish installing the calibration gear, and I've got to set up the database, not to mention the other projects I've got going down here this morning. We're gonna get these two out of the way for a while and get back to work—bring Uncle Howie and come with me. You boys eat your breakfast and forget you ever saw this. And eat quick, we need the room."

There was an awkward silence, until Eightball, who hadn't moved, cleared his throat.

"So uh, with all due respect, Mr. DiSenza, I install point-of-sale terminals. I'm not a mall cop."

"With all due respect, Mr. Shipley, if you don't follow orders I'll see to it you never install another point-of-sale terminal as long as you live. And I have two ways to make that happen."

Eightball seethed, but took possession of Howie and followed DiSenza. The mall manager shoved Meg through the shipping room and double doors into the hall beyond, pausing along the way to grab a roll of packing tape. They were following her planned escape route; too bad she didn't escape first. Still, she took note of the turns, in case she got a chance to come back that way.

After a long walk through the complex, DiSenza steered them through a side door. A young man in a bright blue dress shirt and khaki slacks was eyeing a wall of monitors from a control desk. He jumped up when he recognized DiSenza.

"Stay put, Charles. We've got to park these two in the server bay for a while." He took them through a windowed door into a back room, then held Howie while Eightball, after a whispered apology, taped Meg to an equipment rack. Her arms were pinned back, and the rack was full of running computers. She squirmed and pushed but couldn't budge it. They taped Howie to another rack a few yards away.

DiSenza chased Eightball out and almost followed, but he stopped at the door and cocked his head, listening.

"I thought it'd be noisier in here." He paused again, then glanced down at the tape, and smiled. "Wouldn't want anyone upstairs to hear you two shouting for help." He stepped up to Howie and pressed several strips of tape ear-to-ear over his mouth. Howie's eyes got big and he tried to yell, but it came out like humming a rap song. It wasn't until DiSenza came at Meg that she remembered her nose was completely blocked.

"Please don't! I can't—"

DiSenza hooked her chin and yanked up, cutting her off and catching the edge of her tongue in her teeth. She tasted blood and tried to tell him through the clench, but he either didn't understand or didn't care—she hissed in half a breath before he pasted two strips across her mouth and left the room.

Don't panic.

She first tried to blow the tape off, but it wouldn't budge and the pressure just diverted into her ears. She tried to pull in, with the same result—nothing but stabbing ear pain. She could flex her jaw, but the tape only stretched her cheeks and stayed airtight. Too bad she didn't wear powdery makeup. Or have oily skin.

The previous evening—not her whole life—flashed before her eyes when she realized she'd never tell anyone what she'd learned. Maybe someone would recover her personal witness, at least.

She kept pushing and flexing the tape without success. She looked up at Howie—he was freaking out. But whatever there was to say, they could only say it with their eyes.

You don't want to see this, babe.

Her lungs burned and jerked against the blockage. Sparkles danced around the room, until her head sagged and the sparkles drifted to the floor, fading into darkness.

Chapter 19

Howie tried to scream as he watched Meg's eyes go glassy; when her head drooped and she started convulsing, he could barely breathe himself. The noise of the computers suddenly felt like dead silence. He had to be able to make the kid in the next room hear.

He took a deep breath for one last all-out shout for help. It came out as "hmmmmgh" through the tape, but something else happened, too: his cheek hurt like hell where the tape had pulled out a few beard hairs. He gathered his strength and yelled again, this time focusing on opening his mouth. The tape, or rather, a large section of his beard, ripped loose on one side. "—EEELLLP!" echoed over the drone of the servers.

"HELP! HURRY! PLEASE!" he screamed. The kid's head appeared in the small window in the door, then the door opened and he leaned through.

"Jeez, what's the problem?

Thank God!

"You have to help her! Her mouth is taped shut, and her nose is stuffed. She can't breathe! She's gonna die!"

The kid took an agonizing moment to comprehend what should have been perfectly fucking clear, and then strolled over to examine Meg.

"Hurry! She's already passed out! Please!"

"If this was Mr. DiSenza's idea, I don't think I should do anything."

"He didn't know she couldn't breathe. He just didn't want us to yell. I promise, we won't yell, just take the tape off!"

The bastard stood there for few more eternal seconds, then shrugged.

"I guess I can make it look like it came off by itself..."

He grabbed the edge of the tape, and pulled it partially away. The ripping of glue from cheek sounded painful, but maybe that's what kick-started Meg's lungs. She gasped and gagged, then settled into rapid fire panting, the edge of the tape fluttering with each breath. Finally, she opened her eyes.

Thank God!

"Happy now?" the kid asked. He should have been impressed that he'd just saved somebody's life, but it was hard to tell.

"Yes, thank you! I'll put in a good word with Mr. DiSenza for you."

"I don't need a good word from you."

"I was kidding. But not about the thanks."

"You promised, no yelling."

"No yelling."

The kid gave him one last "I mean it" glare and retreated to the other room. Howie and Meg both sat quietly for several minutes.

She's alive!

"Are you okay?" he said finally.

"I'm okay, don't worry."

"You gave me such a scare."

"Uh, me too." She locked her wonderful eyes on his. "It would suck if I couldn't at least say goodbye."

"You did say goodbye."

She smiled.

"I guess I spoke too soon." Meg took a slow breath and exhaled, looking as relieved as Howie felt. But only for a second, until she glanced down at her chest and back up, urgency in her face. "Howie, we've got to report out to Roger."

She told him about the RFID tag program and her evening setting up gear. "Even Eightball doesn't understand the system. I've got it all on my personal witness—I bet Roger could figure it out. We just have to get out of here and show it to him."

"We should be so lucky. Our jailer was barely willing to let you breathe; there's no way he's going to let us leave."

* * *

Lynn slogged through a knee-deep pâté sea, trying to reach a priceless guitar before the thieves did, while dodging a giant frog as he slapped an equally huge tire iron into the duck liver around her. As her pursuer's shadow loomed, she grabbed the instrument, leapt into her car, and roared away. A split second later, the massive tool crashed down onto the vacated parking spot.

She woke with a start.

Her head nearly exploded with each heartbeat; her stomach was knotted, her mouth dry. She glanced at the clock—8:23—and then dove for the bathroom and the wheel of the porcelain bus. After a few minutes the butterflies were gone, as were all twelve courses of the L'Escargot degustation. The blood had drained from her face, leaving a cool sweat on her cheeks and throbbing forehead. She breathed deeply between echoing dry heaves. Some hangover prevention pill!

To be fair, Roger did say the pill didn't do what they intended. And he only said it blocked the drunkenness, not the hangover. But did he really think that wasn't worth mentioning?

She owed him one.

Lynn hadn't dealt with a hangover since college, but she remembered the routine: ginger ale and saltines until she could get down an ibuprofen. And once the headache was gone, Gatorade to rehydrate and spicy tomato juice to lose the shakes. Unfortunately, that meant a shopping trip; none of that stuff was a staple in her organic household. She checked that Tanya's bedroom door was still closed—not wanting to face her daughter looking and feeling like a wet rag—and tottered into the kitchen.

She managed to hold down some water and a few bites of whole-grain bread. Thinking Ujjayi breathing might help keep her stomach from tossing both, she trudged to the living room, pulled out her yoga mat, and sat.

Breathe.

[Fluttery stomach, pounding head.]

This wasn't a Zen Gourmet review, she told herself. There was no notebook and no need to describe symptoms.

Let it go. Just breathe.

[Gonna hurl.]

Don't hurl! Another badly done meditation session. She pictured gagging the writer's voice.

Accept it, do not judge. Let it go.

[Empty parking space.]

Just let it—

[Empty parking space.]

The car is gone!

It finally registered in her thinking mind. She'd noticed her Civic parked across the street the night before, when she hid the keys…

She rolled off the mat and rushed to the Buddha, leaving the headache behind until she reached the statue, where the pounding caught up and nearly knocked her over. Wincing so hard she could barely see, she lifted the smiling master—*he didn't drink too much last night*—and of course, the table was empty. She knew it was pointless, but she couldn't help quietly cracking Tanya's door to look in—on her deserted bed.

She sat down there, rubbing around her eyes and cheekbones to focus the pain away from her skull. She'd never hidden anything in the Buddha before; Tanya had no reason to look there. She was either lucky, or looked everywhere.

Or got a hint from Phil.

The thought of Tanya cooperating with Phil sent a chill down her already trembling spine. His charisma was perilous enough for Lynn—the limo ride proved that. What would Tanya do when he turned on the charm with her? Besides steal a car…

Lynn returned to the kitchen, found her cell, and punched U - L. The phone rang four times before Roger's voice answered with a calm "Please leave a message."

"Roger, it's Lynn. Call me the second you get this. Tanya's gone—she found the car keys and took off. I'm gonna—"

What *was* she gonna? Withdrawal from the battle was no longer an option.

"—I'm gonna go to the Mall." She hung up and rubbed her eyes. Between throbs, it hit her: No car.

Lynn considered her options for getting to Lexingham on a Sunday morning, and somehow kept coming back to Gerry. It was completely unreasonable after what had happened yesterday, but on the other hand, he did insist that he wanted to help. And if she remembered the philosophy right, *to ask for help is to give the gift of helpfulness.* Gerry loved being helpful, especially to Lynn.

She dialed his number.

"Good morning, this is Gerry."

"Hi Gerry, it's Lynn. Can I bother you?"

"You could never bother me. What do you need?"

"I need a ride. Tanya has my car, and I have to get to the Lexingham Mall. Right away. Can you pick me up?"

"I can be there in twenty minutes."

"Thank you! I'll see you out front. You're a doll."

"More like a gnome."

Lynn hung up, squeezed her eyes one more time, and feebly launched herself into action. Shower, throw on jeans and a shirt, and try to force down some more bread and water. In twenty minutes. After that, she had no idea.

* * *

Tanya sopped up the rest of her poached egg while her father munched his white toast and washed it down with a Bloody Mary, extra horseradish. He'd obviously had too much to drink and not enough sleep—his sunken eyes squinted almost closed against the glare of sunlight pouring in through the Pepper's front window. She wondered out loud if this was worth the trouble she was gonna be in when Mom realized she'd stolen the car.

"Don't let your mother keep you down, Tanya," he said. "Some people are afraid of technology, no matter how harmless or useful. They resist everything—think about cell phones, text messaging, Facebook."

Tanya considered it. Mom's phone was almost ten years old, and she'd never once sent a text message. Showing up on Facebook would be totally creepy.

"And your mother's worse than most of 'em—she's organic.

Nothing's any good unless it was grown in cow shit. From organically-fed cows. By organically-fed farmers, born under the same sign as the damn cows." He laughed, took a big swig of the Bloody Mary, and leaned closer. "But you gotta understand, kiddo, natural stuff is never gonna be big. It can't. It's just too hard to make money. Your mother's kind are gonna die out like the dinosaurs."

That seemed kind of harsh, but sometimes the truth is.

He pointed to her ear.

"Take those earrings you're wearing. Handmade, right?"

"Right."

"Think about the economics. They were hammered out by some starving artisan I'm sure, took some time, and cost a lot of money. It had to, the guy's gotta eat."

"It was a woman."

"Okay, and maybe she's watching her weight and eats less. But she still has to charge for all the time she put into making 'em. She's no factory—her production numbers stink compared to the suppliers for Clones Jewelry. Worse, she can't afford to advertise or open a shop in the Mall, so nobody even knows about her stuff except the new-age hippies who go to craft fairs."

"Like Mom."

"She bought those for you?"

"Yeah, it was my first pair."

"And you like 'em?"

"Yeah." Of course she did—she was wearing them, wasn't she?

"But nobody else does, I bet. They're weird, so they aren't *in*, Tanya. They don't help you look good for the crowd. You can fight popular culture, but you can't be popular at the same time."

Tanya reached up to touch one of the silver-and-ruby earrings. She sure wasn't popular. Did it matter?

"They match the pendant, too, Daddy." She held out the moon-and-star motif. "Clones doesn't have anything as nice as this."

"Puh-leese. Anything as nice as that? I mean, stars and moons are great if you're running with the wolves, but let's talk fashion. You won't see that stuff on TV or in the movies."

"Or at a concert?"

"Whaddya mean?"

"I was at an Actual Musicians concert last night, and—"

"Never heard of 'em."

"—I didn't think so. But they reminded me of you—when I was little. They're like, so intense about the music. And they don't care if it's popular."

"Okay, and they're probably broke, just like I was when you were little."

"Probably."

"Proving my point." He sat back, gulped the Bloody Mary, and reached for the check. "These days, I don't fight fashion—that's why I can afford to buy you breakfast." He signed it, returned the platinum card to his wallet, and pushed back his chair. "But, what I can't afford is the time to hang out here all day."

Tanya felt a sad twinge.

"This is so typical."

"What is?"

"Hearing you say something, and not knowing how to answer, and running out of time. You know, when you used to call, you'd talk about all kinds of stuff and never give me a chance to tell you what I was doing. Or to ask you stuff." She grabbed a napkin and dabbed her eyes. "Like why you never came home anymore."

He jumped around the table and crouched to give her a little hug.

"Honey, I didn't realize."

Tanya sniffed.

"You know, I used to talk with you afterwards, in my head. I'd think up what I should've said, and have these little imaginary conversations with you until the next time. But then there weren't any next times, and it all kind of faded away."

"I'm surprised you remember that."

"I didn't, until I saw you last night. Since then it's been happening again, just like old times."

He looked at her kind of funny, then smiled and gave her another squeeze, this one lingering for an awkward extra moment. He handed her the orange juice, grabbed his Bloody Mary, and clinked her glass.

"To old times," he toasted, and drained the remainder. He set down the glass and picked up his suit jacket. "We'll talk some more when you come in for the program. You're gonna join, right?"

Tanya bit her lower lip. She didn't know what to say.

Just like old times.

"I'll think about it."

"Okay, but don't take forever. Remember, it's a really good deal. I made sure, just for you. In fact, if you come over before work and get there first, I'll tweak the system to give you an even bigger discount."

Tanya choked back the flood of disappointment, built up over ten years of wanting him to be her Daddy again. Now here he was, as if her dream had come true. But the Daddy he was selling wasn't anything like the Daddy she remembered. Or the Daddy she longed for.

And all she was going to get was a bigger discount?

* * *

François had ignored the warning; when Toine found a coffee maker and condiments in the Urban Legion HQ kitchenette, Roger cautioned that the cream was past its prime. But François assumed it was a lie, like Roger's claim that his gamma rays would turn Steve's team to soup. Now he questioned all of his assumptions as he contemplated the foul curds floating in his cup. It had been a long night, and his mood had similarly soured.

He had expected the search team to at least find the gun-collecting country girl and her Jewish boyfriend, but the entire floor was devoid of Legionnaires save the two initial captives. Carl's salesmen did, in fact, discover three secret hiding places, but all were empty, except for a mural on one wall commemorating a "Jack Florey." The name was vaguely familiar but François was unable to place it.

François could almost believe this *was* just an elaborate decoy, and the old man merely a paid house sitter. Yet, he was about to wager his career against it.

"Very well, let us take them away. Carl and I shall accompany the King in Carl's vehicle. Jean-Paul, you and Toine bring Roger in my car." He tossed Toine his spare key bob. "Steve and Lloyd shall remain on guard here—the rest of you may go. We are grateful for your assistance."

François guided his bound prisoners into the lobby and took one last look around. The sunrise over the airport had been spectacular, and now the morning light beamed through the conference room windows and bathed the lobby in a golden glow. Truly, a magnificent sight in a magnificent location. Too magnificent for a decoy.

And the proof of its capture, modeling a blue-sequined jumpsuit, was now shuffling into the elevator, prompted by nudges from a 9mm pistol. François' mood was improving rapidly.

* * *

Lynn twisted slightly toward the Prius passenger-side window, to hide her face from Gerry. She might have covered the telltale dark circles under her eyes with makeup, but she didn't own any. Besides, Gerry might've noticed makeup before he noticed the hangover.

The Prius pulled up to a red light where the Fresh Pond Parkway came down off a railroad overpass and crossed in front of them. The roads were deserted, except for a familiar-looking black Lincoln racing down the bridge. Probably not the same car, Lynn thought, though she'd have to see the inside of the trunk to be sure. But when it zoomed by, she glimpsed an old man in the back seat—an old man who resembled the King. An uneasy tingle crept up the back of her neck.

Twenty seconds later, another, identical sedan roared down the bridge. In the back seat of that car was Roger, though he was hard to recognize with his nose pressed flat against the side window.

Was that supposed to be a nose signal? It couldn't be—all the signs Roger described involved fingers. Assuming he could use his fingers.

Lynn's pulse banged more insistently at her temples. Legionnaires wouldn't drive that kind of boat, or even ride in one, willingly. Plus, Roger and the King were separated. Plus again, Roger might be sending a nose signal. It all added up to something, but she didn't know what—she was as bad at math as she was at Zen.

"Gerry," she said, "I need you to follow that black car."

"What? Why? What's going on?"

"I'm not sure yet. Please."

Gerry gave her that "I'll do it, but only for you" look as the light changed and he pulled the Prius out.

"Think you can keep up?"

"If they don't drive too fast. This isn't built for racing."

The first Lincoln had gotten away, but the second was stopped at the light leading to Route 2 West—it was going the same direction as Lynn. Maybe to the Mall. But Route 2 ahead was a steep uphill climb, and the Lincoln would easily lose Gerry's ecologically-responsible little car.

There was no one else around. Lynn briefly debated the next step in her mind; it deserved more careful consideration, but any reasoned plan would be too late. And too reasonable to work.

"We've got to pass them, Gerry. Run the light. And hide your face as we go by."

"Run the—?"

"Just step on it!"

Gerry obediently swung into the left lane and hit the accelerator. As they ran the light and passed the Lincoln, Lynn ducked low and Gerry looked left.

"Lynn, why are we doing this?"

"I'm not sure, just stay left and keep going."

In the side view mirror, Lynn saw the lights change, and soon the Lincoln was closing the gap in the right lane. A label on the mirror warned "OBJECTS IN MIRROR ARE CLOSER THAN THEY APPEAR."

And a lot more solid, she thought.

Each heartbeat thumped directly into her headache. She double-checked the mirror for a giant, tire-iron-slamming frog.

The Lincoln loomed larger. It was all about timing.

Breathe. Feel the flow.

[Really stupid idea.]

Yup.

Lynn braced herself.

"Stop!"

As Gerry mashed the brake, Lynn reached over and yanked the wheel. The Prius screeched to the right and slowed, at least until the Lincoln crunched into it. The air bags inflated, slamming Lynn's head back into the headrest—amazingly, the impact was nothing compared to her headache. When the bags deflated, the Prius was perched on the curb with the Lincoln's bumper embedded in the trunk.

Gerry moaned. He looked stunned, but he wasn't bleeding.

"Are you okay?" she whispered into his ear.

"I think so. What happened?"

"Stay down—pretend you're unconscious. Trust me. I'll be back in a minute to explain." If she could think of something.

Lynn jumped from Gerry's car to intercept Toine and Jean-Paul jumping from theirs. The back end of the Prius was crushed, but the Lincoln was barely scratched—its airbags didn't even deploy. Lynn could see the scene as an editorial cartoon, with the tiny green Prius labeled "Environment" and the black Lincoln "Big Oil."

Jean-Paul looked ready to kill.

"What are you doing, you stupid bitch?!"

"Stopping you from making a big mistake. Do you know who I am?"

"François told us you work with M'sieur Grady. But we beat you to the punch bowl, no?"

Roger slid out of the open rear door, his hands bound behind his back.

"Lynn? What's he mean by that?"

"She is on our side," Toine said, sneering. "She has infiltrated you."

Roger looked genuinely hurt, and shot Lynn an icy glare. *Good boy*, she thought. *Once you can fake honesty, you've got it made.*

"But," Toine continued, turning back to Lynn, "we have discovered how to get into zeir headquarters, before you did. François will bring ze King to M'sieur Grady, and we will win. Ha!"

It finally sank in: the Frenchmen had actually invaded the Urban Legion complex. And captured the King. And Roger. And Lynn—if she screwed up this charade, she'd end up locked in that trunk again. She suppressed a shudder and forged an irritated frown.

"Wait. François decided to break into Legion headquarters? Without checking with Phil first? I told him we were setting up a mole operation!" She shook her head. "The asshole's ruined the whole thing. I knew Canadians were stupid, but I never expected a stunt like this."

Lynn saw Roger bite down on a smile. Toine and Jean-Paul, on the other hand, bit on the bait.

"What is it zat you mean—Canadian?"

"Canadian. From Canada. Montréal. Spent some time in France, but obviously not the real thing like you guys. You didn't know?"

Jean-Paul and Toine exchanged glances—Lynn could see the gears turning in their heads. Roger gave her a subtle wink and started to slink away.

"Grab him!" she shouted.

Roger broke into a plausible run but allowed Jean-Paul to catch him and drag him back to the car.

"What is it we should do with him?"

Jean-Paul was asking *her* what to do; Roger's brilliant move allowed Lynn to blow the whistle on him, which was enough to tip the thugs' trust over to her. Now she had to use it. For what?

To find Tanya.

She couldn't just say that, of course; there was this complex lie to maintain. Jean-Paul and Toine weren't the sharpest knives in the drawer, but they'd draw some serious blood if they caught her in an inconsistency.

"We take him with us, and go meet Phil Grady as planned. I can probably get him to give you guys a break—you had no idea what you were doing. I don't think François is gonna get the reception he expected, though."

"It will serve him right, ze lying bastard."

The Lincoln looked drivable, so Lynn kept Toine at the wheel and Jean-Paul guarding Roger in the back; she would ride shotgun. She sprinted to the Prius and opened the driver-side door. Gerry's head was still down; he flashed a pathetic look from the corner of his eye.

"Stay put for another minute Gerry. I'm really sorry, I've got to go."

"Huh? Where?"

"Lexingham Mall. I've got another ride; you can go back home."

"What happened?"

"You stopped for a cat, and somebody hit you from behind and took off. You didn't see them. And don't mention me."

Gerry sighed, burying his forehead deeper into the deflated bag.

"You'll explain everything later."

"Of course. And I'll pay for the Prius."

She ran back to the Lincoln and hopped in. Toine pulled back from the crumpled hybrid and roared around it, gathering speed for the impending hill.

Lynn's mind raced as fast as the big Lincoln's engine. Where would she find Tanya? How could she get Roger away from the goons? If she couldn't, how would she deal with Phil, François, and all of her conflicting stories at the same time?

And how the heck would she pay for the Prius?

* * *

Gerry extracted himself from the wreckage. His neck hurt from the initial collision and his nose hurt from the airbag, but as far as he could tell, he had no serious injuries. He was inspecting the damage to the rear end when the police arrived. If they knew he was lying when he told them the story Lynn suggested, they didn't let on; they didn't even question the second airbag. Just for show, he asked them about the chances of finding the hit-and-run culprit.

"Not good," the cop answered. "This kinda thing happens all the time. Hardly ever catch 'em."

"So what should I do?"

"Next time, squash the cat."

As a courtesy, the police measured the skid marks and took paint samples from the rear bumper. They also called a tow truck, since Gerry didn't have a cell phone and wouldn't know who to call anyway. The tow guy gave him a business card, winched the wreck onto the flatbed, and disappeared out Route 2 along with the cruiser.

Suddenly Gerry felt very alone. And stranded, until he realized the Alewife T station was nearby. He could take a train to within blocks of his house.

The few minutes to cross the highway and navigate to the T entrance gave him time to think—enough to make him hesitate at the turnstile. The T would take him back to the center of town, to his home. Which at any other time would be exactly what he wanted most. His whole life was about retreating to his own center.

At the center was peace. And safety.

For him. Not for Lynn. She was clearly in trouble, and it might even be his fault. She'd told him to pretend he was unconscious, but maybe he'd been unconscious long enough. Maybe this wasn't the time to hide from the world; maybe it was time to risk going out to save it.

Or at least, to save Lynn.

He backed away from the turnstile and retraced his steps to the curb. With no cell phone, he had to wait for a cab, a long time coming on a Sunday morning. Finally, a maroon-and-white Boston Checker pulled up to drop off passengers. It had been an hour since Lynn left; with one last thought that maybe he was too late anyway, Gerry waved to the driver. He slid into the back seat and leaned forward.

"Lexingham Mall, please."

Part III

"I cannot, in good conscience, recommend the eggrolls."
— Our Zen Gourmet

Chapter 20

As François guided M'sieur King across the Lexingham Mall parking lot, he regretted his decision to allow the old man's clothing choice. At the time, the blue-sequined jumpsuit had promised a more dramatic presentation to M'sieur Grady; now, François realized it would draw undesired attention.

Fortunately, the atrium was deserted. But it would not remain so for long; thus, he could not wait there for Jean-Paul and Toine to arrive. This circumstance, unfortunately, would require his partners to hold their captive in the car for some time—and the bull Roger would undoubtedly test what little patience Jean-Paul possessed. François was fairly certain that M'sieur Grady would not appreciate a bloody incident outside the Mall on a Sunday morning.

"I guess you know how to get in?" Carl asked.

"I was trained here. Were you not?"

"Nah, I did my stint at the Automotive Division headquarters in Flint."

"I am sorry to hear that."

"Yeah, it wasn't great. The Corporation closed it eventually; I hear the new one in Tokyo is much nicer."

When they reached the Teabury Center entrance, François passed his weapon to Carl and had him wait with the King in the hall; it would be imprudent to demonstrate the entry lock to the head Legionnaire. Behind the closed outer door, François performed the key sequence—*the invention of a twisted mind, certainement*—and heard the solenoid buzz. In moments they were descending the stairs with the door latched behind them. This was safe ground; anyone here seeing the jumpsuit would see a tremendous victory for the Corporation. Those observers would, of course, include M'sieur Grady, and with any luck, his formidable mistress.

* * *

Phil Grady closed his eyes and pressed two fingers to each temple. The four-way combo of Bloody Marys, ibuprofen, Gatorade, and coke was doing its best, but it wasn't up to the challenge of all that wine, let alone the foul-smelling brandy. When was somebody gonna invent a good hangover cure?

He inspected the shipping room, which they'd converted into a microchip injection station. They could close the soundproof door to the cafeteria, keeping the procedure out of sight—and sound— of the girls signing in and waiting their turn. No sense freaking 'em out. Eightball was still setting up the electronics under DiSenza's supervision, but he assured them both he'd be done on time, a half hour away. The only risk factor was whether Tanya would show up before work. After breakfast she'd headed for the Java Jag across the street; Phil had considered shadowing her, but too many other things required his attention.

He stepped into the cafeteria to check on the refreshments. Coffee and donuts would keep the girls happy while they waited; after that, he'd make them even happier.

A burst of plaid and sparkly blue flashed from the stairway entrance, and the drum solo in his skull came back for an encore. *Fuck.* It was François, with a fake Elvis. And a fake somebody else—maybe Buddy Holly, except he forgot the black eyeglasses.

"François. I told you I don't care about your goddamn truffles or your decoy Elvis! What's it take to get that through your Continental skull?"

"But M'sieur Grady, he is authentic! We retrieved this man from a very sophisticated electronic complex in Boston. We are certain he is not a decoy. It is proof to merely look at him!"

"Sideburns and a sequined jumpsuit do not an Elvis make, François. Was he singing *Love Me Tender* in the shower?"

"No." François paused, smug, like a poker player about to lay down a straight flush. "It was *Don't Be Cruel.*"

Phil sighed, resisting the urge to tap his foot to the beat of his headache. François wasn't gonna give in; Phil would have to deal with this, sooner or later. He picked later.

"Okay, but I'm busy for a while, you'll have to cool your heels." He summoned DiSenza from the shipping room; the mall manager's eyes widened at the site of the newcomers. "Don, take François and his royal guest someplace out of the way. François, I assume you can control your hostage?"

François flashed a Glock and nodded.

Wonderful. Sunday morning at the Mall and François was packing.

Don motioned François to follow into the back room. Buddy Holly began to tag along too, but Phil touched his plaid shoulder.

"You, what's your name?"

"Carl. I'm—"

"Car salesman, right?"

"Yeah, how'd you—"

"Stick around. I've got a job for you."

* * *

François pressed the pistol to the King's ribs and followed DiSenza into the subterranean maze. He was aware that Corporation research and development took place here, so he was not surprised to find other people in the complex so early on a Sunday morning. He assumed the early hours were intended to leave time for golf immediately afterwards—most had already donned the appropriate sportswear. Clearly DiSenza was in charge here, since they all stepped aside to let him pass. If they were shocked to see the King, or François, or the automatic weapon between them, they did not show it.

DiSenza reached a metal door and pulled it open before motioning them into the chamber beyond. Once the door closed behind them, he opened a second, thick inner door. A clamor of barking and the odor of fur and feces jolted François backward. The King recoiled, too.

The room was well-lit by overhead fluorescents, almost blinding François at first. As his eyes adjusted, he scanned the space. On the left was a wall of small cages, about half of them containing cats, and three with dogs who barely fit into their enclosures. The dogs, at least, were displeased with the situation, being the source of the manic barking. The cats ignored them.

The floor was a brick-colored conglomerate, like concrete but with a rubbery texture, sloping slightly down from the side walls to a drain grille along the center. Straddling the drain was a workbench with a white plastic table top and a lengthwise stainless-steel shelf. Stacks of Styrofoam trays, a roll of plastic wrap, a tape dispenser, and a label printer were neatly arranged on the shelf, and slotted inserts in the work surface held a selection of knives and cleavers. A power grinder, its square top funnel tellingly larger than the swivel chute at the bottom, dominated the far end of the table.

A bank of freezers lined the right wall. In the near corner, a clear tube ran from the ceiling to a plastic box with a sliding door, resembling a drive-up bank teller's pneumatic transaction system—but larger, as if for very bulky transactions.

François' throat began to tingle.

The King shouted over the dogs.

"This what I think it is?"

"We call it the meat room," DiSenza yelled back.

"Where d'ya get the critters?"

"Hey, it's not like they're filthy strays. They're clean—some of 'em even have pedigrees. But the pet shop can't sell old puppies and kittens. They're gonna get put down anyway, might as well recycle 'em at the food court." He pointed to the delivery chute disappearing into the ceiling. "It was all my idea. It's our way of going green."

François struggled to keep his stomach from erupting. The foul odor and frantic din metamorphosed into surreal symbols of vile American culture.

DiSenza was unaffected and, in fact, seemed cheerful.

"People always complain about fast food, but sometimes the meat is really fresh."

"Why did you bring us here?" François yelled. "We will become crazy, there is so much noise."

"But the noise is only in here," DiSenza shouted. "It's air-locked and totally soundproof. You can shoot this guy if you have to, and none of our shoppers will hear it. Plus, it's easy to clean up—" he pointed at the drain, and then at the freezer with a macabre grin "—and easy to dispose of the body."

François' first thought was to shoot this monster DiSenza, but he held his fire; better to avoid shooting anyone unless absolutely necessary, given the culinary consequences. As DiSenza made his exit, François motioned his captive to a stool and took one for himself nearby. He rested the gun on his knee, aimed at the old man's sternum. This was not his preferred location to hold a prisoner; the difference between it and the L'Escargot wine cellar was astronomical.

The King raised his voice.

"Pretty sad, ain't it? All these animals, I mean?"

"Do not play games with me, M'sieur. I am in no mood."

"I ain't playin' nothin' sir, not while you got that Glock pointin' my way. I just figure we're gonna be here awhile, might as well pass the time."

"You Americans disgust me. I cannot believe you would eat these common house pets."

"Well, we wouldn't—least, not knowin'ly. And it's your Corporation that's servin' 'em." He let François consider that for a second. "Hell, you oughta at least come up with a classy name for it, like, what's that French restaurant name for baby pigeons? Squab?"

François narrowed his eyes.

"Touché, M'sieur."

Chapter 21

Lynn wore a blank expression as Toine cruised past the Mall employee parking section; her own Civic was among the cars there. She felt instinctive relief that Tanya had arrived safely, but Phil and his microchips made the Mall far more treacherous than Route 128. They parked alongside the other big Lincoln, making Lynn wonder if some dealership somewhere supplied huge black cars to all the bad guys.

She took her time climbing out. Her head was still pounding, and the faceful of airbag didn't help.

"You are unsteady, Madame," Toine said with a smirk. "Perhaps you consumed too much of ze wine last night?"

"Actually, Toine, I think it was the cheap foie gras—you really should find a better grade of truffles. But I'll be fine."

"As long as you can march without help." Toine turned away from the car and spoke quietly. "Though the Legion ape is unaware of this, François instructed us to keep him alive. So Jean-Paul and I will both be busy guarding him. Lead the way, s'il vous plaît."

"Ah, but we should try to intercept François. Didn't he tell you where he was going?"

"Not precisely, Madame," Toine whispered. "He mentioned meeting M'sieur Grady at ze Teabury Center. We are unacquainted with zis location, and expected him to await us here in ze parking lot. But your little accident has made us late; how fortunate zat you can show us ze route without him."

"Right. Follow me."

Toine helped Jean-Paul pull Roger from the car, and they fell in behind Lynn. She headed for the atrium, keeping a sharp eye out. She didn't want to come upon either François or M'sieur Grady just yet, even if she had known where to find them. First, she had to deal with the goons.

Master Chuushin would say, *The journey is easier when you leave your baggage behind.*

* * *

With a pair of semi-automatics poking his kidneys, Roger had no choice but to be patient. Besides, it was Lynn who was on the spot. She'd proven herself pretty resourceful so far, but she'd need to come up with something else soon—she couldn't just wander the Mall all day. For now, she calmly led them through the atrium and into the main corridor beyond. She acted like she knew the way, occasionally stopping with a subtle hand signal to Jean-Paul and Toine, to avoid contact with elderly mall walkers.

At one stop, a blue glint from the floor caught Roger's eye. Without moving his head, he took a better look and recognized a blue sequin. He smiled inside at the thought of the King surreptitiously tearing off and dropping the surrogate breadcrumb. There was another a few yards ahead to the left; beyond that were several more, before the trail turned left down a narrow hall.

He couldn't very well mention the sequins to Lynn at the moment, so he remained mute as she signaled and the pistol barrels pushed him forward again. He glanced over at the hall as they passed, noting a few more sequins of the trail as it disappeared into the shadows.

But a janitor was sweeping the atrium with a large push-broom. Roger guessed he'd clean the side hall, too; as a mechanical engineer, he could quickly calculate how little time they had before the guy dumped the last of the King's trail into his rolling gray barrel.

* * *

Ed MacGregor leaned on the kiosk counter, popped another cinnamon Munchkin, and chased it with a slug of Dunkin Donuts regular. He didn't need those expensive fancy coffees; his blend was mostly cream and sugar anyway, and he had the waistline to prove it. He didn't need fancy donuts, either—it was an inside joke among the boys that mall cops should eat mini-donuts and leave the real donuts for real cops. But the smaller size didn't mean he ate less; after eighteen years on the job, his holster belt was under a lot of stress. And his only exercise was twice-a-week target practice at the range, which gave his .38 a much better workout than his abs.

It'd been a long special assignment. Every now and then the boys'd get something like this, watching over late-night deliveries or installations. Nobody ever told 'em what it was about, and they didn't care. All they needed to know was that it paid triple time: time-and-a-half for the overnight, and time-and-a-half, in cash, for not asking—or answering—questions. One long shift was enough to buy a year's worth of Munchkins.

The rest of the guys were trading stories about their night with the obnoxious nerds, but Ed was the envy of all, pulling duty to follow the only girl in the bunch. Unbelievable luck that she was such eye candy—she coulda been a fashion model if she wasn't so smart. Except for having to chase her off a laptop in E-Mart, the night had passed very pleasantly.

Ed was reaching for a napkin when he spotted the small group turning the corner from the food court wing—a redheaded woman with three guys, packed kinda tight together, right behind her. Nothing special, except the only people supposed to be in the Mall this early were shopkeepers and mall walkers. Shopkeepers were at their stores by now, and mall walkers were usually a lot older.

He set down his coffee and stepped away from the kiosk for a better look. The woman seemed to catch his eye—she had some kind of urgency in her face. The guy behind her looked strangely preoccupied, and the two behind him were nervous. He'd seen that look, dozens of times, on the "Shoplifters: Caught on Camera" training DVD. The huge bruise on the fat one's jaw and the equally huge bandage on the other guy's forehead didn't help their respectability.

"Guys. Heads up, north wing."

The other mall cops turned to check out the quartet, now at twenty yards range and closing. Suddenly the woman dove sideways to the floor.

"Help!" she yelled. "Terrorists! They have guns!"

The guy behind her followed her cue, diving to the other side. But he didn't put his hands out, taking the brunt of the fall on his chest and stomach. The reason was obvious: his hands were bound behind his back, in some kind of plastic. Ed quickly focused on the other two as they awkwardly tried to conceal their 9mm Glocks.

With a sound like polite applause for the acrobatic dives, five mall cops slapped their holsters and drew their service pistols. They fanned out instantly—the terrorists could take out one each, but they wouldn't get a second shot off before getting splattered across the You Are Here directory behind them. Ed stepped forward and waved his pistol.

"Hands up, fellas."

The two men glanced at each other, then back at the array of barrels pointed their way, and slowly raised their hands above their heads.

"Ze woman is lying; we are not terrorists!" pleaded the fat one in a thick French accent.

The woman on the floor yelled back.

"Yes they are! They took us hostage! They're armed, for God's sake!"

Ed's partner, Joey, circling behind them to confiscate the guns, nodded.

"And they're French, ain't they?"

The muscular one sputtered as he surrendered his weapon.

"What do you mean? What is wrong with being French?"

"It's un-American," said Lieutenant Sharkey, the shift captain, as he unclipped his handcuffs. He pulled the fat guy's arms down, stretched them behind the man's waist, and cuffed them together. Joey ignored the other guy's snarled threats and cuffed his arms back, too.

"Now," Sharkey went on, "you might have a good reason for comin' in here with them semi-automatics, but I kinda doubt it. We'll just bring you with us and run a few checks—if yer clean you'll have nothin' to worry about. Except maybe a weapons charge. Oh, and hostage taking." He smirked at the captives, then motioned to the other cops. They gathered around the pair and herded them toward the security office.

Ed holstered his .38 and approached the man on the floor. The guy seemed okay, probably thanks to the beer pad. The handcuffs looked like that same high-tech plastic they used to wrap up CDs, but Ed managed to hack through them with his pocketknife eventually. Then, as the woman helped him lift the man to his feet, he got a close-up assessment of her. The terrorists had put her through a hellish ordeal; her nose was bruised and her bloodshot eyes were ringed with dark purple circles.

"How about you come along with me, ma'am? We'll call an ambulance and get you some medical attention. Also, we'll need a statement."

She seemed confused, which was only natural.

"My daughter's here. I just want—I need to check on my daughter."

Ed could sympathize; in times of crisis, most people want to be with their loved ones. He had a daughter of his own, grown up now, but he knew the feeling. Maybe he'd give her a call today, in fact. The statement could wait.

"Okay, but after you see her, come on up to the security office. It's upstairs, at the back corner of the food court. And relax, the excitement's over. Everything's gonna be okay."

The woman looked relieved and thanked him warmly, then she dragged the young man by the arm toward the south wing.

* * *

Roger marveled at Lynn as she hurtled toward the Demografique store. Hijacking Jean-Paul and Toine's car took guts—she'd obviously suffered a concussion in the accident. But the terrorist ploy was sheer genius, made all the more believable by her injuries. And she was playing the frantic-mom-looking-for-her-daughter bit perfectly.

Of course, with the mall cops out of sight, the charade was a waste of time. But no need to stop her; the King's trail led directly beneath the security office, so they couldn't double back to follow it until the cops got Jean-Paul and Toine upstairs. They'd have to wait and hope the sequins weren't gone by then.

"Nicely done, Wonder Woman. That was absolutely brilliant!"

She glared over her shoulder.

"It would've been a lot easier without the worst hangover of my life!"

Crap. That wasn't a concussion.

"We shoulda warned you, sorry."

"Yes, you shoulda."

"In our defense, we did say it didn't cure hangovers."

Lynn turned to deliver another stern look. This time, her eyes were wet.

"Lynn, I'm sorry. I shouldn't joke."

"It's not that, Roger. It's just, if I hadn't been hung over, I wouldn't have slept so late, and I might have stopped Tanya from coming here for a microchip."

"What? She's here?"

"I told her she couldn't come. I even hid the keys. But she found them somehow, and took the car. I saw it in the lot on the way in."

Lynn picked up speed, and Roger kept pace, kicking himself for missing the signs. He'd been so busy promoting her from pawn to superheroine he didn't notice she was just a worried mom trying to save her baby.

Her baby, and all the other girls lined up behind her to become "just like the hooker."

* * *

Lynn peered through the security grille at Demografique. Inside, a middle-aged woman shuffled hangered shirts around a circular rack. No Tanya.

Lynn wiped her eyes with the back of her hand.

"Excuse me!" she called through the grating.

"We're not open yet, ma'am," the woman called back. "Come back in fifteen minutes."

"I was looking for my daughter. Tanya Grady. Is this where she works?"

The woman paused, surprised by the question, studying Lynn. She must have seen the resemblance, but was wary anyway.

"Yes, she's in training. But she's not here yet."

"Wasn't she due by now?"

"Uh, yes. But there's a special Mall program going on today; the girls all get time off to sign up. She's probably there."

Lynn's heart sank. She pressed her face to the grille.

"Where is the program?"

"To be honest, I don't know. I'm just a shop manager; that's a Mall thing. Look, I've got to get ready here, and I'm running late, especially with no help from your daughter. So just come back in a little while, okay? They said it wouldn't take long; she'll be here soon."

Lynn turned to Roger.

"And if she isn't, I suppose we can always track her down by the chip—in her—neck..." She fought back the tears again. Roger was slowly shaking his head.

"Maybe she's not even in the Mall. Last night I overheard Phil say he'd be injecting microchips at some 'Teabury Center,' so I looked at Mall maps for an hour, but I couldn't find it."

That name rattled around under the pounding of Lynn's headache. Where had she heard it before?

Toine!

"The Teabury Center!" she practically shouted. "Toine said that's where François took the King. So she's got to be here somewhere."

Roger's eyes lit up.

"Really? We can find them both, then!"

"But it wasn't on your maps. And it's not on the Mall directory sign—I checked."

"Nope. But we don't need that. The King left a trail—I saw it in the corridor when we came in. Blue sequins, from his jumpsuit."

"He's wearing a sequined jumpsuit..."

"Hey, the King likes his jumpsuits—says they're comfortable. Or maybe he thought ahead. Either way, those sequins will lead us to the Teabury Center—but we hafta hurry, there's a janitor sweeping up the hall back there and pretty soon they'll be gone."

"So let's hurry," Lynn said.

They raced off to follow the King's trail, hugging the storefront windows of the food court wing, out of sight of any mall cops upstairs. Roger took the side hall corner at full speed, where his stomach absorbed a few inches of the janitor's broom handle before propelling it out of the man's hands. The liberated tool plowed several yards ahead, dispersing a pile of dust, straw wrappers, and blue sequins.

"Sorry, buddy—didn't see you there." Roger said. He looked at his watch. "You better finish this up and get out of here. It's almost opening time."

The janitor sputtered curses as he retrieved the broom. Lynn and Roger followed the remaining sequins, one every ten steps, deeper down the hall. The sequins led right, then stopped, at a door marked Teabury—Authorized Personnel Only.

That would be the place, Lynn concluded.

It would have seemed too easy, except that guarding the door was a huge man in a taut suit, with thick, crossed arms riding so high on his massive chest that his biceps were horizontal. He looked like he was expecting someone—probably teenage girls, and certainly not Lynn and Roger. Roger gave the beast an embarrassed grin that said "we're lost" and retreated.

"Well," he whispered, "we found the Teabury Center. That's clearly where they took the King, and I bet that guy has already welcomed Tanya. But we need another entrance—one that's not all plugged up with muscle."

"And how do we find that?" Lynn asked, losing hope. "We can't expect the King to leave two trails."

Roger was staring across the hall intersection; Lynn followed his gaze to a "Facilities Engineering Office" sign. Roger smiled and took Lynn back around the corner, where the janitor immediately clutched the broom to protect his new pile. They nodded politely and squeezed through his sullen stare.

"What now?" Lynn asked.

"The stores are about to open," Roger replied. "We're going shopping."

Chapter 22

Phil Grady set Carl up at a makeshift registration table in the cafeteria, figuring the man's experience with car sales contracts was perfect for getting the girls' paperwork in order—especially the permission forms. Carl was curious about the operation, so Phil gave him the official version, describing the RFID microchips and the discount program. Carl was shocked.

"You're shitting me," he said. "You're gonna give those girls a discount without raising list price first? That's crazy!"

Phil smiled.

"Just wait—pretty soon you'll agree this program is the best thing that ever happened to the Corporation."

* * *

Eightball plugged the last of the network cables into DiSenza's database server and powered up the test gear. The morning had been constant interruptions; mostly DiSenza checking up on him, but also weird stuff, like overhearing Phil's argument with a French guy about an Elvis impersonator. There was also something about truffles and a high-tech complex. None of it made sense, but it sure put Phil on edge—he'd started badgering Eightball to finish sooner. That meant rushing the tests, which, Eightball knew from hard experience, was usually a bad idea.

He fired up the field meter and verified measurements against the installation guide. This setup was different than the stores; it had a bigger antenna and a much bigger power supply. The signal was different, too—stronger, and a stream of pulses at 7 cycles per second on a 200 megahertz carrier.

All night in the stores he'd been wondering how the tiny

subdermal chips could utilize such high power and bandwidth. Now he was even more confused—this was just a registration center, for testing and reading the chips. It should use the same gear as the stores.

All these technical questions were colored by the growing conviction that Phil Grady and Don DiSenza were not playing it straight. Taping Meg and her uncle into a computer room sure wasn't good Christian behavior. He didn't try to guess where Elvis and the French guy ended up.

And, to piss him off even more, his stomach was growling; he hadn't had a bite since last night, and Phil had made him skip the bacon and eggs.

* * *

Ed MacGregor studied the terrorists. Only he and Lt. Sharkey remained to guard them and wait for the hostages; the other guys were too tired, even at triple time, to stick around. At triple time, Ed figured he could stay awake for weeks. But just in case they got sloppy, they'd recuffed the terrorists to a support pole. Nobody'd be taking advantage of a fatigue-induced slipup.

He offered the Frenchmen some donuts, real ones, not just Munchkins. The fat one was interested, but the other guy snarled at him and he backed off. They asked if there were any croissants available; Sharkey grabbed his crotch.

"I got yer croy-sants right here."

Sharkey was such a crack-up.

But they had a problem. Twenty minutes had passed, and the former hostages hadn't shown up. Sharkey did a quick reconnoiter but came up empty.

"No sign of 'em, Ed," he whispered. "What d'ya think we should do?"

The procedure book didn't cover this; your standard terrorists would've planted a bomb or waited for a peak crowd period to shoot the place up. So he and the Lieutenant hadn't sounded the general alarm yet, figuring the hostages would fill in the details. Of course, the terrorists denied everything and explained nothing.

"Can we hold 'em a little longer, Lieutenant? Without hostage statements? Or bodies?"

"Well, they *were* armed, Ed."

"Yup."

"And they *are* French."

"Yeah, that too."

"Shit, they wouldn't even eat free donuts."

"Right."

"That oughta be enough, don't ya think?"

"Works for me."

At least for a while. But the situation wasn't as simple as it first seemed. And whatever it was, Ed was deeply involved. He was gonna be a hero or a fuck-up—it could go either way.

* * *

Toine leaned toward Jean-Paul while keeping an eye on the mall policemen.

"Zey are waiting for Lynn and Roger," he whispered. "Zis is America. Zey cannot hold us without witnesses."

"Except for the guns. And you know that the 'witnesses' will not come here. We have been hoodblinked by the redheaded monster."

"Not exactly. We have only followed ze orders of our manager, François. He has been hoodwinked by ze monster."

"But we are held here, and he is not. We should explanation ourselves to these guards."

Toine had already given this some thought.

"I disagree. I believe zey are merely Mall employees, unaware of ze hidden events around zem. If zey are, in fact, outsiders, we must be careful—despite our situation, it will be worse for us if we compromise ze Corporation. We must contact M'sieur Grady."

This was a problem. The guards had confiscated their phones and certainly would not let them communicate. The stupid Americans actually thought they had terrorists in their midst. There was no choice but to secure their cooperation.

Toine cleared his throat.

"Messieurs, I believe I can clarify zis matter. We are here on important business for our organization—"

"What organization would that be? Al-Qaeda? ISIS? L'Academie Francais?"

"We are working with M'sieur Phil Grady—surely you know of him?"

The guards showed blank faces.

"If you are unaware of ze organization, it is probably best zat you remain so. But I am certain zat your superiors are aware. If you would just call your manager, and tell him zat you have two associates of M'sieur François Spaquel, with urgent news for M'sieur Phil Grady, zey will understand ze situation and resolve it immediately."

They appeared to consider it. He pressed further.

"I assure you zat you will be appropriately rewarded for your assistance."

The fat guard said something under his breath to the Lieutenant, who shrugged and picked up the phone.

Toine could not hear the conversation, but gauging by the simultaneous visual examination, he guessed that he and Jean-Paul were being carefully described to the manager. The guards would clearly remember them enough to identify them later. Toine was new to the Corporation, but already understood that identification by outsiders was strongly discouraged.

He was uncertain what form of compensation the guards would receive for their handling of the "terrorists," but he suspected it would surprise them, and it would not involve money.

* * *

Don DiSenza had just returned to the cafeteria when Lieutenant Sharkey called. The mall cop reported two French, armed, suspected terrorists in custody, who claimed they were working for François and Phil. Don sighed—this wasn't getting any tidier. He made sure the two men had been disarmed, and promised to come up and talk.

"Phil, I've got to go upstairs to the security office. Seems like our mall cops caught a couple of Corporation guys wandering around the Mall, armed."

Phil whirled to face him.

"Armed?! For the love of Christ what the fuck do these people think they're doing? This is a critical operation, with major PR risk, and these assholes are waving pieces around the fucking Mall on a Sunday morning! Doesn't anyone get it? Who the hell do they work for?!"

"They said François—"

Phil's eyes became lasers.

"Of course," he said through a clenched smile. "Look, do you think you could get these shitheads out of my hair, and get this shooting range under control for a couple of hours?"

Don nodded dutifully. He had captured people everywhere; what the fuck more did Phil want?

* * *

Eightball couldn't hold back any longer and stepped through the open cafeteria door. Phil swallowed his next sentence.

"Fuck," he said instead.

"Good to see you too, Axe-man."

"You all done in there?"

"Yeah, except for the questions."

"What?"

"Something evil's goin' on here, Axe-man. People with guns, people tied up with packing tape, hush-hush equipment installations, and RFID transmitters that could cook a hot dog."

"I don't know anything about packing tape."

"Well I just wanna know what I'm involved in."

A cold aura radiated from the former frontman, centered on his steely eyes.

"Eightball, you're an old friend, my favorite roadie of all time. But at the moment, that's all you are, buddy, a roadie. You're getting paid to load in the gear and make it work; nobody's asking you to play any riffs. You are not involved. Am I clear on that?"

Eightball locked eyes with him. Being a good roadie meant two things: understanding the equipment, and sharing the musician's appreciation for the sound that came out of it. Phil wasn't a roadie's musician any more—the gear, and his vision for it, were mysteries he wasn't gonna explain. Eightball had a feeling he was better off not knowing.

"I have one more question."

"What."

"When do I get breakfast? You used to feed the crew, at least."

There was a twitch of a smile.

"Don, bring Eightball up to the food court on your way to security, and buy him some breakfast. He does good work."

Eightball followed DiSenza upstairs, waiting while the mall manager stooped to pick up a few blue sequins from the stair. They hurried out through the Mall hallway, almost colliding with a big guy carrying a shopping bag. There was a red-haired woman with him who apologized for his clumsiness. DiSenza mumbled "no problem" and continued out to the main corridor.

Eightball looked back. The woman seemed familiar, but he couldn't place her. And it might have been his imagination, but he thought she was checking him out, too.

Chapter 23

Outside the facilities office, Roger got himself into character as Lynn mumbled something about trying to place a face. He opened the door and peeked timidly inside, finding a middle-aged man drinking coffee and staring at a computer monitor. The photo frames that adorned the desk were half buried in papers. The man looked up in mid-sip.

"Can I help you?"

Roger smiled and strolled into the office, carrying his recent purchases in a Giftstone bag, which the guy eyed with suspicion. Roger flashed his MIT ring.

"Hi, my name is Roger Landowski—I'm a civil engineering grad student at MIT. I'm doing a research project on mall architecture. May I speak with the engineer-on-duty?"

"That's me. Who's your friend?"

"I'm not his friend," Lynn said sternly. "I'm his aunt. I drove him here—he can't afford a car yet." The engineer gave her a once-over, considering it.

"I don't know why you'd want to study this dump. It's forty years old already."

"My thesis advisor says the Lexingham Mall was a trend-setting fusion of architecture and control systems—way ahead of its time. My research would really benefit from a glimpse at how it all works."

The man shook his head.

"Look, I can't just drop everything and give you a tour, buddy. You'll have to—"

"Oh, I don't need a tour. If I could take a quick glance at the drawings, I'm sure I could get what I need without bothering you."

"I don't think so, son. I'd have to check with my boss and he won't be in till tomorrow."

"Sir," Lynn cut in, "I have to work tomorrow. This was the only day I could give Roger a ride."

"That's not my problem, lady."

Roger stepped forward.

"I can make it worth your while. If you'll let me look at the building plans now, I'll give you this nice barometer."

Roger dramatically lifted the expensive instrument from the Giftstone bag, and dangled it before the engineer. The man was clearly interested, eyes lighting up as he examined the polished mahogany trim and shiny brass fittings. He glanced around furtively, and nodded.

"I guess it's all right." He shuffled a layer of restaurant menus and business cards in his desk drawer, and withdrew a CD. "You can take this over to that PC there, and look at it all you like. Just stay off the Internet, okay? I don't want to get into trouble."

"Don't worry, sir, I'm only interested in the architecture."

As Roger exchanged the barometer for the disc, he nodded at a framed photo on the desk.

"Nice Irish Setter. We used to have one, named Ginger. What's his name?"

"He's a she. Sylvia."

"Great dogs, huh?"

"Yeah, they are."

Roger found the computer in the corner, loaded the CD and opened the first schematic. Lynn whispered in his ear.

"How did you know that would work?"

"There's a standard problem on the MIT Entrepreneurial Physics exam: how to find the height of a building using a barometer. It's a trick question; most engineers come up with typical technical answers: measure the air pressure at the top and bottom and calculate the difference, of course, but also line it up with the building's shadow and triangulate, or even drop the barometer from the top and time the fall with a stopwatch. But the correct answer is to go to the facilities engineer and trade him the barometer for the height of the building. The idea is to get the information you need and establish a business relationship at the same time."

Of course, the building plans were only part of the information he needed—now he had to find another route to the Teabury Center. He scanned through a series of maps showing floor plans, plumbing, electrical conduits, and heating/ventilation/air-conditioning ductwork for both the upper and lower public shopping levels. The wiring channels were extensive; there were data networks and security cameras and other devices—probably including voice projectors—pretty much everywhere in the building, even the restrooms. Many of the connections led to the basement at some point, but when he clicked on that level, a dialog box appeared reading "Authentication required—enter password."

A quick glance confirmed that, for the moment, the facilities engineer was more interested in his coffee and computer than in the grad student and his aunt. Roger smiled at Lynn and typed "Sylvia."

A very different-looking diagram appeared. It had the same general outline as the main building, but this was a maze of narrow halls with hundreds of rooms. Roger pointed out the Teabury Center entrance at the top of a stairway leading down to a cafeteria. He figured the caf was the likely place to do the microchip injections, being closest to the door—the Corporation wouldn't want outsiders to see any more of the hidden complex than necessary. He noted a similar entrance at the other end of the food court wing.

At the top of both stairways was an airlock door system with an electronic keypad on the inner door. Next to that was a set of symbols:

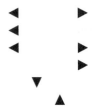

As a mechanical engineer, he had no clue what they stood for—they weren't standard electronic or mechanical parts.

"Any ideas?" he asked.

Lynn shrugged.

"All those symbols are Greek to me."

Roger memorized the room and HVAC ductwork layout, scribbling furiously in his new notebook, though his notes had nothing to do with the information on the screen.

"Just a decoy," he explained. "What student would do this without taking notes?"

"Exactly," said Lynn. "How are you going to remember everything? We'll need that map."

Roger drew back in mock indignation.

"Lynn, the Trail Boys taught me how to read every kind of map known to man. MIT taught me how to memorize 'em." He rubbed his chin thoughtfully. "I just wish it had a little red 'Tanya is here' arrow."

* * *

With twenty minutes to kill between the early breakfast and her Mall shift, Tanya had gone to the nearby Java Jag and plopped onto a couch with a café mocha. She needed to figure out who to trust. And what to do about the microchip. Those were tough questions, and the twenty minutes had stretched into forty. Now she was seriously late for work—if she still had, or wanted, the job.

It was weird how the 'rents were both so intense about it—as if the fate of the world was at stake.

Mom was picky and quirky, but she stuck with Tanya through everything and usually gave her all the responsibility she could handle. But Daddy sure nailed the trendy culture and popularity thing; the Gradys weren't exactly the center of social life in conservative Catholic North Cambridge. Life was boring. She wouldn't even have a boyfriend if it weren't for Michael, from the only other new-age family in town. Out of a thousand kids at school, nobody else wanted to join them at the Actual Musicians concert.

AND THEY"RE PROBABLY BROKE, JUST LIKE I WAS WHEN YOU WERE LITTLE.

Yeah, Daddy, they're broke, and so am I, and Mom, and Michael. But is that so bad? You were a rebel once, too—you didn't care about money!

Tanya had listened to some old Severed Clown Heads CDs at home, and the lyrics weren't just non-pop, they seriously dissed everything about pop. She could understand why he and Mom got together. But when he joined his new company, all that ended. He must've been pretty ashamed of his music; once, she tried to find it on the web but couldn't. It was all gone, like it never even happened.

She sipped, letting the triple espresso shots work their magic. Daddy was definitely rich, while Mom slaved the day shift at a warehouse. On the other hand, Daddy had substance abuse issues—he was pretty hung over at breakfast. Drugs and alcohol were almost as popular as Mall jewelry; did he think addictions were good for business, too?

On the other, other hand, here she was, doing a venti mocha, no fat, no whipped. It was just caffeine, not alcohol, but it was trendy and expensive and marketed just like fancy wines—posters around the shop hyped the pedigree of the beans and nuances of the roast. And Tanya had bought it with money she earned at the Mall—selling trendy and expensive clothes to the barista who served it.

It's just not that simple.

She glanced at her watch—it was time to decide.

OKAY, BUT DON'T TAKE FOREVER. REMEMBER, IT'S A REALLY GOOD DEAL. I MADE SURE, JUST FOR YOU.

Tanya dropped her eyes to the handmade moon-and-stars pendant hanging around her neck. Unfashionable. Nonregulation, even prohibited while working in a Mall store. And yet she loved it—it was beautiful, and made her think of her own unlimited artistic potential.

Potential she wouldn't fulfill if she couldn't afford art school.

She pulled the pendant over her head, unclipped the earrings, and stuffed them all into her purse. Then she hooked on the officially-sanctioned Demografique earrings and marched across the street into the teeth of what Daddy's lyrics called the pop culture grinder.

* * *

Fiona had started out following Phil to the Peppers restaurant, but she changed her plans when his daughter arrived for breakfast. It would be far better to keep an eye on Tanya—she was the key to the test. Phil thought that the experiment was all about the electronics, which was why he considered the permission forms unnecessary management meddling. But Phil didn't get it.

This wasn't about shopping, or even the stores; it was about making the receiver chips popular, just like the Corporation had already done with WiFi itself. The chips had to be universally accepted, especially by new age opponents of technology and pop culture.

Tanya was the perfect test subject—her resistance was obvious. Fiona had watched her from a back table in Java Jag, and she seemed to be thinking deeply about it. But it looked like her rebellious nature was going to win—she was in no hurry to go back to work, or, apparently, to get a chip.

But then Tanya glanced around the coffee shop and at her watch, then stared at her handmade pendant. Fiona held her breath for a moment, until the teen removed all her jewelry, replaced it with standard issue, and headed for the Mall.

Fiona discreetly followed.

There was hope for the program after all.

* * *

Phil Grady loaded the injector gun with the coil of microchips. The state-of-the-art mechanism didn't need to be sterilized between uses: each hermetically-sealed chip packet had a disposable injector needle built in. Pulling the trigger would expose the needle, inject the chip, retract the used needle into its own protective sharps sleeve, and advance the next packet into the chamber.

He set the gun on the table behind the "registration" chair, completely out of sight for anyone sitting there. The microchips were only the size of a rice grain, but the size of the gun would freak out the girls. Even Carl's eyes got big when he saw it.

"Damn! You're gonna shoot 'em in the neck with *that*? Doesn't it hurt?"

"To be honest, it hurts like the dickens. Ever get a splinter the size of a grain of rice?" Phil smiled; Carl was now positively spooked. "But they won't notice it. This room is specially wired; using a signal from this antenna, the chip emits an electronic anesthetic—it numbs the nerves almost as soon as they start to react. Then it pulses a certain brain-wave frequency that wipes out a few seconds of short-term memory. So, they don't remember how much it hurt and walk away thinking it was completely painless."

"That thing can wipe out memory?"

"Yeah, that's why we put it in their neck."

"Jeez. You sure it's safe?"

"Absolutely. I'm gonna plant one in my own daughter, for chrissake. How much safer does it have to be?"

Carl still looked unconvinced. Maybe he had a daughter of his own.

"Okay," the car salesman said, "maybe it's designed safe—what if it's installed wrong? Your mechanic said he didn't understand it."

The man had a point. If Eightball didn't understand it, he might have screwed it up—and if he did understand it, he might have screwed it up on purpose, on moral principle. Phil sure didn't want to give away forty percent discounts if the chips weren't working right. As the old saying went: don't buy 'em dinner if they won't put out.

A test was in order. But the deal was, Tanya would get a chip before the other girls—and he intended to play by the rules. Technically…

They'd have to test it on a *guy*. He decided to let Carl do it.

"Carl, I'd say you're just the skeptic to help me prove this all works as designed. The girls in this program are natural shoppers; it'll be hard to measure how much the discount affects 'em. So let's test it on someone else. How about you and I go upstairs, pick the most sales-resistant-looking guy we can find, and try it on him? A good salesman like you oughta be able to spot the right person."

"I'm not a good salesman, I'm a great salesman. But I'm not a magician. Teenage girls are easy—how are we gonna persuade this 'sales-resistant' test customer to come down here and let us stick a chip in his neck?"

Phil was way ahead of him.

"We're gonna to tell him he's our 500-millionth visitor, and he gets a gift card and a discount card. Then you take his picture for publicity, sitting in this chair"—he twitched his eyebrows for effect—"with me, the Mall President, posing behind him. When the flash goes off, the chip goes in. He won't even know it happened."

Carl rubbed his chin.

"Then we'll hafta take another picture."

Phil laughed. He liked this guy.

"Yeah, and delete the one that shows the injector gun at his neck."

Carl chewed on this for a few moments, then looked up as if he now had the story straight in his head.

"Okay, let's go find us a 500-millionth visitor. We'll need balloons."

* * *

"Thanks again," Lynn said to the engineer as she and Roger hurried out of the facilities office. Roger had suggested that the alternate entrance to the basement was their best bet, assuming there was no alternate sentry guarding it. Unfortunately, it was the long way around. She hoped the basement would be empty on Sunday morning so they could cover the distance back to the cafeteria quickly.

As Roger led her around the corner, he suddenly spun, pulled back her hair, pressed her against the wall, and planted his face onto hers. She was way too surprised to stop him at first, and the footsteps behind him suggested his reason for doing it. In any case, she found herself kissing him back.

Go with the flow, said Zen-mind superfluously as she melted against his lips and body.

Someone snarled, "Get a room!"

The rhythm of wingtips echoed away, and Roger backed off to give her some air. He looked sheepish. But only a little.

"You know," she said, smiling, "When they say 'It's like kissing your aunt,' that's not the kind of kiss they mean. I suppose that was somebody we didn't want to meet?"

"Phil," Roger said. "And the guy who helped François capture the King."

"You said Phil was going to inject Tanya first—personally."

"Yup. In the Teabury Center, which he just left."

"So what does that mean?"

"That means we have a little time before Tanya, or anyone else, gets a chip."

"Or it's already too late."

Master Chuushin would scold her for that. *It is always too early to worry about the future, and too late to fret about the past.* And focusing on finding Tanya would keep Lynn from thinking about either. For the third time in an hour, she and Roger raced through the Mall corridors.

The alternate basement entrance was unguarded and, to their amazement, unlocked. At least the outer door was—the inner door was not only locked, but it had no key mechanism at all. Roger stared at the ceiling, his brow furrowed.

"I expected a keypad—that diagram in the schematic looks like a button sequence. He shook his head, and then dropped his gaze to his feet. A smile stretched across his face.

A few seconds later, Lynn was smiling too. Roger was tapping out the door combination as a dance pattern on the tiled floor.

A great kisser, and he can dance, too.

A four-button video dance game keypad was built into the floor tiles; all this system needed was a catchy tune. Lynn wondered if the lock mechanism had inspired Dance Dance Revolution, or if the game was designed to train future Corporation agents how to open secret doors.

Roger's footwork was rewarded with a buzz and a sliding latch bolt. At the bottom of the stairs beyond the door, they found soda and snack vending machines, and puzzled briefly over a rack full of golf scorecards, until voices drifted from down the hall. Roger yanked Lynn behind a candy machine; the voices approached but stopped at the scorecard rack.

"Okay, Rick, what're we gonna play today? Stow? Or Butter Brook?"

"Let's do Butter Brook—I played Stow last month and I sucked."

The other man chuckled.

"Completely your fault. Okay, today I'm gonna take an… 85. I just triple-bogeyed number 17."

"You sandbagger! In that case, I'll take an 86."

The two men laughed and trudged up the stairs.

Lynn had no chance to ask what "sandbagger" meant before Roger hustled her down the corridor. At the next intersection, they heard more voices.

"This is busier than I expected," Roger whispered. "Time to take the back road."

Lynn had no chance to ask what "back road" meant, either, before she found herself in a room full of pumps and blowers, with huge ducts snaking up through the walls and ceilings. Just like the MIT entrance to the truffle lab; Lynn figured Roger felt right at home.

He quickly proved that by removing a panel from the largest air duct and climbing inside.

"Wait there. You'll be safe—nobody's gonna work on the air handlers today. Or if you want, go back out to the Mall once the coast is clear. I'll meet you at Demografique when I get back."

"I'm not waiting. I'm coming with you."

He glanced into the darkness.

"Lynn, these ducts aren't very big, and they get smaller as we cross the Mall. And there aren't any LEDs along the ceiling—it's dark."

She allowed her eyes to follow the rectangular metal tube as it disappeared into the wall. It had that ominous gym-locker paint color, and now seemed a lot smaller than a few moments ago. Her throat went dry.

"If it's big enough for you, it's big enough for me."

She took an unsteady cleansing breath and climbed in behind him.

* * *

Don DiSenza left Eightball in the food court with a tray of Hello Chicken entrees and proceeded to the security office. Sharkey and MacGregor wearily introduced him to the two "terrorists"; these guys had to be with Spaquel as they claimed—no outsider would know to drop Phil Grady's name. But Phil's outburst made it pretty clear that Jean-Paul and Toine weren't welcome below mall deck—at least, not until his project launch was over. That wouldn't be till midafternoon.

"You're gonna have to wait here for a while, gentlemen. I assure you, François and his, ahm, guest, are not as comfortable where they are." He glanced around at the coffee cups and donut boxes on the desk. "At least you've got coffee and donuts. The best they can do is raw eggrolls."

As Don smiled at his private joke, Toine motioned him closer.

"Zat is all fine, M'sieur DiSenza," he whispered, "but what about our 'hostages,' whom zese guards have set free? François told us zat ze woman was on our side—but he was fooled, and zus, so were we. Now zere are two Legionnaires loose in ze Mall, M'sieur, who know zat François and his guest are here. Zis is a threat to you, no?"

Don stopped smiling.

"What do these former hostages look like?"

As Toine described them, the collision in the hallway flashed back to him. The people he'd bumped were definitely the Legionnaires. And if they'd seen the sequin trail he found, they would definitely try to get below deck.

He called the surveillance room and described the pair, with hopes that Charles could spot them in the public Mall. But there were no electronic eyes on the hidden part; he'd have to search that himself. He asked Lt. Sharkey for a look at the confiscated weapons, and Sharkey showed him two Glock 9mm semi-automatics—serious firepower. Don hefted one and examined the ten-shot magazine. It was full.

"I need to borrow this," he said, tucking it into the back of his belt.

Sharkey's eyes widened.

"You know how to use that?"

"Yes," DiSenza said, and headed for the basement.

Chapter 24

His nerves shredded by the incessant barking, François granted the King's request to approach the meat room dogs. Soft words from the aging country boy soothed the frenzied animals, and eventually he was petting the paws they had extended through the cage mesh. The King returned to his seat and merely watched the dogs watch the humans, letting the peace prevail. But François found the quiet discomforting, as if he now faced a new alliance.

"It is good that you have persuaded them to stop barking."

"Yep. Now that they know we're gonna stick around, they're willin' to just sit with us. Like any dog, all they want is company."

François eyed the butcher table and the stainless-steel grinder gleaming in contradiction.

"I suspect that these particular animals are relieved that we are not wielding those cleavers. They have surely witnessed the fate of others before them. I would guess that they merely wish to live."

"Yer probably right. Guess they don't realize there's more important things. We're all gonna die sooner or later." He returned his gaze to François. "Maybe me sooner than others."

"You seem unworried about this."

"I'm not afraid to meet my maker."

"You are a religious man?"

"I don't know if I'd say I'm religious, but God's seen fit to bless me in a lot of ways, teachin' me to sing and play guitar and all that. I figure it's only fair to try and do some good before I go. And if I don't finish, I have faith that somebody else'll pick up where I left off. You fellas might kill me, but there's a lot more where I come from."

"There are many Legionnaires, but only one King."

"Fact is, there's a lot more Kings, too. You actually think you got the real thing here?"

"Are you saying I do not?"

"Not exactly. I'm just saying it don't matter much—there's a lotta impersonators and we all act the same."

"And you are unwilling even to say whether the real Elvis is dead, or not. Correct?"

"Correct."

François searched the King's eyes for a clue, and found none. But they were the crystal-clear eyes of a man who could be trusted. He would not answer certain questions, but when he did answer, he would not lie. And he knew the answers to many mysteries— one, perhaps, of particular interest to François.

"Can you tell me about M'sieur Jim Morrison? His death in Paris has been questioned for many years. Is *he* actually dead?"

The King's face clouded.

"'Fraid so. What we haven't figured out is who killed 'im."

* * *

Gerry Rutland wrestled his card through the slot and pressed the credit button. He'd panicked as the fare from Alewife quickly surpassed his cash supply, but then he relaxed when he saw the cab's Visa card machine. He only kept his card for emergencies, and, up till now, he'd never needed it. To entice him to use it, Visa kept raising his credit limit until it was much higher than he could ever pay off; he'd worried about it getting stolen and almost cancelled it. Now he was glad he hadn't.

He stepped out from the departing cab's exhaust cloud and took in the expansive façade of the Lexingham Mall. He'd never been in one of these things—how was he going to find Lynn here?

* * *

Phil stood behind Carl, a half-dozen Mylar "congratulations" balloons floating above their heads, and perused the trickle of early Sunday shoppers. Carl was being picky, looking for someone who didn't look like a spender, and Phil was losing patience. He had to get this started soon—any victim would do.

Carl nodded toward the entrance, grinning. He had his guinea pig.

Drifting into the southwest wing was a regular Rip Van Winkle, complete with pony tail, facial hair, and dazed expression as he gawked at the window displays. His clothes, mostly denim, weren't just out of date but a good forty years out of date. If he *had* been sleeping all that time, it was probably from the drugs he did at Woodstock.

Phil was looking forward to watching Carl handle him. The plaid-clad salesman towed the balloons out to intercept.

* * *

Gerry couldn't believe the size of the place—somehow it seemed like an indoor mall would have to be smaller. He was overwhelmed by the soaring glass and chrome, natural light pouring in from skylights high above him, and live shrubbery in brick planters to make the whole thing seem like outdoors. How could they afford this?

He was looking for Tanya's store, hoping Lynn was there, but he realized it would take hours to search the whole building. He'd just decided to ask someone for directions when a man in a plaid clown jacket approached, carrying a bunch of shiny helium balloons.

Gerry was impressed by the customer service. He didn't even have to ask, and they saw he needed help. Maybe malls weren't so bad after all.

"Excuse me sir, may I offer my congratulations? You are the Lexingham Mall's 500-millionth visitor!" The clown offered his hand, and Gerry hesitantly shook it. He wasn't sure what this meant.

"Thank you, but I'm not here to buy anything. I'm just trying to find someone."

This rejection didn't deter the clown; in fact, he seemed pleased to hear it.

"That's quite all right, sir, you'll notice I said visitor, not customer. And we'd like to give you a nice gift, and take your picture with our Mall President for publicity purposes."

Another man, dressed normally, stepped up and offered his hand. Gerry shook it, too, now wondering how to get out of this.

"I just wanted to meet a friend here; surely you could choose somebody else?"

"Nonsense, sir, we use a very scientific method to calculate visitors, and we've been counting all morning. Nope, you are definitely number 500 million, exactly. It would be a terrible shame if you didn't accept our gift—it's a once-in-a-lifetime opportunity, and we've been looking forward to it since number 400 million, six whole years ago. And 500 million is a much bigger deal! Halfway to the billion mark!"

Gerry sighed. 500 million *was* a big number; he'd never get one million customers in his store, even if he stayed open for thirty years. Besides, the clown was very enthusiastic and didn't look like he'd take no for an answer.

"What do I have to do?"

The two men exchanged happy glances and took him by the arms.

"Just come with us to the Mall offices for a few minutes. We'll get your name and have you sign our publicity release. Then we'll take your picture and give you your special gift."

* * *

Phil guided the old hippie to the registration chair. The wall behind it was cleared enough to let it pass for a photo backdrop, and Carl waited in front, armed with a brand-new digital camera. They'd printed up a publicity release and made a big deal of getting the dupe's name and address, all of which they'd feed to the shredder the moment the experiment was done. But—Phil glanced at the name on the sheet—Gerry Rutland wouldn't know that.

They presented Mr. Rutland with a fake preferred-customer 40% discount card and told him it was "magic"—it would work without him taking it out of his wallet. They also gave him a today-only fifty-dollar gift card to get him started. He didn't seem to care, insisting that he just wanted to leave without a fuss.

Carl stood back and set up the publicity shot, telling Phil how to stand, just behind Gerry. Phil reminded Gerry to keep his eyes on Carl and quietly picked up the loaded injector gun.

He placed his left hand on Gerry's left shoulder and held the gun in his right, just behind the man's neck. The long hair could have been a problem, but the pony tail solved it, clearly exposing the scalp behind the ear. Phil pictured a little bullseye just inside the hairline.

"Smile!" said Carl, and as the camera flashed, Phil pressed the gun to Gerry's neck and pulled the trigger.

"Ow! What the heck was… was…"

Carl brought the camera down.

"What the heck was what, Mr. Rutland?"

The old man peered at Carl, then shook his head as if to clear it.

"I don't know—what was I saying? What's going on?"

Carl peered impatiently from behind the camera.

"We were just about to take your picture, Mr. Rutland, for the publicity?"

"Right. Well, go ahead, I'm ready."

Carl shot Phil an impressed look and lined up the picture as Phil slipped the gun back out of sight. This time, Phil merely smiled for the camera.

It was a very sincere smile.

* * *

Gerry shook hands again and escaped down the hall to the Mall proper, the clown's grin lingering in his mind. He'd never met anyone so happy to give him something for free. He examined the gift card—fifty dollars seemed like too much to waste, but it was only good for music, movies, clothes, or electronics, and Gerry didn't need any of that. His clothes were fine, he bought and sold his own music at the store, and—

He remembered the store CD player, choked with flour and buried in the dumpster.

Okay, Mr. Clown, I will use your gift card, he thought. And he'd put their magic discount card to the test, too.

They'd told him he could find all the stores by looking at the categories on the directory. Incredible, to need a map, but this building was bigger than all of Central Square. They even had printed copies in a little rack. He took one and noted an electronics store called Tuneworks, conveniently along the way to Tanya's Demografique.

The young electronics clerk was very helpful, recommending a nice-looking five-disc player for only $119.95. He rang up the sale and Gerry checked the math; the charge was only $21.97 after the discount and the gift credit—it all worked. And as the clown promised, he didn't even have to show the magic discount card; somehow the register knew it was there in his wallet. He felt a little thrill—this was great! You didn't have to be a genius to appreciate getting something for nothing, and forty percent off plus fifty free bucks was pretty close. Of course, there was always the sales tax; even the Mall President couldn't fix that.

Exhilarated at his shopping coup, he felt for his wallet. Maybe he'd pick up something else at forty percent off while he was there.

* * *

Carl followed Phil through underground corridors to a control room lit by a wall of TV monitors. A stylish-looking kid jumped up as they entered, mashing a hand onto his keyboard; the pictures on the screens flashed and settled into a mosaic of storefronts. Phil waved the kid away from the console and took a seat.

"We can see if anybody's used the discount system today, and since there's only one tag out there, it's gotta be our hippie."

He punched some keys and a report appeared on the desktop monitor.

"Ha! He started out with a five-disc CD player, then picked up the complete Enya CD collection. And I bet he's not done." He turned to the kid. "Bring up every monitor you've got on the second floor south wing stores."

The young man rolled his eyes, leaned over the console, and punched a few buttons; the monitors flipped, bringing up interior views of a dozen stores. Carl scanned the array, but he didn't see the telltale blue-jean outfit.

"Maybe he left already, how about checking the parking lo—?"

"There he is!" Phil was pointing at The Chasm, where the old man, carrying Tuneworks and E-Mart bags, was paying for a stack of prefaded blue jeans. Carl had to concede that the discount card was effective—Mr. Rutland was certainly taking advantage of it. In fact, the old man actually seemed excited as the clerk rang up the sale. And when he carried his purchases out past the door-mounted camera, the close-up showed delirious urgency.

After all his years in an auto showroom, Carl could always tell the Shoppers from the Buyers—and he'd never seen a Buyer like this.

"Well Phil, I'd say your discounts work pretty good. He's gonna buy as much as he can carry. Maybe more than he can afford."

Phil looked up and smiled.

"He'll get the money somehow."

Chapter 25

Howie woke with such a stiff neck. He'd been dozing upright, taped to the equipment rack, his chin on his chest. Was it too much to ask to tape his head up, too?

Meg's head was down, too—asleep, he realized after an anxious search for signs of breathing. He wondered how long they'd been out. And what they'd missed.

As he stretched his neck to work out the kinks, a flash of plaid through the door window caught his attention. Two men were leaving the video monitor room. The monitors, which had all displayed store interiors, suddenly changed views. Howie found himself peeking into various restrooms.

"Psst! Meg! Wake up!"

Meg stirred, wincing as she lifted her head.

"Shoot, I fell asleep. What time is it?"

"Like I can read my watch? Meg, this guy is monitoring restrooms now. I can see sinks, urinals, toilets."

"That's pretty damn rude. Can you at least block the view with the stall door?"

"No, that's just it. Some of the views are from inside the stalls. I think there are cameras in the flush sensors!"

"They can't be that perverted."

"Who says? We've got to report this out."

He strained for a better view—he could see faucet sensors on the sinks and flush sensors on the urinals. It seemed that each was looking at the other. His theory was confirmed when a man in denims walked between them, showing up in opposite profiles on the two displays. The man leaned to place some shopping bags on the floor, giving Howie a good look at his face.

"Meg! It's Lynn's friend—the guy from the natural food store!"

"Gerry? What's he doin' here?"

"Well, he bought a lot of stuff and"—Gerry was approaching the urinal, unzipping in front of the flush-sensor camera—"apparently, he's not Jewish."

* * *

Gerry pissed absentmindedly, barely noticing the kids who came in behind him and left quickly. He was thinking about what else he could buy. A new down parka for the winter? Maybe a pair of hiking boots. What the heck, might even be time to buy a cell phone. He finished, zipped up, and turned to pick up his packages as the urinal auto-flushed. But the packages were gone—probably stolen by those kids.

He was surprised that it didn't bother him, but he did have the receipts and trusted that his insurance would cover it. And, somehow, he was actually looking forward to buying the stuff all over again.

He washed up and headed for the door, empty-handed but lighthearted. When he reached the main corridor, he pulled out his pocket map and located Tuneworks again.

* * *

Howie helplessly witnessed the scene from the sink camera. Three teenagers entered the restroom after Gerry, grabbed his bags, and darted out. Strange that the old man never even turned to check on them. Stranger still that Gerry didn't get upset—didn't run out after them, didn't so much as even shrug. He actually looked pleased about the whole thing. The man was either a saint, or a schmuck.

"Meg, I'm thinking something's not kosher here. He just got ripped off, and he couldn't care less. It's like he's on Prozac or something."

"Hard to believe an all-natural hippie like Gerry'd be takin' Prozac."

"A doper he's not, that's for sure. We should get out of here and talk to him."

"We should. Got any ideas about how? I can't even scratch my ass."

Meg was tape-bound to the rack at the upper arms, waist, wrists, and ankles. Howie briefly imagined scratching her ass for her, and decided that bondage enthusiasts might be onto something. This inspired a somewhat repulsive idea, especially considering the risk to Meg if it didn't work. Not to mention what Meg would do to him even if it did work. But it was their only chance.

"Meg, think you can get the guard to come in here?"

"Maybe, why?"

"I bet if you play up to him, he'll let you loose."

He cringed as she delivered the look he knew was coming.

"I ain't sluttin' up to that Chasm mannequin. What the hell're you thinkin'?"

"I'm only thinking about our duty to get out of here and find out what these perverts are up to. So what you don't like it; you should still do it. Just hold your nose"—she delivered that look again—"figuratively, I mean. He's good looking, it's not so bad. And you just have to make promises; you don't have to keep them."

She glared at him, but considered it. Texans always responded to the call of duty, no matter how distasteful or dangerous—a significant disadvantage when negotiating with New Yorkers.

* * *

Things were usually tediously quiet in the surveillance room on Sunday mornings. Other than Mr. DiSenza's urgent scan for some redhead and her partner, and the new guy's search for the old hippie, there was nothing much to watch. Charles nearly dozed, until muffled shouts intruded on his woozy awareness. The girl was yelling for his attention through the thick window, even though they'd promised they wouldn't yell. He cursed and ventured into the server room.

The captives didn't look uncomfortable, given the situation. Maybe they were hungry—they'd been there for hours. The girl nodded for him to come closer.

"Listen," she drawled, "I wanted to thank you for savin' my life before. You seem like a nice guy." Her voice lowered. "And I know you ain't s'pposed to help us, but if you could just do us one more little favor, I'd be willin' to show my appreciation. I know how to make a man happy."

Charles stepped back, shocked, and considered this shapely woman, taped helplessly to the rack. And laughed.

"Lady, you don't know how to make *me* happy. I'm a real man—just like the men I fuck."

Her bedroom eyes evaporated.

"What? You're gay?"

"I might not turn you down if I wasn't—you do look scrumptious, for a woman. Except you should totally lose the tee-shirt; it's got trailer trash written all over it. Now keep the noise down."

The girl scowled, first at him, then at the guy on the other rack. Charles chuckled to himself and returned to his console.

* * *

Howie couldn't hide from Meg's cruel smile, plainly visible through the loosened packing tape.

"Come on, Howie, it's your duty. Just hold your nose."

"But I don't know how to seduce a guy."

"I got news for you—you don't know how to seduce a girl, either. Let your cologne do the talkin', as usual."

"Suppose it doesn't work on guys? Our gay overseer didn't seem to notice it."

"Maybe he was outta range. You just hafta get 'im closer."

"Okay, but what if he just fucks me without letting us go?"

Meg's eyes narrowed.

"*I* took that risk. You ready?"

Never. "Okay."

Meg yelled again, and soon the guard stormed in.

"If you don't shut up, I'm gonna have to tape you back up, even if you can't breathe."

"My friend keeps saying he needs somethin'. But he's kinda

hoarse from sleepin' standin' up, so I can't hear him too well. Will you go check on him?"

The kid took a look at Howie and rolled his eyes. Obviously not interested. Yet.

Looks aren't everything, kid.

Howie mumbled quietly, enough to draw the young man closer, closer… close enough. Howie could see the transformation at the first noseful of cologne—further evidence for the pheromone theory of sexual orientation.

"You're Charles, right?" Howie whispered, going for husky but coming off croupy.

"Yes. And… and you're—?"

"Howard. Listen, Charles, when I first saw you, I thought you were the hottest thing. But my gaydar failed me—I figured you for a breeder. I should have known you weren't—that outfit is fabulous."

Charles was breathing heavier. Howie mentally held his nose, and stretched closer to the young man's ear.

"I need you, Charles. I need your touch. Untape me, now!"

Charles snapped, feverishly ripping at Howie's packing tape bindings.

"Hurry, Charles! I need your kiss! I need your cock!"

In seconds, Howie was free; Charles stood before him, aflame with chemically-induced passion. Howie grabbed the young man's shoulders, gazed into his eyes, and planted a knee into his crotch.

"I knee'd your balls."

Charles sagged to the floor, moaning. Howie freed Meg, and the two of them taped the incapacitated kid to Howie's rack.

"Hey, Charles, I'm sorry. I had to do it. We really do have to get out of here."

"Wait, don't leave me like this. I am like, so horny now. Can you at least leave me a hand free?"

"That's disgusting."

"Oh, right, like you never do it."

"Not me." *Not since I invented the cologne.*

Meg adjusted Charles' bindings so his right hand was just free enough to do what he needed.

"Sorry, Howie, but I know what it's like to be under the influence."

Howie shook off an image of Meg alone and under the influence. He'd thought of something less exciting, but more important: if Meg could be heard yelling in the other room, so could Charles.

"So, Charles," Howie asked, "You can smell cologne, that means you can breathe through your nose, right? You don't have a cold or anything?"

"I'm perfectly healthy—except for the smashed nuts."

"Good enough. I really hate to do this, especially after all you've done for us, but it's necessary."

Howie wrapped packing tape twice top to bottom around Charles' head, holding his jaw shut. Then he wrapped some around the other way, covering his mouth. There was no beard to break the bond.

"We'll let somebody know you're here," Howie promised. He had one more idea on the way out, and went back to tape Charles' head to the rack, to hold it up if he slept.

"Trust me, you'll thank me later."

Meg and Howie snuck back the way they'd come, dodging small squads inexplicably disguised as golfers. They crossed the shipping room, and Meg carefully cracked open the door to the cafeteria. A buzz of teenage voices leaked out.

"Can't go that way," she whispered.

She diverted him over to a freight elevator, and they were on their way. With any luck, nobody entered the room in time to see the floor indicator changing. Or to notice the arrival ding, which was so loud even deaf Aunt Sadie could've heard it.

* * *

Eightball sipped his nectar, recalling how much cheaper it was when they just called it fruit juice, and watched the thickening crowd in the atrium below. It was almost lunchtime and people were streaming in, many dressed as if they'd come straight from church. For some of them, he figured, this *was* church.

The trayful of orange chicken, though it tasted a little gamey, calmed the grumbling of his belly. But not the grumbling of his conscience.

He and Phil went back a long way, to when Phil hired him for his talent, despite his Southie bandmates' objections to the color of his skin. He'd tried to pay that back, working hard for the struggling frontman without much pay. Phil dissed him pretty bad today, but he knew they owed each other. That's why Eightball was sitting here drinking fancy fruit juice and not taped to a computer rack in the basement.

He took another sip. So, were they even?

Eightball wasn't much for crowd watching—lunch was usually on the road, eaten one-handed while he steered the truck with the other. But he couldn't miss Phil and the car sales guy leading some old hippie into the hall beneath the food court. The man wandered out alone later, looking lost. Soon after, a bunch of teenaged girls disappeared into the hall. None of them had come out yet.

He knew they'd all be sporting extra hardware soon. It probably didn't bother them as much as it bothered him, he thought, and wondered if they knew what the microchips really did.

He sure didn't.

For the first time in his career, Eightball had installed gear he didn't understand. In his techie world, that was a sin. He felt guilty as hell.

He was about to put the tray away and the whole episode behind him when two people emerged from the hallway in a nervous hurry.

Meg and Uncle Howie!

They'd either been freed or escaped—either way, they probably knew more than he did about what was going down. He dashed to the escalator, taking it two steps at a time. Meg and her uncle had almost made it to the main wing by the time Eightball pulled up behind them.

"Meg! Uncle Howie!"

The two stopped, turned, and freaked, frantically sizing up escape routes.

"Meg, wait, don't bolt on me." He put his hands up, showing no weapons. Or packing tape. "I don't know what's going on down there, and I don't like it. I want to talk with you. I want to help."

Meg cocked her head, assessing him.

"You trusted me. I'll trust you. Talk."

Eightball caught his breath, and told her about the calibration area and the high-power, weird-modulation gear. She was interested. When he mentioned the Frenchman and his Elvis impersonator captive, she reacted with wide-eyed alarm.

"Holy shit," were her exact words.

Meg quickly grilled him, but he pleaded ignorance—he had no idea why she was in trouble with DiSenza, and he only helped capture her because DiSenza was his client. But now he realized he could trust Meg more than Don.

Uncle Howie didn't believe him—reasonable, given their short, packing-tape-tainted relationship—but grudgingly accepted Meg's reassurance that he wasn't a threat. Meg turned to Eightball and smiled.

"I gotta couple things to confess too, Eightball. First off, this ain't my uncle, he's my boyfriend."

Boyfriend? More like cradle-robber! He had to be almost thirty.

"And I ain't a high-schooler, though thanks for believin' it. I'm twenty-six, and just eight credits away from a Masters in Biology at Texas A&M." She held up a clenched fist. "And if you give me any more of that 'you don't get that stuff in high school math' shit, I'll rap out pi to 23 digits on your forehead. Got it?"

Eightball was so shocked it took him a moment to notice her grin. He grinned back.

"Got it."

Howie coughed.

"I'm so happy you two could make up. But let's not forget Gerry."

They filled Eightball in on what they'd seen on the monitors. He told them about Gerry's visit to the basement with Phil and company. Meg chewed her lip.

"Sounds to me like Gerry's a guinea pig."

"Must be—I'm pretty sure he's got a chip in his neck."

"And apparently," Howie added, "a forty-percent discount really does increase sales."

"Apparently, somethin' does," said Meg, pulling both of them along the corridor. "Let's find out what, before all those girls get their own very personal electronics."

* * *

After confirming that Gerry hadn't gone to Customer Service to report the theft, Meg guessed that the next-most-likely move would be to restock whatever he'd lost. They checked Tuneworks first, and the clerk verified that an old hippie had bought two CD players in two separate visits. There were too many registers at E-Mart to check, so they headed for The Chasm. As they rode up the south wing escalator, they spotted Gerry halfway down the other side, lugging three bags and looking like the happiest man in the world. They caught up with him when he stopped to gander at the down parkas in the Suburban Survivor display window.

"Gerry! Remember me?"

Gerry turned, his face lighting up.

"Yes! Meg, and—I never caught your name. You were in my store yesterday!" His eyes clouded. "Are you okay? I heard you got away in the subway. Lynn was okay last night, but this morning"— he brightened again—"Who's your new friend?"

Meg stuttered for a moment, surprised by Gerry's agitation.

"Gerry Rutland, this is Howie Friedman, and this here is George Shipley—but everybody calls him Eightball. We're kinda worried about you, Gerry. Looks like you've been doin' a mess o' shoppin'."

Gerry beamed and held his loot aloft.

"I have! I have! It's the most amazing thing. You are looking at the 500 millionth visitor to the Lexingham Mall! And I wasn't even here to shop, I was just looking for Lynn—" He twitched, as if remembering something.

Meg took a mental Mall roll call.

Me, Howie, Frenchy, the King, and now Lynn…

"Gerry," she asked gently, "why do you figure Lynn's here?"

"She made me crash my car, and said she was coming here. She said she was okay, but I got worried."

She crashed his car and told him she was okay, Meg thought. *He should be worried.*

Howie pointed to the packages.

"But then you decided, you're here, why not pick up a few things?"

Gerry's mood lifted again, Lynn forgotten.

"Well, yes, that's because the Mall President gave me a prize, a fifty-dollar gift card, and another discount card that gives me forty percent off everything. And I don't even have to take it out of my wallet!"

Eightball moved behind the old man.

"Gerry, did they take you downstairs?" he asked. "Sit you in a chair in a back room somewhere?"

"Why, yes, they did. Took my picture, for publicity."

"Did it hurt?"

"Of course not! That's a silly question."

"Not really, Gerry. They planted an RFID chip in your neck."

Gerry reached up, eyes growing. Eightball gently moved the old man's hand away and examined his neck, nodding as he parted the hair just behind his right ear.

"I'm sorry, I set up the equipment. I didn't think they'd use it on anyone who wasn't expecting it. You sure it didn't hurt?"

"I'd remember if they hurt me. And I'd remember if they stuck something in my neck. What's an 'arf idea chip'?"

Eightball was lost in thought, so Gerry looked to Meg for an answer. She wished she had one. The poor guy was pretty confused now—you never have to deal with this kind of thing in the natural food business. And Meg was pretty sure RFID chips would wind up in his poison cage long before he'd willingly take one in his neck.

"Gerry, we think you're a guinea pig for some warped experiment." She watched doubt cross his face and decided to play her ace. "Lynn is helpin' us get to the bottom of it, and you can help her." She had him now. "We need to figure out what's goin' on here, what they've done to you—why you're spendin' so much money."

"That's easy. It's forty percent off! I never imagined how wonderful it feels to get a bargain like that. At these discounts I can't shop enough!"

Eightball cleared his throat.

"Meg, I think we all oughta go down to Battery Hut and have Gerry buy us a full-spectrum electromag radiation meter. And we should turn it on before he pays for it, and see what that microchip is doing."

Meg glanced at Gerry, who shrugged okay. Gerry would buy anything at that point.

Meg knew the way. She and Eightball had installed an overpowered "reader" there at about three in the morning.

Chapter 26

François found the old man to be pleasant company; if he truly was Elvis, it was no wonder he had been so popular. The King shared tales of his days in Tupelo and the various dogs with whom he had played and hunted. When he encouraged François to open up about his own youth, François resisted.

"It's okay, François—we know you're from Québec. I'm from Mississippi. Neither one's anythin' to be ashamed of."

François sat silent, but not from the immediate shock that the Legionnaires were aware of his false pedigree. What was deeply disturbing was the completely casual way the King had brought it up. As if it actually did not matter to him.

As if he was simply being sincere.

"My neighborhood was far from the country, M'sieur King; there were few dogs, and the only guns I saw were in pawnshop windows and on the belts of strip club bouncers. I was not taught to hunt or sing, but to sheetrock, like my father and brothers. I escaped to the U.S. as soon as I was twenty-one, but I found life no better here. Americans not only discounted our money, M'sieur King, but Canadians ourselves. I received no respect, not even a 'well done' for a perfectly smooth ceiling."

"So how'd you get into the restaurant biz?"

"I grew weary of wallboard, and chapped hands, and lungs caked with gypsum dust. I took a job as a busboy in a French restaurant in Vermont, where the New York clientele could not distinguish me from authentic help. I learned as much as I could by observing the wait staff, but they would not let a Canadian progress beyond clearing tables. So I decided to become French."

The King's gray eyebrows rose.

"I went to France—Lyon—and pretended to be American.

Americans were better tolerated then, certainly better than Canadians. I found work as a busboy, and then as a waiter. After learning the customs and accent for several years, I moved to Paris, and told them I was a Lyon native. I faked it effectively, M'sieur King—I was not questioned, but immediately attained a wait position at a three-star restaurant. I studied the foods and the wine, and learned to manipulate the clientele, especially American tourists, into spending much money. I was rewarded with the job of wine steward, and after great success at that, took a series of positions at ever-more-upscale restaurants. At my peak I was among the highest paid, most successful stewards in Paris."

The King shook his head.

"What I don't understand, François, is why on earth you'd want to come back to the USA after gettin' that far, in Paris of all places. Heck, seems like you'd a been on top of the world."

"On top of Paris, perhaps. But not the world. I was surprised, though I suppose I should not have been, at how much I enjoyed abusing American customers. After fifteen years, I realized that what I truly desired was to return to America and experience Americans' respect. To exact revenge for the injustices of my youth."

"I suppose the Corporation helped you live your dream."

"They recruited me, sharing my contempt for gullible consumers but in turn believing I was as French as champagne. The Corporation pays extremely well, M'sieur King. They brought me to America, where I live comfortably and command the respect of two dozen American patrons every night except Monday."

The King glanced down at François' weapon.

"There's a difference between respect and intimidation, you know."

"Perhaps. And perhaps I do not care."

"I think you do. You strike me as a good guy, François; you just couldn't get a fair shake. You work hard, you believe in quality food and wine. I don't see how you put up with these folks and all their cheap, knock-off crap. They got you so hooked on the money, you sold out your own values. In the music business, we'd say you got good licks, but you've gone commercial. You need a new label."

François could not believe he was hearing this.

"Do you actually think you can talk me into changing sides?"

"No sir, I don't. I can only let you know that we're always open to the possibility, if you ever make that decision yourself."

"You must take me for a fool."

"Absolutely not, François. I'm just giving you the same respect I'd give anybody else. The same respect you oughta give yourself."

François clenched his jaw. In the Corporation, a person at François' level was never given responsibility for his own choices. But that was the only thing the old man could offer.

Perhaps the King, centered in the sights of a semi-automatic pistol, in fact wielded a more effective weapon.

* * *

At the beginning, the ventilation duct was just tall enough to make Lynn think she could crawl quickly despite the total darkness. But every few yards, up ahead, she heard Roger's clothing scraping the points of the protruding seam screws. And despite the warning, she found every screw in the darkness by kneeling on it—other than the ones she gouged her head on.

Actually, the knee pain helped take her mind off the headache, but not off the nightmarish path through the duct system. Her fear of being trapped in small places was now compounded by a fear of getting lost in a maze of small places. Roger clearly had a map in his head and was navigating on instinct. Lynn, on the other hand, always had trouble following maps—she needed turn-by-turn directions. The need for quiet meant she couldn't ask where they were going, but it didn't matter—she'd learned long ago that map people can't speak directionese. A map person would say "get on Route 2 toward Boston"; a directions person would take the wrong Route 2 ramp and soon be heading for Albany.

Lynn felt like she was halfway to Albany, with no exits ahead and no way to back up. She took some comfort in Master Chuushin's advice: *One who does not know The Way must follow one who does.* Roger didn't know The Way, but his way might get them to Tanya.

After crossing a corridor vent, Roger stopped and turned. Lit from below, he looked like the villain in a melodrama as he put a finger to his lips and pointed down. She peered through the grille, just in time to see four men in golf clothes accost a burly man in a jacket and tie. It was hard to tell from that angle, but he might've been the guy they'd bumped into near the management office. His familiar-looking black friend wasn't with him.

She listened to the conversation with growing dismay. This was no melodrama, and Roger was not the villain—the villains were in the hallway below, close enough to spit on.

* * *

Don DiSenza cringed and concealed the Glock as yet another excited foursome approached. The camera scan of the public Mall hadn't located the intruders, and searching the basement on foot meant running into tech teams constantly. Not one team would let him go without a glowing status report.

These were the Packaging guys, and their technology was a mature art—they'd been working with the First Aid Products Cartel for years. Molded-plastic "blister" packs were already impossible to open by hand, and using a knife or scissors on the odd contours of tough polymer naturally caused a cut finger and the need for a bandage. When some people discovered the "can opener hack" on the Internet, his engineers changed the design so openers wouldn't fit right. They even added perforations to make the customers think they could just peel it open from a finger tab; of course, the plastic would break in the wrong place and peel their fingers open instead. A while back, the team had developed a new plastic that maintained a sharper edge with microscopic sawteeth; this edge made the cut deeper and more jagged, requiring a more expensive bandage. But his retail market analyst was claiming that the latest stuff was even more destructive to human flesh.

"...the real miracle here is the material. It's got the same saw edge as before, but the plastic is infused with destabilase—that's the anticoagulant enzyme that leeches use. So when the skin is cut, the—"

"Wait a minute. Anticoagulant?"

"Right. Stops the blood from clotting. Leeches use it to keep the wound open so—"

"I get it. The cut keeps bleeding."

"Yeah, but no major hemorrhaging—that's why we didn't use a serious anti-C like rat poison. This'll just make it bleed a little bit for a week—and use three times the current average bandages per wound. We just confirmed the numbers from last month's test runs." His caddy handed him an iPad, and he punched up a graph that showed bandage sales jumping within a week of the new package introduction. "Not bad, huh?"

Jeez.

"Not bad. The First Aid Products Cartel will love it."

Don smiled to himself as he broke away, envisioning the fat collaboration fee—the team would be able to afford a lot of expensive golf balls with that money. No need to mention that the reason they needed more golf balls was the Corporation's water-seeking ball technology, secretly developed elsewhere.

DiSenza had checked every room in the complex, seeing no one except the most talkative Sunday morning golfers. Maybe the intruders hadn't gotten in—it wasn't like the Mall brochures had a map to the subterranean entrance. On the other hand, a sequin trail from the parking lot was a pretty good substitute. And they might've sweet-talked their way past his guard as easily as they took out Jean-Paul and Toine. They certainly hadn't been seen upstairs, and he doubted they'd just go home.

It was time to face the music and admit to Phil that two Legionnaires were loose somewhere. He tucked the Glock into his belt and strolled into the cafeteria, where he found a crowd of girls, the plaid guy taking registrations, and Phil Grady pacing. He pulled Phil aside.

"We've got a problem."

"Deal with it, Don. I've got a bigger problem—maybe you can help."

"What do you need?" Anything was better than discussing at-large Legionnaires.

"Can you feed a store voice projector from a microphone down here somewhere?"

"Well, the shopping sug-jectors are tied into an MP3 loop, but we can drive them direct from the surveillance room. Sometimes we talk shoplifters into putting the stuff back on the shelf. It's great how they obey their 'conscience' when it's so explicit."

"So you can target a specific person in the shop?"

"Um, yeah—we wouldn't want everyone to put their stuff back." Phil grinned.

"Of course not. That's perfect."

Grady asked the girls if they'd mind waiting a little longer. The general buzz of approval wasn't surprising. A paid break, with free donuts and coffee, and he wanted to stretch it? Duh!

Don noticed Phil's daughter wasn't in the crowd. He had a pretty good idea whose head Phil wanted to talk into.

* * *

DiSenza was surprised to find the surveillance room deserted. Usually you couldn't tear Charles away from the monitors; Don figured the kid had a voyeuristic streak, like all the best surveillance people. It was Phil who commented on the monitor settings— mostly men's room sinks and urinals. Don smiled; *to each his own.* And the view probably explained why Charles was M.I.A.—he'd simply been inspired to go take a leak. Or something.

Don took the chair and the controls.

"Demografique, right?"

Phil nodded, his poker face leaking a little guilt around the edges. Don punched a few keys.

"That's where your daughter works, huh? I take it she didn't show up for her chip yet."

"Not yet," Phil answered, "I thought I'd give her a little reminder." Then with an edge, "Does that violate Corporation procedures?"

"I guess not. Did she get her permission slip signed?"

"I've got it." Phil pulled a folded paper out of his jacket and slapped it onto the console. The signature was readable as Lynn Grady, but very distorted, as if drawn with an Etch-A-Sketch.

"She had a lot to drink," Phil muttered, his guilty look reappearing.

Don let it slide. He didn't give a shit, as long as he had plausible deniability.

He brought up an interior view of Demografique. Tanya was there, refolding sweatshirts near the back of the store. He selected a nearby sug-jector, set the target tracker crosshairs on the center of her head, and clicked the lock button. The tracker icon turned green and followed her head as she moved. He offered the chair to Phil.

"As long as she stays in the store, the tracker'll stay with her, and the light'll stay green. The mike is push-to-talk. Think about what you want to say before you press the button—you can't take it back."

Phil nodded, and studied his daughter on the monitor. Don considered looking in on the server room captives but decided no noise was good news; it was time to check up on François and his Elvis anyway, and get back to hunting intruders.

He patted his lower back, felt the outline of the Glock, and returned to the maze.

* * *

Lynn sensed that the duct was getting smaller as they proceeded further into the basement complex, but that might've just been her rising claustrophobia, or swelling knees. She had no idea how much longer until they reached the basement cafeteria, and a growing panic insisted that it had taken too long and Tanya was already there, getting a microchip injected into her neck. A tiny Zen voice kept her going: *Blind panic is truly blind; truth cannot panic.*

Roger passed through flickering light from a side vent and rotated around. He put his finger to his lips, then tapped Lynn's head and pantomimed talking into a phone. Finally, he pointed through the vent grille.

Lynn slid up and peered into the room below. Phil was seated at some kind of control panel, a wall of video monitors in front of him. On the largest screen was a close-up of Tanya, with a green crosshair centered on her head.

Lynn fought the urge to scream. Crosshairs on Tanya's head!

But Roger's charade had done the job—she understood that Phil was just going to talk to Tanya, not blow her brains out.

Her Zen-mind advised her to pay attention and not judge. Her mom-mind advised her to kick out the grille and kick in Phil's teeth.

* * *

Phil watched Tanya work. For a moment, he reconsidered the plan—it was kind of a shame to do this to her. She was her mother's daughter: healthy, energetic, and even more striking than Lynn. His genes contributed to those good looks, as well as her creativity and stubborn individuality—traits that had long since been drugged and fucked out of her father.

But she didn't understand that. And probably couldn't even believe it.

Which suggested a possible approach, if he could bring himself to use it.

A flash of pink in the corner of the screen caught his eye, and he glanced over just in time to see Fiona lurking behind the jacket rack. Phil smiled and shook his head; he'd flushed her ears, but she still had eyes on him. Or at least on Tanya.

It was a timely reminder of his position. Fact was, the Corporation had rules, and he had needs. He couldn't afford to be sentimental.

He wrapped his hand around the mike and positioned his finger on the talk button.

* * *

Tanya finished stacking the small sweatshirts, saddened that the only design on any of them was the Demografique logo. Fashion wasn't about what looked nice; it was about where you bought it. The stores had turned kids into advertising zombies.

Except me, she thought. *So far.*

She'd picked up and half refolded a pastel blue large when a voice startled her.

IS THAT HOW WE PART?

She turned, thinking that her father had snuck up behind her. The store was empty except for Gina at the register and a blonde lady digging through the leathers.

Weird.

Ever since Gina mentioned that Mom was looking for her, she'd been rehearsing the mother-daughter argument she knew was coming. So why was she thinking about Daddy?

WHEN WE LOOK BACK ON IT, WILL WE WISH WE'D ACTED DIFFERENT? SAID DIFFERENT THINGS? SAID MORE THINGS?

Tanya shook off the wishful daydream. Daddy wasn't there; he never was there, and he never would be there. They were done.

MAYBE THAT'S WHAT HAPPENED TO MOM AND ME. WE JUST STOPPED TALKING. STOPPED TALKING, JUST A LITTLE TOO SOON.

Yeah, maybe that's it. Or maybe you two were just incompatible. Like we are.

SHE COULD HAVE HELPED ME. ALL SHE HAD TO DO WAS TALK WITH ME. WHY DIDN'T SHE HELP ME?

Tanya froze. He was always so aggressive, so confident. She never imagined him needing help before. But it made sense—the confidence was just his stage face.

I CAN BE SAVED. I JUST NEED A LITTLE UNDERSTANDING. REACH OUT TO ME. TALK TO ME.

She'd been so busy fighting off his sales pitch that she never thought about pitching back. Could she convince him to give up marketing and make music again? He knew how to make good music. And she did have something in common with him: they were both artistic rebels. Mom wasn't. Mom couldn't reach him.

I can reach him.

TALK TO ME—SAVE ME, BEFORE IT'S TOO LATE.

She looked again at the Demografique logo in her hand, and then at the sea of conformity around her. If she was gonna save her father, she'd have to save herself first.

She set down the garment and hurried to the back room to retrieve her purse. After swapping her earrings and clasping the moon-and-stars pendant around her neck, she stopped at the register. Gina looked at her funny, obviously sensing that something was wrong.

"I quit," Tanya said.

She left Demografique for the last time and headed for the food court wing, rehearsing what she'd say to her father. He'd think she came to get a discount chip.

She'd straighten that out first.

Chapter 27

François heard the meat room door click; so did the dogs, and they resumed their furious barking. DiSenza entered, gun drawn.

"Just checking that you're still okay here," he yelled.

"And why would we not be?" François yelled back. "We were very well until you disturbed the animals."

"You don't like the noise?" DiSenza asked, sneering. "I can take care of that."

He waved his hand, and three reports thumped François' ears and chest. Blood exploded from the cage wall and the room went silent, save the whimpering of three dogs licking at the stumps where their forepaws had been.

DiSenza had undoubtedly been trained by the same sharpshooting instructor as François—but Jack "Grassy" Knoll always emphasized heartlessness.

"You merely wounded them, M'sieur. Was that a show of compassion, or marksmanship?"

DiSenza shrugged.

"Corporation policy: Don't Kill the Dog." He glanced at the cleavers. "Unless you're gonna eat 'em. But the butcher won't be here till tomorrow, and the meat'll only stay fresh on the hoof." He grinned. "In this case, on the paw. Besides, the Lost Livestock Form is, like, three pages."

François reminded himself that the magazine in DiSenza's Glock might have as many as seven rounds remaining. And there was no Corporate rule against killing people.

"Shooting the dogs was unnecessary, M'sieur. Everything is under control here."

DiSenza let out a derisive snort.

"Not exactly. Ever wonder what happened to Jean-Paul and Toine?"

I have not, François realized with chagrin. The conversation with the King had distracted him completely. And how did DiSenza know their names?

"I expect that they are waiting in the parking lot with our other hostage."

"Expect again. Mall security has them in custody; some red-haired woman set them up as terrorists. She and your former 'other hostage' are running around loose somewhere in my fucking mall."

François jaw stiffened. She had stolen his prisoner!

"I am confident you shall find her with M'sieur Grady. She works for the Corporation, and though we are competing for M'sieur Grady's attention, I have the valuable prize." He waved his own gun toward the King.

"You're too damn gullible, François. She's a Legionnaire."

Impossible! François glanced at the King. His face revealed nothing.

"If I am gullible, then so is M'sieur Grady. This woman told me her story at the dinner she shared with *him* last night. They appeared to be very intimate associates!"

DiSenza snapped his head, and the Glock, over to the King.

"Fuck! You people recruited Grady's ex-wife?!"

What?!

The King replied calmly, by now accustomed to speaking to weapon barrels, even several at once.

"We didn't have to recruit her, sir. She's not just an ex-wife, but a mother, tryin' to protect her child. Did you know Phil was gonna put a microchip in his own daughter?"

DiSenza's eyes shifted sideways. François wondered what these microchips were; management never informed him of such things.

The King continued.

"And do you know what the microchips really do?"

"They're just a fucking discount." DiSenza's eyes were shifting again. "And I wouldn't care if Lynn Grady was MY mother, I'm not gonna let her screw up this operation." He checked the magazine on the Glock and disappeared through the anteroom.

For the third time, François was forced to reevaluate his redheaded nemesis.

"This woman, Lynn, was married to M'sieur Grady?"

The King nodded.

"Then she must be on his side, n'est-ce pas?"

"Guess you never been divorced, have ya, François?" The King smiled, but only for a moment. "When you come down to it, François, this isn't about Lynn versus Phil. It's about Corporation versus Lynn's daughter. Lynn's a good mom—she's always gonna side with her baby."

The King stopped there, his penetrating gaze implying the big question.

Which side am I on?

François averted his eyes, only to recoil from the sight of the blood-spattered cages. He was forced to face the King, whose expression had not changed.

* * *

From the vent above Phil's head, Lynn could only hear his side of the projected mental conversation with Tanya. But she knew the guilt trip would work on her daughter. It always worked on Lynn. Besides, maybe Phil *could* be saved. They cured addicts all the time, right?

At least Tanya wasn't implanted yet. But Phil had left the projection room right after Tanya left her store, both clearly headed for the Teabury Center; when they got there, Phil would be giving her a chip whether she wanted it or not. The ventilation route wasn't fast enough to get there in time to stop him—they needed to break out of the duct and take the hallways the rest of the way.

Roger found the points of the sheet metal screws that secured the vent cover, pressed his MIT ring onto the exposed threads, and pulled back, stripping the screws until they were as smooth as nails. He'd done about half of them when Lynn decided that was enough. She gave him a slight tap sideways, and when he moved over she pressed her head against the opposite wall and kicked, sending the grille and remaining screws clanging to the floor below.

Roger nodded approval and disappeared through the opening. She slid out feet first into his arms; unlike on the subway, he set her down instantly. As they scrambled into the complex, she could only follow, putting complete faith in Roger's mysterious map-person skills. He reassured her with a glance over his shoulder.

"Almost there," he said.

"Not quite," growled a man stepping around the corner. He leveled a pistol at them, and they skidded to a halt. It was the same guy they'd bumped into upstairs and had seen in the hallway through the vent. "And where the fuck do you think you're going?" he inquired.

Lynn stepped forward, feeling the gunman's focus converge with his aim. On her. Was he nervous? Lynn sure was.

"I'm Lynn Grady, Phil Grady's ex-wife. Pleased to meet you, Mr., uh...?"

The man scowled.

"Don DiSenza, and I know who you are."

"Well, then you know that Phil and I have a daughter? I'm very worried about her, Don. I was going to see about stopping her from getting a microchip planted in her neck."

DiSenza glanced sideways, that guilty look that every mother can spot in an instant. This would be a lie.

"It's her decision. And you signed the permission form!"

Okay, two lies.

"Neither of those is true, Don. I never signed any form. And we saw Phil use your voice projector to talk her into meeting him. It didn't sound like she was expecting to get a chip. But it sure seems like Phil's gonna give her one anyway."

She glanced at the dark opening of the barrel, then back to his eyes, and stepped forward again.

"Mr. DiSenza, I'm going to walk past you and put an end to this right now." DiSenza spread his stance and steadied the gun. He'd have to kill her to stop her—he wouldn't do that, would he?

It's possible, said Zen-mind.

"Back off, lady! Don't make me shoot you!"

She continued her advance. He was inching away, until he backed into the wall and couldn't retreat further. The pistol was still aimed at her chest.

"I'm going to go stop this, Don. I won't let you, or Phil, or anybody screw with my daughter."

Everything disappeared into a haze as she focused on DiSenza's eyes. She saw conflict. She was almost close enough to turn the corner, when a shadow of resignation fell across his face. Almost imperceptibly, he adjusted his aim to her heart side, and tightened his jaw.

Shit.

His hand twitched and the gun roared.

* * *

François lowered his pistol; DiSenza dropped to one knee, screaming and holding his hand, while his own weapon spun across the tiled floor. The redhead whirled to see who had saved her, with the ashen visage of one who has cheated death. Which she had.

DiSenza frantically wrapped his tie around his wrist, knotting it with his teeth. He pulled a pen from his pocket and slid it under one loop, and began twisting it into a tourniquet.

"You're a fuckin' double!" he shouted at François. "Damn you!"

"You are incorrect," said François, "I only just turned—when I realized how vile a creature you actually are." He wished he had realized it earlier.

François faced Lynn while Roger scrambled to retrieve DiSenza's gun.

"I have seen many repugnant things today, Madame. I was not going to see a mother killed for the sake of her daughter. I do not know what they are doing to her, but I invite you to go and attempt to stop them."

She stood unsure, undoubtedly still in shock from the shooting.

"Go ahead, Lynn," came the King's voice from behind François. "We can trust him; it's a matter of respect. And Roger, about that job? Now's a good time."

Roger nodded agreement—about the job?—and urged Lynn forward. She took a step and looked back.

"Thanks, François. I guess I owe you one."

François considered this.

"You owe me nothing, Madame."

She met his gaze for a moment, then turned and sprinted down the hall behind Roger.

François approached DiSenza, who had tightened the tourniquet until his hand turned purple.

"M'sieur, I apologize that my T-RP pellet gun was the only means available to make your shot miss Madame Grady. Your tourniquet is an excellent idea, but please note that while it may slow the catalyst trickling toward your heart, it will not stop it completely. As you are doubtlessly aware, the reaction requires very little T-RP, and thus you will suffer your fatal heart attack within a few minutes. I believe your only option for survival lies in your meat room and its supply of cleavers.

"It is convenient that in the meat room, as you have told me, no one shall hear you scream. But keep in mind that your hand is full of poison: please do not be tempted to serve Manager Fingers at your food court. Your trans-fat-clogged customers are no doubt extremely sensitive to T-RP."

"Fuck you, François," DiSenza snarled, and bolted past him toward the meat room. As François watched him flee, he noticed that the King had gone pale and begun to falter. François jumped to his side as the old man sank to the floor, no longer able to hide the bloodstain spreading across his blue-sequined stomach.

"You are hit, M'sieur!" DiSenza's errant shot had found a mark.

"Uh-huh, huh!" the King groaned. "That's one hunka hunka burnin' lead…" His weak attempt at a smile twisted into a grimace. "Guess I shoulda stayed in the meat room."

François hurriedly examined him, heart sinking as he grasped the severity of the wound. There was little time. He swept the King into his arms and ran for the alternate entrance; it was the long way around to the car, but he did not dare risk being stopped by Carl or M'sieur Grady.

"Where we goin'?" grunted the King.

"To the hospital emergency room. Do not worry, we have an arrangement; they will not expose either of us—despite your sideburns and jumpsuit."

"Huh. Or you could just tell 'em I'm a crappy Elvis impersonator, got shot by an outraged fan."

François picked up the pace. Crappy impersonator?
Nothing could be further from the truth, M'sieur.

* * *

DiSenza laid his forearm onto the meat room butcher table, the red tie and purple hand grotesquely contrasted against the white cutting surface.

He'd always done whatever was necessary—to other people—to get the good life for himself. Now, he had to do something horrible to himself, just to stay alive. And without his right hand, the good life was no longer available. It might be better just to die—untwist the tourniquet and let the heart attack happen. He'd never bothered to ask how much that hurts.

Surely not as much as chopping off his own hand.

He glanced up at the cages. The wounded dogs peered at him, silent. Smiling, maybe? Getting the last laugh, he imagined. They were happy with whichever option he chose.

He clutched a cleaver in his left hand. It was awkward. He had trouble filing his fingernails with that hand, how the hell was he gonna chop cleanly through two inches of flesh and bone with it? He'd only get one stroke before he passed out from the pain; if he missed low he'd leave enough hand to poison himself, if he missed high he'd cut the tourniquet and bleed to death.

He reluctantly raised the blade, his fear of death still battling his fear of pain. The fear of pain was winning—he couldn't bring himself to begin the downward sweep. He almost wished someone else would do it for him.

Or maybe he could pretend to be someone else. Pretend it wasn't his own arm under the blade...

That's it, he thought. *That poisoned hand isn't me. I won't feel a thing.*

It's someone else.

Chapter 28

Eightball dug through the Battery Hut antennas until he found a wideband loop. He'd already chosen a battery-powered RF analyzer that could detect any electromagnetic signal from DC to microwave.

He hooked the antenna to the analyzer, under the watchful eye of the Battery Hut sales associate. They told the kid they'd buy whatever they used, and he was too busy adding up the sales total to worry about whether they'd actually pay up. The total was big; the analyzer cost $1200 and the antenna ran another $129. Of course, Battery Hut wouldn't make much profit on that stuff—the real margin was in the eight D-cell batteries.

After firing up the analyzer, Eightball set it to show any signal it could find. The display jumped to life, crowded with noise spikes at all the expected frequencies: AC power, TV and radio channels, 4G wireless networks, and WiFi routers, including the freshly-installed RFID reader at the register. He zoomed in on each signal, made sure there were no surprises, then set a filter to hide it. The result was a flat scan, ready to highlight any new signal that came along. As a check, he pulled out his phone and called voicemail—and a wavy spread-spectrum cell phone pattern appeared on the display.

He nodded to Meg, and she brought Gerry to the register. The old man frowned to realize he had no idea what he was buying, but once he pulled out his credit card the frown evaporated. Eightball was amazed that Gerry would agree to pay for the expensive analyzer; he didn't look like he could afford it, but apparently helping his friend was more important to him than money.

Eightball hit the analyzer's Record button as the associate began to ring up the batteries. As expected, the display showed the

RFID microchip's serial number transmission; nothing peculiar there. But Eightball noticed a signal in the low frequency spectrum, and he focused there as the clerk scanned the antenna package.

A series of pulses popped up at 5.3 cycles per second. They resonated for a few seconds, strong at first, fading away slowly. Eightball called Meg and Howie to look at it, then turned to Gerry. The man was grinning like a doper.

"Gerry, how do you feel?"

"I feel very good, Eightball. Did you see how much we saved on that—whatever it is?"

Meg yanked the antenna out of Eightball's hand and held it near Gerry's neck—as the loop got closer to the microchip, the signal on the screen got stronger. Clearly the chip was generating the pulses.

What the hell for? No chip reader could detect a signal like that.

The clerk finally scanned the analyzer package, and the $720 discounted price appeared on the cash register. A huge pulse signal flooded the screen, ten times more powerful than before. Gerry let out a low moan.

The old man was swaying, eyes closed, mouth open. Howie steadied him.

"Gerry?" asked Meg, "Are you all right?"

Gerry didn't answer right away but just stood there, breathing heavily. Finally, his eyelids quivered open to narrow slits.

"I am soooo fiiinnne…" he sang. "Can we buy another one?"

* * *

Meg bounced her attention between the analyzer screen and the giddy old man whose neck was broadcasting the signal. 5.3 hertz was familiar, somehow. From Texas A&M's undergraduate neuroscience program.

Course NRSC-923. Synaptic biochemistry.

Dopamine and addictive behaviors.

"This thing's an electronic drug," she said. "It's at 5.3 hertz— that's the frequency of the dopamine effect. It stimulates the pleasure center in Gerry's brain—makes him high when he buys somethin'." She glanced down at the fading waveform. "And it's stronger the more things cost."

"So," Howie grumbled. "Now the bastards are hooking kids on shopping."

Meg nodded toward Gerry, who was humming quietly, eyes closed again.

"The kids think it's a discount thing, which helps explain the good feelin' they get. But it's pretty much a shot of heroin. And just as addictive. Maybe more. And I bet Phil's engineers didn't think kids would ever spend so much money—they didn't even put in a limiter."

"Jesus," Eightball muttered. "I can't believe I set this up. We gotta go shut it down. Now."

Meg pictured the crowd of teenagers at dinner the previous night—happy and healthy. Maybe a little materialistic, like all kids, but not shopping addicts. Yet.

"Howie, I'm going back down there with Eightball. Stay here with Gerry and keep him outta trouble. And whatever happens, report this back to the Legion."

"I'll go; God forbid you should get hurt."

"You can't go, Howie—the place is crawlin' with guards. They'll recognize Eightball and me as part of last night's team."

"Except the guy who taped us to the server racks."

"Hey," Eightball began, "I'm really sorry—"

"Yeah, I know you are. You should take better care of Meg this time, okay?"

"We'll stay clear of Mr. DiSenza," Eightball assured him.

"Come on, Eightball," Meg said, inching toward the door, "you know the elevator basement access code. Let's see if we can stop Phil from shootin' up a buncha innocent teenagers—includin' his own daughter."

Eightball's jaw dropped, even as he started to sprint with her.

"Baby Tanya?!"

* * *

Roger steered Lynn against the wall as they approached the shipping room. The cafeteria was nearby, and he was pretty sure the girls would be getting chipped around here somewhere. They crept up to the double doors and peered in.

There was a chair and electronics in the far corner—that would be the injection station. He pointed to it, and Lynn nodded. Near the station was the cafeteria door; beyond that, he figured, waited Phil's intended victims, including Tanya.

The rest of the room looked pretty standard: a freight elevator, workbenches, scales, and a mini-forklift parked in a corner almost buried in empty boxes. It was the only place to hide.

Roger motioned to Lynn and they slipped across to the forklift. As Lynn climbed into the cab, Roger crouched behind it. He pulled out DiSenza's Glock, but Lynn's fierce frown made it clear the weapon was a last resort. He tucked it back into his belt, and they peered over the box pile at the cafeteria door.

* * *

Phil waited in the cafeteria, suffering the teenage clamor; it was hell stalling the other girls while Tanya took her sweet time. When she finally showed, he swallowed his irritation, pasted on his best "I'm a sellout but deep down I want to be saved" look, and feigned surprise.

"Tanya! I was so afraid I wouldn't see you again! I didn't think you were gonna come!"

Her eyes were hard. A scolding was on the way.

Whatever.

"I'm not here for a chip, Daddy. I want to talk."

He went for sheepish.

"Okay, I owe you that. I guess I did all the talking this morning."

"And I didn't know what to say. But I do now."

Phil glanced around. The other girls were watching like this was a prime-time soap. Even Carl was paying attention.

"Can we go somewhere private?" He indicated the shipping room door, got a nod, and guided her through. When the door clicked shut, he casually put his arm around her.

"Don't touch me, Daddy, this is about—"

The rest was lost as he clamped a hand over her mouth and tightened his other arm around her waist. He swung her over to the equipment area and pinned her against the wall with his body, reaching for the injector as she struggled to scream and squirm free. He found the gun and picked a spot on her writhing neck. One shot and she'd forget the whole assault.

He heard a whirring sound and looked up. A forklift was coming at him fast, its twin bayonets shedding empty boxes and rising smoothly toward his stomach.

Lynn was at the wheel.

* * *

When Lynn saw the attack, her maternal instinct and warehouse experience kicked in together: she floored the accelerator, pulled the lift lever, and grabbed the wheel. Tanya took advantage of Phil's surprise and twisted free, giving Lynn an opening—she aimed the right fork at Phil's belly.

"No!" Tanya screamed, and Lynn tweaked the wheel.

The forks slid to either side of him and impaled the wall, the mast crossbar embedding him halfway into the fractured sheetrock before Lynn hit the cutoff. He was pinned, his arms trapped over his head in surrender. She yanked the gun from his shaking grip as Tanya's screams became quiet whimpering.

"What the fuck, babe!" Phil panted. "You coulda skewered me."

"Yes I coulda!"

"Honey! Breathe. You're upset." Phil smiled *that smile*, the one that had always calmed her down. The one she craved all those years. And she knew why she'd turned the forks aside at the last moment. It wasn't Buddhist non-violence. And it wasn't Tanya's plea.

She couldn't bear to lose him forever. *I'm still hooked.*

"It's okay, Lynn," said Roger, climbing out from the box pile. "It's all over now."

The elevator dinged and Lynn turned to see Meg burst through the opening doors. She was shouting.

"Lynn! We found your friend Gerry wanderin' around the Mall with a microchip in his neck. It's like a drug—it triggers the pleasure center in your brain. The more Gerry spent, the higher he got. They turned him into a goddamn shoppin' addict!"

Lynn whirled back to Phil. He glanced side to side, then smiled again.

"It's harmless," he insisted. "It's just making him happy to shop."

"And you were gonna do the same thing to Tanya!"

"I told you, it's harmless."

She glared at the gun. A coil of packets hung from one side, and a single, used packet had emerged from the other. That was Gerry's. The next one was intended for Tanya.

She pressed the gun to Phil's neck.

"So harmless you'd be willing to take Tanya's chip yourself?"

Phil's smile tightened.

"Go ahead, if it makes you feel better. Shoot me!"

She hesitated. *Resentment is poison*, said Zen-mind, *administered by the ego, to itself.*

"You can't do it, can you?" he said with a sneer. "That's why you hippies can't stop progress—you're afraid of everything. Afraid of technology, afraid of the future. Afraid to fight."

Even his eyes were smirking.

"I'm not afraid of anything anymore," she said, and pulled the trigger. Phil grit his teeth and his eyes lost focus. But only for a moment.

"What are you waiting for?" he yelled. "Shoot me! Do it!"

Again? She pulled the trigger, and his eyes rolled.

"It's harmless! Pull the trigger!"

What the hell was he trying to prove? She kept shooting, and he kept asking for more. She lost track of how many chips she fired into his neck and head, trying to wipe out that smile once and for all.

* * *

He blinked to clear the haze. His neck was numb. His *head* was numb. He was trapped by some machine, and two guys were pulling a redheaded woman away from him. She was angry, and looked familiar. One of the guys was black, and bald, and looked familiar too. But he couldn't place any of them. The room was totally strange.

Where am I? he thought. *Who are these people?*

He blinked a few more times.

Who am I?

Chapter 29

Eightball didn't know what to expect when the elevator doors opened. He couldn't have imagined the scene that confronted him: Phil wedged into the wall by a forklift, with Lynn in the cab brandishing an injector gun. He recognized her now as the redhead he'd seen in the hallway—her big clumsy friend was here, too, wading through boxes to get to her. And he even recognized Tanya, though she'd been in diapers the last time he saw her. It looked like he and Meg had just missed the action, and Eightball allowed himself to relax.

But after Meg yelled and Lynn started firing, Eightball scrambled to help the big guy pull her off Axe-man. They tossed the injector aside and set Lynn on the chair, where she hung her head and broke into quiet crying. Tanya rushed to hug her mother.

The cafeteria door cracked open with a burst of hysterical voices, and Phil's plaid helper peeked in.

"Um, there's a couple of spears sticking through the wall. Everything okay in here?"

Lynn's big friend leapt to the door and slammed it onto the man's neck, trapping his head until he could pull the rest of him into the shipping room. In a few more seconds, the man's hands were bound by his own flowered tie—Lynn's friend was pretty damn fast with a knot.

Eightball pulled the forklift away from Axe-man while Meg helped ease him to the floor. It only took a few questions to figure out that Phil Grady couldn't remember a thing.

The plaid guy was staring at the discarded injector gun, its string of used packets curling around it like a cat's tail.

"Assuming you shot all those into Phil, I bet I know what happened. I'll tell you, if you let me go."

Eightball picked up the gun.

"Or how 'bout if you tell us, we won't shoot *you* full of microchips?"

The man's eyes got big.

"Okay, okay! Phil tells 'em the chips don't hurt, but they do. The machines in here make special signals that the chips pump into your brain. First one's a pain-reliever, so it stops hurting right away; and then there's some kind of memory eraser so you forget it ever did."

It all added up.

"Meg," Eightball said, "that's how it worked on Gerry; he didn't remember getting his chip." Eightball pointed to the big antenna next to the chair. "This stuff generates different signals than the stores. 7 hertz, on a 200 megahertz carrier."

"Shoot," Meg mused, "you told me that and I didn't get it. 7 hertz is the synapse firin' frequency for the human brain. I've read theories you can erase short-term memory with it."

"Seems like this proves the theories. And I guess it erases more than short-term memory if you use enough power. Like from ten chips instead of just one." He squatted down next to her, the two of them gazing into the blankness of Axe-man's face. "How long do you think it'll last, Meg?"

"I don't know. But if it really erases memory, it's gone. For good."

For good—Eightball marveled at the pun. Maybe forgetting the corruption of the last ten years would make Phil a better person.

Lynn's big friend stepped up and introduced himself as Roger, then began to introduce Lynn and Tanya. Eightball stopped him.

"I know Lynn, and Tanya too." Lynn was coming out of her funk, staring at him, trying to place him. "I haven't seen either of 'em since the last of the Grunge Tour Diaries." He couldn't help grinning as Lynn finally got it.

"Eightball? I should've recognized you—you haven't changed at all!"

"You either. Tanya, on the other hand..." Eightball flashed back to playing "Trot Trot to Boston" with baby Tanya while Lynn and Phil were bonking in the back of the bus.

Probably not a good time to mention that, he decided.

He looked around at the gear.

"I think the show's over—this shit's done all the damage it's gonna do."

Eightball grabbed a spare power cord, cut off the socket end and stripped the wires back a few inches. He plugged in the other end and jammed the bare wires into a circuit board in the "calibration" system. There was a flash and a pop, and the sound of tiny electronic fragments ricocheting off the inside of the enclosure. A similar operation took out DiSenza's database machine. With nothing to compare tag numbers to, the units in the stores would never trigger a tag again. But just in case, he took pliers to the remaining chips on the coil, crushing them one by one. It was kind of like popping bubble wrap—only much more satisfying.

Roger herded everyone into the elevator, but stopped to press a pistol into the plaid guy's forehead. He reached into the man's jacket pocket and came away with a business card holder.

"Just remember, Carl, we know where you work, and we'll be watching you. You should just forget you ever saw any of this."

Carl nodded.

"You're not gonna leave me tied up here, are you?"

"Don't worry, someone'll find you soon enough."

Meg leaned out of the elevator.

"That reminds me. You know where the surveillance room is?"

Carl nodded again.

"Good. Once you get free, go to the server room behind it, and untape Charles. Bring some paper towels."

* * *

Fiona made her way down the stairs and into the cafeteria, which, to her surprise, was deserted—no Phil, no Tanya, no other teenage girls awaiting their microchips. It had taken a while to convince the massive door guard to let her in, including a few minutes to drain the meager output of his steroid-shrunken testicles. During that time, either the operation had finished or something had gone dramatically wrong. The forklift tines projecting from ragged holes in the wall suggested the latter.

She could hear shouting through the gaps. She drew the T-RP derringer from her clutch and carefully opened the shipping room door.

The shouting was coming from a guy in a plaid jacket, tied up with someone else's tie. He looked like a car salesman. She got his name, and when he mentioned working for Phil, she freed him.

"Thanks," he said, "I was afraid I'd be left here for days."

He told her about the experiment on the old hippie, and Tanya coming for a chip, and the Legionnaires, and Phil's memory.

"Shit," she responded.

So the chips had worked, and even Tanya was willing to get one. But Phil's design team had fucked it up, making the effect too strong. Too noticeable. And the escaped Legionnaires would have spread the news by now—there was no way to cover it up and try again.

The chips had been a long shot, but worth a try; the little electronic amplifiers made it so easy to connect to people. The Corporation would have to keep developing the biological network, which was much weaker and less precise. It meant things would get messy. She was due for a chewing out.

"Shit," she repeated.

* * *

After dropping Gerry off, Lynn navigated North Cambridge side streets, struggling to believe she was actually going home safely. She glanced at Tanya, who was watching the passing houses; Tanya caught the look and came out of her trance.

"Mom, is Gerry gonna be okay? He looked pretty down."

Lynn had never imagined worrying about Gerry—the man was a fountain of positive thinking. But the fountain never had to go cold turkey on a drug addiction before.

"He'll be okay, Tanya. He has Zen techniques to help control his mind."

Lynn could see Tanya wasn't satisfied.

"And I'll check in on him. Often."

"He'll never be the same again, will he, Mom?"

Not really.

"He'll get better. But, you're right—there's always going to be a little piece of his soul craving that high. He'll have to live around it, and try not to let it cry too loudly."

Kind of like the part of Lynn that loved Phil.

Tanya was quiet for a while.

"What's gonna happen to Daddy?"

"Eightball will take care of him. He said he owes him that." Lynn found the next part difficult to say. "But honey, he's not coming back."

Tanya nodded.

"I thought I was over wanting him back," she said. "I guess I wasn't."

Like mother, like daughter.

"That's a hard thing to get over."

Guilt choked Lynn's throat. Shooting those chips into Phil—no, *killing* Phil—violated every Buddhist teaching that even a remedial student knew.

"I'm sorry, Tanya. I shouldn't have lost control like that."

"It was his own fault, Mom; he kept yelling and you didn't know what would happen. And—" Tanya shook her head sadly. "That wasn't the Daddy I wanted back. That was...someone else."

* * *

Don DiSenza came to, finding himself sprawled on the meat room floor. His arm was throbbing so badly he double-checked that the tourniquet hadn't loosened from the pounding pressure. He staggered to his feet, gagging at the sight of the bloody hand on the chopping block.

It's someone else...

Under the watchful eyes of the dogs, he ran the evidence through the power grinder and threw the poisoned burger into the disposer, then ran for the exit. He urgently needed medical attention.

And a story.

* * *

Toine fought drowsiness as the Lieutenant snored at the desk; even a steady supply of cheap coffee and miniature donuts had not kept the mall policeman awake through the afternoon. The fat guard had gone on a third search for the missing former hostages. On the sleeping man's desk, the handcuff key ring was tantalizingly visible atop the equally tantalizing box of donuts; but the pillar to which Toine and Jean-Paul were attached was quite immovable. Jean-Paul was whispering of yet another way he would take tortuous revenge on the redhead the moment they had achieved their freedom.

The door to the office clicked and cracked open, and M'sieur DiSenza peered in. He seemed oddly pleased to find his Lieutenant asleep. He crept into the room and put a finger to his lips; his right hand remained in his suit coat pocket.

There was blood.

Toine tensed for trouble, but relaxed when DiSenza approached the desk and lifted the ring, gripping the keys together to avoid telltale jingling. He required only a few seconds to release Toine's cuff and relinquish the key. Toine unlocked Jean-Paul and the three men made their escape.

They strode through the food court to the escalator as rapidly as possible while remaining inconspicuous. DiSenza whispered that he had injured his hand in a fight with François, and the injury was serious enough to require a ride to the hospital. They exited through the atrium into the parking lot, where they found a problem: apparently François and Carl had both left, taking their vehicles.

Someone shouted behind them.

"Halt!"

Toine turned to find the fat guard ten paces away, in shooting stance and waving his service weapon back and forth between him and Jean-Paul. Toine was familiar with neither the skill nor the will of this potential shooter—and thus looked to DiSenza to establish command. The mall manager paused to assess the situation, then whispered from the side of his mouth.

"Well, gentlemen, time for plan B."

DiSenza suddenly shook his body, bumping both Toine and Jean-Paul aside, and rushed toward the guard. What was he doing? Did he not see the gun?

"Thank God you got here!" DiSenza screamed. "The terrorists got loose! They found me!" He pulled his hand from his pocket— but there was no hand, only a bloody stump wrapped in a necktie. "They cut off my fucking *hand*!"

Toine rolled his eyes.

Not again, he thought.

He began to raise his arms, more as a plea for sanity than a gesture of surrender, when the guard's gun roared and Toine's chest exploded. He crumpled back, on fire with pain and gasping blood. The last thing he saw was the wide-eyed look on Jean-Paul's face, just as that, too, exploded.

Chapter 30

Carl leaned back onto the silk pillow, feeling very much like a King himself. It had been a great week. The plush Graceland setup and his groupie guest were fantastic, but in the big picture, just icing on the cake. A cake that Carl alone was left to enjoy.

Immediately after the Mall episode, he'd set up a little blackmail deal with the mall cops. Ed MacGregor was basking in the spotlight as a patriotic hero and news media superstar; for a monthly fee, Carl wouldn't mention how the terrorists had already been captured and somehow got loose.

And since François was hiding to avoid the Homeland Security investigation of his dead "terrorist" friends, Carl could take full credit for delivering Urban Legion headquarters to his bosses. And as a bonus, he could identify the Legionnaires in the microchipping room. The Corporation would lay a big commission on him once they'd liquidated the whole lot.

But that could wait. For the moment, Carl was enjoying a more personal opportunity. The promise of a replica Graceland tour had been enough for Phyllis to make another set of fake fingers for the elevator, and a couple of C-notes were enough for Lloyd and Steve to find someplace else to go. Phyllis immediately swooned over Elvis' music room and playroom; when she saw the huge velvet-draped bed, it was all over. He'd never gotten laid so easily in his life. Repeatedly, for days.

Phyllis padded in from the bathroom in a King-sized, white-sequined bathrobe. As she laid out her clothes, she warily glanced up at the camera lens in the ceiling.

"Don't worry, honey, I took care of it."

She'd noticed the lenses a few days back. Carl didn't think any electronics were still working, but to placate her, he'd gone around the previous morning and covered all the lenses with a thick layer of her deep red lipstick. Whatever those cameras were watching for, they couldn't see it anymore.

He was considering tearing off her robe for another round when a robotic female voice crackled from speakers in the ceiling.

"Attention! Attention! Armageddon twenty-four command initiated. Twenty-four hour safety time window has elapsed with no movement detected by the ceiling cameras. Final evacuation countdown begun. This floor will fill with polyurethane insulating foam in sixty seconds. If anyone is present, exit the premises immediately. Fifty-nine… fifty-eight… fifty-seven…"

Carl sat up.

"Insulating foam? What the fuck?"

Phyllis dropped the robe and gathered her things.

"Sounds bad, honey. That stuff's hell on your skin—plugs the pores."

"Oh, come on, they're not gonna fill this place with foam! Last week they tried some lame-ass story about radiation melting everybody. Never happened."

"Suit yourself, Carl; it was fun. I'm outta here." Phyllis was decent though not fully buttoned as she disappeared through the gold-trimmed doorway.

"Phyllis! It's just a bluff!"

There was no response; Carl leaned back again.

Insulating foam, my ass.

"…twenty-three… twenty-two…" continued the voice. At twenty there was a hum, and a mechanical blind dropped across the window.

Maybe leaving wasn't such a bad idea. Just in case.

"…seventeen… sixteen… fifteen…"

He leapt up, threw on his pants and rushed to the main lobby.

"…two… one… zero."

Jets of yellow foam erupted from nozzles in the ceiling. Phyllis was already gone, and all the windows were covered by mechanical blinds. He waded through the deepening goo to the elevators and pressed the down button. Good time to use the stairs—he wished he knew the access code. His legs felt warm. *It's insulation.*

When the foam reached his chest, it was clear that the elevator wasn't coming back; upward was the only option. He climbed onto the reception desk, fighting the suction. The shit was sticky. If his arms touched his sides, he'd never lift them again.

The remaining air had to be escaping out the ceiling somewhere. He was scanning for the vent when the jets gurgled and spit, then cut off. The room went deadly silent save a faint, ominous fizzing. He'd lucked out—they underestimated the foam.

He pushed a fiber panel up through the hung ceiling, grabbed the girder above it, and pulled himself out of the brown sea, flopping backward onto the next panel in the hanging grid. Now he just had to find the exit vent before the remaining air got stale.

He grabbed the girder, and pulled himself—nowhere. His foam-covered back was stuck to the panel beneath him, and that was snug in the grid. He could lift it out of the metal frame, but no matter how he turned, it hung up on the grid support wires. He fell back in frustrated exhaustion—and foam squirted around the panel's edges.

The jets had stopped at two feet below the ceiling, but now the foam had filled the room?!

Shit, it's insulation! It expands to fill air space!

He struggled with renewed desperation but couldn't escape the flypaper, which was now solidly stuck into the frame. The fuckers had him.

The fuckers would pay.

It was time to ID the Legionnaires. His arms were stuck down, but he could still pry his phone from his pocket and dial.

Nothing happened. Zero bars.

Foam billowed up in slow motion through the empty panel hole and crept over his legs, his stomach, and his chest. He twisted his head back to keep his nose up, and felt the hissing wave split around his chin like a stream around a stone. It buried his ears, which made his world surprisingly noisier—other sounds were drowned by the pounding of his heart and the last of the air rushing through his nose.

Warm foam crept across his lips. He closed his eyes.

You're not supposed to get this stuff in your eyes, he recalled.

A chemical odor bit his sinuses. He drew in as much acrid air as he could before his nostrils plugged, and held his breath. But as the carbon dioxide built up, his lungs burned and his instincts took over; he exhaled through his mouth, forming a bubble of used air which he reflexively inhaled again. It satisfied his urge to breathe but not his need for oxygen—he continued gasping from the foul pocket until darkness closed in. When the bubble shifted downstream, Carl was only dimly aware of the gagging spasm that sealed his lungs.

* * *

Gerry Rutland worked the register like a tea ceremony, focusing on the procedure and engaging with his customers, to keep his mind off the craving. It was a challenge because this ceremony involved shopping; he felt like a heroin addict preparing shots for someone else.

The good news was, it was impossible to relapse, as far as he knew—the equipment was gone. He could only suffer withdrawal.

Withdrawal was the bad news. Every morning, instead of looking forward to the new day, all he wanted to do was stay in bed and pet his cat.

It had been a week. How long would it take?

He looked up to greet the next customer and found himself face-to-face with Lynn, checking in on him as she had every day so far. This time she leaned across the counter, as only someone so tall could, and gave him a hug.

"Gerry, I told you I'd replace the Prius. Come on out and look."

There was no one else in line, so he nodded and followed her out the back door. Lynn's mysterious new job with Roger, whatever it was, paid well. The day after the Mall, she'd handed him a check for twenty thousand dollars from Interworld Limited, to cover the money he'd spent and the damage to the store.

In the parking lot, Roger waited beside a brand-new, forest-green Prius. He tossed Gerry the keys.

Lynn leaned closer.

"This is no ordinary hybrid, Gerry. We converted the engine to run on diesel fuel. Don't tell anyone you're getting 200 miles to the gallon." She met his doubtful look with a conspiratorial smile. "And if you ever have to race a Lincoln up the Route 2 hill, you'll leave it in the dust."

* * *

Lynn admired the newly repaired and decorated back wall of Nature's Grocery while Roger and Gerry dealt with the Prius paperwork. Tanya had worked all week to complete the giant mural: cowboys on horseback, herding free-range chickens across a landscape of cactus and sagebrush. She was proud that her daughter could capture Gerry's childlike sense of fun, and she hoped the lighthearted mural would help chase away his newfound darkness.

She and Gerry weren't the only ones who liked the artwork; Tanya now had commissions for murals in three other new-age shops around town. Word travelled fast in that crowd, maybe by telepathy. With help from all those crystals.

Lynn and Roger said their goodbyes and headed for the Civic. She toyed with the key while Roger hopped into the passenger seat.

"What now, boss?" Delivering Gerry's car had been the last task on a long list.

"Um, we take a breather and then get to work on the replacement HQ and truffle farm." He'd told her about triggering the foam-fill systems in both places the night of the attacks. And about the new facility, which, while not downtown, promised a remarkable view of the Head of the Charles crew race. "But, Lynn, I'd rather you didn't call me 'boss'."

"Why not? We all work for you now, right?"

"Well, yeah, but, we never called the King 'boss'."

"Of course not! You called him 'King'!"

"Good point. But, this is different. You and I are—different."

Suddenly he was searching her eyes. He was almost aglow, boyish bashfulness radiating from a manly core. She felt the familiar thrill of emotional danger.

What danger? He's a Trail Boy! Was it taboo for someone her age to be hot for a Trail Boy?

"I confess, Lynn, that kiss in the hallway at the Mall, uh, well...

it was kinda rushed, and I *was* trying to hide us both, but, um... I meant it."

Lynn's cheeks flushed.

I feel like a teenager.

Then be one, said Zen.

Okay.

She threw her arms around his neck and let her mind escape into her body. The voices in her head were finally quiet—or at least, she wasn't listening.

Epilogue

"Organic Montréal goodness."
— Our Zen Gourmet

François watched the box truck inch up to the rear of La Crème du Québec, and he smiled when Eightball and "Phil Achsman" hopped out. Phil stacked four bags of unbleached flour onto the bakery racks, then began loading flats of free-range eggs into the refrigerator. François approached Eightball casually.

"M'sieur Achsman is working out well for you?"

Eightball nodded.

"I cheated. I figured out how to trigger his microchips with a modulated WiFi signal. At first I used it as a reward whenever he did well, but less and less as he learned the ropes. I don't need it any more; he just works hard now, and doesn't ask for much in return. Makes it easy to take care of him. Even eats organic food without complainin'."

"And you, M'sieur? You are satisfied with the organic life?"

"Not exactly. I've been moonlightin' as a sound guy for a few months now. But it's with the Actual Musicians, so I can stay sharp without sellin' my soul. And get this—I brought Phil along a couple times, and he's into 'em. He's even learnin' to play guitar. The man's got talent. Born with it, I guess."

"Be careful, M'sieur, that he does not become famous. He will have to change his face, as I did, to avoid his former employers." François grinned to emphasize his stubby new nose and rounded chin. Neither the Corporation nor Homeland Security was looking for a chubby Canadian.

"I'll keep it in mind," Eightball replied. He looked over his order list and glanced around at the open truck. "Lucky we had all this in stock—what's the rush?"

"There is no rush; I requested immediate delivery because I thought perhaps you would care to see some old friends. Is there any danger that M'sieur Achsman would recognize his ex-wife? Especially considering her, ah, role in creating his current condition?"

Eightball glanced briefly at his busy helper.

"Not a chance. Phil Grady is gone."

* * *

Lynn tensed when she noticed François leading Eightball and Phil into the dining room, but the Canadian calmed her with a subtle nod. She knew she could trust him—he'd proven that not only by shooting DiSenza, but by his valiant effort to save the King. He wouldn't stress her out, not in his own restaurant.

And certainly not while Lynn was reviewing it!

Meg and Howie were briefing Roger on their upcoming covert scuba-diving trip to Galveston, but they shut up as the ex-Corporation executive approached the table. Phil nodded politely as he was introduced to each of the Legionnaires, not pausing for even an extra moment as he shook Lynn's hand. He looked handsome, and innocent. Lynn felt twinges of guilt and nostalgia. And maybe love.

But not boredom. Or loneliness. Roger was doing his best to fill that void in her life, as well as a mighty big pair of blue suede shoes for the Urban Legion. The quest to find the Corporation's leaders would continue, but without the King.

Which reminded her—

"François! Take a look at this!"

She set down her ice wine and brought up the photo message on her new smartphone. François leaned over her shoulder to view the picture: A bunch of old men lounging under a palm tree, surrounded by tanned young women in thong bikinis. The men all sported long gray sideburns and sequined swim trunks. In fact, they looked identical, except for the one with the bullet-wound scar on his stomach.

Join the fight!

If the Serious Topics Cartel gets its way, we'll have nothing to read but tomes like *The Non-Illustrated History of Railroad Spikes* or *Harsh: A Memoir*. Fight the forces of gravity by joining the Urban Legion at www.TheUrbanLegion.com, or liking *The Urban Legion* page on Facebook.

You'll enjoy the latest plausibly absurd conspiracies, news about the Urban Legion trilogy (you want to know who killed Tommy, don't you?), and offers and giveaways for sharing the fun.

Don't worry, you won't be required to reply when someone flashes the secret hand signal at a stoplight.

Most of all, please help spread the word about *The Urban Legion* by posting a review on Amazon.com. The author, and future fans, will appreciate it. Thanks!

If you enjoyed this, Please post a review on Amazon.com Thanks! —Dave

Acknowledgments

This book would not have happened without the steadfast encouragement and uncompromising feedback from my wife Gail, the funny conspiracy ideas from my daughter Jen, and the creative design suggestions from my daughter Liz. I cannot thank my team at B. Mirthy & Sons enough, and I especially appreciate the fine work of editor Nina Eppes and cover designer Jack Spellman.

Special thanks to the New Hampshire Writer's Project and my Nashua Region associates, notably Michael Charney of Riddle Brook Publishing for his editorial insights. I am grateful for advice from Jamie Morris, Ed Masessa, Julie Compton, Todd Stump, Namara Brede, Bonnie and Dan Fladung, Winfield Clark, Joan Dash, Melissa Groff, and Mary Russell. The books and seminars of Donald Maass, Blake Snyder, Robert McKee, Arielle Eckstut and David Henry Sterry, Mary Carroll Moore, James Patrick Kelly, and Rebecca Rule taught me much about the craft, and Dave Crary taught me the first rule of comedy.

Long-overdue thanks to Linda Eno for introducing me to Zen, and to Carlos Saavedra for putting my life philosophy into words: "Don't take yourself too seriously."

Finally, I am inspired by Carl Hiaasen, Christopher Moore, Dave Barry, Christopher Buckley, Kurt Vonnegut, Douglas Adams, comedians, columnists, script writers, cartoonists, and Internet jokesters, who put in a lot of effort just to make us all laugh. I hope I can return the favor.